I'LL CARRY YOU

ANNABELLE McCORMACK

This is a work of fiction. Names, characters, organizations, places, events, and incidents are products of the author's imagination or used fictitiously. Any resemblance to an actual person, living or dead, or actual events is purely coincidental.

Copyright © 2022 by Annabelle McCormack

Published by Annabelle McCormack

www.annabellemccormack.com

To all the moms who feel lonely and forgotten. I see you.

I'LL CARRY YOU

I'LL
CARRY
YOU

CHAPTER ONE

I FOUND HER.

Jason Cavanaugh looked up from the text that had buzzed through his phone moments earlier. He tried to control his visible reaction, setting the phone face down on the smooth mahogany table in the boardroom.

Curling his fingers into his palm, he rubbed the back of his knuckles with the opposite hand.

Amanda lifted a brow from her seat across from him. "Are we keeping you from something more important?"

The Powell crew had come to the meeting, including Amanda and her father. Both stared at him with identical steel-eyed gazes. Not that Amanda had any business being here. But since her father had purchased a controlling stake in Cavanaugh Metals, who would protest? The moment Jason's grandfather died, Bill Powell had no one in his way. No one would dare cross him with Thomas Cavanaugh out of the picture.

"Not at all." Jason leaned back in his seat and rubbed his eyelids. He flipped the leather portfolio closed, not bothering to hide his frustration. His plan for his grandfather's forty percent shareholdings had been met with derision, unsurprisingly. *Narrow-minded idiots.* As though they weren't responsible for the terrible shape the company was in. "I think we're done here anyway."

Amanda smirked, tossing her stick-straight dark hair over her shoulder. Her ivory skin contrasted starkly with it, giving her a Snow White-esque look. Not that the bitch was anything like a fairy-tale princess.

More like a vampire.

"We know this is a difficult time for you with the changes in your life and the transition, Jason." Bill Powell stood, setting his hands on the back of the large leather-back chair at the end of the table. "You're not thinking clearly right now. Someone's got to be the voice of reason for you, son."

I'm not your son. Jason narrowed his eyes at the older man. When his grandfather had been alive, Bill had never dared to sit at the head of the table. As though Bill deserved to sit in that chair after the damage he'd done to the company. "I think I made the case well enough, Bill. It's not about the transition. After the lawsuit, employee morale is at an all-time low, and our brand is damaged. A third of our workforce has quit. Your deal with Duncan Motors almost cost us everything. I've talked to the guys at the plant. This is the best path for the company." Jason stood, matching Bill's stance.

Chad Duncan shifted in his seat uncomfortably. *Prick.* Another viper who had taken advantage of his grandfather's failing health toward the end. Even leveraged his way to CEO, too.

Bill's face reddened. "Well, we're not considering employee ownership. Your grandfather didn't specify he wanted that in his will, did he now? And I understand that the will is far from a settled issue." Bill's eyes locked on his, as though to show he knew exactly what the will had said. *And he probably does, thanks to Amanda.* "It's a nice idea, but we'd lose millions with an ESOP. And I didn't buy into this company for that."

Jason's shoulders tensed. When he'd walked through the plant two months earlier, he'd vowed to save the company—not for himself, but for the hundreds of people who would lose everything if he failed.

This plan of making his grandfather's holdings into an ESOP trust wasn't something he'd come to lightly. After all, Jason would lose millions of dollars by doing so. But he had the rest of his grandfather's fortune to soften that blow. And the employees of Cavanaugh Metals had been the ones to make the company successful in the first place. If Jason couldn't turn things around, they'd all lose.

Jason's fingers clenched the leather portfolio. But it was his grandfather's fault this was happening. The old man had ignored Jason's warnings about doing business with Powell Enterprises. They'd long had a reputation for cutting corners.

"My grandfather's will is thirty days from being settled, actually. And we're limping along after that lawsuit, Bill. Our reputation is in the toilet, and thanks to you, *only* Duncan Motors hasn't left us. But I guess since you're double-dipping and Duncan's profits are fine, and you all end up with your pockets full, screw the people loyal to you, right?" He narrowed his eyes at Amanda. "You'd know a thing or two about that, right, Amanda?"

Amanda glared. "You ass—"

"You're being emotional, Jason." Chad lay a hand on Amanda's and frowned. Chad gave him a shit-eating grin. "We've been friends for what, twenty years? You should take some mental health days. I know you're grieving right now, but this isn't the answer."

Like you give a fuck about my mental health.

Jason almost laughed in Chad's face. Instead, he walked out of the office without giving them the courtesy of a goodbye. The click of high heels behind him told him Amanda had followed. She had long legs—she was almost as tall as he was—and caught up within a few strides. "Where are you going?"

He pulled his cell phone from his pocket and clicked on the messages. "TJ's in my office. I have personal business to discuss with him."

"Your business is my business," she hissed, edging into his personal space. Her dark eyes blazed.

Jason looked meaningfully back in the direction they'd come. "Not anymore." He arrived at the door to his office.

She stopped at the door and crossed her arms. "Making some big assumptions by moving into your grandfather's office already, aren't you? You're still CFO—nothing more. Don't be surprised if you have no votes left to decide anything with this company."

Damn the fact that she'd been there when the will was read. "Keep dreaming, Amanda."

"I need to talk to you."

He went inside, slamming the door in her face.

TJ sat at the desk, tennis shoes paired with slacks that went up too high on his legs. Superhero socks showed over his ankles. He was munching an apple noisily.

For good measure, Jason locked the door. "What did you find?" He stalked across the room to his desk, tossing the portfolio down on the top. "Your text was less than clear."

Wiping his mouth with the back of his hand, TJ said, "The 'inconvenience.'"

Right now, it was TJ who was being inconvenient with his cryptic vagueness. Jason scowled and opened a desk drawer. "I pay you to make my life easy. Not for rounds of twenty questions."

"You don't pay me nearly enough." TJ looked bored. "Considering what I found out, my price just increased."

His head snapped up. He leveled his gaze with TJ's grin, which vanished as he saw Jason's murderous expression. "You have about ten seconds before you lose my attention entirely. I didn't come into the office today to waste time."

His lips twitched. Jason should feel bad. It wasn't TJ's fault his proposal to Bill Powell had gone south. But he didn't feel bad. TJ wasn't his colleague. Or friend, even if they got along well. TJ was hired to do a job and paid handsomely for his discretion. End of story.

TJ waited for a beat, as though expecting him to return to a more normal rapport. He bit into the apple again. "I found your brother's ex-girlfriend. And his little bastard kid. Took some digging. Apparently, your brother was using the last name Connor at the time he was with her."

Jason shifted his gaze back to the desk, not wanting to show a reaction to his words. The worst likely scenario. *Goddammit, Kevin.*

He slid his laptop into its case, even though he wasn't planning on leaving. He zipped up the case forcefully and set it on his desk. When he returned a cool gaze to TJ, he hoped it looked as emotionally unattached as he could. "Then there is a kid."

"She gave the baby her last name . . . Klein. There's always a chance it's not his. But look at the photos." TJ slid the file over the surface of the desk.

Jason caught the file before it fell off the desk. This time, he didn't hide his annoyance with TJ. He glared. Thumbing the file open, a few photographs came into view. A little boy, no older than three or four, holding the hand of a woman who faced the other way. Same light blond hair, same piercing blue eyes.

He looked just like Kevin.

Jason's chest squeezed, then he killed the emotion before it could develop further.

The blue eyes were the only thing the Cavanaugh brothers had in common. With dark hair, Jason was the black sheep of the Cavanaugh gene pool. In more ways than one. But not this kid. This kid looked like he had come straight from Thomas Cavanaugh's loins himself.

He could almost hear his grandfather's cackle on his deathbed.

"You won't get a cent from me if there's another Cavanaugh heir. Not one cent."

And he'd made good on his promise. The will stipulated that if any other direct descendants came forward, they'd get it all. Everything. Worst of all, if the heir was Kevin's child and a minor, his grandfather had named the CEO of Cavanaugh Metals as the manager of the inheritance trust until the kid came of age—a safeguard to ensure the kid would get the money and Jason wouldn't take it. Another slap in the face.

Jason's eyes narrowed at the picture. This kid wasn't his nephew. Wasn't Kevin's son. He was nothing more than a broken condom. And a giant obstacle in the way of hundreds of millions of dollars and any say Jason had in what happened to Cavanaugh Metals.

His fist tightened on the edge of the desk, the rage he'd been holding back since his grandfather's lawyer had read the will uncurling into his chest and throat. He didn't look at TJ. Instead, he focused on the smile on that little child's face. The back of the woman who could take it all away. She was slender with long blond hair. In the next photo, she'd turned her face.

Pretty, even.

Not that pretty fooled him these days.

As though some random bitch had ever dealt with the shit

Jason had. Kevin had walked away and left him to handle the fallout. When Kevin had turned up homeless and dead from an overdose on the streets of Chicago, their grandfather had somehow blamed Jason for that, too.

And even though Jason had carried the weight and been by his grandfather's side until his death, the old man had still effectively disinherited him.

Jason straightened. "This woman doesn't know about my grandfather, though, does she?" He flipped the portfolio closed, too sick to look at the pictures any further. If she did, she probably would have found them. Few people would pass up an opportunity at millions.

"I don't know what she knows. But I'm not the only one who's looking. Thanks to Amanda, the Powells are on the hunt to see where Kevin was all those years, too. And they assigned Ned Vickers to investigate."

"Should I be worried?" Jason had to trust TJ would shoot him straight. "How did you find him?"

"Kevin did a decent job covering his tracks. The chances of Ned finding him are slim. I found an old, almost unreadable receipt in Kevin's wallet that you turned over to me, and that helped me get in the general vicinity. Ned won't have that advantage. But you never know—he's smart and been doing this longer than I have."

"If another eligible heir hasn't come forward after ninety days, it's all yours," his lawyer had said. Just thirty days left. It had taken TJ two months to find this kid. How long would it take Ned Vickers?

Jason checked his watch. It was barely noon, but this type of news required a drink. He crossed the large office toward the small table beside the windows. They gave him a panoramic view of Chicago. Jason barely stopped to look. Pouring himself a glass of whiskey, he swallowed it, feeling the burn down his throat. "Where did you find this woman? Somewhere they'll look?"

TJ leaned back on the edge of Jason's desk. "Brandywood. Some sort of hole-in-the-wall town in the mountains of Western Maryland near Deep Creek Lake. I'd never heard of it."

Jason froze. His fingers curled over the smooth surface of the glass. Kevin had been hiding in plain sight. For how long?

This time, Kevin had screwed him over worse than ever. And not just him. If Jason lost control of the company, it would be only a matter of time until all those employees he'd known for years lost their jobs, too.

Jason turned his back to the window, facing TJ. Rage boiled in his stomach. "I have. And it means there's a good chance we're not the only ones who know about this kid."

CHAPTER TWO

THE CRAMPED OFFICE was meant to look bright and cheery, yet it was anything but. Jen shifted in the hard folding chair, holding Colby closer.

Her knee bounced, a leftover habit from her youth that anyone in her family would appreciate as a sign of her nervousness. She stilled it and smoothed a lock of Colby's blond hair from his forehead. His hair was still so light that his pink scalp was visible under it.

She set her chin down on the top of his head. His hair smelled like watermelon kids' shampoo. Wrinkling her nose, she focused on how soft his hair was. She'd never liked watermelon-scented anything, but her mom had bought it for him, so here they were.

Either way, her soft, watermelon-scented child shouldn't be in the principal's office.

The door opened, and the preschool's principal, Miss Tierney, walked in. She gave Jen a polite smile and sat, her chair creaking. "I had asked for an appointment without Colby." She gave Colby a friendly smile that overcompensated her state-ment, her white teeth contrasting with the brown of her skin.

"I didn't have a sitter." Jen set Colby down. She fished into her purse for her cell phone. "Here, baby, take Mama's phone." She slid it open and clicked on a game, all the while feeling Tierney's eyes on her. *Great. Now she probably thinks this is how I parent.* She felt heat climb up her face. "He rarely gets to play these games, so he won't even pay attention to us."

Colby took the game happily and sat on the floor, his eyes instantly glued to the screen.

Tierney observed Colby for a few more moments before folding her hands. She didn't look pleased, but she sighed. "I'm concerned about Colby's behavior. There's been a lot of hitting lately. The other day he drew blood when he pinched one of his classmates."

Jen had already heard about the incident from her friend Lindsay who was Colby's preschool teacher. Lindsay had apol-ogized for having to report the incident about twenty times. Not that Jen blamed her. If Colby had shown up with a giant welt from being pinched, she would have wanted to know which kid had done it, so the other parents probably felt the same way.

"He's been having more nightmares again, but his therapist says he's doing really well." Jen glanced at Colby, her heart fall-ing. How could it be that her angelic son was capable of such violent behavior? He never seemed to fight with his cousins this way.

"Unfortunately, we can't really have him here without an immediate improvement in behavior." Tierney leaned forward, setting her hands on her desk.

"The problem is"—Jen lowered her voice, eyeing Colby—"I need him to be here. I can't keep taking off work while he's on these timeout days."

"If I can make a suggestion, I would look for in-home, one-on-one care. With the issues Colby has right now, he'll face similar challenges everywhere."

No kidding. And other places didn't have her best friend as a preschool teacher. "Unfortunately, I can't afford that."

Tierney bit her lip and pulled out a file. "You can't really afford us, either, Miss Klein. Gina says you're delinquent on the last two payments." She turned the file so Jen could look at the ledger.

Jen's heart rate kicked up a notch, the back of her neck breaking out in a cold sweat. She didn't need to look at the ledger. The invoice amount had caused her to avoid Gina's phone calls a week earlier.

But Christmas was approaching. For the past three years, since Colby had been born, she'd approached the season with dread and anxiety. She couldn't afford this time of year. Hell, she couldn't afford *any* time of year, but Christmas made that disparity clearer.

Jen lifted pleading eyes to Tierney. "Can you give me another month? I have a lot of overtime coming my way from my jobs during December." That much was true. But it also meant having somewhere to drop Colby off on the days Mom couldn't watch him.

"Look, Miss Klein, the truth is we're all pulling for you. And if it were just about the money, that might be something I could wiggle around, but this is the fifth incident this month. The fifth time I've had furious parents at other conferences. We all love you and love Colby, but this isn't the right place for him."

Jen swiped tears from her burning eyes. She nodded a few times, then stood. She didn't need the added humiliation of crying in front of Tierney. "I'll . . . uh . . . we'll go then." She gathered her purse and squatted beside Colby, whose concentration remained unbroken on the phone. "Ready, bubba?"

She lifted Colby and set him on her hip, not wanting the scene of trying to wrestle the phone away from him. Because he rarely got to use it, trying to take it away was always a process. She was embarrassed enough.

She let herself out and hurried down the hall of the small preschool. The walls were plastered with art projects from the different classrooms. Stopping by the door to Lindsay's room, she knelt in front of the cubby. She shifted through it for the gallon-sized plastic bag holding the spare set of Colby's clothes.

Through the open doorway, Lindsay caught her eye. She motioned to the assistant and crept to the doorway, her dark eyes filled with concern. "What happened?"

Jen found Colby's bag and stood, lifting her son once more. "They kicked us out," she whispered. She pasted a tight smile on her face. "But we'll talk about it later." She didn't want to attract any attention to herself. Open-door policies meant any of the teachers from the nearby classrooms could see.

Lindsay gave her a mournful, sympathetic expression and pulled her in for a tight hug. "I'm so sorry. I'll come over after work?"

Shaking her head, Jen shifted. Colby was getting heavier these days, his ankles showing below his pants leg hems. It seemed like he had skipped sizes three and four entirely and gone straight to size five. Another thing she couldn't afford. "I have a night shift at the cabins tonight. Luckily, my mom can take Colby tomorrow so I can work at the café. Maybe after I get off?"

"Don't you have a date with Brad tomorrow?" Lindsay gave her the eager look that she used whenever Jen mentioned a possible romantic attachment. Her best friend's loyalty was heartwarming. Lindsay seemed to want Jen to find a boyfriend more than Jen did.

Jen shook her head. "Saturday." Any excitement she'd felt had been dampened by the news Tierney had given her.

The two women parted, and Jen hurried out of the double-glazed doors. An icy breeze blasted her, throwing her long blond hair over Colby's face. He squirmed, annoyed that his game was being interrupted, and she took the phone away as they approached her sedan.

Colby howled as she put him in his seat. "I wannnnnt it!"

She pushed his shoulders back, desperately trying to pull his arms through the harness straps as he wiggled. "I know you do, but we're all done." His arms thrashed, legs kicking, and he caught her right in the gut.

And this was, precisely, why she never gave her kid her cell phone. Strapping him in, Jen closed the door. Hopefully, no one had seen. She peeked through the parking lot, but the parked cars appeared unoccupied.

Yeah. Only she and Colby were being kicked out in the middle of the day.

Jen lifted a shaking hand to her hair, pushing it behind her ear. She sucked in a deep breath, the cold air filling her lungs and making them ache. One thing at a time.

Getting in her seat, Jen glanced in the rearview mirror at Colby, whose tear-streaked face was red. He'd almost returned to his normal, pleasant self, but he had a hurt look in those ice-blue eyes. Eyes that reminded her so much of Kevin.

She pushed the thought far out of her mind. The last thing she needed right now was to dwell on that asshole. Not right now. Never.

"How about a cheeseburger?" she asked Colby as brightly as she could.

He nodded with a bright smile, and she pulled out of the

parking lot onto the main road. When she got home, she'd go through the linked calendar her mom had shared a couple of weeks ago. Mom's work schedule for the month was on it. Mom only did three shifts at the hospital a week, but with Warren and Alice asking her for help with their two youngest this fall, Mom was tired enough as it was. Jen couldn't expect her to do any more than she was already doing.

Jen pulled into the line at the fast-food place and gripped the steering wheel tightly, trying to relax her shoulders. Earlier this fall, she'd felt relief when she dropped Colby off at the preschool in the morning. Deciding to put him in hadn't been the easiest, but Lindsay was there, and Jen trusted few people as much as her. But shortly after the school year had started, her anxieties had drifted away. Colby only cried at drop-off the first week, but so had the other three-year-olds.

She'd just been a regular mom, swapping stories about how hard it was to yank her kid off her leg. None of the other moms gave her the side-eye, as they did at church. Even people who wanted to be sympathetic still treated her like she was a screwup.

But now, here she was. Jen the screwup. Twenty-three years old, no career in sight, and barely holding on by the threads of the life she'd struggled to sew together. With broken knitting needles, apparently. No wonder she'd failed out of English as a senior in high school. She was terrible at metaphors.

The car behind her honked, and her chin jerked up, her foot mashing the brake reflexively. The car in line in front of her was a few lengths away, the space in front of the illumi-nated menu, open. She glanced back at the car behind her, a fancy sports car with Illinois license plates. Giving the driver an apologetic wave, she pulled up to order.

As she got to the cashier window, an unenthusiastic

teenager mumbled her total, not making eye contact with her. She handed him her debit card. A few moments later, he pushed it back toward her. "It says declined."

"Of course it does," she muttered under her breath. The cold, sweaty feeling was back on her neck. She flipped through her wallet for another card. Her paycheck for the first of December should have hit a few days ago. Just how negative had her balance been?

She hadn't wanted to check the app on her phone to see.

Grabbing her credit card, she handed it to him. *Please let there be some credit left on it.*

A few more beats. "It's not going through." The kid held the card out again.

She popped open the coin holder beside her window. Only about forty cents there. Shifting her gaze to the rearview mirror, she noticed the line of cars accumulating behind her. *Oh, God. Come on.*

Another credit card came back declined. "Um . . ." Jen swallowed, her throat thick. "Can you, um . . . take off the adult meal and leave the kid's one?" Maybe her debit card would go through if it was less?

Now the teenager looked annoyed. He chewed on his thumbnail. "Hang on, I have to ask my manager."

Movement beside her window made her jump. The driver of the car behind her, a tall dark-haired man, stood there. Maybe in his late twenties. *Wow*, he was good-looking.

Great, all she needed. No matter how hot he was, she didn't need an angry man pissing on her. "Mind if I step in?" He reached into his back pocket, pulling out a razor-thin wallet.

Before Jen could say anything, he handed a card to the cashier, who shrugged.

"Y-You don't have to." She'd rather drive off. Preferably a cliff.

"It's my pleasure." Hot Guy flashed her a smile. His piercing blue eyes met hers briefly, then he glanced toward the back seat.

And there it was.

His smile faltered.

Every. Single. Time.

She felt self-confident that she was pretty enough still. But once they saw Colby, most of them took off running. Thank goodness Brad didn't seem to mind that she was a mom. She'd even talked about introducing him to Colby soon.

The cashier thrust a receipt out the window, followed by a greasy bag of food. Food that this guy must not eat often, with a physique like his. Fate had apparently sent him here to seal her humiliation.

Hot Guy took the bag of food. He held out the bag, and Jen took it from him, avoiding eye contact with him. "Thanks," she mumbled. She should be more gracious. But then again, she hadn't asked him for this. Rescuing her only brought more attention to her troubles among other people in line.

Any enthusiasm the guy had about helping her seemed to vanish with her response. He handed Colby's drink to her, then smoothly tapped the window frame, still holding the chocolate milkshake she'd ordered for herself. "Next time, check your wallet before you hold up the line. Cute kid, by the way."

Her jaw dropped as he took a sip of the milkshake and sauntered back to his car with it.

Jackass.

She wanted to run back there and dump the milkshake in his lap. Instead, she drove off, hands shaking.

CHAPTER THREE

JASON STEPPED out onto the driveway and slammed the car door shut. He crumpled the fast-food bag in his hand and walked toward the side of the house. Mildred still kept the trash cans there. Dumping his trash, he wrinkled his nose at the fetid scent and held his hand over his stomach.

He hadn't had a milkshake in years. Spite hadn't been a good enough reason to start now. Still, the outrage on that bitch's face had been enough to make it worth it.

Of all the people to run into. The chances seemed astronomical.

Then again, there weren't any other fast-food places in all of Brandywood, it seemed. And he'd been driving for nine hours. He'd only stopped for gas, and he'd been starving.

A shot rang out.

Jason dove behind the trash can, a terrible shelter, but the first one he saw.

It reeked.

"Put your hands up and stand up, slowly." Mildred's voice was a short distance from him.

He peeked out from behind the trash can. *God, she didn't age, did she?* She didn't look a day older than when he'd last seen her, even though he knew she had to be creeping on eighty. Her hair was bright, curly white, but it had been for as long as he remembered.

Jason held his hands up in front of him and stood. She held a shotgun in her hands and stared down the barrel. "Is that any way to greet your grandson?"

Mildred didn't lower the gun. "If it's the grandson I think it is, then yes."

Then she was still mad at him. Good. Better to get these things out in the open immediately. He threw his shoulders back with confidence. "As it so happens, I'm your only grandson."

The gun lowered slowly, Mildred's creased face paling. A wave of sadness crossed her face, and she marched toward him. She was a foot away when Jason realized what was happening, but by then, it was too late to grab her wrist. Her slap rang into the air, stinging his cheek. Five-foot-nothing, she stared at him with blazing blue eyes. "You son of a bitch. That's how you tell me Kevin's dead?"

"I didn't think you would care." Jason held his cheek. For an old lady, his grandmother could still strike hard.

Now she laughed without a trace of humor. "Ah, of course. Right. I don't care. Because it was me that disowned my daughter. Me, who refused to allow me admittance to her hospital room. Me, who sent back Christmas cards and birthday presents." Mildred scowled, her finger crooking as she spoke. "You sorry bastard. Go back to the hellhole you came from and leave me alone. I've spent the past thirty-five years trying to piece my life back together since your father took my only daughter away from me and your bastard grandfather made sure she'd never come back."

She turned and started back toward the house, shotgun tucked under her elbow.

"Look, the old bastard is dead." Jason followed her up the walkway to her split-level brick home. Thank goodness she lived in the middle of the woods. The gunshot would have attracted neighbors otherwise.

Mildred stopped at the door, glaring at him. "Well, you might want to watch out. It sounds like Cavanaugh men are dropping like flies."

She attempted to slam the door in his face, but he stopped it with his foot. Ouch. He placed a hand on the doorknob. "Come on, Mildred. I just want to talk about Kevin. I understand he might have spent some time with you before he died."

The sadness returned to her gaze. "I don't know what you're talking about."

Tough old bird. It was what his grandfather had always called her. He hadn't understood the term as a kid. When she showed up unexpectedly at his mother's funeral fifteen years ago, his grandfather had put him in charge of getting rid of her. Old man Cavanaugh had called her something different then. *Meddling bitch*, if Jason remembered correctly.

That was the last time he'd seen Mildred.

Jason didn't remove his foot from the doorway. If he did, chances were he wouldn't get her to open the door again. "You don't have to like me, but we have something in common. We both, apparently, gave a damn about Kevin. I'm trying to find out more about what the hell happened to him before he died."

He almost felt bad for putting it that way. He wasn't lying exactly. Every word he'd said was true. She didn't need to know about the inheritance or the reasons he wanted to know about Kevin.

Mildred sucked air between her yellowed teeth, the fine

lines around her lips tightening. Her eyes became like slits. "You found out about the kid, didn't you?"

Shit.

"What kid?" He tried to keep his face blank.

She chuckled, giving a slow shake of her head. "You really think I'm that stupid, don't you? Just like your grandfather." She pointed a finger at him. "You stay away from that girl, you hear? She's one of the nicest girls in this damn town and doesn't deserve you stirring up any trouble for her. If I regret anything in my life, it's the day I introduced Kevin to her. He ruined her life. Leave her alone."

Nicest girl in town. Jason almost rolled his eyes. Then again, Brandywood had people like Mildred running around it —who greeted strangers with shotguns. Bunch of crazy back-country inbreeds.

"Just five minutes of your time." Jason straightened and held his hands up, dragging his foot out of the door. "I drove nine hours to talk to you. I'm not asking for much."

"Nine hours?" Mildred smirked, lifting her chin. "Sounds like something's got you real scared, sonny."

"Mildred, please. I need five minutes."

She squinted at him, one eye practically closing. "Come back next week. I've got a trip to the casinos with the ladies from church coming up this weekend, and right now, I want to spend some time mourning the death of another family member I wasn't given the courtesy of saying goodbye to." She slammed the door in his face.

Jason covered his face with his hands. He should have known better than to come here. She had every reason to hate him. And who knew what Kevin had told her.

He went back to his car and pulled out his cell phone. Barely any signal. Perfect.

Why would a place like this have normal things like Wi-Fi?

Opening a hotel app, he searched for local hotels. Nothing he recognized came up. The closest four-star hotel was forty minutes away, a ski resort. A few fleabag motels and inns with two- or three-star ratings. And some cabins that promised a luxury "glamping experience." They, at least, had almost perfect reviews, Internet access, and were only five minutes away.

He booked a cabin for the week. He wasn't about to go back to Chicago empty-handed. In the meantime, he would lie low here and work remotely. He'd prepared himself to stick it out here as long as it took for Mildred to warm up to him and sign the agreement his lawyers had drawn up. But she better warm up soon. Before Ned Vickers found her. *And then the bitch with her brat.*

CHAPTER FOUR

THE PHONE RANG at the front desk, and Jen lifted her head, blinking. She willed herself awake and disentangled herself from Colby. Ever since the incident the year before where he'd gotten lost in the woods, Colby had suffered from constant nightmares.

He slept with her now, which made nighttimes even more difficult. But it was better than waking up to him screaming from his bedroom. And he didn't fit so well in the Pack 'n Play at the front guest lodge bedroom anymore.

She hadn't taken her socks off, but her toes curled on the cold wooden floorboards anyway as she hurried from the back bedroom toward the front desk. Lifting the phone, she managed, "Front desk, can I help you?"

There was a pause on the other line. Then a male voice. "Were you sleeping?"

Somehow, the question annoyed her more than it should. As though she didn't have the right to sleep. "Can I help you?"

"There doesn't appear to be any hot water in my cabin. I'd

like to switch to another cabin so I can take a shower before bed."

She checked her watch. It was almost two in the morning. Who in the hell took showers at two in the morning? "Uh . . . sir, did you try moving the lever to the other side?" Somehow what people failed to try amazed her. She'd had to visit cabins and explain how almost all the appliances worked at one time or another.

The laugh on the other end was humorless. "Yes, I checked the other side. Went to college, too."

"I wasn't questioning your intelligence." She sighed. Why, of all nights, did she have to have a difficult customer tonight? She would rather put him in a new cabin and explain things to Laura in the morning. She checked the reservation. Single guest. In their most expensive cabin.

Looking at the schedule, her heart fell. "Unfortunately, sir, there aren't any other cabins available. Weekend check-ins include Thursday evenings around here. But all the cabins are serviced regularly. If there was an issue with the hot water, we would have heard about it by now. My suggestion is to let the water run for a bit."

Terse silence sounded on the other end. "I'd like to have someone from the front desk come and check on the water. Within the next twenty minutes. Thanks."

The line went dead.

Jen gritted her teeth. She knew what Mark Dawson, who ran the cabins with his wife Laura, would say. He'd say not to go, that it wasn't worth putting herself at risk to go help a guest in the middle of the night. But the last thing she needed was a guest complaining about her to Laura in the morning. She wanted to wake up tomorrow with new luck and new perspective. Not carry over the shittiness of the previous day into the morning.

Sighing, she yanked her boots and coat on and headed for the door. She pulled the door closed and deadbolted it. Then she locked the outer glass door. No way in hell she was leaving Colby sleeping without several locks. Hopefully, he wouldn't wake up and realize he was alone.

Fortunately, the complainer was in cabin four, which was a short walk from the front guest lodge. A halo showed around the full moon, Orion low in the sky already. She frowned and shoved her hands in her pockets.

She trudged up to the cabin, her eyes burning. This would kill her sleep tonight. Once she woke up like this, she could never get back to sleep.

Cabin four was one of the biggest cabins for guests who wanted more luxury than rustic camping. Why would a single guest rent this cabin? Usually, it was for large groups or families.

The light on the porch flipped on, and the door opened as she approached.

Not this guy.

Complainer and Hot Guy from the drive-through were one and the same. Of course. Why wouldn't it be this way?

Except he wasn't wearing a suit anymore. He had a fitted T-shirt and pajama pants on. And slippers. How cozy. She barely kept herself from rolling her eyes, surprised that he wasn't wearing a fleece robe. *Rich, spoiled jerk.*

The look in his eyes made it clear he recognized her, too. "You," he said simply.

"Jen." She stepped through the open doorway. "What seems to be the problem, Mr. . . ."

"Jason." He motioned her farther in. "I told you. Hot water is broken."

She sighed and made a beeline for the master bathroom on the first floor. Somehow, she doubted he was using the loft bedroom, even though the view was the best Redding Cabins had to provide. This guy liked his convenience. Her guess proved right. A travel case was open on the sink, and an open box of condoms was on the toilet.

Oh. No wonder he wanted a shower. She didn't look to see if whoever he'd brought back was still here because she didn't want to know.

Not her place to judge or even think about guest behavior. She wanted to get out of the cabin as soon as possible. Not that it surprised her he had someone with him. He was handsome. And virile.

Stop it.

She hadn't had sex in far too long. After her experience with Kevin, she'd sworn off sex without some sort of commitment. Not that Kevin hadn't promised to be committed. That was beside the point. Maybe things would get serious with Brad soon enough for that to enter the equation, though. She would welcome the end to her very long dry spell.

This line of thought needed to end. Jen went over to the shower and pulled the lever all the way to the left, turning the spray on.

Jason came to the doorway. He crossed his arms, watching her wordlessly. The muscles in his biceps flexed and were toned and smooth. Not that she was trying to pay attention. Her gaze flitted away, lower, and she stared at the floor. *Goddammit, Jen. Get it together.* She did not want this man thinking she was staring at his package.

"I already did that," he said finally.

A blush warmed her cheeks. "How long did you leave it on?"

"Enough for it to warm up." He scowled. "I don't appreciate the insinuation that I don't know how to use a shower."

She checked her watch, not wanting to talk to him. Should

she acknowledge their earlier interaction? Not doing so made the whole thing more awkward. She gave him a tight smile. "You're not from around here, right?"

"I'm from Chicago."

"Right." City boy. It showed. "The thing is, we're on well and septic systems out here. And the water is coming straight from the well, which is way underground, and it's winter. So it's freezing. Takes a bit for warm water to come out of the faucets because of the lower water pressure." She pointed at the sign on the wall by the shower where this was explained.

She walked over to the shower and put her hand under the stream. The temperature had warmed, so it wouldn't be long now before steam was filling the bathroom. "Give it another minute, and you'll be fine."

With a polite smile, she turned to go.

Jason tested the water temperature for himself. Seemingly satisfied with her explanation, he dried his hand, not saying anything else.

All right. Time to go. She headed for the front door. His footsteps padded behind her. Without looking back, she said, "If you need anything else, let me know."

He hurried to the door. "Wait." He offered an apologetic smile. "Sorry for making you come out here. I really thought it was broken. I swear I let it run like a minute before."

"Yup. No problem." She winced inwardly. He couldn't help that she was a grouch tonight. *Or can he?* He had definitely added to her struggles.

"No kid tonight?"

She frowned, meeting his gaze. Something about him felt so familiar and goose bumps rose on her arms. Not that it was any of his business to ask about Colby. But he seemed like he wanted to be more congenial. "He's at the front guest lodge.

Asleep. That's why I should get going now. Don't want him to wake up and find out I'm not there."

"You left him there by himself?" He raised one dark brow.

She gave him a funny look. The accusatory way he said it made it sound like she'd left him in the middle of the street to play in rush hour. Irritation pricked her shoulders, bunching her muscles there. "Well, when guests demand I pay them a service call at two o'clock in the morning and hang up on me, it doesn't leave me much choice. Next time, maybe run the water for a bit before you assume it's not working. Like I had suggested." *Or read the sign.*

His features darkened. "Thanks again. Good night."

The door closed with a bang behind her.

God, what a jerk. He deserved every bit of her rudeness. Laura wouldn't be happy with her if he complained, though, which he probably would now.

Jen hurried back toward the front guest lodge. His comments about her leaving Colby alone had put her mom brain into hyperdrive, thinking of all the ways he could get up and injure himself.

Worse still, it reminded her of that horrible night a year earlier. Thank God for Sam and Garrett's levelheaded thinking and selfless actions that had saved Colby. She'd never been more terrified in her life.

Jen's hands shook as she unlocked the doors to the guest lodge. She held her breath, listening for the sounds of Colby's frightened screams. Thankfully, she heard nothing.

Shutting the door quietly, she locked the front door and slipped back toward the bedroom behind the front desk. The sounds of Colby's soft breathing reached her, and her body relaxed.

Her coat crinkled as she slipped it off and unlaced her boots. She climbed back into the bed and curled her arms around Colby, tucking his warm body against her. Her mom said it was a mistake to co-sleep with him, that he'd have a hard time transitioning to his own bed later. Mom even suggested that if she ever got married, Colby might feel displaced by his stepdad.

Well, who cared if she never had another man in her bed again?

Kevin had promised all sorts of things, and look where it had gotten her?

She had Colby. She was young with so much life ahead of her, but already she felt he was all she needed. Just the two of them versus the world. And no one would ever convince her otherwise.

CHAPTER FIVE

JASON STEELED himself before he walked into the front guest lodge. If Jen was going to be a part of his everyday interactions while he was in Brandywood, he would have to play nice. He stared at the small ramshackle cabin. Barely over a few hundred square feet. It resembled a log cabin, which he guessed some guests found charming, but he wondered how Jen found enough space to sleep in that place.

She didn't live here, did she?

He'd watched her struggle to pay the cashier at the drive-through the day before. Each time he thought about it, he felt a strange pressure on his heart. Just how poor was she?

He shook his head, the groaning of swaying branches in the trees bringing him out of his thoughts.

Now he really felt like a moron. As a kid, he remembered reading a book about a teacher that the students believed slept at school. Assuming Jen lived here felt a little like that.

He strode into the front guest lodge, pulling the glass door open. A bell jingled his arrival, a Christmas wreath on the door bouncing in the metal wreath holder. He'd been surprised to find a fully decorated Christmas tree in his cabin, too. They apparently went all-in during the holidays around here.

But Jen wasn't at the desk. Instead, a pretty brunette sat behind the desk, staring at her laptop. She was older than Jen, by several years, it seemed. She gave him an easy, practiced smile and greeted him.

"I . . ." Jason set his hands on the counter. "I was looking for the woman who was working the desk last night."

"Oh—Jen. Yeah, she does the night shifts around here a few nights a week. But I'm the owner, Laura Dawson. Can I help you?"

This was his chance to tell the owner all about Jen's rude behavior. He searched Laura's face for a moment, trying to gauge how receptive she would be. *Not very.* His skill with reading body language was something he prided himself on and the way this woman looked made it clear she regarded Jen as a friend.

Better to get Laura on his good side.

"She was very professional. Came and helped me out in the middle of the night when I couldn't figure out how to get the hot water going. I wanted to thank her." Jason reached for a red-and-white-striped mint from the candy dish on the counter.

He'd made the right choice. Laura's dark eyes lit. "She's great. Then again, she's practically family, so I wouldn't expect anything less."

"She's got a kid, too, right? She was telling me about him."

"Yeah, Colby's here on the nights she's working, too." Laura stiffened, and she added cautiously, "I hope that didn't make any issues for you, Mr. . . ."

Thank God. He'd used a different last name when booking the cabin. His goal was to stay hidden from the PI the Powells had hired, if possible, but it had worked out with Jen working here, too. "Sutter." He gave her a taut smile. "And no, the kid didn't cause any issues." He leaned back from the counter, feeling the urge to flee. "Any good lunch recommendations? I figured I'd go explore the town a bit."

"The two best-known places on Main are Bunny's Café and Yardley's Pub. Actually, Peter Yardley and Bunny Wagner are both local celebrities around here. Bunny has a quarterly feature in *This Charmed Life's* magazine, and Peter has a new cable television show with the Happy Home Channel that draws huge crowds. He's got a big baking competition coming up soon, and it's bringing tons of tourists to the area. You one of them?"

"No, actually." It surprised Jason that two locals could have such notoriety, but he said nothing. He'd go to Bunny's. If the Yardley guy was attracting tourists, he wanted to stay away from that. He wanted quiet. Time to think about how to get Mildred to talk to him. He thanked Laura and headed for the door. What sort of name was Bunny's Café, anyway?

Then again, who named a kid Colby Klein?

Not that Colby Cavanaugh was much better, either. Well, the kid wouldn't ever know about that last name.

Lucky bastard.

Jason got into his car and looked up Bunny's, then set the driving directions on. Brandywood had changed a lot since he'd last been here. But it had been twenty years.

Not that Mom had gotten away with bringing him and Kevin here too often. Jason had been fine with it, though. Most of what he remembered was sitting on the orange carpet in Mildred's living room, trying to turn up the volume on the old television while Mom and Mildred fought in the kitchen.

He hadn't wanted Kevin to hear Mom crying.

"You just take those two boys and come back here, you hear? We'll find a way—"

"I can't"—a strangled gasp from Mom—*"I can't. It's not that*

simple. He controls everything I do. There's no way he wouldn't know."

"Then don't go back. Stay with me."

"I can't be without them, Mom. Not without the boys. And he'll take them away. You and I can't compete with his money. He's got a team of lawyers strong enough to mow down anyone who challenges him . . ."

Mom hadn't tried to bring them back to Brandywood after that trip. She'd shut herself in her room, closing the door for what felt like months.

Jason could still remember the notes he'd scribbled and shoved under the door. She hadn't answered a single one.

As he pulled onto Main Street, his phone buzzed in his pocket. He parallel parked into a spot right in front of the café, then checked his phone.

TJ: *What the hell are you doing in Brandywood?*

Jason: *How did you know I was here?*

TJ: *You pay me to know things. Be careful. You could lead Ned there.*

Jason frowned at the phone. He'd thought of that. It was partially why he'd driven instead of flown down here. Harder to track.

Once again, his decision to book the cabin buzzed threateningly in his brain.

He studied the emblem on the steering wheel of his car. Maybe he could talk Mildred into lending him her old car and leave his car covered at the cabin. Even the car felt like a giveaway to his location.

If he could get Mildred to talk to him. She had to have a price. Everyone did. Just because she knew about the kid didn't mean she knew anything about his grandfather's will. Only a handful of people knew the details of that document.

He needed Mildred to agree not to tell anyone else about

the kid. To never discuss Kevin's last name with anyone who came knocking. His grandfather had done his best to expunge his mother's family history from the record, as a matter of privacy. He didn't want anyone looking into the lowly background of the woman Jason's father had made himself a fool over.

Mildred showing up at her daughter's funeral had been horrifying to Thomas. But it had also revealed to Jason how little his grandfather trusted anyone. He'd given Jason the task of removing Mildred rather than risk anyone else learning who the old woman was.

To the rest of the world, Jason's mother had gone from Martha Price to Monique Sutter—a wealthy socialite from California. Only Kevin and Jason had known about Brandywood.

Stepping onto the street, he walked to the meter and then did an about-face. These weren't like the meters in the city that took his credit card or worked by phone app. Did he even have a quarter? He looked through his car.

None. *Fantastic.*

He approached the café. Someone had decorated the large windows on the side with paper snowflakes and garlands, and twinkle lights framed the windows. In fact, all the shops on Main Street appeared to be decorated already.

He held the door for a woman exiting the café and went inside. A long bakery counter and display case showed a variety of baked goods, the full menu written on chalkboards on the wall behind it. The scent of coffee hung in the air, and the grinder screeched as he made his way over to the counter, where a short line waited. Tables were arranged artfully throughout the small space and beside the windows and a row of booths lined one wall. The wall itself seemed decorated with local artwork, which was for sale. *Quaint.*

Jason grabbed a bag of chocolate-covered espresso beans from a display and let his eyes wander the menu. He didn't remember ever coming here. When his mom had brought him and Kevin to visit Mildred, they barely left the house.

He only remembered Main Street from the times they'd driven through it while he watched out the window.

Had he ever even asked to stop?

He didn't remember doing it. Kevin had, though. But that was what younger brothers did—say things the older brothers knew they couldn't.

As the line moved up, the girl behind the counter moved away from the espresso machine with a smile on her face. He stiffened. *Jen.*

Was this girl everywhere?

Maybe she had a twin.

She met his eyes, and her smile vanished. Nope, it was her. The corners of her eyes narrowed, then she set the drink she'd been working on at the far end of the counter and called out a name. When she returned her attention to him, she didn't bother to look up. "What can I get you?"

He placed an order, watching as she scribbled it down in large, loopy cursive. She was probably the type of girl who made hearts instead of dots over her I's. He struck the thought, staring at the top of her head. No, she wasn't. She had too much of a chip on her shoulder for that. Any bubble in her personality had long since popped.

Probably by Kevin.

He paid in cash, and she avoided looking at him. "Thanks, your order will be right up. I'll bring it to you."

Tempted as he was to say something to her, he held his tongue and found his way to a table. He sat and slid his laptop from his case, feeling strangely unsettled. His decision to come to Brandywood had felt so smart two days ago. Like he was one step ahead of everyone else. All he had to do was talk to Mildred, convince her to stay quiet, and go back to his life in Chicago.

Now he wasn't so sure about anything.

Should he feel bad about cutting this woman's kid out of his due inheritance?

Absolutely not. She wasn't a Cavanaugh. The kid was barely one.

He'd worked his ass off for his grandfather and the company. Held everything together when they'd restructured away from his grandfather's dinosaur mentalities into twenty-first-century ideas. Not to mention all the bullshit he'd dealt with.

Kevin had cashed out early, taken off, and disappeared.

A shadow crossed his laptop screen as it powered up. He glanced to the side to see Jen holding his coffee in a steaming, artisan mug. She glared down at him, setting it on the table. "Are you following me?"

Oh. No wonder she'd been uncomfortable. Her concern was totally legitimate.

He gave her an easy smile. "If I told you you're the one person in this town I'm trying not to run into, would you believe me?"

She scanned his gaze, not looking pacified. Crossing her arms, she sat, uninvited, in the chair across from his. "That doesn't answer my question, though. If I were following someone, I wouldn't want to run into them, either. So what is it? You're just a terrible stalker? Or something else?"

"Look . . . Jen." He noticed the nametag on her apron now, which he hadn't seen when she was behind the counter. "I'm not following you. I'm not from around here, so this is weird for me, too, believe it or not. The chances of you turning up everywhere I go seem slim, even for a town this size. So I have to ask . . . are you following me?"

Her deadpan composure slipped and a smile played at the corner of her lips. *Pretty lips.* Full ones.

He looked away.

"Look . . . Jason." She arched a brow and he smirked, leaning back in his seat. She had sass, that's for sure. "I'm sorry we got off on the wrong foot. I should have thanked you yesterday for helping, but truthfully, I was having a shitty day and I was really embarrassed to be your charity case. But thank you, regardless." She stood. "The rest of your order will be up soon."

He watched her go back behind the counter and shifted his focus to the coffee cup. The apology hadn't been expected, and he didn't really want it, either. He'd been happy to embrace the idea of her being rude. Lifting the mug, he sipped the coffee. It was surprisingly good. Not at all like the over-roasted swill he was used to getting from the big-name chain coffee shop at home.

The laptop beeped to alert him to an email. He hit the mute button on the keyboard. He didn't want to deal with Bill Powell right now. Or Chad. Or Amanda.

The thought of Bill Powell as the face of Cavanaugh Metals made him sick. His family's company had been known for years as one of the best metal fabricators in the automotive industry—not cheap, but superior quality. That reputation was something his grandfather had boasted about with pride. Now, with his grandfather gone and the inheritance at risk, Jason had been forced to assume the position of an employee on payroll, helpless to do anything to fix the company and even his own job at risk. An outsider.

He'd warned his grandfather against Bill. By then, he'd been dating Amanda long enough to see Bill's penchant for "cost-cutting corners," as he liked to put it. But the old man hadn't listened. One year after the deal, it had come out that Cavanaugh Metals was no longer producing the same quality materials as before when several cars made with their products were involved in accidents.

The resulting lawsuits and bad press had cost them almost everything. Only Duncan Motors had stayed and that was because Chad was the CEO and the Powells owned large shares there, too. And it only helped the Duncans to have their own metal fabricator at their disposal.

Now Jason had to clean up the mess if he was going to help resuscitate the company his great-grandfather had built. Except the board refused to see it that way. Without his grandfather's shares, it was a matter of time before they fired Jason, too.

Not wanting to imagine the possibilities for that board meeting, he opened a news app on his laptop and clicked on the business section. In college, reading business news had always energized him, given him ideas. Now it strangely felt like drowning.

The clink of porcelain against the wooden tabletop caused him to lift his head once more. Jen set the sandwich and bowl of soup down, wordlessly. He studied her profile. Hard to believe this was the person who had been around his brother before he died. Kevin had overdosed three and a half years earlier. Had he ever met the kid? "How old is your son?" Jason asked, surprising even himself.

Jen pulled silverware out from her apron. "He's, uh . . . three. Just turned three in November, actually."

Kevin had already been dead for over seven months by the time his son was born.

Jen's gaze dropped to his left hand before asking, "Do you have kids?"

"No." He frowned. "Not married."

"Ah." Her lips drew to a line, and she settled her weight on her back leg. "Can I get you anything else?"

"No, I'm good." What was it about this girl who made normal speech difficult? He didn't know what to say to her, and somehow she made his brain go silent. Talking to women was something that came naturally to him.

She hesitated, then added, "I don't know if you need it, but I can add a note for the housekeeper to get you extra linens." He gave her a quizzical look and a blush spread to her cheeks. "I mean at the cabins. For your girlfriend."

"Girlfriend?" He almost spat out his coffee. She'd been paying attention to his activities from the previous night? Or maybe seen a car come and go. The idea of that woman being a girlfriend was ridiculous. Just a casual hookup, no questions asked. He made that much clear to every woman he'd been with recently.

And last night had mostly been about distraction. Seeing Mildred had rattled him more than he'd cared to admit. So he'd gone to a local dive bar and found the sort of company he'd been looking for.

"Boyfriend?"

This time, he threw back his head and laughed. Her blush got deeper. She pinched the bridge of her nose. "You know, forget it. I shouldn't have brought it up. Not at my other job now anyway." She turned to go.

"I'm not gay. And no. Not my girlfriend. Just someone I met yesterday and who won't be back. Not everyone is worth knowing forever."

She stumbled at his words and Jason's hand shot out to steady her. Was she scandalized? She froze and he released her immediately. *Nope, shouldn't have touched her.* "Ope, sorry about that."

Her eyes flew to his. "It's fine." Her eyes grew cloudy. "You remind me of someone I used to know, that's all. Sorry. Not trying to be familiar."

Being in a position where he knew more about her than she did about him gave him an unexpected feeling of control over the situation. He didn't want to toy with her, but he couldn't help but feel amused by their interactions. He crossed his arms. "Someone nice?"

"No, actually." She gave him a pointed look. "You both have that in common."

Yup, he scandalized her. "Ah, a devilishly handsome jerk. I get that a lot. Not really interested in a tip, are you?"

She smirked. "How about I promise not to spit in your food and we'll call it even?"

He chuckled, watching her return to the back. Whatever his brother had seen in this girl, he guessed it had to do something with her quick wit. Or honesty.

Something about the way she said things *was* honest—refreshingly. Maybe she didn't enjoy pretending or had never learned the art of hiding her emotions, but at least he didn't have to guess what angle she was playing. Of course, he was certain that would all disappear if she knew who he actually was. The promise of easy money brought out the worst in most people. And this girl didn't appear to have much money to her name.

Almost concerningly so.

Jason pulled out a set of noise-cancelling headphones and slipped them over his head. Her troubles weren't his problem. If he'd learned anything from his grandfather, it was that there would always be an open hand the second people found out you had money. Filling that hand wouldn't do anything. The lack wouldn't go away and you'd be on the hook for more.

Even Kevin hadn't known what to do with the money his

grandfather had given him. He'd burned through it, drowned his guilt in sex and drugs, and died homeless.

The employees at Cavanaugh Metals deserved the job safety their grandfather had promised them before Powell had destroyed the company's reputation. His grandfather never would have felt the need to bring on Bill Powell if Jason's father had lived. But when his grandfather saw his legacy going to Jason, grief and hatred had blinded the old man.

He didn't want the Powells to destroy what his family had built. But he knew he had to protect his own back first and foremost.

Because the only way to survive this world is to learn to look out for yourself.

CHAPTER SIX

"Is that guy still sitting there?" Lindsay peeked around the high-top and through the glass counter.

Jen wiped down the espresso machine. "Yup. And he's had like four cappuccinos. Apparently, he's not planning on sleeping tonight."

She glanced at Jason furtively. His gaze was still locked on his laptop. Maybe he was a writer? They got a lot of them at the café. Bunny didn't mind as long as they continued to pay for food and drinks. The ones who bought one coffee and used the Wi-Fi all day—those were the ones they *all* grumbled at.

But he seemed too wealthy to be a writer. Unless he was famous. He'd rented out the most expensive cabin and drove a fancy car. Even his clothes seemed expensive. Not that Jen would know about brands. She shopped at the consignment shop, and Colby got most of his clothes as hand-me-downs from Warren's kids.

Lindsay bit her lip. "He's not bad to look at." Her own eyes twinkled. "Maybe you should go over there and talk to him again. I swear I saw him peeking at you."

Jen untied the apron from her neck. Her feet ached, and her head throbbed. All she wanted to do was go home and soak in a bubble bath. Fortunately, her mom had volunteered to keep Colby overnight, which was especially generous, considering she was watching Colby tomorrow for her date with Brad.

"He's passing through town. And I think things are heading in a good direction with Brad. Want to come over and watch a movie?" Jen asked Lindsay. "I unexpectedly have the night free."

Lindsay shook her head. "My grandfather wants me to come over and check out the menu he has planned for the Christmas special." She rolled her eyes. "He's becoming such a diva."

"I'm surprised he hasn't outright forbidden you to come visit me in here. A Yardley at Bunny's. Think of how bad it could be for business if people found out." Jen grinned and looked back at Bunny, who was busy cleaning out the roaster.

"I heard that." Bunny didn't look at the two younger women. A bead of sweat gathered on her forehead, so she wiped it away and gave Lindsay a cross look. "And he's not becoming a diva. He's always been one. If that man's head gets any bigger, they'll be able to use him for a float at the parade on Main next year. And you can tell him I said that."

Jen and Lindsay both burst out laughing. Bunny Wagner and Peter Yardley's feud had been going on for as long as anyone could remember. But neither Jen nor Lindsay was naïve enough to think there wasn't anything to it. Bunny and Peter actually loathed each other.

Bunny's resentment had only grown, though, when the Happy Home Channel had noticed Peter's work with *This Charmed Life* magazine. They'd given Peter his own television show, which only brought him more tourism and traffic in town.

Wiping tears of laughter from the corners of her eyes, Lindsay straightened. "Speaking of which, did you hear about the baking competition my grandfather's show is hosting as part of his televised Christmas special? At his new store?" She dug through her purse and pulled out a crumpled flyer, which she pushed into Jen's hands. "You should totally sign up."

The paper crinkled as Jen smoothed it out against the counter. The prize money swam in front of her eyes, her jaw dropping. "Twenty-five thousand dollars?"

Lindsay gave a giant, exaggerated nod. "See what I mean? It's being sponsored by *This Charmed Life* and Happy Home Channel. The magazine got such a great response last year to the Christmas cookie thing Sam Doyle did, so they wanted to do a big Christmas thing in Brandywood this year, too. And with Grandpa's show and his store, they thought it would be a good tie-in. But sign-ups are only through the weekend. The first round of the competition will be on Wednesday. Then they do the final the week after and they announce the winner at the special, after Christmas."

As Jen got excited, a line from the flyer leaped up at her. Her heart fell and she met Lindsay's eyes. "Why is it couples only?"

"To handicap me," Bunny said in a flat voice, passing by them. She glared at the flyer. "At least, that's practically what Peter told me. He didn't want me to enter, so widows need not apply."

"Sorry, Bunny." Lindsay's apologetic expression confirmed Bunny's story.

"I guess that means I'm out, too." Jen pushed the flyer away.

"Why don't you get Brad to sign up with you? You can totally do it together." Lindsay replaced the flyer in her purse.

Would Brad be willing? "I don't think he bakes, though." To be honest, he had talked about little outside of his work as an accountant. Which was probably the most boring job that Jen could think of, but hey, he wasn't struggling to pay his bills.

"You'll carry the team no matter who's on it. Best damn baker I've ever trained," Bunny muttered, passing by them. The door to the kitchen swung behind her as she went through it. The rare compliment was enough to warm Jen's heart. Bunny didn't give out praise about baking if it wasn't earned.

"Do you think we count as a couple?" Jen leaned her hip against the counter. "We've only been on three dates. He only just kissed me last time." And it had been a nice kiss. Little boring, like him, but nice. God, she really needed to have sex. This whole *not* having it was becoming too big a thing in her brain. Had things really been that good in the past? Maybe she was conflating the whole thing. Should she lower the threshold on what "commitment" meant?

"You totally count. Sign up. You can do it tomorrow when you go on your date. You're going to the pub, right? There's a sign-up sheet there. I think it's fifty bucks to enter, though."

Jen shot her a warning look. Bunny had to know Jen went to Yardley's, like everyone else in this town. But she'd prefer not to deal with the consequences of Lindsay bringing it up. The sigh that she breathed felt defeated and empty. "That settles it. I don't even have five bucks. I can't enter."

Lindsay pulled her checkbook out. "I'm writing you the check." She reached for a pen from the cup beside the register.

"Not a chance." Jen pulled the pen cup away. "There's no way that I can ask any more of anyone. I can't keep expecting my friends and family to bankroll me through life."

Lindsay nodded toward the seating area. "Looks like your stalker is gone."

Jen looked up, surprised. *Why did she feel disappointed?* The table Jason had occupied for hours was empty. He'd packed up and gone in a blink as though he'd been in a hurry. "You know who he reminds me of?" She grabbed the spray bottle and rag to go over and clean the table. "Kevin. There's something about him. Today he said, 'not everyone is worth knowing forever' and followed it by 'ope'—made me almost fall over. Kevin used to say both things."

Lindsay stuck her lower lip out, biting it gently. "I think comparing cute guys to someone you used to be in love with is normal. Even if they're like, you know, total opposites. It's not like 'ope' is some super original phrase."

That was true. And Kevin had been the first guy she ever believed she'd loved. They hadn't been together that long, really, but he'd been fun and exciting. Different from the usual breed of guy she found here in Brandywood. Maybe that was it, actually. She had a thing for guys who weren't from here. Trust Lindsay to put it into perspective. "I don't know. I think it's the eyes. And that he's from Chicago."

"Again. Chicago." Lindsay over-enunciated the word. "Not like Paduka or Massapequa. Plus, he's unbelievably hot, so I could see you overanalyzing all of this because of that, too." She grinned. "But since he's a stalker—"

"And I know nothing about him."

Lindsay smirked. "In that case, why don't you tell me how that kiss with Brad went?"

Jen surveyed the café. Thankfully, it wasn't crowded, and her shift ended in a few minutes. She reached under the counter for the envelope where she stashed her tips. Bunny was known for paying more than the usual meager restaurant wages, and she didn't make them tip out since, usually, it was only one or two people working the front. But tonight had been unusually slow. Not much there. Not meeting Lindsay's eyes, she shrugged. "It was fine."

"Not a great kisser?"

Jen cringed. "I mean, I don't know." She made her way to the tablet on the wall, where they logged in and out of work and entered her code. "He's nice. But I miss the excitement I used to feel—like if I wanted to stay up all night talking about nothing and everything with a guy, I could. Or take off for the weekend. Now I'm just a mom with a babysitter, checking the phone to make sure I haven't missed a call. And frumpy. I feel so freaking frumpy. On the last date I went on with Brad, Colby smeared peanut butter on my sweater right before I left him at my parents' house. I washed it off, but I felt so gross. And you know how much I love Colby." She met Lindsay's gaze, thankful that their friendship allowed her to complain about things like this almost guilt-free. Lindsay wouldn't judge her or think she was selfish or think Jen didn't love her son enough.

Lindsay studied her. "There's nothing wrong with wanting to feel feminine. And sexy. Maybe you do need a little more mysterious hotties from out of town right now than sturdy potential husbands. You deserve to have fun, Jen."

Jen rolled her eyes. "A stalker's hotness has its limits, you know."

"But apparently, talking about him is enough to distract you." Lindsay waved a folded check between two fingers. She gave a sneaky grin and hurried toward Jen's coat over on the coatrack. The money for the contest.

"Lindsay!" Jen stamped her foot as her friend stuffed the check in her pocket.

Lindsay blew her a kiss and pulled her own coat down. "Pay me out of your winnings."

"Hold up. Let me clean off this table, and I'll walk out with you to the parking lot." Jen moved to the table Jason had been occupying. She'd already cleared most of it earlier, and only the last coffee cup remained. She lifted the mug, and a neatly folded bill showed under it. He'd paid for his food at the counter, so he clearly meant this as a tip.

He'd tipped her one-hundred bucks.

Her fingers hesitated over the bill. She'd only ever received such a large tip on a couple of occasions. Did he still feel sorry for her after the drive-through incident?

But she'd been such a jerk to him.

She could use the money to enter the baking competition. Not have to owe anyone, including Lindsay, anything else. Jen pocketed the tip and cleaned the table. As she put the supplies away, Bunny came back out of the kitchen. "Travis is covering for me tomorrow, don't forget. You may need to get here a little early in the morning to show him the lay of the land."

"Sounds good. Have fun at the casino. I already clocked out." Bunny's grandson, Travis Wagner, was one of her closest friends on the planet. Much as Jen loved Bunny, Jen also relished the times when Travis oversaw the café.

"Don't forget the boxes," Bunny called as Jen grabbed her purse.

Jen went over to the counter and grabbed two heavy cardboard boxes loaded with food from the counter. Lindsay came up beside her. "For Pete's sake. Let me carry one of those."

The two women headed for the door of the café. Just as they got there, Jen almost ran straight into Jason, who appeared distressed.

He appeared to be in the middle of a phone call but pulled the phone away from his face and hung up when he saw her. "You okay?" she asked, frowning over the top of the box. Whatever strange magnetic pull she had toward him, right now, he was in her way, and her arms hurt from the weight of the box.

"Yeah. My car's been towed." Jason looked back and forth between the two women. "Can I carry those for you?"

"Sure." Lindsay plopped the one in her arms into Jason's.

She pressed a kiss to Jen's cheek, a twinkling gleam in her eye. "Call me later, okay?"

As Lindsay walked away, Jen's heart sank. Lindsay probably thought she was doing Jen a favor by giving her a moment with a handsome man. She hadn't told Lindsay the full extent of her interactions with Jason.

Jason took the box she carried, and Jen shook out her arms. "Where were you parked?" She scanned the street. The twinkle lights from the Christmas decorations sparkled in the windows of the shops on Main, but the sidewalks were crowded tonight, especially heading up toward Yardley's.

Trust there to be some Christmas event going on. Fridays brought that sort of excitement for most people, after all.

"Right here." Jason pointed at the empty spot in front of Bunny's. "I forgot to feed the meter. You all tow quick in this town."

"Actually, that's a tow zone after four o'clock." Jen nodded toward a sign on a lamppost. "But if you want, I can give you a ride back to the cabins."

"You'd do that for the schmuck who made you come turn on the hot water at two in the morning?" Jason's eyes glinted with humor.

He had been a schmuck. She shrugged. "No. But I would do it for the guy who came to my rescue in the drive-through. Even if you took my milkshake."

He grimaced. "I do feel a little guilty about that. And for being an asshole. I'll have to make it up to you."

"It's fine. I could have been more gracious. Besides, you tipped me too much today. Which means I'm in your debt again. If I help you, I'll be out of your debt. Maybe then whatever cosmic force that keeps throwing us in each other's path today can be satisfied, and we can return to our merry lives."

Jason fell into step beside her. "How do you know it's merry?"

She gave him a sidelong glance. "Your life?" Her breath fogged the air in front of her. "I don't. But you don't look miserable."

He didn't respond, shifting his attention to the boxes he carried. "What's in here? It smells good, whatever it is."

"Yesterday's leftovers. I'm taking them to one of the local nursing homes."

"Don't nursing homes charge exorbitant fees to the elderly, thus paying for the food they give them?"

A harsh view, especially for a guy who appeared wealthy. But not completely incorrect. "It's not that type of nursing home." As they continued down Main Street, the sidewalks grew more crowded. People were sitting in folding chairs on both sides of the streets, cones closing a section of the street.

Jason exchanged a look with her. "Is there something going on down here tonight?"

Jen scanned the crowd. She didn't remember the schedule of events for December this year, but once December started, it was nonstop Christmas-themed events. "Looks like it. Here, follow me. I'll try to navigate us down the sidewalk through all these people."

"Excuse me," she said, attempting to part the sea of people on the sidewalk. Moving through the stopped crowd was nearly impossible, especially with Jason carrying two large boxes. People were clapping and singing. They didn't hear her.

Having had enough with the crowd on the sidewalk, she skirted around it. Finding a break in the folding chairs, she pushed onto the street and started to cross it. Jason followed her.

It took about thirty seconds for Jen to realize she'd stepped onto the set of a street play. She froze. Couples were dancing on the street, wearing vintage costumes. One actor wore a nightgown and an old-fashioned nightcap, looking disheveled as he stood in the center of the street, watching the merriment beside another actor.

Of course. The street production of *A Christmas Carol.* Her parents had always brought her when she was younger. It was one of her favorite Christmas traditions in town as a girl.

And right now, she was standing in the middle of the scene.

Another actor traveled between the couples, carrying a large bough of mistletoe. He held it over each of their heads, and they each stopped, on cue, to kiss for the clapping crowd.

The actor neared where she and Jason stood. With a twirl, he held the bough over them.

Jen's eyes widened. It wasn't unusual for the street actors to pull people from the crowd into various scenes, and people usually participated enthusiastically when selected. Jason had a bewildered look beside her. "What's going on?" he asked in a low voice.

The actor continued to hold the bough over their heads with a wide smile on his face.

Jen turned toward him, her cheeks flaming. "It's a play." She kissed his cheek, quickly.

The crowd booed, and the actor held out his hand at their response, encouraging the boos. Now the rest of the actors surrounded them, dancing in a circle around them as the crowd chanted, "Kiss! Kiss!"

This might be her worst nightmare.

Jason seemed to have caught on to what was happening. His sharp gaze pierced hers. "Fezziwig's ball?"

"Yeah, and we're a part of it." She eyed the manhole cover a few feet away, trying to figure out if it was possible for her to move it and jump inside.

"All right." The unreadable mask on Jason's face melted

into an easy, practiced smile. As though he had years of practice performing. "This ends faster if I just kiss you, right?"

She nodded. *He was going to kiss her?*

Then again, this guy brought random women back to his
room. A kiss probably wasn't that big of a deal to him.

He set the boxes on the street, and the crowd cheered, the
chant growing louder. She didn't want to look out at the sidewalk. People she knew were out there. *Oh my God.*

Jason pulled her closer, slipping his hands on her waist. He
searched her eyes. "Is this okay?"

Was it? That he'd asked for her consent surprised her. Most
guys sort of just did that head-tilt-and-lean-in.

This. Was. Mortifying. "Yeah. Let's get it over with."

He hesitated, his eyes focusing on her lips. Then he pulled
her closer, dropping a soft kiss on her mouth. His lips were soft,
warm, and surprisingly gentle. She closed her eyes automati-
cally—or squeezed them shut.

And her heart gave a giant lurch. Goose bumps rose on her
arms, and her spine tingled.

When she realized the crowd was cheering and she was
frozen in place, she drew a sharp breath, relaxing into his arms.
Her mouth softened to his, and she kissed him back, her pulse
pounding.

Jason pulled away after a few seconds. Or maybe a minute.
She had no idea. The whole thing felt as though she'd passed
out. An odd expression was in his eyes, and the dancers had
moved on, satisfied with their performance.

"Um . . ." she stammered, then pressed her lips together.
They continued to tingle.

What in the hell had just happened?

Jason leaned down and grabbed the boxes. "We might want
to get moving before the ghost of the Christmas past drags us
away."

Nodding, she willed her feet into action. She hurried across the street toward the parking lot where most of the store employees from Main Street parked. "No wonder your car got towed," she finally managed. There wasn't any street parking left in town. "They probably thought you were trying to get around the rules."

Jason didn't respond right away. "They do this sort of thing a lot?"

She looked back at him as she reached her car, her face still burning. *It was a good kiss.*

She had to stop thinking about it. "Yeah, you know. Christmas. Thanksgiving. Pretty much any holiday is an excuse for a small town to celebrate." Jen popped the trunk. "You can put those boxes down in there."

"Sounds like an exciting place to grow up." Jason put the boxes into the back of her car and straightened. He closed the trunk.

Yeah. Great place. Until you become the one everyone was whispering about. She unlocked the passenger side. "If you don't mind, we can drop them off at the nursing home before I take you to the cabins. They're on the way." She climbed into the driver's seat, and he got in beside her.

She glanced back into the back seat, hoping he wouldn't judge the state of her car. Not that she'd ever been the neatest car owner, but life with a toddler had made it ten times worse. She was certain the Goldfish and Cheerios would be stuck between her seats forever. And Colby had a habit of putting his muddy shoes on the back of the passenger seat.

He shut the door. "Yeah, that's fine." Buckling his seat belt, he asked, "So you take donations to the nursing home?"

"My church runs it." She started the engine. "It's for the elderly poor—people who can't afford housing and would be homeless. They run entirely off donations."

He set his laptop bag on his lap. "So you're a do-gooder, huh?"

She pulled out of her spot. "I wouldn't say that." She threw him a smile. "I just deliver the food." If there was anything she hated, it was false humility. She didn't really even like talking about the charity work she did. Kevin had always told her it was his favorite thing about her. When he'd left, she'd nearly quit it all, too angry with life and him to continue. Now she mostly did it out of habit.

Why did this guy keep bringing thoughts of Kevin to mind? Almost four years and she'd struggled to forget him. Kept hoping one day, he'd turn up again. Take a damn interest in his son.

A damn interest in her.

She pushed the thought away, flipping the windshield wipers on to clear some of the fog from her windows. "I take it you're *not* a do-gooder."

Jason winced. "Ouch. What makes you think that?"

"To begin with, because the term do-gooder is a pejorative." She came to a stoplight, which cast a red glow onto Jason's face. With his dark hair and light eyes and complexion, he looked a bit like a devil. A charmingly handsome devil.

He didn't meet her gaze. "I give plenty of money to charity."

"Because it's a good tax write-off?" She knew his type.

This time, his eyes narrowed. "I don't think we know each other well enough to discuss my taxes, but thanks."

She gritted her teeth. Their conversation had quickly gone south—and she'd felt strangely jovial after he'd kissed her. Why did she have this inexplicable reaction to him? She wasn't normally like this. Especially not with strangers. She replayed her words. She must have sounded so judgmental. "I'm sorry," she breathed, releasing a sigh. "I'm not exactly having the best last few days. My son . . . he's been getting into trouble in preschool, and they kicked him out."

Jason glanced back at the empty car seat. "What is he chain-smoking and cutting class?" He laughed. "Didn't you say he's three?"

The laughter thawed the tension between them. The mental image of Colby doing those things made her grin. "No." She shook her head. "He's pinching other kids."

"Wow, they set that bar real low these days, don't they?" Jason shifted in his seat and stretched his long legs out. He sobered somewhat. "I don't know much about kids or preschools, but I'm sure that can't be easy."

"It sucks." She pulled into a space in front of the nursing home. "But it's fine." She swallowed, her throat feeling tight. "Truthfully, I can't really afford the school, anyway. Childcare is crazy expensive. But my friend Lindsay was his teacher, so at least I knew he was with someone I trusted." Why was she pouring her heart out to him now? "Sorry. More than you asked for. I talk too much. I'll be right back." She turned the car off and opened the door.

Jason got out, setting his hands on the top of the car. He looked across it toward her. "Why don't you let me carry those in for you?"

"Okay." She tried to regain her composure, feeling rattled. Not that this was anywhere close to a date, but she hadn't spent much time one-on-one with a man she considered especially sexy for a while. And Jason intrigued her.

Jason helped her get the boxes out of the trunk. "So what's your story?" She studied his face. "What brings you all the way from Chicago to Brandywood?"

"Some family business." He gave her a polite smile. "And I heard about some fantastic cabins in the mountains I had to visit."

She grinned. If he was wealthy, Redding Cabins were probably unimpressive to him. "They are world-famous. We specialize in the cold shower for men clearly not in need of one." She regretted the comment immediately, her palms breaking out in a sweat. She *had* to stop commenting on his sex life.

His azure-blue gaze showed a mixture of amusement and shock. "That's the last time I'm making a service call when I know you're at the desk."

"Good. I'm there Sunday, Wednesday, and Thursday nights. I'll be able to get much better beauty rest if I know I can turn the front desk phone off." They reached the brightly lit front entrance to the nursing home, and she held the glass front door for him.

"Fortunately for you, I'm only here for a week or two. And if I can wrap up my family business before then, I'll be gone even sooner." He gave her a jaunty smile.

Just passing through then. No one interesting ever stayed.

"Hi, Victor," Jen greeted the security guard at the front desk. She tilted her head toward Jason. "He's with me. Just dropping food off in the kitchen."

The security guard gave her a nod. "Always good to see you, Miss Jen. Go on back."

Jason followed a few steps behind her as she went through the familiar maze of hallways. As she turned a corner, she nearly ran into Bertie Hillsbury on her walker. Bertie gave her a hug, her bony arms tight around her neck. She smelled like rose-scented lotion. "Jen! Oh, I missed you, honey! When you bringing that baby in to see us again?"

"As soon as I have a chance. He's been busy drawing Christmas cards for you and all the ladies."

Bertie sized up Jason. "Well, looky here. You brought me a new boyfriend, did you?" She gave Jason a big wink. "Just my type." She posed, showing off her nightgown. "I'm ready for our date, sweetheart. Where you taking me tonight?"

"Flying you to Paris," Jason said smoothly, without missing a beat. "Plane's out back."

"Ohhhh." Bertie squeezed his forearm. "Oh . . . nice, strong muscles. I like this one, Jen." Her guffaw seemed to bounce off the floral wallpaper as she continued down the hall, the walker squeaking with each step.

Jen continued forward. Something about watching Jason with Bertie was oddly endearing. And he probably had the money to fly a date to Paris. If he made her that offer . . . *stop it, Jen.*

She shouldn't be thinking about this random stranger this way. Her pace increased. Jason caught up with her. "Don't leave me behind in this place." He glanced over his shoulder at the direction Bertie had gone. "I have a feeling I'll fill my date book for the year a bit too quickly."

She gave him a wary glance. "When you go making promises of Paris, no wonder." They reached the kitchen, and she flipped the light on. Two large commercial refrigerators hummed on the other side. "Put the boxes right in here." She held the door open to one of them.

Jason offloaded them and wiped his hands on his jeans. "That's it?"

"That's it." She closed the fridge door. "I usually let the director know I've dropped the food off. But that should only take another minute." She leaned her hip into the fridge. "See? Just the delivery girl. I don't buy the food. Bunny does. I can barely take credit for most of this."

"Doesn't mean you're not a do-gooder." Jason glanced around the kitchen. She followed his gaze. The area was clean but cold and metallic. The kitchen here always made her a little sad. It was functional, of course, but held none of the warmth of a home. Instead, it served only as a place to prepare food.

"I always wonder about the kitchens these people left behind," Jen mused. She gathered her hair back into a ponytail. "Seems heartbreaking to never think about making another family dinner again, doesn't it?"

An odd expression crossed his face. Then he answered, "Yeah, sure does." Not a trace of conviction sounded in his voice.

They went back in the direction they'd come, silence between them. She didn't know much about him—or how he felt about family—and how he'd reacted made her think he might not be too close to his family. She should have been more sensitive. As they climbed back into the car, the awkwardness grew. She gave him a tense smile and drove. "Hey, so, back in the town with the *A Christmas Carol* and all—"

"Don't worry about it. I can't tell you how many times I've found myself in the middle of a play being asked to kiss a pretty girl. Pretty much my normal Friday night."

She didn't really want to know what his normal Friday night was like. She looked over at him, and a snort of laughter choked out of her throat. He grinned at her. "Yeah, well, mine usually involves waking up on the couch and finding myself watching some sort of cartoon two hours after my son has fallen asleep."

"Those Smurfs are basically like sleep therapy."

He clearly knew nothing about modern cartoons, but she didn't blame him.

She pulled up in front of his cabin. Would he linger in the car? She wasn't ready to say good night yet for some strange reason. "I'm pretty sure Laura has a list of the Christmas events at the front desk. I can grab you one if you want." *Stupid, Jen. A single, hot guy like him won't be interested in Christmas festivals and tree lightings.*

An easy smile tipped at his lips, the hint of a dimple on his left cheek. *God, stop staring at him.* "Are you going to be there?" he asked, reaching for the handle.

She shook her head with a rueful shrug. "I don't have a ton of spare time right now."

"Then I'll probably pass." He checked his phone and frowned at it. Snapping his head up, he met her gaze. "Thanks for the ride."

He gently closed the car door, silhouetted against the porch light as he walked toward it. The implication that maybe he'd have gone to those Christmas events if she was there wasn't lost on her, but he'd seemed to realize he'd put his foot in his mouth and hightailed it out of the car.

Maybe whatever attraction she had toward him wasn't completely one-sided.

Or maybe it was wishful thinking. She'd spent enough time self-pitying her lack of desirability the last few days. And Lindsay was right: she longed to feel desired again.

Jen let out a slow breath and chewed on her lower lip, watching him for a few seconds before she threw the car into reverse. Whomever Jason was, she was thankful he was passing through. He'd seemed cold and indifferent—*judgmental*—when she met him. But back in the nursing home, she'd sensed kindness and a decent sense of humor. *And he could certainly kiss.* No, it was good he wasn't staying in Brandywood. Jen knew her kryptonite.

CHAPTER SEVEN

KISSING JEN KLEIN had been a monumental mistake.

Jason pulled his heel back, stretching. The dim haze of dawn barely lit the road to the cabins, the route he'd taken on his morning run. Though the cabins were nestled in the woods, they weren't so far out from the historic part of Brandywood, as he'd discovered on the six-mile trek in the morning.

He pulled one arm over the opposite shoulder, filling his lungs with the wintry morning air. He'd always hated running in the cold, but he hated not running more. And this morning, he'd needed to pound his frustrations out with sprints so fast they made his sides ache.

Somehow, kissing Jen felt a bit like breaking a rule even he hadn't broken before. And worse was the way his body had responded to her.

He'd enjoyed it.

He wasn't supposed to enjoy kissing his brother's ex-girlfriend. And he definitely wasn't supposed to enjoy being around her.

That damn kiss. It was like opening a bar of the world's

finest wine and only having one tiny taste. Just enough to confirm that he wanted more. That one taste made him a drooling idiot.

Both facts troubled him in different ways. She wasn't his type at all. But he never would have guessed she'd have been Kevin's, either. Kid notwithstanding, she seemed like the type of girl who didn't get into trouble.

He'd wanted to warn her off the night before, let her know to stay away from him. He didn't want to like her. And he'd seen the hint of pleasure on her face. She didn't mind being around him, either.

Damn Mildred. If she'd just talked to him and let him leave, he'd never been forced to deal with Jen. This complicated things in ways he didn't want to face. He didn't want to be sympathetic to Jen or her problems. Screwing his brother didn't make her entitled to the Cavanaugh family fortune or business. If that were true, a long line of other women would also qualify, both from his and Kevin's exploits. Jason was practically a saint next to Kevin, at least when they'd been in college.

Kevin's reputation was known. Jason guessed it was part of the reason his grandfather had changed his will the way he had. That and the fact that Jason had dared discuss with the old man some changes Jason planned to make someday to help bring things into the 21st century. The mere idea of his life's work in Jason's hands had been an "affront" to his grandfather's legacy.

He'd ended up doing worse in his paranoia by giving Bill Powell a controlling stake.

As Jason's running shoes collided with the gravel up the driveway, he felt his frustrations slipping back into his crowded mind. That was the worst part of this situation. Even if he wanted to feel sympathy for Jen and her son, giving away his inheritance would screw over everyone at the company who needed the changes Jason wanted to make.

Jason approached the cabin he'd rented, which had the architecture of a chalet. He hadn't bothered to look at the view from the loft, despite the promise on the website that it offered "stunning views" of the mountains. The Appalachians hardly impressed him.

As he drew closer, he noticed a car parked outside the cabin, an electric car that fit into Brandywood's sea of trucks and SUVs as well as his sports car did.

TJ sat on his front porch, swaying on the swing. He'd extended both arms on the back of the swing and wore an impish grin on his face.

How had he tracked him down so exactly? Jason scowled at him, wiping the sweat from his forehead with the hem of his shirt. "What're you doing here?"

"I came to warn you. I tried calling, but your phone went to voice mail. Lucky for you, I figured the drive was worth it for my favorite client." The smirk on TJ's face made it clear he fully intended to bill Jason for the drive. He rubbed his bearded chin. "Ned's in town."

Jason shot him a quick look before unlocking the cabin. What sort of place didn't have electric keys these days? He slipped the key back into his pocket, processing TJ's words. The news should surprise and worry him more than it did. But really, if TJ had found him, it wasn't that surprising that Ned had. "Why?"

"Because your car license plate showed up at an impound lot."

Right. Because, of course.

He set his mouth to a line. "Come on in."

"I told you, you were playing with fire by coming here." TJ slipped in behind him. "Interesting place, though. Definitely not where I'd expect to find you. You planning on staging a *Butch Cassidy and the Sundance Kid* when they come for your money?"

Jason stalked toward the kitchen. He rummaged through the fridge and pulled out a plastic water bottle. The cap popped as he opened it and he took a swig. "They didn't have a normal hotel in town."

"You mean they didn't have a five-star luxury hotel in town? There's a difference between what you consider normal and what everyone else does." TJ sat on one of the barstools at the open kitchen countertop.

"All right, get on with it. Clearly, you're interested in telling me more than the fact that Ned is here. We both know you could have done that with a phone call."

TJ shrugged, reaching into the basket of complimentary fruit. He plucked out a banana and turned it upside down. "You know most people peel their bananas wrong? Watch a nature show. This is how the monkeys do it." He popped the peel off the bottom and took a bite. "I could have told you everything by phone. But I figure it's our one and only time to hang out."

"That and you can charge me for travel." Jason set both hands down on the counter, facing him.

TJ chuckled. "And I can charge you for travel." He took another bite of the banana. "You were right about Amanda. She's pregnant."

Instant, purple rage curdled in his throat, the back of his neck tensing as he mashed his teeth together. "That bitch."

One more way she could ruin his life. Cunning, manipulative *whore*.

He never should have married her. But she'd been model-like gorgeous and they'd shared all the same friends. A perfect match, according to everyone. And it made his grandfather happy. Jason should have known then she was no good. His grandfather had a way of pushing Jason toward things that suited his interests more than Jason's.

"It's hundreds of millions. You called it." TJ chewed noisily.

"It's not mine." He had called it. He'd known the instant Amanda heard about his grandfather's will that she'd try something like this. The will had been about as clear as mud about the whole thing anyway and if there was a case to be made, she'd try to do it.

"Are you sure?" TJ dipped his chin, scrutinizing him closely.

Jason's eyes narrowed. "She's been fucking Chad Duncan for years. Ninety-nine-point-nine percent positive it's his. And I'm willing to bet a paternity test on it."

"Ninety-nine-point nine isn't one hundred."

He was aware of that fact. And hated it. "Thanks, genius. You know I didn't get to be CFO because I'm not familiar with numbers."

"Still." TJ shrugged. "Between her and this whole thing with Kevin, whatever inheritance you have could wind up in court disputes for years."

Jason rubbed his eyes. "Years the company doesn't have before the Powells and Chad run it into the ground." He finished the water bottle and crumpled it in his fist, the plastic crackling. "What are my options?"

"I'm a private investigator, not a lawyer. What the hell do I know?" TJ leaned back in the stool and swung his feet on the counter. "But you might want to talk to yours."

Jason's head throbbed. This was quickly snowballing into a monster of a situation—one that he had little desire to direct. He glared at TJ. "Since you've made yourself so useful to me with this and clearly have time on your hands to be here, what do you say to the proposition of handling this for me?"

"You know, I'm not your personal assistant." TJ crossed his arms. "I also don't care about your business."

"Yeah, but you're the only one I trust."

TJ chortled. "Now you're sounding like your grandfather." He tossed his head back and forth as though weighing the offer. "How much are we talking?"

Jason strode back toward his room. "Double whatever I normally pay you."

"Triple," TJ called out. "And I need someplace to stay. You have an extra room?"

After peeling his shirt off his head, Jason balled it up and threw it on a pile on the floor. Triple, then. TJ knew he had the upper hand. It was feeling like everyone did. "Fine," he called back out the door. "But you're not staying with me."

He pushed open the shower door and started the shower. Of course, the damned thing would remind him of Jen now. She'd been so irritated with him when he'd called for service in the middle of the night. Of course, if he'd known she was the one at the desk, he would have waited until someone else was working.

Or taken a cold shower.

Of course, that reminded him of the other time he'd showered quickly after waking up with a massive hangover and having slept with someone he wanted to avoid.

He fisted his hand, wishing there was something he could punch nearby. He had never intended to get back into bed with Amanda. They'd been *done* for a long time.

But he'd been drinking too much the day of his grandfather's funeral. And she hadn't seemed so unappealing then. In fact, the entire episode had been one of their more pleasant interactions recently. And it would bother him less if he could be certain that he'd reached for that condom because he'd been expecting the pregnancy claim. Access to all of his grandfather's wealth?

It was too good of an opportunity for her to pass up.

But he couldn't quite remember. He'd had way too much to drink. His celebration of finally being free of that old bastard.

A paternity test might take care of Amanda's claim if it wasn't his, but she'd played her cards well. She knew the ninety-day limit as well as he did. And determining what constituted a legal heir could very well end up in court.

He stepped into the spray of the shower and grabbed the bottle of shower gel he'd brought with him. Normally showers were a refuge for him. Even as a teenager, whenever things got bad enough, he could hide in the shower and step away for a while. Showers let his brain shut off the thoughts and memories that the therapists hadn't been able to help with. It was the only time he enjoyed being near water.

But not now. Now all he could think about was how to get the upper hand.

And if he had to pick between Jen and Colby—Kevin's actual son—and Amanda, the choice was no contest.

At least Jen appeared to be a decent human being. Maybe she was hiding a more nefarious side. Some people who did religious or charity things were the biggest hypocrites he'd met. Then again, those tended to be the ones who liked to talk about it. People like Jen—who demurred when talking about it—were the ones who usually actually meant it. Of all the people involved, she might be the most reasonable.

But what would involving Jen mean?

He let the water run off his face. He hadn't shaved for a couple of days, and the temptation to let the hint of a beard come in was strong. Maybe he'd fit in better here. He chuckled at the absurdity of it. How had Kevin slunk his way through this town? The whole of it was the antithesis to everything he knew of his brother.

Kevin had loved loud parties, fast women, and even faster drugs. The overdose hadn't surprised Jason.

But the woman Kevin had a kid with . . . she was a surprise. Unless she was hiding something.

Now he really sounded like his grandfather.

He slammed his hand against the spigot, shutting off the water. He didn't want to involve Jen in this. Each person involved made things more complicated. If it weren't for the damned Powells, he'd be able to breathe, but they were strangling him, making the whole thing more tenuous for the people of Cavanaugh Metals he actually cared about.

People he'd known all his life. People who had comforted him after the deaths of both his parents. They were the reason he had stayed in Chicago for so long—to absorb the blows his cantankerous grandfather delivered as he'd grown increasingly more unstable and deluded about who was out to get him.

If it weren't for the people in the company, he'd wash his hands of it. Walk away like Kevin had.

He could almost hear his grandfather's smug laughter. *"Yeah, right, Kevin. You'll come back with your hand out. Neither you nor Jason could survive five minutes out there without my money."*

He grabbed a soft towel and stepped out of the bathroom, toweling off as he went. He had to talk to Mildred. Find out what had really happened to Kevin when the money ran out. Kevin hadn't come to Brandywood by accident, that's for sure. But what it all meant had broader implications than he allowed himself to consider before.

CHAPTER EIGHT

Yardley's was entirely too packed for this.

Oddly enough, Jen had been dumped at Yardley's before, by her first boyfriend, at age fifteen. But she hadn't expected to be dumped tonight by three-date Brad, of all people.

God. She'd shaved her legs tonight. *For this?*

Could she even be dumped if they'd only gone out three times? They weren't an official anything. Which was exactly why she shouldn't have signed up for that baking competition without asking him. *Shit.*

Jen tried to focus on Brad's moving lips, her brain going to the sound of live music in the bar beside the main dining room. She squeezed her eyes shut briefly, trying to unscramble her thoughts, which had dulled by the two glasses of wine she'd had during dinner, then looked back at Brad.

"So let me get this straight. You brought me out to tell me you don't want to keep dating me?" She stabbed her cheesecake with a fork, though she had lost any appetite she had for it. "You couldn't have told me by text? Before you spent the whole evening talking like nothing was wrong?"

Brad shifted with discomfort, loosening the collar of his button-down shirt. He'd buttoned the top button, no wonder. "Look, it's a lot of jumping through hoops. We can't talk at night because you're working or sleeping with your kid in the bed. I'm looking over my shoulder at all times because everyone has warned me about the sudden parking and speeding tickets I might get from your police officer brother. And then, this whole thing with that kiss? My mother was the one who called to tell me about it. What was I supposed to say to that?"

Her eyes narrowed at him. "You could have asked me what happened."

Brad leaned forward. "She wasn't the only person who saw it, Jen. And it's not like people don't know about you."

What. The. Hell.

She envisioned grabbing her glass of water and tossing it in his lap. Her hand shook as she reached for it and sipped it, trying to take a calming breath. "It was a harmless kiss with a stranger. Because the crowd was chanting."

"Three dates, well over several hundred dollars, and I can't even get to second base. Now you're telling me you were making out with a stranger to make people cheer? My mom said you looked like you really enjoyed that kiss."

"Glad to know you were trying to buy your way into my pants." She stood, yanking her purse from the back of the chair. She reached into her purse. The only thing she had was a fifty-dollar bill—her change from signing up for the baking competition before Brad arrived earlier that evening.

Her heart fell. Another fifty dollars she didn't have to waste, down the drain. She threw the money on the table. "Don't worry. I can pay for myself. Keep the change and make sure you give the server a good tip. Most people tip twenty percent, you know."

Cheap asshole. She'd wanted to hide her face when she'd seen the last few tips he'd left.

Brad didn't even look apologetic. "You're not exactly a known catch, Jen. Everyone whom I've even told about dating you says I'm crazy for trying."

Asshole.

Dammit, Dan. Warren, too, to a lesser extent. Her brothers had made her basically un-dateable. After the incident with Garrett the year before, Dan had sworn to never get involved in her love life again—but by then, the damage was too great. Dan beating up a man he thought she was interested in had made the rounds faster than she could control the spread. Her pathetic dating life had dwindled to online matches who lied on their profiles and guys like Brad.

Mad as she was at Dan and Warren, they were her brothers. They did it because they loved her.

Brad was just a dick.

She wished she could overturn the table and make a big scene as they did in the movies. For once, she wished she had the gumption to really put a jerk in his place. She'd been screwed over on one too many dates, by one too many assholes.

His panties were seriously in a twist because she'd kissed Jason during *A Christmas Carol?*

"Just so you know, maybe the reason I looked like I enjoyed that kiss is because that guy knew what the hell he was doing." It was the only thing she could think to say. Her throat tightened, her lack of imagination frustrating her as much as Brad was. Instead, she turned and fled through the tables at Yardley's, determined not to cry.

Brad didn't deserve her tears.

She made it outside and yanked on her coat, so flushed with anger that she practically didn't need it.

Brad had picked her up, and she was *not* going to have him

drive her back. The heels of her nude pumps wobbled as she traipsed down the sidewalk toward Bunny's. Travis would still be there—it was only a little past nine—and he'd drive her if she asked.

"You're not exactly a known catch."

Ouch. Not that she'd never had insults hurled in her direction, but why such vitriol?

Brad must have been furious about that kiss.

Angry enough to dump her without bothering to talk to her about it first. And be a first-class asshole about it. She could understand being bothered by the kiss, especially hearing about it from someone else. But the rest was unforgivable.

She hugged her arms to her chest. She was tired of all this. Tired of getting her hopes up. Tired of failing. Tired of being the girl who screwed up. Between the impossible standards of her brothers and being held to constant scrutiny, she would always fall short.

She hadn't been the first woman to have an unplanned pregnancy with a deadbeat dad.

On days like this, she wanted to find Kevin, wherever the hell he was, and scream at him.

Whatever he saw in her that had made him leave, she couldn't comprehend a reason he would skip out on even meeting their beautiful boy. Of all the ways she'd failed, that was the one that hurt the most: she'd failed to give her son a good daddy.

She couldn't let herself continue going down that train of thought. Nothing good ever came from it.

The familiar bell on Bunny's Café rang as she stepped inside. Most people couldn't wait to leave their jobs when they were off. They didn't spend their time off at work.

Travis was still behind the counter, wearing the bright blue uniform apron. After all these years of him stepping in whenever Bunny wasn't around, it still made her laugh to see him in it. He was a mechanic and owned an auto detailing shop the rest of the time, a trade he had picked up from his father.

He frowned when he saw her and looked at the clock on the wall behind him. One dark eyebrow quirked. "What happened?"

Jen glanced around the café. Only a handful of customers were here tonight . . . their big rush was usually around lunch. Weekend nights attracted the occasional moms catching up over coffee and first dates, but rarely the dinner crowds.

She sighed and left her coat hanging on the coatrack. "I got dumped. If it counts after three dates."

Travis winced, his warm brown eyes sympathetic. "Truth time?"

She nodded. It was their way of telling each other hard truths without the other getting offended.

"I didn't like him anyway. Anyone who wears sockless boating shoes with pastel pants—there's no coming back from that."

A giggle erupted, and she curled her arms on the counter, pressing her forehead against the cool wooden surface. "Ugh . . . why do I always pick the worst guys?"

"Did you even like Brad that much?"

"No." She chewed on her lip. "But right now, I'm willing to settle."

"That's your problem right there." Travis pulled an éclair from the glass case and slid it toward her. "Be more like me. Miserable and alone, but completely confident in that decision."

Her eyes met his, and she rolled them. "No. Your problem is you're afraid of the girl you're in love with. I don't have that problem. I just have no one to love."

She went behind the counter and grabbed a fork. Travis

had shared his feelings about Lindsay with Jen years before, but they didn't talk about it often. Travis and Lindsay had even hooked up once. The result? Now she could never hang out with her two best friends at the same time.

"I'm not afraid of her. I'm afraid of her family. And she's afraid of mine. Until the Hatfields and McCoys decide to give it a rest, what chance do we have?" Travis grabbed a mug. "Latte or cappuccino?"

"Latte, thanks. And I think you're both still being ridiculous. Also, if not her, I'm sure there's a long line of women who'd appreciate you. If I met a guy who could fix my car and make me breakfast, I'd marry him tomorrow."

Travis smirked. "You wouldn't, though. Because despite your claims to the contrary, you don't want to settle. You're picky. You always have been." The frother whirred to life, hissing steam and gurgling milk.

"According to Brad, I'm not that great of a catch."

Travis's face darkened. "What a prick."

"He was mad because he heard from his mother that I kissed a guy during the play last night." She summarized the situation with Jason briefly and added, "But it was nothing and meant nothing to me. He could've at least asked."

Blinking at her for a minute, Travis studied her features. "I agree Brad was an ass. But . . . you're sure it meant nothing?"

That warm feeling, the aching of her palms like her nerves were misfiring, resurfaced. Nothing. Jason, the douche who called for service and had hookups with strangers. Yeah, it meant nothing, right? "I'm totally sure."

"Okay, well, don't look now, but a guy is standing outside the café window looking at you. And for the last thirty seconds, I'm pretty sure he's been trying to figure out whether to come in and talk to you." Travis poured the espresso into the frothed milk and slid it toward her.

She couldn't help but look. He was right. Jason was out on the sidewalk.

Their eyes met briefly, and she froze. Snapping her eyes back at Travis, she caught the hint of laughter in Travis's expression. "Nothing, right? I told you not to look. Looks like he's coming in."

"What's he doing here?" she muttered under her breath. She sipped her latte, wishing she hadn't had that wine with dinner. It didn't take much alcohol for her to get too chatty these days. Maybe the coffee would counteract it.

"He knows you work here." Travis shrugged and walked back toward the kitchen.

"Hey, Jen." Jason stood only a few feet from the doorway with his hands in his coat pockets. "I didn't expect to see you here."

She turned toward him. "Well, I do work here. Except I'm not working today. I mean, right now. I was working earlier. And you know I work here, so I'm guessing maybe it might have occurred you'd run into me?" Yeah, she needed an upper. She took a big, hot swallow of latte, and it burned the roof of her mouth.

Choking it back, she tried to suck in some air to cool it down and looked around for a napkin. She coughed a few times, sputtering on coffee. *Real elegant, Jen. Graceful.*

Jason slid up beside her and pulled a napkin from the holder beside the register. He handed it to her. "You okay?"

She didn't look at him as she tried to clear the coffee from her lungs. At last, she gave him a tense smile. "I may never taste anything again, but I'm fine. So what are you up to?"

"Just came to take a picture of the space I parked in yesterday. I don't think it was marked clearly, and my lawyer wanted me to . . ." He trailed off as though he sensed he sounded self-indulgent. "It doesn't matter."

She wiped her mouth, checking her blouse. She'd dripped coffee on her shirt. A ticklish feeling spread to the back of her neck. She'd also worn a lower-cut top in case her date with Brad went in that direction. And, yup, Jason had noticed, too. His eyes cut from her boobs back to her face.

Great. "I-I was on a date," she explained, as though she needed an explanation for why she'd dressed in a more revealing outfit.

"Were?" Jason checked his watch. He had more scruff on his face than the day before and it was sexy.

Oh, God. She was doing it, wasn't she? Fumbling over her attraction to this casual-sex indulgent, just-passing-through stranger. *Very bad. Stop it now.*

"Yeah, well, it turns out when you kiss a stranger in the middle of the street while the whole town watches, the guy you're dating doesn't take it so well." Jen flashed him a grin. "What can you do?" Travis came out of the kitchen and started cleaning the bagel toaster. The look on his face made it clear he had been intently listening.

Jason rubbed his well-defined jawline. Such a good jawline. She focused on his eyes as he said, "I'm so sorry. Want me to . . . talk to him?" He grimaced as he finished the sentence awkwardly, as though he knew it couldn't possibly be a solution, but he felt obliged to offer anyway.

"No, it's fine." She released the words in a rushed breath. "He was a jerk anyway. And now I know." Okay. Enough. Before she made a bigger fool of herself. She straightened, then reached behind the counter, helping herself to a plastic to-go container and a paper cup. She slid the éclair into the container and poured her coffee into the cup. "I'm going to take my dessert for one home. Maybe there's some cheesy movie about a prince masquerading as a pauper in flannel at Christmas on."

He smiled, and that hint of a dimple made her pulse do things it really shouldn't be doing.

"In light of costing you a date, can I get you a drink?"

She popped the top onto the cup. She had a drink. Coffee. Something to sober her up, reminding her of her single-mom life and to move on. Her eyes darted to Travis.

Travis gave her a hard look, one she understood well. *Go.*

"All right." *Mistake.* "Where to?" *Mistake, mistake.*

Jason looked over at Travis. "Where's a good place for drinks? I went to some dive bar called The Bench the other night."

"You should try Yardley's." Travis turned away again, but not before Jen caught the glimmer of furtive laughter in his eyes. "Just a short walk."

She grabbed her coat again and slipped the boxed éclair into her purse. Grabbing the coffee, she called out a thank-you to Travis, then started forward, Jason a few steps behind her. No way in hell was she going back to Yardley's fifteen minutes after one date with a new one.

Though she would pay to see the look on Brad's face if he heard about it.

"I would offer to drive, but my car's still at the impound lot." Jason fell into step behind her. "I had someone drop me off in town."

"It's really not far." Jen pointed down the block to Yardley's, coffee cup in hand. The frigid December air was doing nothing to her cheeks. She examined the cup, her tongue still feeling scalded. Then she tossed it in a nearby trash can. She shouldn't have wasted the cup.

She glanced at Jason. "Get your family situation figured out?"

"Not really." Jason didn't look at her, as if doing so would breach some cryptic code known only to him. "Things have actually gotten a bit more complicated." He glanced in a shop window displaying a Christmas train setup. "They go all out on Christmas here, don't they?"

"Yeah, it's sort of a thing. Especially this year. You know. Parade of lighted boats on the lake, carriage rides, tree lightings. There's even a couples-only baking competition in a few weeks, as cliché as it sounds." One that she'd have to watch from the sidelines. "But you'll probably be gone by then." She hoped he'd correct her.

"Probably." Jason rubbed the back of his neck. "Speaking of Christmas, I feel like I should apologize about that whole kiss last night."

Was he purposely avoiding eye contact with her? He seemed embarrassed. No, that wasn't it. "You didn't make it happen. It's fine."

"But it ruined your date tonight."

"Probably better in the long run." She gripped the strap of her purse. "I don't have a ton of time to waste on dates that aren't going anywhere."

His brow furrowed. "So dates with you are for serious contenders only?"

She grimaced, realizing how it had sounded. "I mean . . ." She bit her lip, trying to think of a better way to put it. Then she defaulted to her comfort zone. "Not all of us are experts at finding random partners the first night in town."

Now the corners of his lips twitched. "Who says I'm an expert?"

"Aren't you, though?" She flashed him a knowing look.

He shrugged. "Casual is easier. No messy goodbyes." His gaze pierced hers. "You've never just . . ."

Her cheeks grew warmer. "Just what? Hooked up with a random guy?"

"Basically, yeah."

She'd pretty much invited him to have a conversation about her sex life. This was why she needed to butt out of his. She shook her head. "Nope."

"And how's that going for you?" They got closer to Yardley's, and the beat of the drums from the live band sounded into the night.

She stopped, cocking her head to the side. She should feel shyer than she did right now. Noticing her lips were dry, she dug through her purse for a lip gloss. "Honestly?"

Jason's eyes followed the movement of her hands as she uncapped the lip gloss and applied it. "I wouldn't want anything but."

Was she really having this conversation right now? Maybe the fact that he was a stranger—a stranger she'd kissed—made it easier. "Honestly, I haven't had sex in a really long time, and it's driving me crazy."

A satisfied smirk came to settle on his face. "See? Casual is better. You don't have to wait for the 'right' person, if that even exists."

She paused on the sidewalk and eyed him. "So you don't believe in love and marriage and monogamy and all that?" All the things she was waiting for. *Because you can't afford to be selfish, Jen. Someone else is affected by everything you do.*

He shrugged as they started walking again. "It's not all it's cracked up to be."

Jen raised a brow. "You've been married?" He seemed too young to be divorced. But some people married young and divorced right away. Maybe that was what it really was: he seemed too fond of the bachelor lifestyle to have ever been married.

"A monumental mistake." Jason stretched his shoulders back. They reached the door, and he held it open for her.

As she passed him into Yardley's, she felt oddly thrilled to be coming back here with him. A hot, mysterious stranger in town? That she'd been seen kissing? Let them talk. She'd earned the right to have some fun after the crap week she'd had.

They went to the bar and ordered drinks, but there was standing room only. Finding a corner against the wall of coasters to stand near, Jen slipped her coat onto her arm. "Here, I'll take that from you," Jason offered. He hung both their coats at a nearby coatrack, then returned with their drinks. He nodded toward the coasters. "What's that about?"

"It's an old Brandywood tradition. When you're an official couple, you go up there and tack a coaster with your names written on it. The owner leaves it up forever, so it's not anything to be taken lightly. Think of it like the lock thing people used to put on Parisian bridges, sort of."

"Except it annoyed the ever-living shit out of Parisians, and they were always cutting locks off and throwing them out," Jason remarked dryly, clearly unimpressed with the senti- mental gesture.

Trust him not to care about sentimentality. She twirled the stem of the glass of wine. She should have switched to some- thing that would make her less woozy, but she might throw up. Watching Jason take a pull from his beer, she analyzed his features. What was it about him that made her feel so at ease?

"So how does the casual thing work?" she asked when he stepped closer to her. "One night, no repeats?" That was the situation with the woman the other night, right?

Jason gave her a questioning look. Then he smiled. He'd probably had braces because no one had teeth that straight. Slinging back another drink, he shrugged. "It would never work for you."

Cocky bastard. She glared. "I didn't say I was considering it." She had totally been considering it, but he didn't have to know that. A one-night stand might be exactly what she needed. Someone to make her feel wanted, who never had to meet Colby. She was smarter about sex than she'd been when she got pregnant.

And Kevin had taught her that being in a loving relationship didn't stop the other person from walking out on you.

"You're too set in your ways. You want romance. This isn't romance. It's just sex." Jason's eyes drifted over the names of couples on the coasters tacked to the wall. "That—that's you. I bet you even have a coaster up there with your name on it, don't you?"

Yep. She purposely avoided scanning the wall for the coaster Kevin had put up there. She sipped her wine. "I'm currently fifty dollars in the hole from entering that couples-only baking competition as a newly party of one. I'm willing to consider my options."

Jason cringed. "You're making me feel even guiltier about that kiss, you know."

She rolled her eyes. "Don't be. I'm glad you kissed me." Maybe it was the alcohol or the forced proximity, but she was enjoying the intimacy of their no-holds-barred conversation. "First decent kiss I've had in a while." Without waiting for a reaction, she lifted her chin toward the crowded bar. "So show me how it's done. How do you find your one-night stand in a throng like this?"

Jason stood shoulder to shoulder with her, facing the bar. "What makes you think I can teach you?"

"You're the expert, remember?" She stared at the sides of her glass as she swirled the white wine around.

"You make it sound like I go around bragging about my exploits."

True. She only knew about his behavior because she'd walked into his bathroom. And then pried. And pried some more. Before she could apologize, he went on, "It's a look you exchange, you know?"

She almost choked on her wine. "No, I don't know." Had anyone ever given her that look? Her thighs tightened.

Jason leaned closer, his lips only inches from her ear, his breath warm on her cheek. "Okay, it's a feeling. Like the two of you are all alone in the room, but you're ready to find a place to tear each other's clothes off."

Oh . . .

Yes, she knew that feeling. She was having it right now.

She turned her face toward his, her chest growing tighter, her pulse faster. Her eyes dipped to his lips. "And then . . ."

A smile curved his full lips. "And then you go fuck."

Her breath caught. Red-hot tingles shot up her spine, a warm flush spreading to her core.

He lifted his beer to his lips and took another drink.

She tore her gaze from him. *Enough already.*

They stood in silence, facing the bar together. Then she felt his fingertips brush against hers, his hand at his side, like hers.

His touch was like electricity, shooting goose bumps up her skin. But if he was touching her hand, she wasn't imagining the chemistry between them either, was she? He had to be feeling it, too.

Or maybe it was because she'd practically demanded they talk about sex.

She shifted her hand away and turned her head to look over her shoulder at him. "You make it sound like it's super easy. If I tried that, I don't think I'd have a single taker."

His eyes drifted over the crowded bar. "You mean to tell me that if you make it clear to one of these small-town guys that you want them to take you home tonight, they'd be foolish enough to say no? I call bullshit."

She raised a defeated hand. "I'm serious. I don't think they would."

He guffawed. "No single straight man is going to tell you no. Hell, I bet even most of the married men would go for it. Have you looked at yourself in the mirror lately?" He leaned closer, his lips so close to her ear that they practically grazed the sensitive skin there. She suppressed a shiver, her breath catching. "In fact, I'm willing to bet good money you could get a guy faster than I can find a woman to take home."

When she turned her face toward his, he was tantalizingly close. She shifted her gaze from his lips. "How much?"

"How much am I willing to bet?" He grinned. "It wouldn't work. All you'd have to do to win is not try, which is what you want anyway." He paused, looking over her shoulder. "How about we do first person to find someone to take home wins twenty dollars instead?"

She held back a laugh. "You call that good money?" This was ridiculous to consider, wasn't it? Except he made her feel daring. *Alive.*

"I call that not wanting to lose too much of my money on a bet I know I'm going to lose. You're sexier than you seem to think, Jen. And it's not that hard to talk a man into sex."

The way he said it made her legs feel wobbly. But he might have a point. After all, it had been *her* rules that had kept her from jumping into bed with someone casually. "All right." She raised her chin daringly. "But I have an advantage. These people know me on some level. Small town, remember? How do you know I'm not going to go find a friend and tell them about our bet so I can win your money?"

He threw his head back and laughed. "First, because that's not the game we're playing. Second, because you're honest enough that you felt the need to admit that to me. Anyway, I don't think you've convinced me you're up for this anyway."

Before she could answer, the band struck up loudly once again, making conversation more difficult. She didn't know if she welcomed the interruption or not. Tapping her foot to the beat, she avoided looking at him. Was he right about her? Was she incapable of letting loose and having a fun, if forgettable, night?

Couples were making their way out to the dance floor, and she let her gaze wander over them. *Who am I kidding?*

Even if she was pretty, that still didn't solve the problem of her undatable reputation in town because of Dan. Anyone considering taking her home for the night would have to be crazy. *Unless they aren't from around here.*

She stepped away from Jason, more conscious than ever of his presence. She didn't have to look back at him to feel his eyes trailing her as she circled the dance floor, pretending to examine potential partners.

But to her surprise, when she glanced up at him, Jason had one elbow against the bar, already in conversation with a pretty brunette who worked at the yoga studio.

"Goddamn him," she muttered, pursing her lips. So much for him being attracted to her.

She tossed her long hair over her shoulder, looking at the men at the bar more earnestly, hoping to catch someone's eye. Isn't that how Jason said it was done? She paused by a row of high-top tables, feeling lost. This wouldn't do anything to help her self-confidence.

Her gaze flitted toward the bar once again. Jason wasn't there anymore, but the brunette was. Jen cocked her head to the side and scanned the bar, then the dance floor.

Jason wasn't anywhere to be seen.

This is stupid.

She shouldn't be here with him in the first place. And she'd turned a perfectly nice offer for drinks into this, once again screwing things up.

Jen looked for a clear spot on the bar to leave her wine. With one final swallow, she marched to the bar and set her glass down. Going back over to the coatrack, she searched for her coat. But Jason's coat was still there. She turned to see Jason excusing his way past the crowded bar toward her. His eyes met hers, and he offered a warm, questioning look. "Are you leaving?" He leaned down toward her so she could hear him.

She straightened. "I just . . ." She shook her head. Trying to talk over the music was almost impossible. Should she admit defeat now? That he was right—she wasn't cut out for finding someone random to hook up with?

The song ended, and the bar patrons clapped. As the music transitioned to a slow crooner, Jason curled his fingers against hers ever so lightly. He stepped closer. "Want to dance?"

There it was: that feeling of intoxication when he touched her, a flutter of nerves in her stomach. Grateful that he didn't mention their bet, she nodded. "All right."

His hand grazed the small of her back, his strong fingertips splaying against that sensitive area right above her waistline and settling there, gently. As he pulled her closer to him, her heart hammered wildly in her chest. If she was honest with herself, the bet had been dumb. Because she wasn't a one-night stand kind of girl. Especially not to prove a point.

And her attraction to Jason was distracting her.

As they swayed to the music, Jason's thumb trailed over her skin, right at the hem of her shirt. "I thought you'd already found someone to take home," she admitted, hoping the stab of irrational jealousy she'd felt wouldn't come through. She tilted her head toward the brunette at the bar.

Jason's cheek brushed her own, his hand tightening. "No, I

asked her where the ATM was. You were giving up that easily, huh?"

She swallowed, her mouth dry. His featherlight touch on her back was making goose bumps rise on her skin. Not that he was *just* a stranger. She worked at the cabins and saw strangers all the time, especially at this time of year. And ever since Peter Yardley had turned into a celebrity, Redding Cabins were booked solid. Laura was even talking about expanding. Strangers were a part of her life.

No, there was something about *Jason*. And if she was going to be bold, she should do it with him. "Actually . . ." Her lips grazed his jawline. "It so happens I was already having a drink with the guy who caught my attention."

His hand stilled, his body close enough to hers that she felt the taut muscles of his stomach stiffen as he slowed them to a stop. "I'm not a good option for you, Jen. You'd get hurt."

"Then why are you dancing with me?" She tipped a smile at him, drawing her face back so she could scan his eyes as she led him back into the dance.

His expression was guarded, his movements less fluid. "Because a beautiful woman like you shouldn't be on the sidelines of the dance floor, especially when I cost you your date tonight."

She laughed, not buying it. Whatever chip he had on his shoulder that made him occasionally ruthless and insensitive, he'd also shown a different side. She pushed her hips closer to his and felt her confidence level climb. Even if he didn't want to admit it, his arousal was clear. She tugged at his earlobe with her lips ever so gently, feeling sexier than she had for years. "So if I told you I wanted you to take me home, you'd say no?"

She recognized a few couples on the dance floor eyeing her and gave them a satisfied smile. *Let them talk.*

Jason groaned, sucking in a shallow breath. "And you think

you don't have what it takes." His palms clamped her hips as they swayed. "How much have you had to drink tonight?"

"Three glasses of wine. Over two hours, though." Her eyes locked with his. Did he think she was going to regret the decision later? "I'm not drunk, Jason. Besides, I'm only talking about one night. And then you can forget me, right?"

She'd had enough to drink to make some bad decisions. But she welcomed the decrease in her inhibitions tonight. It was fun, and she was so tired of being "undatable Jen" and playing by the rules.

He released her and stepped back, scanning her face. After a moment, he gave a taut nod, his face unreadable. "Right. If you're clear that's all this would be."

As though he wants to prove I'm forgettable. She shrugged. "That's all it would be."

He pulled out his phone. "I have to call a ride." A few taps of buttons and he was pushing his phone back into his pocket. "Two minutes. Ready?"

She grabbed her coat and followed him out the door, because why not? Colby was safe with her mom, and she wanted to feel like a sexy woman, not just a mom. *And I shaved my legs.*

CHAPTER NINE

WAS it possibly the dumbest thing he'd done yet? Yes. But she didn't look like pretty Jen tonight. Tonight, she was jaw-droppingly sexy. And some idiot had let her go—*looking like that.*

Jason had to get her out of his system.

But more importantly, he *could* forget her. He'd be stupid to deny he was attracted to her. And right now, that attraction was ruining his ability to think clearly. If he slept with her, he'd move on. Just like he did with every other woman.

She was visibly nervous as she slid into the car's back seat beside him. Not a bad nervous. But an alluring innocence to it made him want her even more. Yet now that she had left the bar with him, that confidence seemed to slip a bit.

He reached over and took her hand, interlacing their fingers. The action made her visibly relax, and his heart settled at a steady pace. "My cabin okay?"

She nodded. "I don't know that I've ever gone into a cabin when I haven't been working." Her pupils were wide in the darkness, her blue eyes almost diminished by them.

"You work a lot, don't you?" His thumb brushed

against the fleshy part of her palm, and her fingers tightened in response. Keeping her talking was a good idea. He wasn't used to women who were nervous like this anymore. Reminding her of their connection would set her at ease.

"Six days and three nights a week." She fidgeted with her purse. "The cabins are the undemanding job. Mostly, I get to sleep and man the phones. Sometimes there's a late check-in, but they give us a heads-up if that's the case."

"And the rest is at the café?"

"I split my time between serving and the kitchen. I prefer baking, but the money is better for serving. More tips." She pulled the éclair out of her purse. "Actually, I made this earlier this morning when I was at the café."

"That's impressive." The idea surprised him. He didn't know why. But it seemed like an advanced skill for someone who mostly took orders and answered phones.

She popped open the container and broke off a piece. "Want to try it?" She held it out to him.

He wasn't the biggest fan of sweets, but he didn't want to offend her by saying so. Taking it from her, he ate it. The flavor was incredible, the delicate pastry melting against his tongue. He swallowed. "This is amazing."

"Thanks." She licked the pastry cream from her fingertips, and he almost groaned. *God, this woman.* The freaking car needed to go faster.

"I'm serious. I don't eat a lot of desserts, but this is one of the top ones I've ever tasted." He wasn't exaggerating to get in her pants, oddly enough. Did he sound genuine? It barely sounded sincere to him, so there wasn't any way she would believe his motivation. "I'm really not just saying it. You should open your own bakery."

"I want to, but it's not so simple." A wistful expression

lingered in her eyes. But something else. An ember of excite-ment that he sensed she didn't discuss often.

"Because you don't want to compete with your boss?"

"That's part of it. Bunny taught me everything I know. Setting up my own bakery might really hurt her, and she's like family to me." Jen played with her necklace. "But it would be amazing to have a place on Main that I could call my own. There's this old hardware store that used to belong to Colby's great-grandfather, and it would be perfect. But the building needs a ton of work, and I just don't have the money for some-thing like that. I could never get a business loan." She sighed. "Someday. Maybe." Her lips tipped in a smile. "You have some left right here." She leaned over, brushing some crumbs from his lips with a featherlight touch.

Now she was just messing with him.

The power dynamic between them was unusual. She seemed to take it back from him effortlessly but not in a commanding way. *Aggressive.* That fact was unbelievably alluring.

He reached for her fingers, then kissed them smoothly. He returned their intertwined hands to her lap, grazing her thigh. "No wonder you were going to enter a baking competition."

Her sigh was an unhappy one. "Yeah, but I can't now. It's for couples only. I was hoping to ask my date." Her eyes darted to the rearview mirror toward the driver. The driver kept his gaze level with the road, clearly aware of the intimacy of their behavior.

She'd been hoping to ask the idiot who had let her go tonight. Jason felt a twinge of guilt. "Maybe next year?"

She shook her head. "It's not like a yearly thing or some-thing. It's being sponsored by a cable television network and has a twenty-five-thousand-dollar prize. Which I could really use right about now. But I guess it's not meant to be."

"Well, it's not twenty-five thousand dollars, but"—he fished a twenty from his pocket—"I grabbed this from the ATM for you because I knew you would win. Which you did, actually. So congrats."

She laughed, pushing the money away. "No way. It was a tie."

He smirked and rolled it up, then shoved it in her purse. "A bet's a bet. I would have expected you to pay up."

They pulled up in front of the cabin. Thank God TJ had found some seedy motel that had a room available. Of course, if TJ saw who Jason had brought back, he'd probably call him insane.

And maybe he was insane.

He wasn't used to this level of overanalyzing who he took home. After TJ had shown him the footage of Amanda and Chad together, he'd sworn he would control the circumstances of any encounter with a woman. Never give them hope for something more.

But he'd been clear with Jen. The rest was on her.

He unlocked the door and let her step in before him.

Now her lack of experience in this sort of situation bubbled closer to the surface. That woman he'd brought back from the bar the other night had practically ripped his clothes off at the door.

Jen was gripping her purse strap as though it were an anchor.

He really needed to hit up a liquor store if he was going to be staying here for much longer. He unzipped his coat and took hers. Setting them on the sofa, he reached for her hand. "Why don't we sit down?"

She didn't move from her place. "I'm not very good at this." She pushed a strand of hair behind her ear and gave him an apologetic look. "I'm sorry."

He came up beside her and set his hands on her hips. "We don't have to do a single thing you don't want to do." Her reluctance now was disappointing but unsurprising. Still, it would take a lot more than a run to get this night out of his system. He'd let himself fantasize about her. That was never a good idea if sex wasn't really on the table.

She rubbed her arms. "I've never slept with a guy I barely know."

Was she shaking? The idea of it filled him with a mixture of awe and fascination. But he was losing her here. He'd been right about her. She liked romance. No-strings-attached sex was too much to ask from a girl like her.

But it didn't have to be a mad dash to the bedroom, either. He could give her a little romance if that was what she wanted. He left her side and went to the fireplace, thankful it was gas. With a flip of a switch, it roared to life with a *whoosh*. Going over to a basket, he grabbed a blanket and set it in front of the fireplace. He sat facing the fireplace, his knees bent in front of him. Looking over his shoulder at her, he said, "Want to sit here and warm up?"

A smile curved her lips, and she came toward him, then sat. She curled her legs to the side. "You're trying to make me comfortable, aren't you?"

"Is it working?"

She laughed lightly. "Maybe." She leaned back on her hands, away from him. "You know, I admit I don't really know what to make of you. There's this one side of you that's standoffish and kind of a jerk."

"Ouch." But he probably deserved that. He couldn't really deny he'd been that way toward her.

She shrugged. "You and I both know it's true."

He gave a slow nod. "But?"

"But there's another side, too. I mean, I can't imagine you're this charming with all the women you hook up with. You'd be leaving a trail of broken hearts and shattered dreams."

She had a point. "Are you trying to talk me out of this?"

"No." She bit her lip. "Just trying to figure out why you're being nice to *me.*"

That was way more complicated than even he could unpack. Before he could speak, though, she leaned forward, her fingertips against his. As their fingers interlaced, his pulse picked up a notch and he met her gaze.

Why am I being nice to her?

She was beautiful, but she was also dangerous. Just being with her meant risking everything. But the brush of her thumb against his was incredibly alluring.

Maybe a little danger appealed right now.

He scooted closer to her and pushed a strand of hair behind her ear. "Why shouldn't I be nice to you?" His thumb skimmed her jawline.

She shrugged. "Well, the guy I was on a date with tonight told me I basically wasn't worth the trouble. I don't even know why I'm telling you." There was a flash of hurt in her eyes, though, something that needed soothing.

Probably why she's here.

Her words brought a jolt of anger to him. Some asshole had said that to her? Stranger still was the fact that she felt like she could confide that to him. He didn't know that he'd done much to deserve her trust. The flames on the fake logs in the fireplace danced like translucent, molten ghosts, stirring up the embers of something he hadn't felt in a long time. He clenched his jaw, blinking away from the fire.

"Sounds like that man is an idiot." But he was the wrong person to soothe that hurt, and he didn't know what the hell he was doing. Still, they were here. He leaned forward, his lips finding his way to hers, and her mouth melted against his, soft and yielding, drawing him deeper toward her. This was an area he felt confident in. He pushed away the nagging thoughts that wanted to snake their way in. Her lips were warm, full against his, less timid than he'd imagined she would be.

Her mouth opened to his as his tongue tasted hers. As her arms tightened around his neck, his hands slid around her back, dipping low on the small of her back and trailing over her thighs. He wanted to feel those thighs around him and taste every square inch of her. As his lips trailed to the curve of her jaw, his hands slipped under her shirt.

"Jason?" She pulled back from him, searching his eyes. Her lips tipped in a smile. "I want to do this. I want to fuck you."

Holy shit.

Those words coming out of her mouth were the biggest turn-on. Ever.

Apparently, the pretty do-gooder had a wild side.

Their mouths collided again, this time without tenuous hesitation. Her tongue darted into his mouth, stroking against his as the sexual tension between them built, simmering to a hot boil as his hands moved up to cup her full breasts. Her bra was lacy—and in the way.

He was determined to be cool and detached. If she was here for sex, that was what she would get and nothing more. Then he could go on with his life.

Jason tugged at her top, then slipped it over her head. She wore a lacy black bra over perfect breasts. No doubt she'd worn lingerie for her date.

"What's the name of the idiot who broke up with you tonight?"

She gave him an odd look. "Brad. Why?"

"I need to find him and thank him." He reached behind her. As he deftly unhooked her bra, his palms replaced the lace fabric, and he slid his hands over the fullness of her breasts, her nipples hardening at his touch. She moaned lightly into his mouth as she unbuttoned his shirt.

A shrill ringtone made them both flinch. *Not mine.*

Jen pulled her face away from his, blinking as the phone's ring brought her back to reality. She was breathless, her face a soft pink. "I should get that," she whispered, dropping a full, luscious kiss on his mouth as she slinked away.

He had never hated a phone more. He was going to kill whoever was dragging this gorgeous, topless woman away from him.

She dug through her purse for her phone and pulled it out. Cursing under her breath, she turned it on. "Hey, Mom." Her frown deepened, and she turned from him, covering her breasts with her arm. "Well, can you put him on?"

He stood and stared into the flames, setting his hand against the stone façade of the fireplace.

"Hey, buddy." Jen's voice dropped to a soft, singsong tone. "You okay?" She listened for a few beats. "No, I know, buddy, come on. You're with Mom-Mom. She'll snuggle you."

Colby. *His nephew.*

He rubbed his eyes. What the fuck was he doing?

Shit.

Money aside, this whole situation was quickly spiraling out of control. Jen might be all right with having sex with him, but she didn't know who he was.

As her quiet coaxing on the phone ended, he straightened. A soft rustle came from behind him, and he turned to find her slipping back into her bra. "I have to go."

As much as he wanted her, his relief at her words felt like guilt coursing through his gut. "Okay."

She didn't meet his eyes as she grabbed her top. "My son has night terrors. Normally, he doesn't spend two nights away from me. But my mom kept him last night because he was excited to spend some time with his cousins. This means tonight, he's just not really having it. He started thrashing, and my parents woke him up, and now he's inconsolable."

"Yeah, it's never good to wake up a kid with night terrors." At her questioning look, he stammered, "My younger brother used to get them." Especially after their father's death.

His younger brother, the father of her child. He was glad for the dark, feeling the blood draining from his face. In fact, Colby had probably inherited it from Kevin.

"I don't think I ever had them, so my parents didn't know what to do." She grabbed her coat. "I'm so sorry." She took a few steps toward him, then paused as though unsure of how to handle the situation.

It wasn't like they could pick up where they'd left things. Her lips twisted regretfully. "I had fun, though. Sorry to leave you like this."

He gave her a practiced smile, trying to act more gallant than he felt. "Maybe we'll do it again sometime. Let me call you a car?"

Again sometime? So much for being gallant.

What the hell was he even saying?

"Hey, for what it's worth, I had more fun tonight than I've had in a long time. And this evening really didn't start like that."

He fumbled for an answer. *More fun than in a long time?* She didn't want to be pitied, but, God, something about the way she said that made him feel worse. He'd flirted with her and shared a few kisses.

But if he was honest, he'd had fun, too. And the strange tug of regret he felt at her leaving wasn't something he wanted to feel.

The time spent waiting for the car was almost torture. He

wanted to pull her back into his arms, kiss her until she refused to go without finishing what they'd started.

At last, headlights shone into the front windows and his phone buzzed with a notification. As though he hadn't noticed.

She chewed on her lip, then glanced back at him. "All right. I guess I'll just see you around."

He nodded, keeping her at arm's length. What was he supposed to say? His shoulders tensed. "Good night, Jen." A flash of hurt crossed her features.

She started to let herself out, then stopped as though caught by an impulse. Crossing the space between them, she tilted her head to the side and stood on her tiptoes.

She pressed a kiss to his cheek, then dragged her lips over to his ear. "You better not leave this town before we finish this." She stepped back with a coy smile on her mouth. "We're on pause. Not stop. Got it?" She pulled her phone out. "What's your number? I'm texting you later tonight."

A chuckle rumbled in his chest. *This woman.* Giving her his number was the total antithesis of casual sex, but he gave it to her anyway. She slipped out into the night, and he watched her go, his jaw tight. He didn't want to get enough of her, and it was killing him.

CHAPTER TEN

"Mommy, can I play the caterpillar game?"

Colby's voice sounded behind Jen, and she turned to look at him. He was already dressed for church, and she was still in her pajamas. Thank goodness for her mother. She grabbed a brush from the dresser and brushed his wavy locks to the side. "Maybe just for a couple of minutes while Mama gets ready."

He held his hands out eagerly. Grabbing her phone from the dresser, she smiled to herself. She'd exchanged a few sexy texts with Jason throughout the night, and for the first time, she'd woken up feeling a little more hopeful about her dismal love life. But she didn't want Colby to come across them, even if he couldn't read. Closing her messages, she opened the game app and handed the phone to him.

He left the room with a bounce, traveling down the hall-way. She closed the door behind him and went to the closet. Keeping some clothes here came in handy on days like this.

She'd spent the night at her parents' house rather than dragging Colby to their apartment in the middle of the night. Something about sending secret messages to a guy while spending the night in her old bedroom at home made her feel like she was in high school again sneaking around, though.

And it was precisely why she didn't want to move home. Her parents were wonderful and helpful, but she'd struggled too hard to prove she could make it on her own. Have her own freedom. She was sick of always being the screwup who had to come home with her hand out.

She threw her hair up into a ponytail and then started on her makeup. Knowing that a guy out there thought she was still sexy enough for a random hookup felt like a confidence boost. Especially when it was a man like Jason. She'd never met someone like him before.

A few minutes later, a soft knock sounded on her door. Checking her watch, she frowned. If she didn't step it up, she'd make her parents late for church. "I'm almost ready, Mom." She went to the door and opened it, then startled.

Dan stood at the door, arms crossed. What was her brother doing here?

"Hey." She grinned. "What's up?"

Dan waved her phone. "You got a text message while Colby was playing with it."

She felt the blood drain from her face as she reached for it. *Oh no.*

Holding the phone back, away from her, Dan's dark eyes grew even darker. "Who's Jason?"

She snatched the phone from his grip. "None of your business."

"It's my business when your son tries to figure out how to clear the message 'still woke up wanting to fuck you' from his game." Dan's eyes flashed. He looked down the hallway and stepped inside, lowering his voice. As he closed the door, he hissed, "Can you imagine if Colby had given that to Mom or Dad to clear?"

"It's still none of your business." But his words found their mark. A stab of guilt went through her. "And thank you for not saying anything to them."

She cleared the message from her screen and put the phone face down on the dresser. Her face burned. If there was one person she didn't want to have this conversation with, it was Dan. She wished he would leave, but his stance made it clear he had no intention of going anywhere. He crossed his arms. "So who is he? I thought you were dating some guy named Brad?"

"Brad dumped me." Jen shrugged as though it was old news. It really wasn't, but it felt like it. "Because I kissed Jason on Friday."

"When did this happen?" Dan looked less than pleased. God, no wonder her brother intimidated guys. He filled up the entire door frame. And he was a cop.

"When did *what* happen?"

"When did Brad dump you?"

"Um . . . last night." Jen searched under the bed for her heels.

"He dumped you last night? And you're already exchanging texts like this with Jason? Jason who?"

"Jason . . ." What had he said again? "I think he said his last name was Sutter." This sounded awful.

Maybe because it was bad.

Dan's eyes bulged. "You don't know his last name?"

"Sutter. Definitely Sutter." She grimaced. Dan was clearly unconvinced. "Anyway, um, so after work the other night, I drove Jason back to the cabins because his car got towed, and we ended up in the middle of the street during the *A Christmas Carol*. It wasn't like we meant to kiss."

"Why to the cabins?"

Trust Dan to catch these details. "Because that's where he's staying." She balanced on one foot, then the other, pulling her heels on.

Dan drew a sharp breath. "When exactly did you meet this new guy?"

God, he was grilling her. But she was used to this annoying questioning from him.

He wouldn't like this. She should just lie. But if he found out she'd lied to him, that could just be worse in the long run. "Thursday."

"What the actual fuck?" Dan stormed closer, his face red. "You meet a guy Thursday, kiss him Friday, then spend Saturday night with him?"

She leveled her gaze at him. It sounded irresponsible and horrible when he put it that way. And it was also true—almost, anyway. But still. "It's none of your business who I sleep with. Do you give any of your buddies at work this sort of inquisition when you swap stories?"

Dan raked his fingers through his hair. "You're not a dude, Jen. You're my sister. I give a damn what people are saying about you." He scowled. "And you should be better than this. You have a kid. You can't afford to expose him to whoever, whenever."

Now her own temper flared. "Did I say I was in a relationship? Or introducing anyone? You've made it impossible for me to date in this town, big brother. And now a rich, handsome stranger comes into town and isn't afraid to have sex with me. Forgive me for considering the option. I know you'd prefer for me to be a frickin' nun, but I happen to enjoy sex, same as everyone else our age."

Dan crossed his arms. "Real mature."

"Oh, shut up. Don't tell me you've never thought about screwing someone for fun. You can pretend to be a robot all you want, but you're not."

They squared off, and finally, Dan stepped back, letting out a frustrated breath. "I don't want to know the details of your little arrangement. But can you please promise you're being safe about it?"

Yes, because I've messed up everyone's life by having unprotected sex before. She'd learned her lesson. She narrowed her gaze at him and pointed at the door. "Out of my room."

"Jen, sweetheart! We have to get going," Mom called down the hallway.

Dan didn't move. "Look, Mom and Dad have been through a lot with you. You're right—it's your life, and I can't stop you if you want to be irresponsible. But don't expect them to foot the bill if you screw up."

She followed him out the door, so angry with him it was a struggle not to slap him. "You know, it's not like you've never screwed up and put other people through hell with your actions. Remember how my baby almost died because of you?"

Stopping at the top of the stairs, Dan stared at her, hurt in his eyes. He took a shaky breath. "I'm trying to protect you. You deserve better than some asshole who wants to use you for a one-night stand. And you know I'll regret that until the day I die."

"I can take care of myself." She had forgiven Dan for his actions the year before because she knew he hadn't forgotten the terror she'd experienced for those hours when Colby had been missing. But it was hard to let go, especially considering Colby's night terrors. She lived with his *horrible oversight* every day. Dan did not. And she was angry.

She pushed past him, hurrying down the stairs. Colby waited for her at the bottom, looking up at her with bright eyes.

"Mommy, can I have the game again? Uncle Danny took it from me." He held his hands up.

She shook her head. "No, we're all done with Mommy's phone right now." She helped him into his coat.

"Can I ride in Uncle Danny's police car?" Colby looked at Dan as he came to the bottom of the stairs.

"No, Pop is going to drive us." She pulled his winter hat down over his ears. Letting him ride with Dan was easy enough, but she was too angry with her brother to let Colby go with him.

"Pwwwwwwease?" Colby whined, holding his arms out to Dan. "I want to ride in Uncle Danny's car."

Dan set his mouth to a line. He gave Colby a sympathetic look. "It's up to your mom."

"And Mommy said no." Jen yanked her coat on.

As Colby cried, Dan's face softened. "For God's sake, don't punish the kid because you're mad at me. I can drop him off at the church on my way to work."

She couldn't control much right now, but she could control this. Forgiving Dan didn't mean that she had to forget the havoc his actions had wreaked on her life. Letting her anger get the better of her, she said, "I'm not punishing anyone. He's just going with me. He's my responsibility, end of story." She picked Colby up and stormed out, leaving Dan behind.

CHAPTER ELEVEN

FOR THE THIRTIETH time in the past ten minutes, Jason checked the notifications on his phone. After a night of messaging that had kept him up most of the night, Jen hadn't replied to his last text for a few hours.

Turning it off, he plugged the phone into the charger on the nightstand and got out of the bed, where he'd been working on his laptop. He could use a few hours away from his phone. Most of the time, it felt like an electronic leash that he couldn't get away from fast enough. Now he was like a teenager staring at his message app, willing for three little dots to appear and let him know she was talking to him again.

How in the hell had this happened?

He didn't believe in love at first sight but definitely lust at first sight. And he had a severe case of lust.

Not that it was even at first sight, really. But it hadn't taken long.

This had to end. He'd come to Brandywood to talk to Mildred, not get involved with his brother's ex-girlfriend and her kid.

Last night had only made it worse. A thousand times worse.

He dressed in his gym clothes, feeling a bit like someone had kicked him in the balls, and pulled the hood of his sweatshirt onto his head. No amount of fantasizing about her had helped last night. Without a car or a phone, his options were limited. He felt driftless and completely displaced.

As he stepped outside, he sucked in a deep breath of chilly mountain air. Some of the other cabins had fires going, and it perfumed the air with the scent of wood smoke.

He considered going for a run, but a run would probably end up taking him into town again. He didn't want to go into town, didn't want to be wandering the streets of Brandywood if Ned was skulking around. TJ had promised to find out where Ned was staying and keep tabs on his activities, but the chance of leading him to Jen and Colby was stronger now that he'd gotten involved with her. Come to think of it, TJ probably wouldn't want him turning his phone off.

But he needed the mental break. Nothing about that inheritance was clear anymore. Maybe Jen did deserve something. She was clearly struggling financially.

He headed into the woods, where dried, fallen leaves crunched under his running shoes. He nodded a hello at a couple walking their dog nearby.

If he could trust her, maybe Jen could help him do what he needed to do with the money for the business. Getting her on his side might be the safest way to go about everything. He'd set her and Colby up comfortably.

The sound of moving water up ahead made him freeze. He searched for the source. Just a stream. Nothing to get his heart beating as abnormally fast as it was. The water moved quickly, the ground near it muddy, as though the rain levels were higher than normal, and the stream couldn't absorb it. With how deep it was, there had to be a river nearby. Or it led to the lake.

He exhaled slowly, refocusing his brain away from the black thoughts.

Fucking ridiculous. He was thirty years old. A stream shouldn't do this to him.

When Amanda had found out he hated the water, she'd purposely scheduled the company picnic at Promontory Point on the shores of Lake Michigan. She said she wanted to help him get over his fears. Except she hadn't put it so nicely. *"It's embarrassing that you won't go boating with my friends. You're a grown-ass man."*

He headed back toward the cabins. A run into town might be preferable, after all.

A cop car was sitting in front of his cabin.

He put his hands in the front pocket of his sweatshirt and casually walked up toward the cabin. A cop was standing on his front porch in full uniform. He was a tall, intimidating man with a strong square jaw.

"Can I help you, Officer?" Jason approached the porch.

The cop turned and stared at him with a look that seemed to bore through his skull.

"You Jason Cavanaugh?" the cop asked.

"Yes, sir." The formality of his response was second nature. His grandfather had been a stickler about that sort of thing.

"Mind if I ask you a few questions?" The cop shifted his weight, the floorboard creaking under his feet and his black work boots.

Jason didn't love the idea of inviting this guy inside his cabin, but he didn't want to have a conversation out in the open, either. Had he broken some law he didn't know about?

He nodded and unlocked the cabin, letting the officer in. He flipped on the light in the living room and pulled open the blinds. Dust motes swirled in the streaming sunlight, bouncing against the warmth of the wood-paneled walls.

"I'm Sergeant Dan Klein. I think you know my sister, Jen."

Jason stiffened. He turned slowly. Not because he'd mentioned Jen. But because he'd called him by his last name when he'd first addressed him. Jason gave him a flat, hard look. "What do you want?"

Dan crossed his arms. "I want to know what the hell you're doing with her." His eyes narrowed. "She mentioned you and that your car was towed. That your last name was Sutter. So I looked up the cars that were ticketed and towed the other day but didn't find any Jason Sutters. Found a Jason Cavanaugh, though. So I looked you up."

Jason felt his throat go dry. He took a step back and rubbed the back of his neck. "Listen . . ."

"I'm not finished," Dan gritted through his teeth. "Imagine my surprise when I dig into who Jason Cavanaugh is, and I find a picture from an obituary of another familiar face. Another prick who didn't give my sister his real last name, apparently. And now that I know, it all makes a lot more sense why I could never find a trace of him."

Kevin.

Jason pinched the bridge of his nose. This was worse than he'd even assumed.

Dan's face reddened. "What the hell am I supposed to tell my sister? That the man she's been hoping will show up someday again is dead? Or the even better part? That his *brother* is here is in town, trying to fuck with her, too?"

Jen was hoping Kevin would come back? Was she still in love with him?

"That's not how it is." Jason gave him a level glare. "I had no intention of messing with her."

"I don't know what sort of sick game you're playing here, but you have no idea what your asshole brother put her through. She almost died giving birth to his son. And he wasn't anywhere to be found. She's broke and my nephew has no dad, and you're over here toying with her." Dan reached for his shirtfront and grabbed it in a fistful, yanking Jason closer. "I don't think so, pal."

"I'm not trying to toy with her," Jason managed. Despite his instinct to pull away, he steered himself to calm. Dan wasn't acting in any official capacity, but cooperating with him would probably be smarter. And make his own life easier.

"Just trying to sleep with her." Dan didn't loosen his grip.

God, he didn't want to admit that to this guy. But Dan had asked nothing, and there was nothing to deny.

Dan's voice lowered to a threatening whisper, close enough to Jason's face that Jason could smell the stale coffee on his breath. "What the hell are you doing in town?"

Jason's mind raced for an answer. Anything that made reasonable sense. "My grandmother," he finally said. "I came to see her."

"Then why stalk my sister's workplaces? You knew who she was before you kissed her at the street play, didn't you?"

How did he know about the kiss? Then again, the guy who had dumped Jen had known about it. Word seemed to travel exceptionally fast around here. Dan was definitely not someone he wanted to involve in his personal business. "Yes."

Dan's grip—amazingly—grew even tighter. The fabric dug in around Jason's neck. "Explain how you're not messing with her."

Jason narrowed his gaze at him. "I will when you get your hands off me." He needed the time to think anyhow.

Dan's fingers uncurled slowly, and he stepped back. Jason had served as the cooler head throughout his life, learning early on that explosive anger only fed off more anger. Pissing Dan off would only make things worse. Jason pulled the front of his shirt down, away from his neckline.

He scanned Dan's face. There was a faint resemblance there, one that he could see now that Dan had told him he was Jen's brother, but not too close. Probably the same way Jason and Kevin had been. But Dan had clearly known Kevin, and his attitude toward him would definitely impact how he saw Jason.

Something close to the truth would be the best bet. With Ned in town, it wouldn't help to have Dan as his enemy. Dan knew Kevin's real last name now, and that Colby was his son. Both things made Dan a threat he had to neutralize.

Jason relaxed his posture. "Want to sit down?"

"Not really."

Not surprising. Dan probably was accustomed to using his stature to his advantage. The more Jason could treat this like a casual conversation, the more it would disarm him.

Jason turned and went over toward the kitchen island, where the coffee machine waited. "Coffee?"

Dan's angular face followed him suspiciously, his eyes wary. "No."

The small bag of coffee was French vanilla-flavored, and Jason frowned as he ripped the foil top. "I found out about Colby and Jen last week." He grabbed a spoon. Now that he wasn't so close to Dan, he felt remarkably more in control. He'd dealt with men like Dan before. "As soon as I heard that my brother had left behind a child, I drove down."

The heels of Dan's shoes dragged against the hardwood floor. "And you decided to stalk Jen?"

Jason gave him a quick glance, his brow furrowing. "No. My intention was to talk to my grandmother first and find out what she could tell me. We've been estranged for years, so I couldn't call. But she's apparently out of town." He spooned coffee into the filter. "Running into Jen right away was unexpected. I never intended to get involved with her." He couldn't tell Dan that she'd been into the idea of a one-night stand.

"But you did." Dan crossed the room toward him. He squinted, a tired expression on his face. "And she has no idea who you are, does she?"

"No, she doesn't." Jason put the coffee maker on and came around to the other side of the island, leaning back against it. He crossed his arms. "But I'm going to tell her everything."

Holding his hands up, Dan shook his head emphatically. "Hang on, I wasn't trying to say you needed to do that."

What? Jason furrowed his brow. "You don't want me to tell her?"

"I'd prefer for you to get the hell out of this town, but there's not a lot of control I have over that. But do I want you to bring up that jackass brother of yours? Not particularly. She's finally put that to rest. It took her a while to get over him, though. He *is* dead, right?"

Jason blinked at him. He peered at him, trying to make sense of his words. "He died over three years ago."

"Right. And you're not planning on staying long, right? I know you're not looking for a long-term thing here with my sister. You have a life in Chicago. You'll be out of her life soon enough."

Just what had Dan looked up? No way he could know about the will—that was all done behind closed doors. But he wasn't wrong, either. He hadn't given Jen the impression he was searching for a relationship. They'd talked about a hookup. Jason cleared his throat. "I'm not planning on staying, no."

Dan rubbed his thumb into the opposite palm as though thinking. Had he even thought out his reasons for coming here? Jason wasn't so sure Dan knew what he was doing here. "Are you telling me you're fine with—"

"I'm telling you I don't want you to tell her who you are, so don't get carried away."

Jason waited for a few beats, the tension in the back of his neck increasing. "What are you doing here, then?"

Dan walked over toward the island, his shoulders drooping. He pulled out a stool and sat. "That depended on what you told me. Your brother didn't leave a good impression, and that's putting it nicely."

Unsure of what to make of Dan, Jason strolled back to the coffee maker. He poured a cup of black coffee and let the steam uncurl from the surface, waiting to sip it. "I'm not proud of what my brother did to Jen. It's part of why I came here. I wanted to find out more about the circumstances. To be honest, Kevin disappeared seven years ago, and I never spoke to him again. I don't know much about what he did during that time period or where he was, and this was my first clue."

Silence filled the space between them. Dan stared at his hands, clasped in his lap. "I'm sorry, that can't have been easy."

"It wasn't." Jason gave him a curt nod and sipped his coffee. "But what're you gonna do? Siblings don't always listen to other siblings—especially not younger ones."

Lifting his head sharply, Dan met Jason's gaze. He wasn't dumb, that was for sure. "No, they don't." Dan's mouth twisted, then he drummed his fingers against his thigh. "I love my sister. I want to protect her, which you seem to understand. But Jen is tired of me trying to protect her. She'd kill me if she knew I was here."

Jason didn't doubt that part. Dan was intimidating as hell. No wonder a woman like Jen had a dating problem. Dan had likely done his fair share of cock-blocking in the past.

He sighed. "I don't want to interfere. But I don't trust you, either. I wouldn't be able to live with myself if I didn't come and see what you were about. So I can't stop you—or her—from doing whatever the hell you want. But my sister doesn't deserve one-night stands with men who are lying to her. She deserves a lot better than that. And then some."

The conversation was fraught with the potential of making his life more difficult, but Jason didn't quite know what to make of it. Dan made him feel as though he should feel guilty, but Jen was a consenting adult who could make her own decisions. He'd been stupid to give her his phone number because it extended the situation beyond one night . . . but it had also been fun.

The inheritance part of it all complicated things. "Can I ask you a question?"

Dan frowned. "What's that?"

They'd made a tenuous peace, and Jason didn't want to backtrack to angering Dan, but his curiosity burned. "What was Kevin like when he was here with Jen? I'm assuming you knew him."

A shadow crossed Dan's features. "I didn't know him well. He was quiet. Didn't talk about himself a lot."

The opposite of what Kevin had been before he left home. Still, not what he really wanted to know. "Yeah, but . . . what was his relationship with Jen like? Were they serious?"

Dan scowled. "How serious could they have been? No sooner did she tell him she was pregnant than he hightailed it out of here. Left no return address. Phone disconnected. Believe me, I tried to find him." Dan stood again and glow-ered at Jason. "Jen's a good person. Easily taken advantage of. She went right on believing Kevin would turn up again for a good year after he left. Thinking something must have happened."

Jason stared at the inky blackness of his coffee. "She wasn't entirely wrong. He died before Colby was even born." Not that Kevin probably had ever had any intention of going back. Dan had confirmed what Jason had suspected. The relationship hadn't been that important to Kevin in the first place.

That knowledge didn't bring him the peace or relief he thought it would have.

"How did he die?" Dan asked.

"Homeless. From an overdose." Jason prayed Dan wouldn't make another comment about how wonderful it was that his brother was gone. As much as Kevin had his problems, he'd also been his brother and closest friend.

Chad Duncan had proved to Jason that even the people you thought of as friends could turn around and stab you in the back. *Smile to your face and then fuck your wife in your bedroom while you're away on a business trip.*

Dan shifted his weight. "Is Mildred Price your actual grandmother?"

Jason nodded.

"Then I guess she's been lying to Jen the whole time, too. They see her once or so a month for lunch. She's had more than ample opportunity to tell Jen the truth." Dan released a frustrated breath. "But whatever reasons the old coot has for doing that, I think that's more than enough people knowing that Kevin's dead, wouldn't you say?"

Whether he wanted to tell Jen more, Jason wasn't in a position to argue. Dan unknowingly held damaging information to Jason's claims in the whole inheritance mess. "Mildred just found out about Kevin's death, actually. So I don't know what, if anything, she's lied about."

"All right. I'm happy to make you the liar in this scenario." Dan gave him a hard look. "Don't fuck with someone special. She's been through enough." He left the cabin. As Jason stared at the space he'd vacated, a strange mixture of relief and guilt filled him. He didn't want to lie to Jen. But that was exactly what he'd agreed to do.

CHAPTER TWELVE

SHE MUST HAVE TAKEN TOO long to text him back. Then again, his lack of response could also be a lack of interest. He might have found someone new. Gone out to lunch, met a girl in town, and taken her back to his cabin. That was his MO, right?

But his texts hadn't appeared as delivered either.

Jen's throat was tight as she gripped the steering wheel, glancing in the rearview mirror at Colby. He caught her looking and flashed her a smile.

His smile did wonders for her heart. Always had. There were times, especially when he was a newborn, that he'd look at her with those big blue eyes, and she'd whisper to him, *"You saved me, buddy."*

She looked back at the road. Maybe Jason's phone had been disconnected? A knot of pressure pushed in on her ribs. *Nope.* The likelihood of his phone being disconnected wasn't huge. Unlike her, he probably had the money to pay his bill. She'd gotten another text from the phone company saying her bill was late on the drive over.

Everything was late. Her rent, her electricity, and of course, the preschool her son could no longer attend. *Crap*. What was she going to do tomorrow? Mom was working and Dad had a meeting. She'd even asked Laura Dawson and Sam Doyle. The sisters both loved Colby like a nephew and watched him occasionally. But they, too, had been busy.

No one she'd texted had been available.

She'd have to call out of work. She couldn't do that to Travis, though. Bunny was out of town, and Jen did most of the baking when that was the case.

Maybe Travis would be all right with Colby coming with her?

Really, she didn't have time for worries about why Jason hadn't answered her all afternoon. And it didn't matter that she'd be a stone's throw from him tonight at work.

She wasn't about to go over there and see if he'd brought back another fling.

Ugh. She wasn't supposed to be jealous of an imaginary date with a guy she'd known for a few days. A guy who had clearly told her that what he looked for in women was sex only.

She didn't want Dan to be right. She wanted to have fun and—

Crap.

Why was Jason sitting on the porch of the guest lodge? It was dusk, but she saw him clearly enough, right there, on the rail of the porch.

Her heart dipped. She pulled up to her parking spot and killed the engine. As she climbed out of the car, she tried her best to look breezy and laid-back. As though she hadn't noticed his lack of communication. Casual meant not getting hung up on things like that. Clingy emotions would probably repel him.

And you can't afford to get attached to a guy who's leaving soon.

Getting Colby out of the back of the car meant a few extra moments to settle her thoughts. Colby hopped out of his seat the moment she'd unbuckled him, reaching for his favorite train on the floor of the car. He grabbed it and then slipped out past her onto the gravel. "Hang on, Colby! Wait for Mommy." She grabbed his backpack and her overnight bag, then closed the door.

Colby ran up to the guest lodge, then halted when he saw Jason. Colby hung back, waiting for his mother. Jen reached for Colby's hand and smiled at Jason. "Hey there."

"Hey." Jason didn't exactly return a smile, but his eyes were warm. "That's right, you're working tonight." He looked good, even in a sweatshirt and gym pants. Considering how baggy his clothes were meant to be, his muscular frame filled them out well. And she'd seen him with his shirt open—he had the muscles to back it up.

But he seemed cold. His hands were stuffed into the front pocket of his sweatshirt.

He said it as though he hadn't been sitting waiting for her. Which meant what, exactly?

"Um, yeah." She stepped onto the porch beside him. "What's up?"

"I went for a run and locked myself out of my cabin."

Oh. She tried not to feel deflated. Of course, he was a runner, though. He looked as though he hit the gym hard on the regular. The lights were on in the guest lodge. "Isn't anyone here?"

He nodded at a small sign on the glass door front. Laura had written her phone number on a piece of paper with the message, "Be Back Soon!"

Jason cleared his throat. "I left my phone charging in my cabin, so I couldn't call the number."

Well, that was something. Maybe it explained why he

hadn't bothered to text her. The keys on her key ring jangled as she unlocked the front door of the guest lodge. "Sorry about that. Have you been waiting here long?"

Colby pushed into the cabin and bounded toward the back room right away. Jen smirked. As he got older, it never ceased to amaze her how he had his own agenda and plans for everything. She set their bags down behind the counter and then unlocked the cabinet where they kept the keys.

Jason came up to the counter slowly, his eyes unreadable. He watched her silently. Did he not know what to say? Had they made things awkward?

She fished one of the spare keys for cabin four out of the cabinet. She held it out to him, and his fingers brushed against hers as he took it. A sizzling, electric feeling rose in her skin, goose bumps the aftershocks of his touch. She met his gaze, pulling her hand back, then gave a quick glance to the room where Colby was busy setting up the train set from the box he'd pulled out from under the bed.

Moistening her lips, she gave him a taut smile. *What did you do today? Nice day?* Nothing seemed to be an apt question.

"So what do you have going on tomorrow?" Jason dropped the key into his pocket and broke the silence.

"Actually, I'm not sure. I work at the café, but"—she looked back at Colby and lowered her voice—"I don't have anyone to watch Colby. I'm trying to figure it out."

His eyes, fringed with dark, long lashes, narrowed. "Don't they have apps for babysitters these days?"

She raised a brow. His inexperience with children and parenthood was showing through. "You'd think." Then she shook her head and added, "But even if they did, I'm not comfortable leaving Colby with just anyone. Especially because I left him with a friend last winter for a few hours, and he got lost in the woods during a snowstorm. It was terrifying. That's when his night terrors started."

"That sounds awful." A thoughtful look crossed his face as though her words had a deeper impact. He leaned forward on the counter on his forearms. "Can you call out?"

"Only if I really want to leave my boss scrambling and upset with me. But I don't know if I have much choice." *Crap.* With her having to do the baking, she'd have to get to the café extra early. That made the logistics of childcare even more difficult.

He hesitated, his eyes flickering over at Colby. "Do you need a hand? I mean, not that you know me well enough to watch your kid, but I can try to help in some capacity. Maybe sit and entertain him in the café if he doesn't mind watching cartoons on my laptop? If it helps you."

This definitely broke the rules of casual hookups, didn't it? She hadn't expected that level of thoughtfulness or problem-solving from him. And she *really* shouldn't take the offer to mean something more than it did. She did her best to keep her expression completely even. "Don't you have work or something?"

"I'm working remotely." Jason shrugged. "Besides, I'm taking leave. The only reason I'm logging in hours on this trip is that it's my family's business, so I like to keep my head in the game."

"So you're a compulsive workaholic who works on vacation?" She leaned forward on the counter on her forearms and elbows, closer toward him, clasping her hands. "The list of things I know about you is getting a little long for comfort."

"And those include?"

"Let's see. You're from Chicago, drive a nice car, go on vacation by yourself in small towns off the beaten path—

presumably because you have family nearby—and have terrible taste in coffee."

He guffawed. "What's wrong with my coffee?"

"It's black." She rolled her eyes. "Which everyone knows is the quintessential drink of choice of a workaholic, by the way. All the caffeine, none of the fun."

"It's healthier," he defended wryly.

"Ah, yes, you're also a runner—and probably a health nut, from the sounds of it—and you like your women commitment-free."

He set his hands down on the counter and straightened. "And you claim not to be stalking me."

They shared a laugh, and she bit her lip, smiling.

She didn't need to know much about him to know she was extremely attracted to him, which wasn't a great thing. He was leaving sooner rather than later, but she didn't want to put the brakes on whatever pulled her toward him, either, because he had somehow made her feel so alive. Desired.

His offer to help her with Colby was intriguing, and if she was honest, a bit of a relief. Even if she didn't accept it, he'd been sweet to offer.

And Jason isn't the sort of guy who comes off as sweet.

But if she was even going to consider it, she would have to start by introducing him to Colby. See how Jason even interacted with him. She didn't have to make a big deal out of it to either of them, especially since Colby was only a few feet away. And she appreciated that fact. One less thing to overanalyze.

"Well, if it doesn't interfere with your running diet, I'm going to order a pizza for Colby and me. You want some?"

He hesitated, then gave a brief nod. "All right."

She wouldn't read into the hesitation. If he didn't want to, he'd say no, right? She dipped her chin. "What do you like? We usually get cheese. I doubt we have any deep dish or whatever it is y'all eat in Chicago." She wrinkled her nose. She'd always hated deep-dish pizza, which felt like a soggy mess.

He chuckled. "I like tavern pizza, actually. Deep dish is for the tourists. But cheese is good for me." He watched her as she pulled out her phone and started the order. "See, you can add that to your list about me."

"Great. You like soup, sandwiches, and tavern pizza. But really, I'm missing all the important questions like . . . what fictional family do you wish you could join?"

He gave her an amused look. "What sort of question is that?"

"Fine. Coffee or tea? Morning person or night? Lake or beach?" She finished the order on her phone and pushed back from the counter.

He eyed the chairs behind the counter, then came around and sat, stretching his long legs in front of him. "Coffee, morning, and neither."

She sat beside him. They were simple wooden chairs—not comfortable for sitting for long stretches, but fortunately, she rarely had to sit behind the counter during Sunday night shifts. Most people checked out Sunday at 11 a.m. or Monday after she'd gone. Sunday check-ins were rarer. She might get a few stragglers later in the evening, though.

"Neither?" She gaped at him. "You don't like the beach or the lake? What sort of American summer travesty is that?"

His gaze clouded. "Let's just say I'm more of a winter person. I'll take a ski lodge or the mountains any day."

"What about swimming pools at resorts and hot tubs? Those both seem right up your alley." She threw him a teasing look. "You know, lots of bikinis."

Any ill humor she'd dredged up by mentioning the beach seemed to vanish in a twitch at the corners of his mouth that hinted at humor. "Pools are about on par with the beach. But hot tubs are an exception." He lowered his voice to a deep, suggestive rumble that Colby couldn't hear. "And I generally prefer those without bikinis."

"I'm shocked." She felt a blush warm her cheeks. "You know there's a hot tub in your cabin, right?"

"I do." He rubbed his neck. "I may need to go out tonight, see if I can't find some company for it."

His teasing look made her feel strangely close to him, and she resisted the urge to slug him playfully in the arm. "Oh, I'm happy to give you all sorts of advice about the wonderful locations for romance in Brandywood. There are prime spots everywhere, like under the bleachers at the high school football field and the old, abandoned cars in the woods."

Jason reached over and traced a fingertip over her forearm. "Romance is overrated."

Her heart raced. Right. She had to choose her words carefully with him. Did he feel like she was trying to push him toward something he wasn't interested in? His actions seemed to contradict his words. "And why is that, exactly? Dark and twisty romantic past? You know, in books and movies, it's always the guys who protest romance who fall the hardest."

He laughed. "Maybe. But that's the problem, isn't it? Life isn't that fairy tale. When the lust fades, it's not picnics in the park and dinners at the best restaurant. It's not even that thrill of a great night together. If you never get carried away with the idea that those things will remain in the first place, then maybe you can just enjoy life a little more. That and the sex is better."

She searched his face. He'd dodged the question, admitting little. Did he mind that she was trying to figure him out? He hadn't run away yet.

If she let herself think about it more, she wasn't sure that she wanted to introduce Colby to him. He was leaving, so what was the point? Just another way for her to think of Jason in a way that she shouldn't. But it was too late for that now. She'd invited him for pizza. She would tell Colby he was a friend of Mommy's and leave it at that. Hopefully, Jason wouldn't become Colby's new favorite person to ask to see again. And somehow, she doubted Jason would, given his life philosophy.

Would Colby find it strange, though? She'd never had any other guest at the cabins join them for takeout at the guest lodge. And Jason had also offered to help her the next day, which was potentially a huge deal. If she could figure out a way to make it work. She'd never leave Colby alone with anyone she barely knew. But maybe if Jason helped entertain Colby at the café for a few hours as he'd suggested? If she could at least get the baking done in the morning, she could leave Travis in good shape for later in the day.

She checked quickly to make sure Colby wasn't in view, then leaned across the space between the two chairs. Holding his gaze, she brushed a kiss on his lips with the softest touch. "I've thought about finishing what we started all day."

He cradled her chin and returned a warm kiss. "Right back at you."

She smiled, then leaned back in her chair. She didn't want to question what they were doing. For so long, she'd overanalyzed every step of every potential relationship to where things lost spontaneity and fun to fit into a plan. Not that her plans had worked out. She'd been trying to fit square elephants into the round heads of a pin.

She took a deep breath, switching gears. "If you really are around tomorrow, I might find a use for you. Even if it's just having another set of eyes on Colby at the café in the morning. I can probably bring him to work with me but trying to keep him occupied while I work isn't exactly easy. The tough thing about only children is that they don't have siblings to entertain them."

Jason looked over his shoulder toward Colby and nodded. "My brother and I used to spend all day playing together, which made boredom less frequent." A strange look crossed his face, and his lips drew to a line. He pulled his gaze from Colby abruptly. "But yeah, I can try to help."

She stood, remembering the sign Laura had left on the door. "You have a brother?" She crossed the room to retrieve the sign.

"Had." His voice was clipped, with a tone of finality that made it clear he didn't want to discuss it. "He left years ago, and I never saw him again."

She peeled the tape off from the glass, lingering there to think. "I'm sorry." She looked over her shoulder at him. "I have two brothers. Both are older than me. They've been overprotective pains in the ass all of my life, but I've always appreciated them, too."

"Are you close with them?" Jason crossed his arms. Those strong biceps. She had to stop imagining him with his shirt off. Nothing was going to happen tonight. Another night of sexual frustration.

"I am. Especially my brother Dan—he's closest in age to me." She didn't want to think about the way she'd treated Dan earlier today, though. She'd text him an apology later. "My other brother Warren has kids, so I probably see him more often these days. Colby is a huge fan of his cousins."

Almost as though he'd heard his name, Colby wandered out of the back room. He came up to Jen, his hair sticking up in twenty different directions. "Mommy, my tummy is hungry."

"We have pizza coming." She ruffled his hair, then squatted beside him. "In fact, Mr. Jason is going to stay here and have pizza with us. Isn't that fun?" She pointed at Jason. *There. Done.* That wasn't so hard, was it?

Why did she feel the need to hold her breath?

Colby gave him a wary glance.

Jason leaned forward in his chair. "Were you building trains in there?"

Colby nodded shyly.

"I ride a train to work every morning where I live. It's my favorite part of the day. You ever been on a train before?"

Scratching his nose, Colby looked at Jen, then looked back at Jason. "We went on a big train for July."

"That's right." Jen gave Colby an encouraging smile, raising the pitch of her voice. It amazed her that he remembered. He'd also spent the holiday adorably calling it "July" rather than the Fourth. "We went on that steam engine on the Fourth of July."

"Can you show me the trains you were building?" Jason peeked back toward the bedroom.

The bell to the front door rang, and Jen stood as a guest wrangled with the glass door. Out of the corner of her eye, she saw Colby lead Jason to the room, talking animatedly about his trains.

She focused her attention on the man who came into the guest lodge, then started the check-in process with him. Jason and Colby chatted together, Colby noticeably excited, and her heart squeezed.

The truth was, she'd never introduced any of the guys she'd been on dates with to Colby. Brad had only ever seen one picture she'd pulled up for him on her phone.

Maybe it was the circumstances of him staying where she was, but she was excited about seeing Jason playing with Colby.

She pulled her thoughts back toward the guest in front of her and slid the key toward him. "Is there anything else I can help you with, Mr. Vickers?"

The man shook his head. "No, thank you. Have a good

night." As he turned to go, the door to the guest lodge opened. A driver with her pizza. Good timing.

She took the pizza from the driver, then carried it back to the room. She and Colby usually ate on the bed while watching TV together. Then Colby would take a shower and go to sleep.

Pausing at the doorway, she leaned her hip into the door frame. The heat from the pizza box warmed her sleeve, the scent of it making her stomach growl. But Jason and Colby were sitting on the floor together, and Colby was playacting with his trains. Jason watched him with rapt attention.

A pang pierced her heart, making it hard for her to breathe quite right.

This was why she hated Kevin. He'd left Colby without a father, something every boy needed. She was lucky that Colby had her brothers and her dad, but that right there was what Kevin walked away from. *Complete focus from a dad.*

CHAPTER THIRTEEN

"FOR A SMART GUY, you're really stupid sometimes." TJ breezed past as Jason held the door for him. Outside, dawn was hinting on the horizon line. TJ walked straight to the kitchen, helping himself to a coffee cup. "It's because you think with your dick whenever you see a pretty face."

"Good morning to you, too." Jason rubbed the sleep from his eyes. He'd slept later than he normally did—he was almost always up by five at home. What was it? Like seven?

Shit. He'd told Jen he'd meet her at the coffee shop by eight. His hand traveled to his chin, the stubble itchy. He still hadn't shaved and wouldn't have time to this morning. Almost five days without shaving and he was looking like he was intentionally growing a beard.

But given TJ's words, he knew where this was heading.

"Ned Vickers checked into one of these cabins last night. Did you know that?" TJ rummaged around the kitchen, making himself at home as he had previously. "I mean, of course you don't know that. I know that. But anyway, I figure you have approximately"—TJ checked his bare wrist, as though he was checking a watch—"an hour before he knows exactly where you are. And that means you have maybe ten minutes after *that* before he knows about your brother's ex and the kid. Because you can't seem to stop hanging out with the one person in this damn town who could completely screw you."

Jason stared at him. Trust TJ to know. He didn't want to have to explain himself, though. "It's slightly more complicated than that. And how did you find out?"

TJ laughed and gave a bow. "You pay me to know these things." Then he busied himself with making coffee. "French vanilla? Gross. I bet it's a light roast, too." He looked over his shoulder. "I've seen her, man. I'd tap that, too. The whole brother's ex thing is weird, but she's pretty enough to get over it. But is she a screw worth hundreds of millions? Nope."

He didn't like the idea of TJ talking about Jen like that, but defending her felt like he'd be giving too much away to TJ. Jason sank into an armchair in the living room, facing his PI. More than anyone right now, TJ understood his situation in its entirety. That his PI had become his most trusted advisor almost elicited a chuckle from him . . . if it hadn't been for the gravity of what he was saying. And that he felt the need to defend Jen. "I haven't actually slept with her."

"None of my business. And also, not the point. You came down here to keep a lid on your grandmother, right? Instead, you've led Ned . . ." TJ paused, grinning. "Led Ned. That rhymes."

Jason scowled. TJ's quirky behavior was a lot less amusing at this time of day. "Yeah, I get it. But Mildred's not in town. What was I supposed to do? Follow her to the casino? The woman literally took a shot at me when she saw me."

"I don't know. A casino might've been a good option. Pretty sure she can't shoot at you there." TJ shoved his hands into his pockets and came around to the other side of the island, leaning against it. "Still doesn't explain why you took up with Kevin's ex."

"Why do you care?" Jason shot back. He sounded as defensive as he felt, and he cringed.

TJ lifted a thick brow. "Because you're my best and wealthiest client. I have a vested interest in making sure you keep the source of your fortune."

Jason smirked at his honesty. But it was also one thing he liked about TJ. He'd never held his opinion back, which was useful. Jason had spent most of his life surrounded by people who were too afraid to tell him the truth about anything—or too accustomed to lying, like Amanda.

"Any luck with the paternity stuff with Amanda?" Jason crossed his ankle over the opposite knee. Another case of stupidity on his part. He should have known she wanted something more than to "end things between us on a high note."

Their sex life had been the *only* high note of the relationship. The only note, really. They'd never connected on anything else and had argued constantly about politics and finances. And then he'd found out Amanda was sleeping with Chad, which meant nothing left to stay for.

"All I know is that she was having some tests. Getting the results are a little harder, even for me. But she's going to need to prove it's yours soon or have her lawyers raise that question in the courts."

"And on the off chance it's somehow mine?" Jason's throat tightened at the words. He didn't believe it could be possible. Even Amanda wasn't that lucky, and he doubted he'd been that stupid.

"Then, assuming they don't find out about Kevin's kid, your kid would get everything."

Jason could strangle Amanda for this. "With Chad as the trustee?"

"No, your grandfather only specified that the trust would be managed by the CEO of Cavanaugh Metals if it was Kevin's kid. Probably so he wouldn't step on your toes if you and Amanda had decided to have a kid, is my guess. You would manage the trust if it's your own child. Chad's only the trustee if Colby is the heir."

"But even if it was my kid, Amanda would be the puppeteer." She would use any child they had to control and manipulate him, goddammit. Eighteen more years of Amanda controlling his life in every way was enough to make him want to run away and hide. In some ways, that would be the worst scenario possible. He'd hate for the business to go under if it all went to Colby with Chad as the trustee, but at least Colby and Jen would wind up with a comfortable life and be taken care of.

Jason straightened. "What if . . ." He scanned TJ's face, analyzing the risk of asking TJ more. But he needed his advice and knowledge here. "What if people found out about Colby?"

"He would have the birth date in his favor. As the oldest, he would be the heir." TJ crossed his arms. "But I thought the whole point of you being here was to stop that from getting out."

Clearly, TJ didn't know where Jason was going with this yet. The back of his neck tensed. Jason clasped his hands together, setting his elbows on his knees. "And what if Colby was my son?"

TJ scrunched his features as though taking a few minutes to connect the dots and failing. "How could he be your son?"

"I could adopt him. Marry Jen. Then a paternity test could prove he's actually a Cavanaugh, and I'd be the trustee."

Staring at Jason as though he'd gone nuts, TJ blinked rapidly. "I don't know if any of it is that straightforward or if you're a complete genius." He shook his head as though trying to clear his thoughts. "I'll have to talk to your lawyers. But it's possible. Except for the obvious problems. Amanda might lose her shit, especially if she's carrying your child. And you'd have to get Jen to agree to it."

"It's not my kid. It's Chad's." Jason let out a slow breath, puffing his cheeks. He didn't feel like a genius. He felt like an asshole. Jen longed for romance. And Dan wanted his sister to forget about Kevin.

If he propositioned her with this, he'd effectively be ignoring both things.

But if he wanted to save his company, what other choice did he have?

"You said it could be yours. If it is and you move forward with this idea for Jen and Colby, won't it mean you're screwing your own son?"

Jason stood. "It's not my kid." He said it with a finality that he hoped made it clear he no longer wanted to discuss it.

TJ crossed his arms. "I know you, Jason. You're not the type to abandon your kid, no matter how much you hate Amanda. You should consider that option seriously before you do something you can't undo. If it's your kid, you're going to completely change your mind once it's born. You're going to want to be a part of their life."

What would it take to make TJ drop the issue? Irritation prickled his shoulders. Narrowing his eyes at TJ, Jason snapped coolly, "Not all of us get fathers. We deal with it."

"Right." TJ pursed his lips and walked back around to the coffee maker. He poured himself a cup, then looked around for the creamer. Pausing, he glanced back at Jason, a gleam in his green eyes. "But something tells me part of the reason you're hanging around your nephew is that it bothers you that your brother left him fatherless. And that he's some of the only family you have left."

Asking TJ to find out where Kevin had been had opened a

door Jason hadn't expected. He'd given TJ access to parts of his own past and history he didn't want anyone rooting around in. The damage was done there—TJ would always see that side of him now. But Jason wasn't about to allow TJ to keep bringing it up like he actually knew him.

Jason rolled his shoulders. "I'm hanging around my nephew because my nephew's mother is very fuckable. End of story." The words sounded as acidic coming out of his mouth as he'd intended them to sound. He swallowed the guilt down with the acid.

Regardless of his intentions, TJ had hit a nerve.

No child should be forced to grow up without their father's love.

CHAPTER FOURTEEN

JEN SCOOPED the starter from the crock, weighing it on the scale. No matter how many years she'd been working with it, feeding it, storing the discard, the whole process felt a little like she was working with a hungry child in the kitchen. The sourdough bread bowls for Tuesday's clam chowder special were usually started on Mondays. Today, it was up to her to make sure they were prepared.

She moved the starter to the mixing bowl, then added warm water and flour. When Bunny had first taught her how to bake bread, Jen had watched in amazement as Bunny seemed to measure out the precise amount without weighing it. Bunny had told her that after over forty years of making bread, she knew by feel what the right weight was.

Eight years later, Jen understood what she'd meant. She'd gotten there faster than eight years yet still measured everything just in case, but she didn't really need to. Some day, she might feel brave enough if she was working in her own kitchen. But in the same way that Bunny was the best mentor Jen could have ever asked for, she also expected precise results.

"What do we do now?" Jason's voice cut through Jen's thoughts.

She looked across the kitchen toward the stove, where Jason held a wooden spoon above a pot. Colby stood on a step stool beside him.

She still couldn't believe he'd shown up here this morning.

Wiping the flour from her hands onto the apron, Jen crossed the kitchen and peeked into the pot. A yellowish lump of dough had formed in the center. "It looks pretty good." She turned off the heat and grabbed the wax paper sheet she'd gotten ready for him. Laying it flat on the counter beside the stove, she spooned the dough out onto the wax paper.

"Knead it on the wax paper until it gets smooth." She turned and then held back a smile at Jason's blank expression.

"What the hel—heck does that mean?" Jason quirked a brow. "You sure this is going to work? I bet that toy store up the street has playdough, you know. I don't mind buying some."

She choked on her laughter. "I know. I was in charge of making playdough for the preschool. It'll be fine." She wasn't entirely sure it would come together. Somehow, the mixture looked lumpier than when she made it.

"Can we add the blue now?" Colby asked eagerly.

"Not yet. Really soon." She pushed her palm flat against the dough. "Knead. Like this. Except not yet. It's still too hot. My hands are used to handling hot stuff."

Jason shot her an amused look. "I bet."

She felt her cheeks warm and cleared her throat, giving him a warning look. "Also, I'm going to move you to that smaller table over there. Lunchtime is starting soon, and the kitchen is about to get really busy." As it was, the cooks were shooting Jason looks like they were wondering what the hell he was doing in there. She tried to stay out of their way. Cooking always took precedence over the baking, and they would need her help during lunch today.

This had felt like a great idea when the morning had started, and things were relatively quiet. But now that the kitchen was at full speed, it felt stupid and dangerous. A kitchen was no place for a toddler, even at a place like Bunny's where everyone knew and loved them both. Jen suspected the only reason no one had said anything was because they all knew Travis was one of her best friends.

Jason gave the lump of misshapen, hot dough a disgusted look. "I was thinking, what if I walk Colby down to that bookstore a few stores down? I saw on my run yesterday that they have a story hour at eleven."

She bit her lip and caught one of the line cooks giving her the side-eye. Would Colby be safe?

"Behind!" Molly, the server working the lunch shift, called, passing them with a tray of hot soup. She scowled at Jen as Jason tucked Colby out of her path.

Jason must have noticed the looks, too, if he'd suggested the story hour.

As much as Jen felt guilty about letting Colby out of her sight, it might be a better idea than keeping Jason and Colby in the kitchen during lunch hour. "What do you think, bud? You want to go to story hour at Miss Annie's?"

Colby's face brightened. "Yeah!"

She helped Colby down from the stool, then untied the apron from his neck. "Sounds good. But if you need anything at all—"

"I know where to find you." Jason gave her a reassuring look. "I promise I'll bring him right back."

As they headed out the kitchen door, Travis passed them on his way in. He held the door for Jason and then let it swing shut behind him. Jen met his gaze and looked away, her face feeling hotter. "I know what you're thinking."

Travis crossed his arms and came closer. "You don't know."

"I do. You're thinking I'm being an idiot. That I shouldn't let my baby out of my sight with a man I hardly know." Jen returned to her station. She'd played that argument over and over and over in her head ever since that day Colby disappeared. And as much as she'd felt judged harshly over the past three years for being the "single mother," not a soul had said a bad word *about* her—*to her knowledge*—regarding that night. In fact, since then, she'd felt as though everyone had been a little more attentive to Colby's location. So she'd hoped that those extra eyes would be on Colby now as a virtual stranger led him to the bookstore.

"No, I wasn't thinking that, Jen, but clearly, that's where your head went." Travis had followed Jen to her station and tilted his head. "I was thinking how nice it is to see you finally trusting people again."

She cringed and gave him a one-eyed squint. "Have I gotten that bad?"

Travis simply nodded slowly.

"Ugh—it's the worst. Speaking of which, my anxiety is going into hyperdrive. Can you call Annie and ask her if Colby got there safely? Jason took him to story hour."

Travis laughed and pulled his phone out. Less than a minute later, Travis flashed a picture of Colby and Jason sitting on the braided rainbow rug in the children's area of the bookstore. "From Annie. See? You can calm down. Go back to that progress I thought you were making."

Despite Travis's teasing, it set her heart at ease to see Annie's picture. And made her heart throb. "I really like Jason. But he's not in town for long, and then I'll probably never see him again. And he probably doesn't feel the same way. We talked about spending a night together and not getting into a long-term thing. But I have this weird gut feeling about him. He seems like someone I can trust, and Colby was strangely very comfortable with him."

Spilling her heart out to Travis was easy. Like Lindsay, he'd been there to pick her up off the floor a thousand times before. Sometimes literally. One time in her late teens, Travis had been forced to go into the ladies' bathroom at The Bench and carry her out because she was too drunk to stand. Then he'd taken her to Lindsay's house to spend the night so Jen's parents wouldn't kill her for underage drinking.

"He's spent the morning hanging out with your three-year-old, Jen. Trust me when I tell you he likes you."

"Then you don't think I'm being stupid?" Jen held her breath, hoping. Her instincts kept screaming at her to slow down, to be more cautious, but maybe if Travis thought it was all right for her to jump into this without overthinking it, she'd feel more validated.

Travis winced. "It's not stupid. It's . . ." He released a slow sigh. "I don't want you to get hurt. And you don't know much about this guy, right?"

Her heart fell. She'd hoped he wouldn't say this. "You think he just wants to sleep with me?"

"He definitely wants to sleep with you. He wouldn't be doing this if he didn't." Travis's eyes were warm. "But that's not what I'm saying. I'm saying that I'd hate to see you finally open up to and trust someone only to have it set you back in the long run. There's a middle ground between being too cautious and running off an airplane with a backpack instead of a parachute."

Jen finished feeding the starter and then put it away. She reached for a pastry bag to fill éclairs. "So what do I do? It's not like I can ask him to stick around. Should I talk about where this is going before I let things go any further?"

"Not unless you want to scare him away permanently." Travis chuckled. "I was thinking maybe an actual date. You said you all stayed in Yardley's for what—ten minutes?"

"Yeah, but we had pizza together last night."

"With Colby. Watching cartoons." Travis gave her a sympathetic look. "But you need a date. One where you can get lucky if it goes well."

"First, I can't ask my parents to watch Colby for a date and tell them I might not come back that night, so they should just keep him all night. They'd be pissed."

"Then don't plan on staying the night. That's not what this thing you're having with this guy is, anyway. Wrap up dinner early, go back to his place, and then go home. And if it helps, I'll watch Colby."

That was true. Her mind didn't need to go to a long night together. She gave him a grateful look. "But doesn't that make me a horrible mother? Colby spends enough time away from me as it is. For me to be pawning him off on you so I can get laid . . . that makes me a shitty mother."

Travis slipped his arm around her shoulder. "It just makes you a person. You're not shipping him off for a month or even a week to a boarding school either. It's one evening. One date. Give yourself permission for a quick fling. You have to take care of yourself, too. Otherwise, you can't be the best mother anyway. No one can run on an empty tank of gas."

Travis looked back toward the kitchen doors. "I should go back out there. But I'm serious. Get that date and get to know the guy a little. Just tell me when. I'll clear whatever I have planned for you."

As Travis went back into the front, Jen snipped the end off a pastry bag. She set it over a cup, folded the edges over the side, and filled it with pastry cream. Getting lost in work was the peaceful part. She didn't eat too many desserts these days— she'd had more than her fill of pastries and cakes—but she still enjoyed the creation process.

Thoughts of Jason and Colby crowded in, though. The idea of having the date Travis had suggested was exhilarating, actually. She had to stop trying to think of the long term.

Give yourself permission for a quick fling.

They'd also lost the spontaneity and mystery of Saturday night. How would Jason react if she asked him out on a date? It seemed to break whatever fragile rules he had for women. Did he take the women he hooked up with on dates? Or was it more like he'd implied at Yardley's: finding someone at a bar? If it was the latter, the idea of a date might repel him.

The start of lunch hour left her little time to worry about it, though. She shifted her efforts over to helping the cooks, plating meals, and packing to-go containers as the orders came in. She barely could wave as Jason snuck back in to let her know he and Colby had returned and were grabbing a table.

When the rush died down, she left the kitchen for a few minutes to go check on Colby. He and Jason were seated at a booth in the corner. She hung back for a moment near the doors.

Except for the color of their hair, Colby and Jason looked like they could be father and son. They wore similar expressions: self-satisfied smirks, their laughter twinkling in their sharp blue, intelligent eyes as they laughed about something. Even with him only being three, Jen could tell Colby was smart. He had a way of understanding things that shocked her sometimes.

The moment made her heart melt as Jason said something to Colby, then stole a piece of a brownie from his plate.

A wave of anxious, breath-stealing nausea smacked her,

crowding her lungs. She was letting herself get carried away by thoughts of Jason.

Travis was right. She needed to set some ground rules. Especially now that Colby had met him. Rules that might be better fleshed out with a date. This was a short-term fling, and that was that. She wasn't being dumb and irresponsible, and she hated that Dan's words hung on the fringe of her thoughts.

She walked up to the table, managing a weak smile. "How's it going?"

Colby had the remnants of a grilled cheese sandwich in front of him but was busy digging into a brownie. Whatever Jason had eaten had been polished off, but she guessed it was a bowl of soup and a sandwich, from his order the previous time. He ate healthier than she did. And worked out more, too.

Great. Another thing to be self-conscious about.

"Guess what, Mommy! Mr. Jason got me a book!" Colby held it up, a story with a cartoonish dog on the front.

"Wow, did you say thank you?" Jen kept her gaze level with Colby.

Colby mumbled a thank you, going back to the brownie. Jen mouthed, "Thank you," to Jason.

The corners of his mouth turned up in a smile, but he looked away as his phone rang beside him. Checking the phone, he frowned. "Um, I gotta take this. That okay?"

"Of course." Jen stepped to the side to let him pass. He answered before passing through the front door to the café, then hurried out to the sidewalk.

She sat on the side of the booth Jason had vacated. "Did you have fun with Mr. Jason?"

Colby looked up between a bite of brownie, his face covered in chocolate. "Uh-huh. Can we go home now?"

Tension pushed up her esophagus. Poor Colby had barely been home since Thursday afternoon—no, Wednesday. She checked her watch. "Mommy will be done working in another hour. Do you think you can wait that long? I bet we can play with your playdough. I finished that batch for you and gave it to Uncle Travis to hold for you behind the front counter."

She didn't want to tell Jason that she'd had to start the playdough all over again. He'd made a good attempt. Colby swung his legs around the side of the booth, eagerly heading toward the front counter. "Wait, wait, wait." Jen grabbed him by the back of the shirt, then wiped his face with a napkin. He grumbled, then she took his hand and led him to the front counter.

Travis was busy with a customer, and he directed Colby to sit at the front barstools for single diners while he waited for Travis. Surprisingly, Colby seemed all right being patient and took out his new book. Jen walked a few feet back toward the table where he and Jason had been to clean up some of the food Colby had spilled on the floor. Not that they went out to restaurants often, but Jen was always hypersensitive to how much food Colby spilled on the floor while eating after having worked in food service for so long.

But Bunny's was like a second home for him. Except, not really. Because he had three "second homes"—her parents, the guest lodge, and the café. And he spent more time in all three places than in his actual home. Not to mention that his actual home—their apartment—was the fourth place that she'd rented since Colby's birth.

And she was still struggling to pay her bills. How far behind was she on rent? Not to mention everything else.

She released a shallow breath that couldn't encompass the actual sigh she needed for her life. What was she doing? No matter what she tried, she was constantly failing.

A shadow crossed the table, and she didn't look up as Jason sat back down. "Hey there."

Except it wasn't Jason.

She looked up sharply. A familiar man sat there. She frowned. He'd checked in to the cabins the night before.

He was middle-aged with a touch of gray in the light-brown hair of his temples. His hair was short, as was his stature, but he was slender. His dark eyes were analytical. "How are you?"

"Fine." She scanned the café. The lunch crowd had died down, so there were plenty of open seats. What was he doing?

"Ned Vickers." He slid a business card across from her. "I'm a private investigator. I was hoping I could ask you some questions since you're the only local I know."

The only local he knew? She fingered the edges of the business card, which was made of heavy card stock and embossed. Not at all like the cheap business cards she'd printed at home for the cookie business she'd tried to start a couple of years earlier. These were expensive.

She eyed him warily. "What do you want to ask me questions about?"

Before Ned could answer, Jason sidled up right beside her. He slipped his arm around her shoulders. "Hey, babe."

Babe? Despite the instant comfort of Jason's protective stance, her brain fumbled to catch up. Jason reached his free hand over. "Hi, I'm Jason."

Ned looked from Jen to Jason. Then he stood awkwardly. "Sorry, I didn't realize this seat was taken." Giving Jason another look, he slipped away and sat at another table.

"Geez, I leave you for two minutes, and men come out of the woodwork to hit on you," Jason said smoothly. "Even with that costume on."

"Oh, um." She laughed, suddenly acutely aware of her messy ponytail, hair net, and chef's coat. "Watch it, buddy. You insult the cook, and you might live to regret it."

"You know, you keep threatening that." Jason's eyes

gleamed. Then he looked at the empty booth seat. "Where's Colby?"

"At the counter waiting patiently for Travis to give him the playdough you all made." She threw Colby a glance and smiled at the sight of his feet swinging. "And what can I say? I lean into stereotypes. They say writers kill off people they hate in their books, and people in food service take their revenge out on the food you eat. Just consider yourself lucky that I'm not a baker who likes to write."

"I didn't know you hated me."

Jason's arm still weighed against her shoulder, and the warmth of his body tempted her to lean in closer. Plus, he smelled like *Old Spice* and . . . mmm. She leaned in and whispered in his ear, "I'm more than happy to prove that I don't." She pulled back with a self-satisfied grin. "I gotta get back to work. Thanks for helping me out with Colby. I think I can handle him from here."

Jason groaned softly. "You're killing me, you know that?" He gave an exaggerated sigh. "What did that guy want, by the way?" He took a glance over his shoulder at the table Ned had scurried away to.

She shrugged. "I don't know. Says he's a private investigator." She motioned to the card he'd left on the table.

"Huh." Jason ignored the card and reached for her hand. "What are you doing tonight?"

Everything about his touch made her want to delay going back to the kitchen. Her gaze darted to Colby. Travis had taken the playdough out and grabbed him some cookie cutters. Thank God for Travis.

"Colby and I are just hanging out at home. Why?"

"Can I take you out?" Gentle pressure from his fingertips shot sparks up her core. "I have something I want to run by you."

"Uh . . ." His words were intriguing. And he was asking *her* out.

But Colby also hadn't had a normal night at home for the last few days. Even if she was doing a shoddy job of it, she couldn't deny Colby some stability for a date with Jason. She sighed. "I really can't. Colby needs some time at home, I'm sorry. It can be a little hectic managing everything, so I like to make sure he gets the time he needs with me."

His eyes flickered, something in his gaze unreadable. Then he nodded and squeezed her hand again. "What about tomorrow night?"

If she said no, would he ask for a different day? She didn't want to take that risk, either. He could leave by then. And she had Travis's offer on the table. "I'd have to find someone to watch Colby, but it should be okay. What time?"

"I can pick you up. My assistant is working on getting my car out of the impound lot. Where should I meet you?"

"I'll text you my address." This time, she really needed to go. Jason had a way of making her want to forget she had any responsibilities. She hurried back to the kitchen, her heart feeling remarkably light. One date. That would be enough, right?

CHAPTER FIFTEEN

Jason waited in the cabin's darkness, the hood of his sweatshirt over his head. The motherfucker was taking his time coming in through the door.

TJ had been happy to teach Jason how to pick the lock. He'd even reset the paperclip Ned had put in the doorjamb to tell if someone had been inside. Having TJ around in Brandywood had proven to be useful in more ways than one. They'd spent most of the day together, following Ned to see what he was up to.

And TJ had swept Jason's cabin for surveillance equipment, which had been an unpleasant surprise.

The scraping of the key against the lock stopped, and Ned opened the door. The light flipped on, then he jumped, seeing Jason leaning against the wall of the front door with his arms crossed.

"What the hell, man?" Ned's face reddened. He slammed the door behind him.

"You're not the only one who can slip around locks." Jason pulled a ziplock bag of electronic devices out from the pocket of his hoodie and tossed it at Ned's feet. "I did a sweep of my cabin. Took plenty of photos to prove you're trying to record me illegally, though. Which should be helpful."

Ned lifted the bag, his face scrunching at the liquid inside the bag. "Is that water?"

"Water. Piss. Whatever I got out of my toilet." Jason put his hands back into his front pockets. "I don't know what the hell you think you're doing here in Brandywood, but it's time for you to leave, Vickers."

Ned dropped the bag of cameras with disgust on his face. He lifted his chin. "You know exactly what I'm doing here, so why don't you cut the crap. And as soon as your dear old grandma comes back into town, we'll sit and chat."

His words were chilling. What else had he found out? Dan wasn't the only person who remembered Kevin. If Ned asked enough people, he was bound to find someone who recognized a picture of Kevin. And if they knew about Kevin, they might know about Jen.

"You stay away from my grandmother, you hear? And my girlfriend." Jason glared at him menacingly. "Or next time, I won't just be breaking your toys." TJ had been the one to suggest that Jason continue the girlfriend ruse for now. Ned probably wouldn't immediately jump to the conclusion that Jen was his brother's ex, especially since it made Jason look reckless.

Which he'd been.

He'd been so goddamn reckless.

But Jen was involved now, like it or not.

As he stepped onto the porch, Ned called out behind him. "Amanda's going to be real interested to find out you have a girlfriend. She says you blocked her number. You're going to want to talk to her if you're smart."

Jason looked over his shoulder. What the actual fuck? She

was really pushing this whole pregnancy scam, wasn't she? But the implication that she'd be upset about Jen was just one straw too far. They were history. *And she doesn't have a heart.* "Amanda can go fuck herself. And so can you."

He stalked back to his cabin, half expecting Ned to follow him. Instead, he was left alone with his thoughts and the cold seeping in through the fabric of his sweatshirt. The wood smoke from fires and the occasional hoot of an owl brought back memories of summers from long ago—camping trips and the trips to visit Mildred. Things had ended with his father.

The cold cut his throat, and he peeled the sweatshirt off as he reached his car. At least he didn't have to go to the trouble of hiding it now. He'd already dressed for his date with Jen and had even shaved. But it was more than nerves that ate at his gut as he started the engine.

If he told Jen the truth now, she'd think he'd been lying to her the whole time. Which wasn't completely inaccurate. Omitting the truth was still lying.

He shifted his car into gear and pulled onto the main driveway. He'd loved driving this car from the minute he'd pulled it off the car lot. The muscle memory of shifting and the smooth feel of the leather steering wheel against his hands always worked wonders for stress.

It'd been the first thing he bought for himself after his split with Amanda. He couldn't stomach the thought of the other car he'd owned. Or the way they'd christened it in a parking garage in Chicago.

But maybe he'd deserved what he'd gotten with Amanda. He wasn't any good, and his whole reason for being here in Brandywood more than proved that.

How could he start anything off with Jen by explaining that everything she thought she knew about him was a lie?

Jen had been sweet, listing the things she'd tucked into her memory about him. What was he even thinking? He wasn't *starting* anything with her at all. He simply wanted her.

Temporarily.

Because that's all you're good for.

His fucking grandfather's voice sneered at him.

Jason slammed the palm of his hand against the steering wheel.

It hadn't been enough that his grandfather blamed Jason for everything going to hell. Hadn't been enough that he hated Jason.

He still remembered standing next to his grandfather at his father's funeral. A ten-year-old boy, sniffing, tears flowing freely.

"Quit your crying. That should be you in that box," his *grandfather had said.*

And now, his grandfather had reached those claws out from beyond his own grave and was still sinking them into Jason's life.

Nothing he'd ever done had been enough to make his grandfather happy.

Jason worked himself up into the worst of moods by the time he pulled up in front of the apartment complex where Jen lived. He was in the mood to run ten miles or pound his fists into a punching bag.

He was in the mood to fuck, especially since he hadn't seen Jen for twenty hours. Her texts last night had definitely made him horny.

His blood boiled hot as he stalked across the parking lot, thinking about Jen. Maybe they should skip the restaurant and room he'd booked them at the nearby ski resort and just stay here.

He hardened as he thought about her on his lap in the cabin the other night, her voluptuous, perfect breasts rubbing against his chest. He'd strip her down, find the nearest surface to prop her up on, peel her panties off, and then bury his face between her legs.

Jen opened the door to her apartment a few moments after he knocked.

Her hair was down in waves, and she wore tight jeans and a sexy black top that plunged into a deep V. *Perfect.*

Then he noticed the flecks of mascara on her cheeks and the puffiness of her eyes. Her lips, too.

She'd been crying.

He froze, thinking of Ned. Had he gotten to her already? A flash of panic rose in his chest.

"What happened?" Jason stepped in and closed the door behind him.

She hugged her arms to her chest, which had the unintended effect of making her breasts more pronounced. He'd have to ignore them for now.

Jen took a shaky breath. "I'm being evicted." She grabbed the paperwork from the console table by the front door. "When I got home today, this guy was waiting who served me the papers."

Taking the papers from her silently, Jason felt his pulse return to a normal pace. He scanned the papers, then looked over them at her.

Even crying like this, she was gorgeous.

She held a hand to her forehead, her cheeks red. "I'm so embarrassed." She turned away. "I mean, I don't have to ask to know you clearly aren't struggling, and here I am, working two jobs, and I can't even keep my own place."

Jason refolded the papers and then pulled her into his arms.

She cried against his shirt. She was right. It wasn't fair. She worked harder than anyone he'd met. She was so soft, yet so incredibly strong. Feisty, yet kindhearted. The feminine scent of her shampoo reached him as he pressed his chin to the top of her head. Even that he liked. Everything about her made him want to take care of her.

"I'm assuming you don't have the money for the back payments?"

She shook her head and sniffled. "God, I must look terrible." She stepped back and reached for a tissue. "No, I don't. And I still owe the preschool, too. I got buried in credit card debt and hospital bills after Colby was born. I had pre-eclampsia and ended up needing to be in the hospital for forever. And I couldn't work during and after the pregnancy. Everything just piled up. And I've spent the past few years trying to get unburied, but I . . ."

Can't do it on your own. As she shouldn't have to.

No wonder Dan hated Kevin.

She grabbed the eviction papers and crumpled them up, then stomped on the ball. "I'm so sick of it."

Jason watched her outburst. Despite her anger, something was amusing about it, and he repressed the urge to smile. He reached for her hand. "How much do you need?"

She wiped the remnants of tears away and scanned his gaze. She squeezed his hand and let it go. "If you're thinking of lending me money, don't. I like you, Jason, I really do. But I'm not taking your money. As it is, I'm going to have to move back in with my parents and live off their help again for a while. And they've been really generous. My mom paid off two of my credit cards only for me to max them both out again."

Despite the inherent absurdity of it, he understood her pride.

If she only knew who he really was.

But would she hate him? He'd have to explain why he'd come to Brandywood. Have to dredge up everything about Kevin. And even if he got her to agree to anything, the money for Colby would take months or years to access after a long bout of legal wrangling.

She needed his help now.

When he didn't respond, she gave him a brave smile. "I'm going to go touch up my makeup. Sorry to be such a wreck when you found me. Make yourself at home."

As her footsteps faded down the hall, he stepped a few paces into her apartment. Despite the presence of a toddler, it was neat and organized—well decorated, too. The furnishings were simple but clean. The only thing that even seemed remotely out of place was her chef's coat on the back of a chair.

If giving her the money she needed wouldn't work, he'd have to find a way that made her feel as though she'd earned it. But with sex in the equation, it complicated everything. He had every intention of sleeping with her—it was a question of when, not if.

And if he didn't tell her who he was soon, she might never forgive him.

But if he told her now . . .

Was there some in-between? Would she be more forgiving of his lie of omission if he let her in a bit more? If he could reduce the scope of what she didn't know about him, she might see why he'd waited to tell her. Maybe.

He raked his fingers through his closely cropped hair. He didn't know.

Trying to predict how a woman would react was about as accurate as a weather forecast a month out.

When she came back out to the living room, she held a

peacoat over her arm. "Ready to go?" She grabbed her purse from the table.

"Before we do, I have something to propose to you."

She arched an eyebrow. "What's that?"

Jason came toward her and took her hands in his. "What do you think of the idea of being my girlfriend for the next few weeks?"

She gave a scoffing laugh as though she'd never heard something so strange. "What?"

"I can probably extend my leave for a bit. I still haven't been able to resolve my family matter. And I"—he pushed a tendril of hair away from her cheek—"I sort of cost you an opportunity that could have helped you."

She narrowed her gaze. "What are you talking about?"

"The baking competition."

Her face lit, unexpectedly. She let out a relieved breath. "Oh my gosh, you scared me there for a minute. The baking competition. I honestly didn't even think about that. I signed up on a whim, and Brad didn't bake anyway—"

"But you do. And you're good. You could probably win."

She smiled widely. "I saw you making playdough today, Jason. I'm not sure you're up for the challenge."

"You just tell me what to do, and I'll do it. And then, when you win, you can feel completely entitled to the entire twenty-five-thousand-dollar prize since I was basically a handicap." Jason cupped her face with his hands. "You could accept that, right?"

"Would you do that for me?"

"For the girl who didn't spit in my food when I wasn't looking? Anything." He kissed her lips gently.

She returned his kiss, her lips warm and inviting. As the kiss deepened, she tilted her head back toward the bedroom. "You sure you don't want to just stay here?"

Don't tempt me.

But he wasn't about to let her know what an ass he really was. Not after she'd been so vulnerable with him.

"And miss our date?" Jason held her coat for her and helped her into it. Then he swatted her gorgeous ass. "Not a chance."

CHAPTER SIXTEEN

"ALL RIGHT, TWO TRUTHS AND A LIE." Jen sat forward in her seat, holding her wineglass in one hand. Hard to believe it was only eight o'clock. She'd told Travis she'd pick up Colby at eleven. Which felt a bit too late. Travis had told her not to worry about the time, but she couldn't help checking it.

Jason leaned across the table with the last spoonful of crème brûlée. "Let's see. I graduated from college at age twenty. I've climbed Mount Everest. And chocolate and peanut butter is my favorite flavor combo."

She took the crème brûlée he'd offered and grinned. "Don't expect me to suddenly take up running because you're my fake boyfriend, by the way. Which also means you probably shouldn't feed me all this dessert."

She hadn't had this much fun on a date in a long time.

Then again, she'd never been to such an expensive restaurant. She'd nearly fallen over when the server had handed her the menu.

And since they were there on a Tuesday, they seemed to have most of the restaurant to themselves. On their one side, a wall of floor-length windows gave a view of ski slopes. With the clear night and full moon, the view was gorgeous.

She refocused on his answers, squinting at him. "You know, we might not make it. Because I have a feeling you don't like chocolate and peanut butter."

"Hate it." Jason smiled, then signaled the server. "And you, of course, love it."

"Because I'm not crazy." Could she even pretend to date a guy who hated chocolate and peanut butter?

"Chocolate and mint is a far superior combination. Not that I really like chocolate all that much."

She winced and put one hand over her heart. "Maybe this was a bad game." Then she leaned closer. "You really climbed Mount Everest?"

He nodded, then sipped his wine. "A buddy of mine from college wanted to do it. I was the only friend he had who didn't mind the cold. So we did." A shadow crossed his face. "But it feels like a long time ago."

Jason slipped a card from his wallet, then handed it to the server. Between the bottle of wine and the food, they must have run up a bill of a few hundred. The ease with which he handed the server his card without even waiting to look at the bill was stunning. She swallowed the last sip of her wine. "You're not some sort of con artist who pays for dates with one woman while running up another woman's credit, are you?" She gave him a teasing glance.

He chuckled, grazing her fingers with the knuckle of his forefinger. "We should probably send Natasha a thank you for this amazing meal. Oh, damn, I shouldn't have told you her name."

She laughed. "Well, if you are, you made a poor choice in women this time. I still maintain I'm completely underdressed for this place. I'm in jeans."

"I sincerely doubt the server has been staring at your jeans this whole time. His gaze has been distracted by two objects due north."

She shot him a look, then pulled out her purse to reapply her lip gloss. But she'd caught the server staring at her breasts, too. And his banter with her made her happy. "So tell me this—you said you're a CFO. But Everest must have been expensive." Asking if he'd been born into wealth was gauche and nosy, but it would explain a lot about him.

"My great-grandfather started a family business that did well. It's been in the family since then."

So he'd grown up rich.

"You know, I rarely date rich guys." She rubbed her lips together to smooth out the lip gloss. "In fact, the last guy I was dating—Brad—was apparently keeping a running tally on how much he'd spent on me. But he was an accountant."

Jason leaned back in his seat. "I think we've established Brad was an idiot." But he gave her a humoring expression. "What sort of guys do you normally date?"

"Broken ones." She threw her hands up. "I seem to be a magnet for guys with issues. Colby's dad was a drug addict when I met him."

Jason stiffened, his steel-blue eyes flicking up toward hers, then back down. The server arrived and laid the check presenter on the table. Jason busied himself with signing it, and Jen felt a trace of tension constrict her chest. Did he think she had a past like Kevin had? "I—I mean, I was never into drugs. Just so that's clear. I never even smoked—"

The look Jason shot her silenced her. "I wasn't thinking anything bad about you." He put his credit card away, then stood, holding his hand out for her. "Ready to go?"

She nodded briskly, then took his hand. Once again, his touch steadied any feeling of being off kilter. He led her from the dining room, then straight toward the elevators. They climbed inside, and she asked, "Where are we going?"

"To the room I reserved." He pushed a button, then lifted his phone to a scanner on the elevator. The elevator started up.

She'd assumed they'd go back somewhere tonight but had figured it would be to his cabin. He'd rented a room at the lodge? "I didn't pack a bag," she said. "And I have to pick up Colby."

He gave her hand a reassuring squeeze, her fingers tight between his. "I know. And we don't have to go up if you don't want to. I just thought it might be nice to have some time alone."

The elevator chimed to announce their arrival, opening to a hallway with only a few doors. Jason led them to one of them and used his phone against the scanner on the door. A beep and flashing green light came from the scanner, and Jason unlocked the door. The lights were already on inside, revealing the largest suite Jen had ever seen. The décor was modern and lavish, the living space in the room bigger than her apartment.

Two double doors led to a bedroom with a massive bed, perfectly made with plush white bedcovers. The same floor-to-ceiling windows that had been a feature point of the restaurant were here as well, but a door led to a balcony, and there were curtains to be drawn for privacy.

Jen stepped into the room, her eyes falling on the champagne and chocolate-covered strawberries on a table beside the sofa. This room must have cost a fortune.

And he'd booked it just to spend a few hours with her?

She spun to face him as she set her coat and purse down on a nearby chair. "I'm not going to lie. I feel a bit like I'm in *Pretty Woman*."

He smirked, then set his phone down on the table. "You're a lot prettier than Julia Roberts, to start."

She went up to him and placed her arms around his neck. Nervous energy was ricocheting down her limbs, making her feel a little unsteady. They'd talked about what came next. Yet now that they were here and the opportunity was perfect for it, she felt strangely awkward.

What if she didn't live up to his expectations?

Dinner had been wonderful—they'd talked about favorites and swapped some stories—but it hadn't felt casual. And she hadn't even come close to laying out guidelines on how things should go with Colby, especially since he was going to do her the favor of entering the baking contest as her boyfriend.

Jason set his hands on her hips, then slid them forward to slip his hands into her back pockets. *Damn, that was sexy.*

"You seem nervous." He scanned her gaze. "We don't have to—"

She kissed him to shut him up. Not a passionate one, just a soft brush on the lips. His lips curved upward in a smile against hers. "Why don't we look around the suite? I've never been in a room like this."

Taking his hand, she pulled him from the living room into the bedroom. The bedroom also had a balcony door. On the opposite side, it opened to an enormous bathroom, complete with a Jacuzzi. She let her fingers glide over the complimentary soaps and shampoos. "When I was a kid, I used to beg my dad to bring these back to me as souvenirs from his business trips."

Jason came up behind her and slipped his arms around her waist. They were in front of the mirror, and she stared at their reflection as he kissed her neck. Her eyes closed, and she reveled in the feel of his lips against the soft skin by her jaw, trailing upward. She turned her face toward him, and his lips descended on hers.

Her heart slammed into her ribs. Something about seeing them together in the mirror was more of a turn-on than she'd expected. He was hotter than any guy she'd ever dated, and somehow, she felt beautiful and sexy as a result.

His kiss was commanding and purposeful, his mouth opening against hers. His tongue stroked against hers, determined and sensual, the taste of wine still on his lips.

She pressed back against him and pushed herself against his groin, rubbing against the hardness she found there. He pulled away briefly, scanning her gaze. "Is this okay? I don't want to rush you if you're not ready."

Whatever his thoughts on one-night stands were, his approach caused her core to melt into a pool of hot liquid. She nodded. "I want to."

"You don't know how much I've been dreaming of fucking you." Jason deftly unbuttoned her pants. He set his chin on her shoulder, watching her in the mirror. As he slipped his hand down into the front of her pants, she tensed against him, her eyes widening. They both watched in the mirror now, and his hand dipped lower, pushing past the skimpy fabric of the thong she'd worn.

She knew she was wet, but his fingers glided against her with skillful ease as he pushed one, then two inside her. She gasped, and his other arm braced against her breasts, pushing against them. Watching the pleasure she took from his touch seemed to embolden him, and he pulled one finger back against the tender spot that throbbed against him.

Her knees almost buckled. Still, he didn't release her. His fingers continued to glide in and out, pushing deeper and rubbing against her with command. Pressure built within her. She hadn't been with anyone for so long, so it wouldn't take much.

"Oh my God, Jason," she moaned.

Jason paused, one finger still inside her. The other finger pushed against her, back and forth, then in a circle, her own wetness the only slickness he needed to elicit electric jolts from her. She opened her eyes and met his in the mirror.

He wasn't just finger-fucking her.

He was claiming her.

The possessiveness of his grip, the intensity of his gaze locked with hers, and then her orgasm mounted, lifting her higher until she could barely stand. His arm kept her upright, her knees shaking as he refused to relent and release her.

The lights in the room seemed to flash with her climax, and she melted back against him, a feeling of complete satiation filling her. *Oh. My. God. That was incredible.*

Her breath was ragged as she came down, her heart pounding through her shirt. He kissed her temple and chuckled softly, the vibration in his chest against her back. "You're so fucking gorgeous when you come, you know that?"

What was she even supposed to say to that? Thank you? He'd just given her an incredible orgasm and hadn't even removed a single article of clothing from her.

"Thank you," she stammered and then opened her eyes once again. Her face was flushed, her lips redder.

He grinned, then led her away from the bathroom toward the bed. "We're not even close to done."

She still felt wobbly, but she slid onto the bed.

"Be right back." Jason went out the double doors toward the living space. When he returned, he had the champagne and chocolate-covered strawberries in his hand, along with two champagne glasses.

He poured them each a glass of champagne, then set it on the nightstand.

Was there a sexy way to take jeans off? She should have thought this through more before she planned her wardrobe. Her button was still undone, and she pushed the fabric from her hips, then pulled them off her legs. Dropping her jeans to the side of the bed, she said, "I absolutely can't stand when people leave cabinets and drawers open. It's my biggest pet peeve. Your turn."

Jason blinked, then gave her an amused look. He pulled the Henley he'd worn off in one swift, fluid motion, revealing his well-sculpted abs and chest. He was one of those men who genuinely looked better without a shirt. Not because he didn't look good with a shirt. She might come again just staring at him, if that was possible. "I hate Lima beans."

She rolled her eyes. "No fair, you already gave me a good one."

"Fine. You get a bonus one." He shrugged, those strong biceps showing every ripple of muscle. "My biggest pet peeve is when other people are late."

Such a good quality. Also, so the opposite of her. "I'm always late." She pulled her own shirt off, and the room suddenly felt colder than before. Goose bumps covered her torso. She sat back on her heels and dropped her blouse, enjoying Jason's eyes on her body.

She'd worn the sexiest lingerie she had. "I lost my virginity when I was fifteen. To a senior on the football team. Then he broke up with me and told the entire football team about it."

"How is it that you don't hate men?" He winced, then unbuttoned his own pants.

"I hate some of them." She shrugged, then crawled toward him.

He took in her position, and she could see the lust burning in his eyes. "Remind me to fuck you just like that before we go." He pushed his pants from his hips, and her eyes went to the bulge in his black boxer briefs. "I lost my virginity when I was sixteen. My grandfather was out of town, and I threw a party. Of course, he came back early and found me having sex in his bed with my high school girlfriend."

"That can't have gone over well." She pulled him down to sit beside her.

"It didn't." He leaned over and held her chin between his forefinger and thumb. "He transferred me to an all-boys boarding school."

"Well, I guess it's a good thing you're not gay, or that would have totally blown up in his face." She set her arm over his shoulder. They both chortled, and she pressed her forehead against his.

"I think it works out for both of us that I'm not gay." Jason took her wrists and pinned her back to the bed. "Now, I'm going to take off the rest of your clothes, and you're welcome to tell me two facts . . . later."

"As long as you tell me one." She nodded toward his boxer briefs.

"Deal." He lowered his mouth to hers again. Her lips moved against his, her tongue colliding with his as his hands released her wrists and then slid to her breasts. His thumbs brushed against her nipples, over the fabric, and she moaned.

His fingers quickly unlatched the hooks, and he pushed the bra away, revealing her breasts to the cool air. He pulled his head back, staring at her breasts. "You are spectacular, Jen."

His head lowered, and he kissed her nipples, one after the other, sucking on them until white heat curled through her. His hands pulled the thong from her hips, and he parted her legs with his knee, his fingers seeking her entrance once again.

As his kisses grazed lower, she trembled. He paused briefly, taking her in with his gaze, then pushed her knees so they were bent, her feet flat against the comforter. He dropped his head between her legs, his kisses gentle, then more demanding as his tongue explored further. "Jason . . ." she breathed, and he held her hips.

"You taste incredible," he whispered against her, pushing two fingers inside her.

As his tongue stroked her, her hips rose against his mouth, her body feeling like it was floating as the movement drove her to heights that made her moan uncontrollably. She dug her fingers into the top of his head, gripping his hair. "Jason—"

"Yeah, babe?"

The term of endearment almost undid her. "I want you inside me." She looked down at his head, nestled between her legs, his eyes cutting to her with full control of what he was doing to her. "Please."

"Soon," he promised, and then his tongue stroked her harder. She groaned, her hips rising against his mouth, and he locked her there, holding her hips as her body tried to get away from the incredible rise of spectacular bliss that poured through every nerve ending of her legs, making her feet tingle, rising through her in waves. She was moaning louder than before, crying his name.

Her heart didn't slow as he lifted his head, then kissed her mouth. "You're so wet. And I've wanted you for days. So it might be rough, is that okay?"

She nodded. She wasn't sure when he'd taken off his boxers, but staring at him now, her own lust took control. He was bigger than she'd expected he'd be. As he reached for a condom in his jeans, she tried to catch her breath.

Once he'd covered himself, he pushed her legs apart once more, holding her hips. He encircled her entrance, pushing against her with gentle pressure, and then he took her in a swift motion.

Oh my God.

She closed her eyes, the pressure of his length hitting deep inside her, ripping a scream of pleasure from her throat. She'd forgotten how good this could be.

Had it ever been this good?

He pushed harder and harder, her hips rising to meet her movement. Then he stopped, pulled away, and she gasped at the lack of him. He flipped her onto her stomach. "Can you get on your hands and knees again?"

She nodded, and his palms cupped her ass, and he pushed inside her once again, going deeper this time.

Thank God they were in a suite. Her volume was too loud. She was practically screaming cries of pleasure as he drove deeper. One hand slid around her hip and down between her legs, playing with her once again. "I want you to come again for me," he told her. "I'm going to keep fucking you until you come again."

She drove her face into a pillow, holding it against it as he continued to pound against her, his hand relentless in stroking her until he'd brought her to another height of pleasure, shattering her completely.

His own release came soon after, and he stilled, then withdrew, collapsing on the bed beside her. His chest heaved, his eyes closed.

Jen lay there, out of breath, then reached out for a chocolate-covered strawberry. She took a bite, then turned her face toward him. "Two things."

He laughed. "I don't know if I can even talk right now."

She could barely think straight, the euphoric feeling of pure bliss still cascading over her body. "Number one, sex with you is better than this chocolate-covered strawberry. Which is the actual best chocolate combo of all, by the way, so that's saying a lot. And thank you." She offered him the rest of the strawberry.

"Thank *you*." Jason opened one eye. He grinned, then finished the strawberry. "And I concur."

She smiled. "You concur with what?"

"Definitely the strawberry thing. Best combo. But also—sex with you. I may be addicted."

He was probably just saying that, but she still liked to hear it. "And number two . . . I really like you, Jason Sutter. And I don't think that's going to end with tonight."

CHAPTER SEVENTEEN

Jason had really messed up this time.

He'd messed up before. Lots.

But not like this. He shifted the car into fifth gear as he merged onto the highway. The cold light of dawn made him feel ill.

Jason Sutter.

He'd almost broken right there and told her everything. Which would have probably completely freaked her out, given that they'd just had sex, and she didn't even know his last name.

How would she ever forgive him for this?

She couldn't forgive him for this.

He didn't forgive himself for this.

What could he say? *"Hey, Jen. I lied to you about my last name. It's Cavanaugh. Like my brother, coincidentally. Except he told you it was Connor. That's right. You're sleeping with your ex-boyfriend's brother. Yep. We're both liars. And your son, well, he's my nephew. He's also inherited hundreds of millions of dollars . . ."*

His brain stopped at that point. But he wanted her. He

didn't want her for one more night of sex. They'd fucked twice after that and it hadn't been enough.

He wanted to make her smile. To hear her tell him about losing her virginity while she did a striptease. Or her biggest pet peeve.

He wanted to watch her pretend he hadn't messed up an entire batch of playdough. Who made their own playdough anyway?

She did.

She was gorgeous, articulate, and fun.

And he'd enjoyed the time he'd spent with Colby, too. He hadn't known what to say to him, but the kid didn't seem to mind.

Jason pushed the car faster, speeding past a slowpoke in the left lane. One night with Jen had made things infinitely worse.

Jason Sutter. She was going to hate him.

Just as much as he hated himself.

"What sort of guys do you normally date?"

"Broken ones."

He lifted his eyes to the rearview mirror, caught himself looking at it. Little did she know.

After he'd dropped her off, he felt as though he'd unraveled, the frays that had been wearing on the edge of his life tugged loose. She was unlike any woman he'd ever been with. And not just because the sex had been good.

The connection he felt with her went beyond that. To describe it wouldn't do it justice.

His phone rang. TJ. He pressed the button on his steering wheel to answer. "What's up?"

"Where the hell are you now?" TJ's voice crackled, the service in the mountains less than reliable.

"On my way to West Virginia. I need to find my grandmother, even if it's at the casino."

"Then turn around. I'm sitting outside her house. She got home late last night."

Jason cursed. The next exit wasn't for a few miles. "All right." His shoulders bunched, the tension in his chest like an acidic knot eating its way through his core. "Actually, don't stay there. I need you to make sure Vickers doesn't talk to Jen."

"I'm not going to even ask how your little outing went last night."

"Thanks, Mom." Jason pushed the gas down, watching as the speedometer climbed higher. "I don't want Vickers within ten yards of her or anyone in her family."

"You know I'm not a bodyguard, right? Also, that's a lot of people. Have you considered the alternative?"

"Which is?" The gray of the morning was turning brighter but not less gloomy. With the cloud cover that had rolled in overnight, Jason doubted the sun would make an appearance today.

"Coming clean."

"I'm going to tell her. I just have to figure out a way how."

"You're like that Bible guy. You know the one with the plaques?"

Jason squinted. "Moses?"

"Yeah. Him. Holding your hands up and trying to keep a tidal wave back. Except you don't have magical powers and shit."

"Your theology might be a little lacking, TJ."

"Not the point. The point is you can't stop this from getting out. All you can do is mitigate the outcome. She's probably not going to take it so well since you've been screwing her both literally and figuratively, but the longer you don't tell her, the worse it's going to be."

"You're aware I actually have a therapist?"

"Free of charge. Actually, nix that. Maybe I'll add it as a

line item and then back charge you on all the advice I've been giving you."

"Later." He hung up as he veered toward the exit lane.

The phone rang immediately again, and Jason picked it up without looking. "Eat a dick, TJ."

"Jason, it's Bill Powell."

Jason stiffened and glanced at the dashboard. Of course it was. He cringed. "How can I help you, sir?" Truthfully, he'd wanted to tell Bill to eat a dick for a while, so maybe it wasn't the worst mistake ever.

"We've been trying to get in touch with you, and you've been unavailable. Now I know you're going through a tough time with the death of your grandfather, but enough is enough, son."

"I'm not your son," Jason snapped, downshifting as he got closer to the stop sign at the end of the exit.

"Listen here. I don't know where you are or what the hell you think you're doing—"

"Cut the bullshit, Bill. You know exactly where I am. You sent Ned Vickers to follow me."

"And he tells me you've taken up with a girl in your mother's hometown."

Jason drew a sharp breath. The implications of that sentence were a lot to unpack. Ned had not only told Bill about Jen, but he'd outed his mother's hidden background, too. To the Powells. Who cared about things like breeding and lineage. That Bill Powell could destroy the beloved image of Jason's mother among their social circle was a threat.

"My fiancée, actually," Jason managed. TJ hadn't exaggerated the part about this spiraling out of his control.

Lies, lies, and more lies.

The pause on Bill's end was prolonged. Amanda was his daughter, after all. He'd give a shit about it. "Jason?"

"Yes, sir?"

"You're fired. You'll get an email to confirm what we've discussed here."

The line went dead.

Jason pulled the car over onto the shoulder. Getting out, he slammed the door, feeling the need to rage at something, someone.

He was literally alone on the side of the road.

He slammed the fleshy part of his fists against the window, beating the glass. They'd wanted him out for a while. Their plan all along had been to kick him out. With Thomas alive, two Cavanaughs were more than enough to keep things just so. But with his grandfather dead and Jason's stake being so uncertain, they could do whatever they wanted.

They would dissolve the company even faster without him.

He tore his sunglasses from his face, rubbed his eyes, then forced himself to swallow a few deep breaths and climbed back into the driver's seat.

He had to talk to Mildred. This time, he wouldn't take no for an answer.

————————

THE DOOR to Mildred's house opened, and she stood there, still clad in a nightgown, hair up in curlers.

Jason crossed his arms. "No shotgun this time?"

She gave a weary sigh. "What do you want?"

"Five minutes of your time."

Mildred gave him an impatient look, then pushed the door open.

"You're going to let me in?" He stepped through the doorway. An old scent from his childhood came toward him. Like the combination of cedarwood and mothballs.

Mildred put a hand on the rail and continued up the stairs without looking back at him. "When a dog has the runs, do you let it shit on your front door where everyone has to step through it?"

What the hell did that even mean? Jason closed the front door and followed her. "I'm the dog in this scenario?"

Mildred gave him a look, her eyes gleaming. "You're the shit. Thomas Cavanaugh was the dog. He's the one that formed you into this." Mildred gave a tired wave of her hand toward him. "It doesn't have to make sense. I'm old enough to string words together and just have everyone assume I don't have the brain cells left to know what I'm saying."

She reached the top of the staircase and continued shuffling toward her kitchen. "Want some breakfast?"

He gave the back of her head a puzzled glance. She seemed to sense it and gave him another look, with a shrug. "You are my grandson. It's not my fault you don't know me at all."

Mildred. His only living relative. The thought hadn't occurred to him before. Besides Colby, anyway.

She walked over to the kitchen and pulled out a pack of cigarettes. With shaking fingers, she lit one and took a long drag.

"I didn't know you smoked." He observed her quietly, then sat at the worn, round kitchen table. There was only enough room at the table for four people. The chair creaked under his weight, the legs wobbling enough that he pictured himself falling on the red-and-yellow linoleum floor.

"I only smoke when I'm stressed. And don't you tell me anything about how it'll kill me. We all have to die of something, and I've lived long enough. Somehow, I keep outliving everyone."

Jason chuckled. Instead, he held his hand out for a cigarette. He rarely smoked and mostly cigars when he did.

Somehow the idea of sharing a smoke with Mildred was strangely comforting. She gave him a toothy smile. The package crinkled as she set it down on the table, lighter beside it.

Lighting one up, he leaned back in the chair, taking in the kitchen. The geese and chickens on the wallpaper had remained in his memory. The taste of tobacco was bitter in his mouth, the smoke stinging his throat. Mildred set out a glass ashtray and then sat beside him. "So you want to know about Kevin."

The woman didn't beat around the bush. He nodded.

Mildred tapped her cigarette. "You sure you're ready to hear it?"

He leaned forward on his elbows. "Why wouldn't I want to know about how my brother lived the last years before he died?"

The wrinkles around Mildred's mouth cut deep lines as she frowned. "Kevin was in an awful state when he came looking for me. Took me three months to get him clean and sober. Then Jen gave him a reason to want to live." Mildred wrinkled her nose, a bitter look settling into her features. "I always told Martha that man would ruin you boys. But she was just as afraid of him as you were."

"Well, he's dead now." Jason watched the ends curling in at the tip of the cigarette in his hand. "They're all dead. And Kevin's son is my grandfather's heir." He'd spent the entire night thinking about it. Lying would never have gotten him anywhere with Mildred. If she found out the truth later, no nondisclosure agreement, no payoff would keep her silent. She'd proven throughout the years that she couldn't be bought.

Mildred didn't react, her chest rising and falling with soft breath as though he'd been conversing about the weather. "Except nobody knows Colby is a Cavanaugh. Which is why you turned up the moment you found out."

She was as quick as he believed. Something about it gave him a satisfied feeling. His mother hadn't been dumb either. Just stuck.

"Exactly. Grandfather didn't know about Colby. He just knew Kevin went missing for a while. So he put in his will that if there was any other direct descendant, they would get everything, the shares in his company and his entire fortune. But if not, it goes to me."

Mildred watched him for a few moments and then burst into laughter. Jason had been expecting an unusual reaction, but her outright mockery was hard to swallow. He watched her humorlessly, his jaw clenching. She laughed until there were tears in her eyes and then snuffed out her cigarette in the ashtray. "This is quite a situation, Jason. You must feel a bit like the brother of the prodigal son right now."

He gave her a tight smile. *Couldn't have put it any better himself.*

"So Colby is worth a few hundred million and . . . what? Inherits Cavanaugh Metals?"

Jason extinguished his cigarette, no longer in the mood to sit and share anything with Mildred. "A portion of it. My grandfather sold a majority stake a few years ago to Powell Enterprises."

Mildred nodded slowly. "And you're worth a few million? I'm assuming they paid you well, at least for the last few years. But you probably spent it, thinking you'd have a nice inheritance coming your way." She winked. "I saw that car you were driving the other day."

She wasn't too far off. He had put some away in the bank and retirement accounts. But the bulk of his personal wealth was in investments and property. "That's not the point," he said, bristling. "Mildred, that money can't just go to Colby."

Mildred climbed out of her chair again and shuffled to the fridge. "Scrambled eggs?"

He didn't answer, and she pulled out a carton of eggs from the door. As she shut it, he went on, "The company . . . my grandfather made a terrible deal with the Powells. I want to convert the entire company to a one-hundred-percent employee-owned. Set up a trust with my shares and use some of the money my grandfather left in his will to buy out the Powells. It's not even for me. It's for the people who have put their whole lives into Cavanaugh Metals and are going to lose their jobs with the way Bill Powell is running things. I don't care about the legacy. I don't care about the money—"

"That's not true. You do care about the money." Mildred snorted and gave him a pointed look. "Otherwise, you wouldn't be here."

"I don't want to see a couple of hundred good people out of work because my grandfather was a controlling asshole who didn't listen to me about the Powells. And that's why I need your help, Mildred. The Powells hired an infamous private investigator to see if they can find out if there's anyone other than me who stands to inherit."

Mildred cracked a few eggs into a mug and pulled a fork from a drawer. She turned her back to him, dragging a cast iron frying pan from the oven. "Your brother"—she set the pan on the grates of her stove with a bang—"he left Jen because he didn't want your grandfather to ever find out about Colby."

Her words stole the breath from his body. "What?"

Cutting a piece of butter, Mildred threw it onto the pan. She didn't look at him. "You heard me. He loved that girl. Loved the baby she was going to have, too. I could have murdered him for leaving, but I can't say I didn't understand it. I think it damn near killed him." She pulled a couple of slices of bread out of a bag and pushed them into the toaster.

When Mildred turned to look toward Jason, red rimmed her eyes. "Kevin never wanted Colby to grow up the way he did. Never wanted your grandfather to get one finger on Jen or his son. So he picked up and left in the middle of the night so Jen wouldn't know where he'd gone. He swore me to secrecy."

Jason's throat tightened. He didn't want to think about it. Didn't want to imagine the desperation.

Didn't want to register what it meant.

Mildred poured the eggs onto the frying pan and pulled out a spatula. "I know Thomas is dead now, and all I can say is good riddance. But if he thinks he can get his claws on my great-grandbaby from the grave, he's got another thing coming. I don't want Jen to know about Kevin. Just tell me what you need me to do."

Jason set his elbows on the table and covered his face with his hands. "God, Mildred, why couldn't you just have talked to me when I first got here?" He felt sick. Mildred would have helped him. Kevin had loved Jen. All of it was too much. He'd ruined things and made them impossible to fix.

Silence settled between them, the only sounds the gentle scraping of the spatula against the pan and the clock ticking on the wall. A plate clinked, and Mildred stopped in front of Jason, setting a plate of scrambled eggs and toast on the table. She took a deep breath and set her hand on his shoulder. "What did you do?"

Jason stared at the food she'd made him, too nauseated to eat. But he didn't want to offend her by not taking her peace offering, either. He lifted the fork, his mind drifting over the mental image of Jen in his arms. Images he didn't want to erase. Words seem to strangle his throat. At last, he managed, "I started a relationship with Jen."

Mildred's eyes narrowed at him, and she sat across from him once again. "What sort of relationship?"

He wasn't about to discuss his sex life with his grand-mother. But he lifted his gaze to hers and gave her a hard look, one he knew she was wizened enough to understand. Her face fell and she shook her head. "There must be some sort of curse on your family name. Cavanaugh men just keep coming to Brandywood to ruin and steal their best women."

Her eyes misted. "You look like my Martha, you know that?" She clasped her hands together, her thin and wiry frame seeming smaller. "Kevin didn't. He was the spitting image of your dad. But you—you took after the Prices."

"Mom never really talked about her family." Jason shoved a forkful of eggs into his mouth, chewing slowly. It was better than he expected.

"How could she? And she died when you were so young."

Fifteen. He'd been fifteen. But his mother had changed after his dad's death.

He closed his eyes, not wanting to think about it. She had just stopped living, really. Stopped going outside, stopped going to parties. She'd wasted away and had been even thinner than Mildred had been when she'd died. An acute case of the flu and pneumonia had been enough to undo her. But her death had started long before then, with her broken heart.

Mildred was clearly lost in her own haunted thoughts. Her jaw moved as though she was grinding her teeth. "If he'd just have let me see her. Talk to her. I could have helped her. I was her mother, for God's sake."

When his grandfather had talked about Mildred, he'd always used some name. *"Crazy old bat,"* or *"backwoods country loon."* Something like that. That voice had shaped Jason's teenage years.

He'd been ashamed of Mildred when she showed up at his mom's funeral. Ashamed of her clothes, her hair. Everything. Ashamed of the way she wore her grief openly and loudly.

And never once had he stopped to think about the person underneath that earthen, crusty veneer.

His guilt sat in his stomach heavily with the food he'd eaten. He cleared his throat and set the fork down. "Mildred, I —" He could barely get the words out. "About Mom's funeral .. ." He couldn't form the apology she deserved. How could words ever be enough?

She sighed, then reached for another cigarette. "Do you mind if I smoke while you eat?"

He shook his head.

"The truth is, Jason, I was angry with you. I gave up on you. Both of you. Until Kevin turned up on my doorstep. Then I knew. Kevin told me everything, you know." Her hand shook as she lifted the cigarette to her lips. "And you need to understand something. You are not a bad person, Jason. And your dad's death—"

"I don't want to talk about that, Mildred."

She chewed on the end of her cigarette, then gave a curt nod. "When you're ready, I'll be right here." She set her elbows on the table. "Now let's get back to Jen. That was pretty quick, don't you think?"

Resisting the urge to face palm, Jason continued his breakfast. "I don't even know how it happened."

Mildred blew out a puff of air, her lips vibrating in a scoff. "Oh, come off it. If you don't think I know how it happened, you're out of your mind. I know exactly what happened. You took one look at her, and your penis took over."

Jason blinked at her. For an old lady, she was surprisingly .. . candid. Perceptive. He choked on his guffaw. Then he stammered, "Maybe. But the problem is that the asshole the Powells hired to find out about Kevin is here in town now. He followed me. And he knows about you. It's only a matter of time before he finds out about Jen and Colby."

Mildred looked confused. "So if he knows about me, what are you doing here?"

"I need to figure out how to tell Jen about Kevin. And the inheritance."

"You haven't told her anything?" Mildred squinted at him.

"No."

"Then it's already too late. You've been lying to the girl. She's never going to believe anything you have to say now." Mildred shrugged.

He needed to tell her about the idea of asking Jen to marry him. And the paternity issue with Amanda. But their frail peace might not survive that last part. "Help me. She knows you're Kevin's grandmother, doesn't she?"

Mildred nodded, flicking the ash from her cigarette into the ashtray. "We have dinner a couple of times a month. And I see her at church. I'd help with Colby more but my joints aren't what they used to be."

"She's being evicted. I have to help her." Jason finished the last bite of toast and scooted his chair back. He stood and crossed the kitchen. Grabbing a clean mug from the dish rack, he filled it with water. "And even if I do nothing and Powell's guy catches on to the situation with Jen, my grandfather instructed that the CEO of Cavanaugh Metals would manage the trust for a minor heir that wasn't my son. Colby probably would see next to nothing until he's eighteen. Maybe even longer."

"And you want to—"

"Marry her. Adopt Colby. Not for romantic reasons. Just as a financial and legal transaction."

She didn't react, her gaze analytical. "But wouldn't the trustee still be the CEO fellow?"

Jason shook his head. "Not necessarily. My grandfather's will stated that on the off chance I had a child, he or she would be the heir, but I would be free to manage their estate. The Powells would probably take it to court, but my lawyer thinks I have a solid argument."

Mildred crushed out her cigarette. "Sounds like a hopeless mess. You shouldn't have gotten involved with Jen."

He shifted, gazing out the small kitchen window. His grandmother's house backed up to the woods—woods that looked overgrown with brush and thorns. An ancient deck on the back of her house was covered with green mildew, the boards lifting. Did she have anyone to help her with this place?

"Noted." He gave her a taut smile.

"I'm serious. And Jen . . ." Mildred shook her head. "I don't know what that girl is thinking. She already went through enough with Kevin. You'd think she'd learned her lesson." Mildred stood, then came to stand beside him. "The longer you wait to tell that girl the truth, the more she's going to be convinced you only want her for the money. Which is true, isn't it?"

The grimness of her words made him wince. "I want to help her. More so now than ever. If Kevin left because he loved her, she deserves a lot more than she's been dealt."

"That's all very nice, Jason. But would you be offering to marry her if you didn't want the money? If you didn't have a vested interest in the whole thing?"

No. But this isn't just about me. His grandfather was an ass, but there was a way to keep the integrity of what his family had built intact, especially for the employees who had dedicated their lives to it. *And for me, too.* And he hated the idea of the Powells winning.

"You want my advice? Walk away. Sure, she might end up struggling for some years. We'll all pitch in to help, though. You stay, and you're going to destroy her. She made a mistake and slept with you. Okay. She hasn't gotten in too deep. But another broken heart?"

"And what if she's okay with marrying me for money?" Jason narrowed his gaze at her. She'd given him nothing else to work with. Could he offer Jen such a cold transaction? He cared about her. But everything else that came along with marriage wasn't really on the table for him.

Been there. Done that. Never again.

"She may be willing to. She may." Mildred patted his hand. "But money doesn't hold people together when the love you ache for is gone. I'd tell you to ask your mother, but we can't, can we?" Mildred let his hand go and rubbed her bony knuckles. "I'll tell you what. If the truth is what you want to tell her, I'll help you find a way. But I'm going to have to think about it."

CHAPTER EIGHTEEN

JEN GROPED in the dark room, looking for Colby. Finding her cell phone, instead, she checked the time. *Ten thirty?*

Holy crap, she hadn't slept in this long in years.

She rolled over in the bed, her eyes adjusting to the dim light. Travis must have blackout curtains in his room. By the time she'd arrived the night before and with a few glasses of wine and champagne in her system, Travis had insisted she spend the night. Colby was asleep anyway, he argued, and she could have his bed.

The low buzz of conversation in the adjoining room told her Travis must have gotten up early with Colby. *Poor Travis.* She'd taken off work because she had no one to watch Colby, and Bunny had come back from her trip. But she'd never intended for Travis to miss another morning of work for her. She sat up, combing her fingers through her hair. The champagne had left her with a mild headache.

Jumping out of bed, her thighs twinged with pain. *Ouch.* The muscles on her butt hurt, too, and she smiled at the memory.

Travis had lent her a T-shirt, and her bare feet were cold against the hardwood floor of his bedroom. Her toes curled as she found her clothes on the floor. She changed quickly and pulled a hair elastic from her purse. She threw her hair into a messy ponytail. Grabbing her phone again, she looked through her texts. Nothing from Jason.

His last text to her had been a quick one to let her know he was on his way the night before. She stared at the screen, her thumb hovering over the keyboard. Should she text him?

I really like you . . .

She bit her lip hard. What the hell had she been thinking? Nothing like the high of an orgasm to make you utter stupidity.

Had she freaked him out?

She slid the phone into her back pocket and grabbed her shoes. She didn't feel like putting heels back on this morning. Opening the door to the room, she blinked at the relative brightness in Travis's living room. He and Colby were sitting on the couch, watching cartoons.

Travis eyed her with a knowing grin. "Morning, sleepyhead."

Colby didn't look up as his eyes were focused on the screen.

"Don't look at me while I'm doing the walk of shame." She crossed the room to his kitchen. "Do you have any orange juice? My mouth tastes like chalk."

Travis hopped up from the couch and joined her in the kitchen. He grabbed her a glass while she rummaged through the fridge. She avoided his gaze, pouring the juice, and then sipped it. "Don't look at me."

"Why not?" Travis crossed his arms.

"Because I know what you're thinking."

Travis gave her a serious look. "I'm not Lindsay. I won't try to get every detail out of you or whatever it is you women talk about."

"Don't worry, I'm not about to share details." Jen chugged the rest of the orange juice. "But I may or may not have told him I wasn't feeling so casual about him." She grimaced.

"Yikes."

She inspected her empty glass. "I know."

"This is the guy who told you he's only into one-night stands, right?"

She nodded. "But that was also after he asked me to be his fake girlfriend for the baking competition."

Travis's brows shot up. "Fake girlfriend?"

"He feels bad for the whole thing with Brad. And I told him about the eviction." She'd told Travis about that whole mess the day before when he picked up Colby.

"And you said?"

Jen moseyed over to the sink and washed her glass. "I said yes. It's twenty-five thousand dollars. And I need it. He said I could keep all the prize money since he doesn't know a single thing about baking. Which reminds me. I need to tell Laura I'll be late to work tonight."

"So Mr. One-Night Stand—"

"Jason."

"Whatever. He tells you he wants to get in your pants. Then he hangs out with you and your toddler, watches your kid while you work, and takes you out for a ridiculously expensive dinner."

"That room he rented at the resort was seriously nice, too."

Travis shook his head. "Exactly." He frowned. "Jen, I hate to break it to you, but this guy's words don't match his actions. Which is fine in the sense that he's clearly into you. Not so fine in the sense that he's more than likely hiding something. Not to mention, his life is in Chicago. Nowhere near Brandywood. He could be married."

"No, he told me he's divorced." She stared at Travis, then

rolled her eyes. The last thing she needed was for Travis to get as overprotective and paranoid as her brothers. "What are you talking about? What on earth would he have to hide?"

"I don't know. You don't know. That's sort of the point, isn't it? You know next to nothing about this guy. He told you he's a CFO, but what company? He went to UPenn, but when? You have no way of verifying anything about his identity."

Determined to prove him wrong, she pulled out her phone. She typed his name, followed by "CFO" and "Chicago" into the search engine.

Nothing came up.

The refrigerator seemed to buzz more noisily.

Travis came and stood beside her, his arms still crossed. She moved her back toward him, feeling defensive. "His company might not be based in Chicago."

"Except that he told you he worked there, right?"

He'd told Colby he took the train into work every day. Which meant an office. A sinking feeling went through her. "Maybe they're not online."

"Maybe they're not a real company. Any company big enough to have a CFO is online, Jen. This isn't the 1900s."

She typed in "Jason Sutter" then "UPenn."

Still nothing.

She closed the browser and put her phone away. She looked toward Colby and lowered her voice to a whisper, "This is stupid."

"Is it, though?" Travis gave her a wary look.

"Not everyone is online. Just look at Kevin."

Travis set his hands on her shoulders. "That's the last person you should use as a yardstick of upstanding behavior." Travis squeezed her shoulders. "You're going to hate me, but I think you should ask Dan to look into him."

"No way in hell." Jen emphasized every word. She shot

Travis a betrayed look, then left the kitchen. "Come on, Colbs. We have to get going."

"I'll drive you back." Travis reached for his keys.

"I'm good, thanks." Jen pulled her coat on. "I can call a ride and get my car seat from your car." She'd left him with it last night in case of emergencies.

"I'm driving you. You don't need to waste your money on a ride." Travis's voice was flat. He shut off the TV, then helped Colby into his coat. "I'm not trying to make you mad, Jen. I just want to make sure you're not—"

"I know." She put her hand on Colby's shoulder and jutted her chin. "Everyone thinks I can't handle anything. And that I make terrible judgment calls. But just let me be happy for like ten minutes, okay?"

Travis opened his mouth to argue, then snapped it closed. He nodded.

The drive back with him was tense, and she felt like a brat as she waved goodbye to him. He was the only reason she'd been able to go out with Jason last night. She should be grateful. But his words had also rattled her.

Rather than go inside, she re-installed the car seat into her own car and then plopped Colby in it. She needed to go get boxes for packing. Maybe if she listed her furniture for sale, she'd scrape together enough money to pay for some of her rent.

She didn't want to even think about the fact that Christmas was coming up.

Getting in the driver's seat, she checked her phone again. Still nothing from Jason.

She closed her eyes, releasing a slow breath. "Come on, Jason, please." Her voice was a breathless whisper.

Starting the engine, she pulled forward and out of the apartment complex. She watched Colby in the back, staring out the window, his feet swinging gently in his car seat.

What was she doing?

She'd been so caught up with Jason. Too caught up.

Dan was her brother, and he loved her. He'd never seen eye to eye with her about her boyfriends, but he'd also been right about her boyfriends 100 percent of the time. He made mistakes—some huge ones—but he was a respected person in town.

And he genuinely loved Colby.

She went a block farther, then made a U-turn, heading toward the police station. Hopefully, Dan would be at the precinct.

CHAPTER NINETEEN

YARDLEY'S COUNTRY DEPOT was vibrant with Christmas decorations, customers, tourists, and contestants—not to mention a camera crew. Jason scanned the long glass display window where Jen had told him to meet him. She wasn't there yet.

Two long folding tables sat on either side of the main doors with a pair of older women at each. One table had a sign taped to it that said, "Guests and Tickets," the other "Contestants."

He may as well get the materials he and Jen would need as contestants. If he'd known it would be this crowded, he would have arrived a half hour earlier at least. She wasn't kidding about being late to things.

He got in line at the contestants' table when a familiar man stepped up beside him. Dan Klein. He wasn't in uniform, but he still had a commanding presence.

"What did you tell her?" Dan didn't look at him.

Jason's brows drew together. "What?"

"She came to me today. Worried. Asked me to investigate

you." Dan crossed his arms. "I told you to let the past stay in the past."

What the hell? Why would—

He had the urge to catch himself against something, but since Dan presented the only option, he just straightened. Could Ned have talked to her? TJ had been following him all day. He would have known if Ned had talked to Jen.

What could have spooked her?

"Did you tell her?" Jason's voice was strained. Maybe it was why she hadn't shown up to the competition yet.

Dan shook his head slowly. "But I don't enjoy lying to my sister. So I'm going to ask you nicely. Again. Stay away from her."

The person in line in front of Jason finished, leaving the space at the table vacated. "Last name?" a woman intoned in a dry, unenthusiastic voice.

"Klein." Jason lifted his gaze and met Dan's eyes. "I promised to do this contest with her."

"I know." Dan's mouth set to a line. "And I know about the eviction and her debts. You're still not doing her any favors by staying in town."

Dan's stiff nod signaled the end of the conversation. He strode off into the crowd of the store. Jason turned back to the check-in table. The lady handed him a canvas bag with the name of the store printed on the side. Whoever was running this operation had a good handle on marketing, that's for sure. The line to the cashiers was almost around the store.

Colby found him before he could turn around. His arms snaked around Jason's leg, and Jason stiffened, startled. He looked down, then put his hand on the top of Colby's head. "Hey, dude."

Jen was a few feet away with two other adults right behind her. The way they looked at him, expectant for an introduction, almost made him feel like a teenager standing at the door for prom. Jen smiled. "Jason, these are my parents. Betty and Robert Klein."

Parents, he could usually handle. Even parents of a girl he had no interest in dating long term.

But the parents of a woman like Jen?

He felt intimidated as all hell. He put on his most charming smile and held out his hand. "Nice to meet you. Jen's told me all about you." Had they even talked about her parents? Did he remember something about maybe her mom working as a nurse?

Jen looked a lot like her mom, who was of similar height, with blond hair that had long since gone gray. Neither of her parents was overwhelmingly tall, so where the hell had Dan come from? Her father was an affable-looking man with a trim gray mustache and glasses. He had a sharp look, his hair wispy. He shook Jason's hand with a firm grip. "Call me Bob. Jen tells us you're in finance."

"That's right." His eyes darted to Jen's face briefly. She didn't give away any sort of concerns with her body language. Why had she gone to Dan?

"What company? I work as a consultant for the FBI in financial crimes, so I'm in the Windy City a lot."

Of course. Because why wouldn't he be? He held his breath momentarily. It wouldn't help to lie about this. "Cavanaugh Metals."

"Really?" Bob drew his face back. "I've met Tom Cavanaugh before." He gave a brief chuckle. "He's a tough son of a bitch. Good businessman."

The chances of Jen's father having met his grandfather. The skin on the back of his neck prickled, and Jason's smile was tight. "He actually passed away a couple of months ago." Before the conversation could continue, he lifted the canvas bag and set his gaze on Jen. "I checked us in. They said we need to be over by the baking center in ten minutes."

Was that relief on her face? She slipped her arm into his. "See you later, Mom and Dad." Then she kissed Colby's cheek. "Behave, okay?"

Colby threw his arms around Jen, and she squatted to hug him. "I love you, Mommy."

Jen kissed his cheek. "I love you, too, bud. Maybe if you're lucky, Mom-Mom will buy you a candy cane."

Colby gave a wide grin. "Two candy canes!"

"Don't push your luck." She kissed him again, then stood. "*After* the show is done," she murmured to her mom in a low voice that Jason barely heard.

As her parents and Colby walked away, Jen turned to him. "I told them we've been together on and off for a while but that we finally made our relationship official. I didn't want them thinking I've lost my head with a guy I just met, especially right after I just asked them if I could move back in."

"Got it," Jason said. Her face looked pale. "Everything okay?"

Her gaze followed the direction her parents and Colby had gone. "I was just worried you might not be here when we showed up."

Jason bent his head toward hers and kissed her. "Of course I'm here." He interlaced their fingers, tugging her deeper into the store. "Why wouldn't I be?"

"It's just that"—she kept her gaze low—"I didn't hear from you all day. I mean, even after I texted you the instructions for tonight, all you answered was 'OKAY.' And I-I didn't know if things were okay."

He paused mid-stride. *Crap.*

He'd been out of the dating game too long. And when he'd taken women back home recently, they knew better than to expect a message. They didn't even get his phone number in the first place.

Jason had spent the entire day thinking of her and the situation with her and everything to do with her.

And he hadn't let her know.

None of that would make for a good explanation, though. He reached across his chest, rubbing his opposite shoulder with his free hand. "They fired me this morning. So I had a lot on my mind." He took both her hands, pulling her closer. "I promise, all I dreamed about today was you. And I won't let it happen again." He kissed her as though they weren't in the middle of a crowded store.

"You got fired?" She pulled away, her eyes wide. "Are you okay? What happened? I'm so sorry, I had no idea."

"It's fine. The company hired a CEO a few years ago that I don't get along with too well, so I've been expecting it." That was putting the whole thing mildly. All the half truths made him shift with discomfort. None of this was straightforward anymore, and he'd started to feel like he was drowning while trying to keep up with the lies. "The good news is that I can stretch my visit out here to Brandywood longer."

"I don't love the reason for it, but that makes me happy, at least." She gave him another kiss, enough to send his pulse racing, and a man bumped into them.

"Get a room," the man muttered, stalking past.

Jen pulled away, then covered her mouth with a gasp. "Oh my God." Her eyes were wide but gleeful as she looked at Jason. "That was *Brad*."

"As in the idiot who dumped you the other night for kissing me?"

She nodded, her cheeks reddening. "He's going to think I was totally cheating on him."

Jason wrapped his arms around her, then kissed her jaw. "I'm more than happy to confirm his worst suspicions."

"Stop. My parents are over in the audience." She pointed toward the middle of the room, where a large section of the store was corded off. About ten rows of folding chairs had been provided, but they were full, and there was standing room only.

Beyond the folding chairs was an elevated area—not as high as a stage, only about one stair step up. But wide enough to accommodate what looked like a full, well-stocked kitchen. Ten small but stocked kitchen islands had been set up across the space, each with a stand mixer. "The guy who owns this place, Peter Yardley, got a deal with the Happy Home Channel to make a cooking show. He built this to accommodate his filming schedule."

Jason frowned at the large cluster of contestants in the contestant holding area beside the stage. "There are more contestants than stand mixers."

"I think they said they're going to do a few rounds of quizzes to eliminate people before anyone gets to cook."

Jason froze. "Individually?" He didn't know a damn thing about cooking.

Her grin widened at his discomfort. "By team. So as long as you smile and look pretty, we should be good to go." She winked at him, then pulled him into the holding area.

TWO HOURS LATER, Jason felt more out of his depth than he'd felt in a long time. They'd made it through the first three rounds, which had whittled the crowd of over one hundred and fifty contestants down to ten. Because it was being televised, the contest had drawn entrants from the tristate area, and Brandywood was bursting at the seams with tourists.

The owner of the store, Peter Yardley, was acting as the host and chief judge of the competition, with two other people from the magazine and channel as judges. He was speaking to the camera now, and Jason could see why the magazine had chosen him to work with. Despite being an older man, he was charming and had a magnetic personality. Considering his obviously successful bar and the Depot, he clearly had a shrewd eye for business.

He reminded Jason of his grandfather.

As Jen sorted through the ingredients at their station, Jason eyed the crowd. Besides Jen's family, he'd spotted Mildred come through the door. He avoided looking at her, but he saw her now, sitting in the back corner of the seated section.

TJ was there, too. And Ned.

Ned didn't hide his presence, and it wasn't as though Jason could kick him out.

"Ready?" Peter motioned to the contestants. "Time to bake!"

Jen turned to Jason. "Hold on. Let me help you tie your apron on." She pulled an apron from the canvas bag he'd gotten during check-in, also emblazoned with the store name.

"I don't think I've ever worn an apron in my life," Jason muttered back to her. She'd tied one on herself without blinking. He wasn't used to doing anything he didn't excel at. Anything he couldn't do, he just didn't. The kitchen was not a part of the house where he'd ever spent any time. "What am I supposed to do? I can't just stand here next to you as I did during the quiz stuff."

"I'll talk you through it. I got us through the other part, didn't I?" Jen gave his hand a reassuring squeeze. She looked at the assignment card and read it out loud to him. "Make a signature pastry that is an expression of both people in the relationship."

Jason blinked at her. "Come again?" The blush that spread on her cheeks was enough to make him grin. "You know what I mean. Good God, your parents are over there."

She planted a kiss on his cheek. "I know what you meant. And I'd be happy to do the other one at another opportunity. Right now, let's bake."

"Bake what? I don't understand what the hell that means. Don't we need a recipe?"

"I am the recipe." She checked the clock. "We barely have enough time for this because they have to sit for a while before we bake them."

Her mind was clearly going at a speed he couldn't keep up with. But she was skilled in this without the slightest self-doubt. He liked how confident and clear-minded she was even though he felt like an idiot.

In order to keep the streaming and live audience entertained, the camera crew stopped by each of the tables three times during the baking part to interview them. They were the last station on the end, which meant they had some time before they came for the first interview.

Jen was moving with a quickness he couldn't follow, cracking eggs. She separated the whites from the yolks into two separate bowls. He stood next to her, using the cart to shield him from view. "Give me something to do."

She didn't look up. "Okay, grab that sieve from the side of the cart."

He set his hands on the cart, then checked the side. He looked back at her. "What's a sieve?"

"Strainer." Her focus remained on her work, but she'd finished the eggs and had moved on to opening a bag of powdered sugar.

He saw two options—one that looked like a fine net and another with wider holes. "Which one?"

She opened a small bag labeled almond flour and jutted her chin toward the fine net. "That one."

He set it next to her. "What are we making?"

She weighed her ingredients out in a bowl on a small kitchen scale. "French macarons." She gave him a jaunty grin. "Chocolate French macarons, to be exact. One with peanut butter buttercream, one with mint buttercream, and one with strawberry buttercream. Hand me that big bowl over there."

The fact that she'd come up with that so quickly deserved a medal by itself. If they'd given him two days to come up with something to bake with that prompt, he'd probably still be wearing a blank expression when they returned for the final product.

Despite his lack of any skill, they fell into a routine quickly enough. She'd spent enough time in a kitchen ordering other people around, and he could fetch things and move things as she finished with them.

As the camera crew neared stopping a few stations down, Jason slinked beside her. "Should we figure out a couple story?"

She frowned, pulling the bowl of merengue she'd made away from the stand mixer. She grabbed a whisk. "I don't have time to talk to them. I'll let you do most of the talking, and I'll just go with whatever you say."

She'd just made his job easier in so many ways. He could kiss her.

By the time the crew reached them, she was piping macarons onto the parchment paper. Peter stepped between them and put his hand on Jen's shoulder. "Last but not least, we have this special lady, who is my favorite baker in town, Jen." The audience clapped.

Had the audience been clapping and interacting before? They must have been. Jason had paid little attention because he'd been so distracted by what Jen was doing. But now that all eyes were on them, he noticed everything about the audience. Noticed Jen's family. Noticed Ned leaning forward from his spot over by a display of cookbooks.

Peter looked over Jen's shoulder. "I don't have to ask what you're making."

"No, you don't." Jen smiled, giving him a brief glance, then continued her piping.

"I'll ask you about them in a second. First, I think the question everyone here in Brandywood has been wondering is who this handsome fellow to your left is."

Jason shook Peter's hand. "I'm Jason."

"Jason, you're not from around here, correct?"

"No, sir." The lights seemed brighter, hotter. Jason had been on live television before. He'd partied with celebrities and been invited to soirees and done press conferences.

His heart felt as though it would pound out of his throat.

"And how long have you and Jen been together?"

He shot her a smile. "A long time. But long-distance, which has been tough." His grandfather had taught him that. *"When they ask a question you don't want to answer, give them something vague, then distract and redirect."*

"Oh, sure, sure. That's always a hard thing for relationships. Where're you from?"

Peter was a natural, and his calm demeanor was all Jason needed to find his footing. No one had ever accused a Cavanaugh of lacking social grace or confidence.

Now he really sounded like his grandfather.

"Chicago. But it's getting harder to stay away from Brandywood." He stepped closer to Jen and rubbed the small of her back.

"I have it on good authority that you two were recently an accidental part of one of our best Christmas traditions here in Brandywood—the *A Christmas Carol* street play. Care to replicate the scene you were in for all of us?" Peter reached from behind his back and lifted a sprig of mistletoe.

A red blush was spreading to Jen's cheeks, but the audience was loving it. Peter was doing them a favor—giving them a chance to be rooted for—and Jason could see it in Peter's eyes.

"All right. If I can wrestle that pastry bag out of Jen's hands." Jason winked at her, then held out a hand toward her.

She put the bag down and took his hand. As he pulled her closer, he wrapped one arm securely behind her back, then dipped her for a kiss. Their lips connected, and the audience cheered, which electrified the energy of the entire room.

Any nerves Jason had melted away as he kissed her. He was having fun . . . in the most unexpected of ways.

He brought her upright. Jen's eyes were glued to his, bright with laughter.

If someone had told Jason a week earlier that this was where he would be, he wouldn't have believed it for a second. In Brandywood, doing a baking competition, pretending to be dating the gorgeous single mother of his nephew? With Mildred in the audience, no less.

He felt like he was living someone else's life.

And even more strange, it felt like a life he'd actually enjoy. One he didn't deserve.

His throat tightened as he glanced at Colby in the audience, watching him and Jen with rapt attention.

. . . *the life Kevin should have had.* And once again, Jason felt like he was the wrong person to be living.

CHAPTER TWENTY

Jen braced herself for Lindsay's tight hug. As her friend wrapped her arms around her, Jen saw Jason chatting comfortably with her parents and Colby. Jason was getting a lot more trouble than he'd signed up for, that's for sure.

"I'm so proud of you," Lindsay said without letting go. Then she pulled back and grabbed her hands. "You're going on to the semi-final. I knew you would. You're totally going to win this thing."

The crowd at the Depot was clearing. Jen waved to Bunny, who gave her a thumbs-up. She'd have to thank Bunny later. Without her tips and tricks, she'd never have pulled it off. "I had no idea the whole town would be here." Jen shook her hair out of her ponytail, a feeling of exhaustion sweeping over her. "That was intense."

"You did amazing. And—um. We seriously need to grab some drinks and talk about that man you had at your side. This whole text exchange we've had going on about that situation does not do him justice." Lindsay nodded toward him. "I think he loooooooves you."

"Stop." Jen couldn't stop the smile that came to her face. "We're . . . friends."

"Friends who can't keep their hands off each other?" Lindsay looked skeptical. "Whatever you call your little arrangement, you two have some serious chemistry."

Jen bit her lip. She hadn't had the chance to update Lindsay on what had happened with Jason the previous night. "Actually"—she lowered her voice—"we slept together."

Lindsay's eyes widened, and she smacked Jen on the arm. "See? I told you. When did this happen? How did you not tell me about it! How was it?"

"Last night. And I didn't have a chance. And amazing." Jen squeezed her hand. "I promise to send you the full details later. And I don't know about drinks because my life is completely upside down right now. I'm moving back in with my parents this weekend, so maybe you want to come by?"

Lindsay's cheerful expression faded. "Oh, honey. I'm so sorry."

"It's fine." Jen didn't want to think about it. "It's going to be fine. If I can win this competition, then I can pay off the rent I owe and the preschool and have some left over."

"You're going to win for sure." Lindsay gave her another hug. "Call me later, okay?"

Jen left her by the stage area and made her way over toward Jason. She came up beside him, and Colby turned to her. "You win, Mommy!"

She lifted him into her arms. He was growing so tall it was getting hard to lift him. "Not yet. There's one more round, and then we have to wait a whole week to find out who won during Mr. Peter's Christmas special. Then hopefully Mommy can win."

"Do you two want to go out and celebrate your success?"

her father asked Jason. "Betty and I can watch Colby if you do."

"I don't have a lot of time before I have to get to the cabins for work." Jen exchanged a look with Jason. He'd spent his whole evening on her so far. Would he want—

"That would be great," Jason said, slipping his arm behind her. He did the role of boyfriend well.

Her mom took Colby from her. "I'll give him a bath." She kissed her grandson's sticky cheek. "Candy canes this time of year—they seem to end up on faces more than in stomachs. Oh, don't forget, Jason. Sunday dinner at five. If you can make it, we'd love to have you."

After saying their goodbyes, Jen watched them leave, then turned to Jason with a frown. "It's occurring to me that I need to think of some better way to handle this with Colby. He just saw us kiss up there—and I don't think he's ever seen me kiss anyone like that."

"That makes sense. What do you want to do?"

Despite the dying crowd, it still felt a bit too crowded for this conversation. "Probably no PDA in front of him, but we can talk about it more when we go."

A sudden pulse of noise and activity drew her attention away. Jason straightened, looking in the hubbub's direction, by the backend of the folding chairs. His face paled. "Oh, shit." He started toward the small group of people who had made a circle.

Jen followed him. Someone was lying on the floor beside the chairs, but she couldn't quite see over the people gathered there.

Jason pushed his way through, then bent beside the figure. "Mildred. Mildred, can you hear me?"

Jen got past a few people, then got close enough to see. She froze. Millie Price lay there. "Oh my God!" Jen dug through.

"Millie!" Was she okay? Kevin's grandmother had always been an enormous source of support for her and Colby . . .

She paused, staring at Jason. Millie had opened her eyes now and lifted her hand to pat Jason's cheek with familiarity and tenderness that stole her breath.

She lifted a shaking hand to her forehead, then squatted a few feet from them. Her chest felt as though someone had tied a belt around it, pulling it tighter and tighter.

How had Jason known Millie's name?

Dan was there now, but her head buzzed with such ferocity that she could hardly absorb the scene in front of her. She'd seen her brother in the crowd, but he'd seemed to come out of nowhere. "We've called an ambulance, Millie, okay?"

Millie sat up, shaking her head. She touched her forehead. "I don't know what happened. Everything just felt dizzy." She gave a sharp look at Jason, holding his hand with a tight grip. "I'm much better now."

"I think we should still have you checked out at the hospital," Jason told her. His face was flushed, and he didn't look at Jen.

"No, no, I'm fine." She let go of Jason's hand and held her hands out to Dan. "I'm sure Sergeant Klein can see me back to my house."

Dan leveled his gaze with her as he helped her stand. "Millie, you're going to the hospital."

"We can talk about it." She smoothed out her dress. "See? Perfectly fine."

Dan didn't release her arm. "Let's go sit in a chair, okay?"

As they moved over to a nearby folding chair, the small crowd that had gathered around Millie wandered off, satisfied.

Jen didn't move from where she'd squatted on the floor. Neither did Jason.

She closed her eyes. He obviously had met Millie—but no

one in town called her Mildred. She was *Millie Price,* and her name carried with it the weight of her antics and personality.

Which meant he already knew her.

He'd come to Brandywood for "family business."

She felt sick.

Opening her eyes, she cleared the knot from her throat. "You're Millie's—"

"I'm her grandson."

Jason still didn't look at her. His shoulders fell, and he rubbed his fingers over his jaw. At last, he lifted his eyes, his gaze apologetic.

The impact of his words was like a bludgeon to the head. She felt so dazed she couldn't think straight. *Millie's grandson.* She stood shakily and whirled around. Dan was still a few feet from her, watching her. He gave her a comforting look. "Just stay here," he mouthed.

Had he heard Jason? If so, Dan was smart enough to put it together. Who knew—by now, he might know something else about Jason. His gaze told her he knew *something.*

But she didn't listen, feeling so nauseated that she couldn't stand still. She bolted from the Depot, not waiting for Jason.

Jason followed her outside. "Jen." He was only steps behind her, and the sidewalks of Main were a bright blur of Christmas lights through her tears.

When he caught up with her, he grabbed her elbow. "Wait up."

She whirled to face him. "Who are you?" Her words were a demand, not a question.

Jason dropped his hand. "Jason Cavanaugh."

Liar. "Not Sutter?"

He shook his head. Then he took a step toward her and added, his voice low, "I'm Kevin's brother."

His words were like a death knell. She already knew. Millie

only had one daughter. But Jen had also never spoken Kevin's name to Jason.

Kevin's brother.

Oh my God.

She covered her mouth.

Jason held her shoulders. "I didn't know how to tell you and—"

"Don't you dare give me excuses." She wrested herself away. "You *lied* to me."

He rubbed his eyes and nodded. "Yes, I lied. But I—"

"Kevin's last name is Connor." Had everything he'd told her been a lie?

Jason stared at the thick covering of clouds in the sky. "Cavanaugh, actually. Like mine. It was a stupid lie."

What? Why had Kevin lied to her about his last name? Had Millie known? She looked back toward the door of the Depot. She didn't know that she'd ever discussed Kevin's name with Millie, actually. The only time that might have qualified was when Millie came to see her and Colby at the hospital after he'd been born.

"What'd you name him?" Mildred asked, peering down at the little bundle in Jen's arms.

"Colby. Klein. Like me."

"Good."

And that was it. Neither of them had gone into the specifics of Kevin's last name. Neither of them had a reason to. Jen closed her eyes, unable to look at Jason.

Kevin had never mentioned having a brother, had he?

Maybe he had. She could hardly remember anymore. Aware of the number of people still on the street, she spun and started her flight again.

Tears stung her eyes as she thought of all her conversations with him. The ample opportunities he'd had to tell her the truth. She put a hand to her throat. She'd had sex with him, for God's sake. More than once.

Colby was his *nephew. Same color eyes.*

Who was Jason? Why was he in Brandywood? He'd been lying about so much. Was Kevin using him to spy on her? Maybe he finally had decided to make a bid for custody. The thought made her tremble.

As Jason fell into step beside her, words spilled from her chest as she walked. "I don't leave Colby by himself in the guest lodge too often, you know. Almost never. And I rarely date. And no, I haven't slept with anyone else since Kevin. I don't make a habit of that. And . . . and the preschool stuff? We're working through it. I have him talking to a therapist, and as soon as I find another childcare option, we'll be totally fine financially. December has a lot of overtime opportunities for me. The eviction . . ."

Oh, God.

She'd given Jason every tool to destroy her with.

"I'm not—" Jason's eyes moved to her hands. "You're shaking."

Jen swiped her tears away and stopped by the small park on Main—really just a few benches and streetlamps and trees. In the back, a small bridge overlooked the river that flowed alongside the city.

She gave Jason a pleading look. "I love Colby. More than life itself. And I don't mind Kevin wanting to be a part of his life if he wants. God knows I dreamed about it for . . . well, years, actually. Colby deserves a dad. But"—her face grew more serious, less vulnerable—"he can't seriously think he can waltz in here. I don't have time for games anymore, and neither does Colby. I refuse to even entertain the idea of introducing them if there's a chance he'll disappear again."

Jason was silent. The silence was thick and uncomfortable, and she wanted Jason to say something.

Anything.

At last, Jason lifted his blue eyes to her. Eyes that were just like Kevin's. Just like Colby's.

No wonder she'd thought they looked like father and son. *Stupid, stupid.*

How could she have missed something so monumental?

"Jen, I don't know how to tell you this, but . . . Kevin's dead."

She gripped his forearm to steady herself, gasping. *Dead?*

It'd been almost four years since she last saw Kevin. And she'd spent most of the time hating him. But she'd never thought he was dead. Not really. She choked back another cry, then wiped her eyes, leaving a streak of mascara across her fingers. "How?"

He unbuttoned the top button of his coat as though he felt hot, despite the frigid December temperatures. "To be honest, I don't really know much about it. He left home over seven years ago. Barely came back while he was in college and just vanished after a while. Then I got the call one day to come down to the hospital and identify a man in the morgue. It was him."

She fought for composure, then found a nearby bench to sit. "What did he die of?"

Jason didn't sit beside her, his posture rigid. "An overdose."

Oh, Kevin.

His demons had come back to haunt him, after all. She shuddered, the cold permeating her uneven breaths and invading every inch of her skin. She almost didn't want to ask her next question, but it burned in her throat. "When?"

Jason looked back toward a group of passersby on the sidewalk. He waited until they'd moved farther away, then stepped closer. "About three and a half years ago."

She hugged her legs to her chest, setting her face on the tops of her knees. Before Colby was even born. He hadn't even made it to his son's birth.

This whole time, she'd been furious with a man who was dead.

He would never come back. Was never going to be a part of his son's life.

She'd mourned Kevin years before when he'd left. But this . . .

A crushing pain gripped her heart. She'd loved him so much. She didn't stop the tears. Her shoulders shuddered with broken sobs.

The bench creaked as Jason sat beside her. She didn't fight him as he wrapped his arms around her, pulling her close. Much as she was angry with Jason, her head was spinning from all the shocks to her system at once. Her feet slid off the bench, and she buried her face against his coat, breathing in his scent, which had felt so familiar and comforting just minutes before.

She'd tried to do her best to learn more about him, and he'd hidden the most important thing she needed to know. Jen clenched her jaw. Jason had slept with her knowing all this about her, while she knew nothing.

Her hurt was difficult to process, to understand. A gust of icy wind sent the bare branches of the trees scraping against the stone of the buildings beside them. The air dried the icy trails of tears on her cheeks. The desire to know more about what had happened to Kevin consumed every other emotion.

"I was afraid—" Her voice filled with tears. "I was afraid that he'd gone back to using." She sniffled, wiping her nose with her sleeve. "He just seemed so different from any of the guys I knew around here. Didn't know a thing about fixing cars." She chuckled softly. "But we could go to museums and get lost in them for hours. He was the only person I'd ever met who would stop at the historic signs—you know, the ones on the side of the road that tell you about the important stuff that's happened there?"

"Did he ever talk about his family?" Jason leaned back against the back of the bench, his arm still around her.

"Not really." Jen cleared her throat. "He would just get really sad and close up entirely when I asked about it. He said something about his dad drowning, though." She winced, immediately remembering Jason's dislike of water. *No wonder*. "I mean, your dad. Sorry, I probably shouldn't bring it up."

Jason looked away as though willing himself not to think about it. He got to his feet. "Yeah. That was a long time ago." He held out his hand to her. "I know you probably don't want to be around me, but if you'd like to talk . . . can we continue it inside somewhere? You're shivering." Then he added with a pleading expression, "Please."

She stared at his hand, her anger at him flowing back to him now that the shock about Kevin had ebbed. She shouldn't have let him comfort her. Not after the way he'd lied to her. "Did you know who I was when you met me?"

"Yes." Jason put his hands in his pockets.

The succinctness of his response felt honest but only made her eyes narrow as she remembered her fears about stalking her. "Then you actually were following me?"

"No." Jason drew a sharp breath through his nose as though affected by the cold. "I just kept running into you. I didn't come into Brandywood to meet you. I only found out about you and Colby the day before I came into town, and my goal was to talk to Mildred."

She stood and lifted her chin. "And somehow, instead, you conveniently found and flirted with me—and then fucked me?

Even though you knew I didn't know Kevin was dead. Even though you were basically lying to me about who you were."

"Jen . . ." Jason took her hand, but she yanked herself free from his grip.

"Don't you dare touch me." Jen glared at him. "The thing is, this whole time I've been questioning myself since I met you. But maybe being cautious and waiting for someone who actually deserves my limited time wasn't the world's worst plan." She backed away, ready to flee. Her teeth chattered, almost more from emotion than from cold. "Do me a favor, will you? Stay away from Colby and me."

CHAPTER TWENTY-ONE

THE DOOR to Mildred's house swung open, and Jason crossed his arms as she peered out from behind the door. "What are you doing here?" Mildred asked. Her white hair was set in pink foam curlers, and she wore a nightgown as though she'd been in bed.

Jason let out an exasperated sigh. "What in the hell do you think I'm doing here? I just spent the last forty-five minutes trying to find out what happened to you. You were gone from the Depot when I went back, and then I checked the hospital and swung by the police station to find Dan Klein—"

"I'm flattered. Sounds like you were worried about me." She winked. "But I'm just fine, honey. Thanks for checking. Good night."

She started to shut the door, but Jason shoved the toe of his shoe in the doorway before she could, wedging his way closer to her. "Shouldn't you be in the hospital?"

Mildred scrutinized his expression, a faint smolder of surprise in her eyes. "You don't really care, do you?"

"I . . ."

The thing was, he hadn't even really considered that possibility. When he and Jen had gone their separate ways after that disastrous conversation, the only other thing he'd been able to focus on was finding Mildred. His shoulders loosened. "I care, Mildred. You scared me back there."

"It was all part of the plan, sonny. I'm in perfect health. How'd it go with Jen?" Mildred gave him a bright grin.

She pretended to be sick?

Dumbfounded, Jason stepped back. His arms flexed as he set his hands on the back of his neck. "Are you serious?" A bristle of annoyance replaced his surprise. "Do you have any idea what you did? Jen is furious with me. And I had to tell her about Kevin being dead. She said she never wants to speak to me again."

"Well, what did you expect to happen? The girl wasn't going to be thrilled to find out you lied to her." Mildred gave an exaggerated shiver and looked over her shoulder. "My warm bed is calling me back. Glad I could help."

"Mildred, this isn't funny." Jason's eyes narrowed at her. "I don't know what to do." The hurt in Jen's eyes, the way she'd looked at him with a mixture of contempt and confusion. She believed the worst about him.

And the thought of that was eating a hole inside his stomach like battery acid.

The night before, she'd been in his arms and said she liked him. He didn't know what he was doing with her anymore. He'd thought he could rid himself of the attraction to her with one night, but it was like she branded his skin with her touch.

And the whole situation with the inheritance . . . he'd made a nightmare out of it. "What do I do?" He didn't mean to ask aloud, his voice barely above a whisper.

Mildred pursed her lips. "Apologize. Then leave her alone. Kevin loved her, and he let her go. So can you." Mildred yawned, reaching up and clearing a cobweb from the light beside the door. "Why don't we have lunch in a few days? Before you go back to Chicago. You can tell me all about how it went."

Jason nodded and stepped back from the door as she shut it. He set his hand on the closed door, fighting the urge to knock and ask her to let him inside. Mildred's advice had been concise but also something he didn't want to hear.

But we don't have that sort of relationship.

Yet here he was on her doorstep.

He hurried back to his car, the engine still making mechanical clicks as it cooled. He was no more a doting grandson than she was a nurturing grandmother who offered a warm embrace when he needed to vent.

JASON FINISHED off the breakfast smoothie he'd gotten from a juice bar and tossed it into the trash bin outside. The smoothie hadn't helped the feeling of nausea that had settled in his stomach since the night before.

He'd gotten a lousy night of sleep, tossing and turning most of the night. When dawn had come, he'd wanted nothing more than to send Jen a text message and see if she was still working at the guest lodge. She'd been so close all night.

Instead, he'd waited until nearly ten to leave his cabin, which meant he'd been starving by the time he reached Main Street.

Running his hand through his hair, he released a tense breath. The quaint buildings of the historic street were decked out in Christmas tinsel and lights, the crisp air of the last few days of fall laden with the scent of pine and sugar from baked goods somewhere. He smirked. *Probably Bunny's Café.*

"What am I even doing here?" Jason murmured in a low, almost inaudible tone.

He zipped his jacket higher.

Striding past his car, he headed down Main Street, unsure of where to go. Jen was probably working, and he'd done enough to her. Space was probably a good thing until he could figure out how to apologize to her.

Then came the hard part: telling her about the inheritance. Given how she'd reacted to the news about Kevin, he no longer had any confidence that she would take it well.

Once you tell her, she'll be out of your life for good.

Jason's gaze fell on one of the few buildings on Main that didn't exude the holiday cheer surrounding them. Instead, the building seemed more like he felt: bleak, dark, empty. The windows still had the remnants of vinyl lettering from some sort of mailing and copy center, but that business was long gone. But across the doorway and windows on either side, the historic name of the building was still there, stamped in wood. *Price's Hardware.*

"There's even this old hardware store that used to belong to Colby's great-grandfather. It would be perfect."

Jen's musings about the building where she longed to have a bakery had slipped past Jason in terms of impact. *Colby's great-grandfather.* Hell, that could have been her grandfather for all he knew, though the phrasing wasn't quite right. But she hadn't meant her grandfather. She'd meant his.

He had exactly one memory of his mom's father, and he didn't know how old he'd been. Just that he was sitting at a dusty old counter and had fallen, hitting his head. But his grandpa had scooped him up, set him back on the counter, and given him a lollipop.

He couldn't have been very old. Mom's father died when he was three.

Jason crossed the street, heading straight for the building.

He couldn't picture Mom's father if he tried. But Mildred had said he looked like the Prices, and he imagined someone looking like him, palm on that brass-handled door. Day in, day out, going to work.

Does Mildred still own it?

He knew nothing about this part of his history. Nothing about who that man had been.

If Mildred owned it, would she be willing to sell it? He peered through the glass. Jen was right. The place was a wreck. The walls appeared to have been taken down to the studs, then covered with thick plastic. Wires hung down from the ceiling.

This was where Jen wanted to have a bakery?

Wreck was a generous term. Dumpster fire was more accurate.

"You thinking of taking up real estate here in town?" a voice came from behind him.

Ned stood a few feet behind him, hands in the pockets of his peacoat.

Jason stiffened, then looked back at him through the window's reflection. "I'm not interested in discussing my personal affairs with you, Vickers."

"Affairs. That's an interesting word, isn't it?" Ned stepped forward so they were shoulder to shoulder. "You told Bill Powell the girl in town here is your fiancée, didn't you? That's the story you're trying to spin here?"

Jason gave him a sardonic smile. "No comment."

"You know I'm going to get to the bottom of what you're doing here. And who that woman is. I hear she has a kid."

"There you are." TJ sauntered up toward Jason, then handed him a paper bag with what appeared to be a sub inside.

He reached into the breast pocket of his jacket and pulled out an envelope, which he handed to Ned. "This is for you."

Ned lifted a brow. "What is it?"

"Restraining order. Stay away from my client and stop stalking his girlfriend." TJ winked at Ned and set a hand on Jason's shoulder. "Ready to go back to your car?"

Whatever TJ's quirks, Jason really couldn't pay him enough for all he did. Jason didn't bother to give Ned a second look as he headed down the sidewalk with TJ. When they were out of earshot, Jason asked, "Was that a real restraining order?"

"Yup. But it doesn't mean he'll stay away from Jen."

"Vickers knows Jen has a kid."

"It was only a matter of time." TJ stopped abruptly and snatched his sandwich back from Jason. "My cheesesteak is getting cold."

"Keep him away from Jen and her family."

"Jason, I'm going to say this again as nicely as I can. I'm not a bodyguard." TJ peeled back the foil paper from the sandwich and took a bite. "It's over. Go home. Consider this one a failure. You're going to lose."

Jason backed up toward his car and shook his head. "Cavanaughs don't give up, TJ."

"Until they make bad decisions and destroy their lives."

Jason cringed and unlocked the car door. TJ couldn't possibly know how closely he grazed the truth. "You just keep doing what I pay you to do, TJ. It'll be worth your time if you succeed."

He climbed in, wanting to shut himself away from TJ's comeback. As Jason started the engine and sped away from the curb, he couldn't shake the gloom that settled over him.

Go home.

And then what? Let Ned find out about Colby without telling Jen about it first?

He could survive losing the company well enough, even if his grandfather's loyal employees wouldn't. He'd find another job, sell some investments, make some others.

But it wasn't just about that anymore, was it?

His mind felt like it was spinning. As he turned off of Main Street and headed back toward the cabins, a road sign that had brought him from the highway caught his attention. That was all he needed to do. Hop on that highway. Drive home. Leave it all back here. TJ could pack up his belongings at the cabin if necessary.

And he'd go back to Chicago where there would be no Ned, no ghosts from his past, no Mildred. Only forward and onward.

Without Jen and Colby.

He continued toward the cabin, unable to turn the car around.

Coming down here had been the last desperate act of a drowning man.

The metaphor stung, and he gripped the wheel more tightly.

"You should have been watching Kevin. You're always busy goofing off. Clowning around. Well, look what your worthless clowning around has cost us now, Jason."

His grandfather's voice seared into his memory, sang in his ear as the car rumbled over the gravel road.

He pulled the car to a stop and sat in the car, his hands gripping the wheel so hard that they hurt.

You're a jerk.

A failure.

Worthless.

He drew a sharp breath and lifted his head, staring at the dash.

Go home.

He put his hand on the shifter to throw the car into reverse when a movement from the porch of the cabin caught his attention.

Jen stood from the front porch swing and started toward him.

CHAPTER TWENTY-TWO

THE CAR CHIMED as Jason opened the driver's side door, and he climbed out. Despite the pounding of her heart, Jen lifted her chin calmly, trying to give him the steadiest look she could muster. She set her hands on her hips. "Why do you call her Mildred?"

Jason stopped mid-step and gave her an odd look. As though he'd expected a different question. And maybe it was a strange thing to ask first. But she'd spent the night and the entire morning in the café going over everything in her head. Kevin had called Millie "Gran."

That Jason had called her Mildred felt like one last-ditch attempt to continue his lies. Which meant he'd never intended to tell her the truth about who he was until he felt his back was to a wall.

Jason took a few slow steps toward her. "We weren't close to her as kids. I only saw her a handful of times that I even really have a good memory of. Grandma just never stuck."

She studied his features. Now that she knew he was Kevin's brother, the hints of the resemblance were unnerving.

There wasn't that nearly identical look like Dan and Warren had, despite being a few years apart, just something familiar.

Sadness crept into her heart once again. As she'd cuddled with Colby the night before, she'd allowed herself to *really* think about Kevin for the first time in years. They'd met at a church picnic, and Jen had been drawn to how different he seemed from the other guys she knew. He was older than her by four years, too, and she'd been an inexperienced nineteen-year-old who was easily swept off her feet by a guy who could talk about Paris and Amsterdam and Bali . . . *because he'd been there.*

"Kevin called her Gran." She crossed her arms. "It just seems like another way you were trying to lie to me."

"Kevin was younger than me." Jason's eyes were flat. "He remembered less." He gave her a tense smile. "It wasn't Mildred's fault. My grandfather was a proud and difficult man. He didn't like her and did his best to keep her away from our family."

Millie was well-liked by the community, but she had a quiet, reserved side and didn't let a lot of people in. When Jen had started dating Kevin, her mother had dragged out her high school yearbook and looked Martha Price up. Martha was a couple of years younger than her mother and had left town shortly after high school, never heard from again. Even Millie didn't talk about her.

Sadness washed over her. Millie's daughter had been separated from her. Even her own grandson didn't call her by any affectionate title. It was a wonder that she wasn't filled with bitterness and anger. Jen regretted the times she hadn't made more of an effort to let Colby spend time with Millie.

Tension settled between them.

"You should have told me the truth," Jen said, her voice sounding less angry than she intended it. She'd been angry.

And sad. And then angry once more while she was at work and couldn't concentrate on a damn thing. Bunny had sent her home early, sensing Jen's distress, which was just one more thing to worry about because Jen couldn't afford to lose the pay.

Because her mom wasn't expecting her to come pick up Colby until later in the afternoon, she'd driven around aimlessly, trying to get her head on straight.

And then she'd ended up here.

"I know." Jason's eyes were veined with red, as though he hadn't slept well. *Well, that makes two of us.* He deserved to lose more than one night of sleep.

"I don't know that I can trust you again." Whatever they'd had was over. He couldn't be a casual fling because he was her son's uncle, not some hot mysterious stranger like she'd thought. When he left here, it wouldn't be like their connection would stop. "I don't . . ." She gulped another breath, trying to slow her thoughts. Laura wouldn't want her having a shouting match outside a cabin, and she felt herself losing the ability to remain calm.

"You used me. I'm not even sure why. But you took advantage because you knew who I was when the reverse wasn't true." She took another step toward him, hugging her arms closer. Despite her best efforts, her voice rose in pitch. "Explain it to me, Jason. Help me understand how you could just get involved with me, knowing that I could never just be that one-night stand girl you claimed you wanted. Was it just to screw with me? It feels so . . . I can't even verbalize how wrong it feels."

Jason looked away, his eyes reflecting the gray sky and looking less bright than usual. "I didn't come down here looking to get involved with you."

He could say that, but then why? Why carry on with her? "But we are involved now, Jason. And I don't just mean the fact that we slept together. I mean this whole stupid baking competition and that you're my son's uncle, which, by the way, I don't know how in the hell I'll ever explain that one to him. I don't kiss any of his other uncles the way I kissed you at the Depot in front of him."

"Well, I hope not. Considering they're your brothers." Jason's voice was dry, the hint of a smile curving on his lips.

"This isn't funny." His joke only stoked her anger. "Don't you get it? No, I guess you don't. There's a little boy involved here. A little boy who maybe you don't give a shit about and if that's the case, fine. You're not obligated to. God knows Kevin didn't stick around. But for you to come here and do what you did? It feels like a sick joke."

Her anger burned up her chest. She'd parked at the guest lodge, which she was thankful for. She needed a moment to walk off her mounting fury before getting behind the wheel of a car again. Giving him a look that she hoped was scathing, she started forward. She shouldn't have bothered to come here. Seeing Jason only made things worse for her.

Jason's hand shot out as she brushed beside him, his fingertips catching hers. "Jen, wait."

She stiffened, closing her eyes. She didn't want to feel anything for him.

Jason didn't release her fingers, and she didn't pull away. "I've been trying to figure out how to tell you the truth the last few days. And the more I tried to find a way, the more I didn't know how."

She threw him a glance over her shoulder. "Yeah, well, you should have thought of a way before we fucked."

"It wasn't that easy." Jason's hand tightened on hers. "I didn't plan what happened between us; it just happened. And, yes, I'm the type of selfish asshole who lets it happen. You and Colby are both better off without me in your lives. I spent a good part of the morning trying to come up with a way to apologize to you, and everything I thought of fell short of what you deserve. There's nothing I can do to apologize."

She pulled her hand away, throwing her hands up in exasperation. "You could start by saying you're sorry. You haven't even tried those words, Jason! God, it's not that hard to do the bare minimum decent thing here." She searched his gaze and then shook her head. Was he incapable of saying he was sorry? He was awfully arrogant. Maybe he didn't have much practice. But it didn't excuse him.

He stared at her, silent, clearly struggling to speak.

A choked, overwhelming feeling gripped her. Whirling around, she scanned the nearby wood line, then took off at a sprint, desperate to get away.

She'd avoided these woods since Colby had disappeared in them. But they offered a desolate comfort to her now, of just being away from Jason and everyone. *Everything*.

Avoiding the path that would lead downhill to the stream, she took the trail that led to the cliff known by locals as "Redding's Bluff" even though it was in the state park beside the cabin property. A crunch of leaves sounded behind her.

"Jen, wait." Jason was close behind, but she didn't stop.

"Go away." She swiped a few tears from her eyes. *God, I'm such an idiot.* She ran, thankful she was in her work tennis shoes and jeans.

"Will you stop?" Jason grabbed a fistful of her jacket, but she wrested herself free.

"No. I mean it, Jason." She continued her uphill trek, dodging past barren tree branches and brush with spindly thorns. "Leave. Me. Alone."

"I'm not letting you run off into the forest by yourself. The last thing I need is for you to fall off a cliff or get attacked by some axe murderer out here and have that on my head." Jason didn't even sound like he was struggling with the trail, which was her luck. He was a runner, though, so this was probably nothing for him.

She slowed, unable to verbalize her response while running.

"Why do you care? You're just planning on leaving, aren't you? Anyway, I'm a small-town girl from the country. You city boys seem to think that there's nothing but serial killers hanging around here instead of good-hearted people who realize the value of a life without so much noise." She broke through the crest of the hill, out of breath, then gripped the trunk of a maple where the forest let out onto the rough sandstone of the mountain cliff.

She couldn't appreciate the view through her tears. Thick gray clouds blanketed the sky. But in the distance, a few sunbeams streamed down onto the tops of the naked trees, branches swaying as a strong, icy blast of wind wound past them.

Jason came up behind her and set his hands on her shoulders. "Jen, I'm sorry." His voice was raw, strained. "I don't even know how to tell you—"

"It's not that hard, is it?" She turned to face him, still trying to catch her breath.

He cupped her face in his hands, wiping the trail of tears away from her cheeks with his thumbs. "I'm so sorry, Jen. I didn't want to hurt you. I don't want to hurt you. I'm just no good. I'm sorry."

He didn't say it in a self-pitying way. It was more like a statement of fact. He'd accepted this way of thinking about himself. That he was inherently rotten.

"What made you think this way about yourself?" She moistened her dry lips, searching his eyes. Kevin had struggled with his darkness, too, but he'd turned to drugs to soothe his pain. And that was when she saw a very distinct difference between the brothers. Jason believed his darkness. Jason had . . . accepted it instead. She didn't know which was more dangerous.

What had happened to them? She reached up, placing her hands on his wrists. "I may not know much about you, Jason, but you're not a bad person. I don't know why you think you are."

"Because you don't know me." He leaned down, pressing a kiss to her forehead. The stubble of his jaw brushed against her skin, and shivers crawled up her spine.

As though he sensed the response of her body to his, he pulled back, just slightly, as she raised her chin, lifting her lips toward his. His mouth descended on hers, not a kiss of wild sexual passion but something more.

Need.

She didn't want to forgive him. Didn't want to pretend it was okay for him to have done what he'd done to her.

But her hands slid from his wrists and found their way around the back of his neck, clasping on to him as the wind whipped around them, their bodies melding together until she felt like they were two warm souls who had found each other amidst the emptiness of the expanse. Both of them broken.

He didn't want to reveal any depth, it seemed. His words said that he wanted her to believe he couldn't be better. But she didn't believe it. Couldn't. Her back pressed to the tree trunk she'd been gripping as he pinned her there, his arms tight around her, one hand splayed on the small of her back, the other digging at the hair at the nape of her neck.

As Jason dragged his mouth away, he managed again, "I'm sorry."

Her lips grazed his jaw. Her mother had once told her how forgiveness had a way of changing the life of the person on whom it was bestowed. And maybe she wasn't street-smart or worldly like Jason, but she knew some things he didn't. She'd known unconditional love. She'd received it from her parents and given it to Colby.

What little Kevin had told her and Jason had confirmed, neither of them had been that fortunate.

Holding on to her hurt wouldn't help her. If Jason wasn't planning on staying, she'd just be left with that anger, and she'd stew until it turned into bitter resentment. *And she'd done that once before.*

Setting her forehead against his cheek, she skimmed the back of his neck with her fingertips, her hands cold. "I'm still angry, Jason. But I forgive you. So if you need to go back to Chicago now and just forget us, I'm not saying it won't hurt. But I'll be okay."

Jason's jaw tensed, and he held her closer. With his closeness, she could feel the pounding of his pulse at his neck. Then he murmured, "I won't be okay."

His fingers wound their way around the hair at the nape of her neck, and he drew her head back to stare into her eyes. "Jen, I didn't sleep with you under the pretense of things being a casual, one-night-only event. It might have started out that way, but I couldn't stay away from you. Even when I really should have. What I'm trying to say is—"

She drew him down toward her, cutting off his words with a kiss.

He doesn't plan on just walking away.

A strange sense of relief crested in her mind.

I couldn't stay away from you.

The tenderness of her kiss dissolved quickly, their mouths meeting with strong, rushed passion. Their tongues collided as Jason hoisted her up, her legs wrapping around his waist.

He doesn't want to leave.

And she didn't want him to. Whatever they'd started by getting together the way they had, she didn't want to stop. She wanted to feel his lips against hers, to hear his jokes and witty comebacks.

Text him all night.

She wanted to watch him make playdough with her son and feed him chocolate-covered strawberries and have him dip her for a kiss in front of a crowd.

And she wasn't ready to let go of that yet.

He pinned her against the tree, the rough bark catching on her jacket, her jeans less flexible than she wanted. Keeping one hand on his neck, she slipped the other hand lower, popped off the button of his jeans, and tugged at his waistband. She slid her hand down and wrapped her fingers around his firm length.

God, she wanted him.

And not just because she knew how good it could be between them.

The aching emptiness resurrected with their fight last night nagged at her. But being with him made that pain dull.

Jason drew back, searching her gaze. "This is what you want? We should probably talk some more. We can go back to my cabin—"

"This is what I want." She drew him back down again for another kiss. "Right here. Right now, Jason. I want you."

He set her down, unbuttoned her jeans, then pushed them and her underwear from her hips. She pulled her shoes off, staying in her warm wool socks because it was cold, then stepped out of her pants. He unzipped his pants, freeing himself from the boxer briefs below them. Jen practically jumped back onto him and he lifted her, wrapping her legs around his waist. He grimaced and stopped, his forehead against hers as the tip of his shaft found her entrance. "Ugh, goddammit. I don't have a condom here." He drew back, his breath shallow.

He was tantalizingly close, and she ached for him. Catching her breath, she squeezed her eyes shut as he shifted her on his hips. Her legs tightened around him. "I'm on the pill," she whispered against his cheek.

"Are you sure?" His heart pounded against her breasts, her nipples hard in her bra. She longed for his touch. Too many clothes, but then she had never had sex in the middle of the woods like this, especially not in the cold. She shivered, but she also didn't care.

Being with him made her feel sexy. Unlike she'd ever felt before—but maybe it was the strength of his body and the hardness of his taut muscles. How wet he made her. But she also knew he'd been with other women recently. "Do you always use protection?"

"Always." His mouth found hers again, then he pulled back with a groan. "I'm driving myself crazy like this. I'm going to put you down."

"I want you, Jason." She nestled her head in the crook of his neck. She clasped her legs tighter. "Please."

He groaned and held her gaze as he positioned himself against her again. Taking her in one hard thrust, she cried out, her fingers digging into his shoulders. "Oh, God," he groaned. "Jen, you feel so fucking amazing." He pumped into her, grinding her back against the tree, her hips rocking against him to receive every thrust, her need for him slick and undeniable.

Something about being out here in the woods in broad daylight was animalistic, as though this view was made for two lovers drinking in the wild. She moaned, and he pushed deeper, relishing in the feeling of the bare, hard ridges of his length inside her, lost in the pleasure as it passed through her body.

She rocked against him harder, lifting her hips off his just slightly, exposing the sensitive nerves against him. As they found a rhythm, a deep, throbbing lightheaded feeling spread through her and built. She was on the verge, and he thrust harder, faster. "More," she managed, moaning louder as the sensation simmered to a hot breaking point.

She sensed him thickening, his own release approaching, and she dropped her head back, her hair catching the bark as a simmering hot climax tingled through her nerves.

Jason slammed himself one last time, and she nearly doubled over as she reached the peak, pleasure washing over her body as he pulsed inside her and released with a groan. She cried out his name, and her lips found the curve of his neck as she clung to him tightly.

When he stilled, she drew her mouth away, still connected to him, the remnants of pleasure sizzling through them like lightning unleashed.

As he lowered her to the ground, her legs wobbled, and she braced herself against him. He kissed her temple, and he reached down for her discarded jeans. As he handed them to her, he caught her in another kiss, this one sweeter, more tender than before. "Thank you," he said, when he pulled away, then kissed the backs of her knuckles.

"For sex? No problem." She gave him a sheepish grin.

He chuckled, but his eyes were more serious. "For being you. And forgiving me. I swear I'm going to make it up to you, Jen."

Jen pulled her jeans on, more conscious now that they were on a hiking trail that could attract company. "You already did," she teased. But as she caught the unreadable expression in his eyes, she couldn't help but feel a spark of worry that she could no longer afford to ignore.

Do either of us know what we're doing?

CHAPTER TWENTY-THREE

"You look happy, Jason." Mildred lifted the cup of iced tea to her mouth and sipped it through a straw.

Jason leaned back into his seat at the restaurant he'd taken her. He'd driven one town over, not because he didn't like Bunny's or Brandywood, but because he wanted the privacy.

Happy? He was happy. He'd spent the past three days finding every creative method of spending time with Jen. They'd fucked all over Brandywood in his car several times and at the guest lodge once Colby was asleep. The damned chairs behind the front desk weren't comfortable, but they were better than nothing.

Of course, they barely had time. Jen didn't want to sacrifice time with Colby, so their meetups were between her jobs and in the little spare time she had.

He felt like a teenager. But he didn't want to stop, either.

And it wasn't just the sex, something he knew he could get on the regular when he wanted. Facts. But it was Jen herself. She'd been through so many tough times in her life, yet she had a vitality about her—*raw exuberance*—that wasn't something he'd ever experienced in a woman. She was warm, real, nurturing, and kindhearted. And he found it hard to imagine ever letting that go. Letting *her* go. *Kevin had been much braver than I could ever be.*

TJ was irritated and exhausted with him. Trying to keep Ned away from Jen was proving to be a challenge. And Ned wasn't keeping a low profile, either. He seemed to slink around everywhere.

"She makes me happy." Jason sipped his Coke and then bit into one of the french fries on his plate. "I've never felt so much for anyone so quickly."

Mildred laughed. "Oh ho, really?" She rolled her eyes. "One week and you're in love. Sonny, I think you're confusing nooky with love."

"I didn't say love." His lips parted at her words. "Mildred—"

"Don't you think it's about time you call me something else? Grandma is just fine, thank you."

I'll give that some thought. He couldn't really fathom the idea of calling her Grandma after all these years.

"I know it's not love. That would be ridiculous. But I care about her in a way I haven't really cared about anyone. Maybe ever."

"Care about her so much you've told her the whole truth about why you came to Brandywood?" Mildred lifted her crab cake sandwich.

He'd *meant* to tell her. The thought had kept him up almost every night. But then he remembered the sweetness of her words and the way she'd forgiven him in the woods. He didn't want to say anything until he was sure he'd found a way to assure her forgiveness again.

When Jason didn't respond, she gave a self-satisfied smirk. "Didn't think so."

"I'm going to tell her." The acid in the back of his throat was back. It'd been there each time he thought of this subject. Which was often.

"I can't pretend to faint every time you need to tell the girl something you know. Which, by the way, you still haven't thanked me for. What'd you think of my performance? I think I should get an Oscar, no?"

"It was brilliant, Mildred," he deadpanned. "I still haven't decided if I'm actually thankful for that, by the way."

"No? Seems to me she's still running around with you, so it couldn't have done much harm."

She was right, in a way. The sex had only gotten better, but by not telling Jen the whole truth that night, he'd delayed the inevitable. "I want to ask her to marry me. I'll explain about the inheritance then—and I'm hoping that since we've deepened our relationship, it'll be enough to get us through any problems that might arise."

"Marry you!" Mildred cackled with a piece of crabmeat clinging to her lips. She shoved it into her mouth with the edge of her forefinger. "You think it will be 'enough to get us through any problems that might arise.' And here I thought you were the smart grandson."

Jason narrowed his gaze. "It's my best shot." He tugged at the collar of his shirt, his gaze traveling over the nearby restaurant patrons. The restaurant was a small family-type place, where tables were close enough that someone could easily eavesdrop on their conversation. Not quite the privacy he wanted. The jangle of silverware and dishes and low conversations filled his ears.

She shook her head. "You really know squat about women, don't you?" She leaned forward and hissed, "I don't care how magical your penis is, son. She's never going to trust you again."

This time, he felt his face grow hot. He'd never met an old lady that talked like this. "Is that really necessary?"

"I am who I am, Jason. Your grandfather thought I was a coarse, trashy woman, and I loved every second of making that pig squirm. So maybe I leaned into it a bit. I'm too old to change now."

"And the ladies from your church are fine with this?"

She tossed up her hands. "Who knows? That's why I go to church, right? Forgiveness and such." She wagged a finger at him. "Which is saying more than you. Who knows when you last stepped into a church. And now you're dragging that poor Klein girl right into temptation with you."

"I said I wanted to marry her." Jason's fist curled at his side. Why did she have to be like this? He'd felt they'd gotten somewhere the last time they had a genuine conversation. And now here she was, putting on a show again. She was exhausting.

"And I said that ship has sailed. The cat's out of the bag. The cow is out of the barn. Elvis has left the building. Pandora's box—"

"I get it." Jason mowed her down with a cutting look.

She took another bite of her sandwich. "I get carried away sometimes."

"You don't say." He was forgetting why he'd asked her to lunch in the first place.

Mildred adjusted the strand of pearls around her neck. "My Martha enjoyed performing, too. You know that's how your father met her, didn't you?"

He picked up his burger with both hands. "No, I didn't." He knew little about how his parents had met.

"She was singing in a band in her high school. They won a regional award and went on to a national competition. One where hoity-toity schools like the one your father went to mixed with the kids from small towns like Brandywood. Can't recall the name of it right now, but it doesn't matter. Your mother was a real artist, you know. Always painting and singing and playing the violin."

No, he didn't know. He never recalled her singing or playing the violin. Not once. Painting, occasionally, but never in front of him. Of course, she'd spent the last year of her life shut behind a door.

Her straw slurped in her tea. "Anyhow, your father heard her singing." She covered her heart with one hand and closed her eyes exaggeratedly, swaying. "Fell in love. Which is apparently what you Cavanaugh men do when you see a woman you like. Your grandpa John courted me properly. Took me out for a full year before asking my daddy to marry me."

His mouth curved in a smile. His father had fallen for his mother that quickly. "And then what?"

"And then your father stole her from me, that's what. Martha came home telling me how she was in love. Instead of going to the local college, she graduated a few weeks later and eloped. And that was that. I lost my baby girl." Mildred's voice dropped, and she lost the joyful expression in her eyes. "After that, every time I wanted to see her, I had to make an appointment. She was young and vulnerable. Just turned eighteen. Your grandfather made that new identity for her, and she would have twisted herself up into a pretzel trying to please him—and your father."

Eighteen? Huh. He'd never thought about how young his parents were when they'd gotten married. But the implication that his mother had been some shallow, immature, and uncaring daughter who had abandoned her parents bothered him. "There must have been some other reason she didn't mind leaving her life behind." He bit into the hamburger, then chewed slowly, staring at Mildred analytically.

Mildred's eyes grew teary. "If you're implying I didn't love my daughter enough, you can stop right there." She glared. "I'd kick you under the table if it didn't mean I might break my toe. Your mother was the apple of her daddy's eye. She couldn't do a single thing wrong. That man died of a broken heart after she left."

Jason swallowed. Her words reminded him of his own thoughts about his mother the other day. "I wasn't trying to imply you were a negligent mother."

"That house I live in was the house she grew up in, darling. Not too much to look at, is it? We didn't have much—always struggled. And then your father came by and the world he took her into—jets to Iceland and weeks in Bora Bora or Hawaii. Days spent buying whatever she wanted, doing anything she wanted. Never having to worry." Mildred sighed. "And before all that glimmer wore off, she had you boys. She really needed nothing else. Your father adored her, and she loved you boys. Gosh, did she love you."

So that was it? His mother just left without looking back? "Didn't she try to come back at all? To visit?"

"At first." Mildred rubbed her forefinger against her thumb, dusting the crumbs off her fingers. "Then each time she came, she seemed to get more uncomfortable with home. First, she didn't want to sleep there. She'd book a hotel a whole hour away just because they had sheets with the right thread count. Tried to send people to fix things around the house—poor John just felt awful when she did that."

Jason set his hamburger down. "So you're saying she became a pretentious snob who put money above the only family she had?"

Mildred gave him a hard, knowing look. "Is that so hard for you to believe?"

The hair on Jason's arms stood on end as he stared at her.

How she'd turned this around on him, he wasn't sure. But she had. He'd come down to Brandywood with the same mindset.

"I want to do right by Jen and Colby, though. And you, too. I want to get to know you better."

"Now. But those weren't your original intentions, were they?" Mildred smiled at the passing server. "And if Jen ever finds that out, what do you imagine she'll think?"

"She doesn't need to know that."

She clucked her tongue. "I thought you wanted to tell her the truth."

"I do. And I'm going to. Speaking of the truth and ways to tell her, part of the reason I wanted to talk to you today is that I found out you own some prime real estate on Main Street in Brandywood."

Mildred threw her head back and laughed. "Oh, why am I not surprised? You want whatever the shriveled hag can give you since old limp dick didn't leave you anything."

"Thanks for the crude assessment of my character, but no."

"Well, I'm sorry to tell you, sonny, but I've already decided to leave that disaster to the town of Brandywood. It's a worthless headache that only costs me money I don't have in property taxes every year. Stopped even being able to get a renter for it about four or five years ago. I would have gotten rid of it, but no one will buy it off me in the condition it's in. And to make it worse, the damn thing is on the National Register of Historic Places, so any updates to the place have to go through so much red tape that I'm going to let those law-making idiots deal with it themselves."

"I already know most of that." Jason crumpled his napkin and tossed it on his plate. "I didn't know who you intended to give it to, but it didn't take me too much research to figure out you'd probably benefit more if I burned it down for the insurance money."

Mildred quirked a brow. "Is that what you're suggesting?"

She seemed game for that.

He chuckled. "No." Setting his forearms on the table, he leaned forward. "Jen mentioned that she'd love to fix it up and make a bakery out of it one day. I don't know if the building caught her eye because of Colby or you or what, but obviously, she can't afford to update it. But I can."

"So you're going to buy a building that's worthless and fix it for her? That's a hell of a bribe."

Jason bristled. "It's not a bribe. It's just something I want to do for her."

"She might see it as a bribe. I'll think about it, though. We'll have to talk numbers."

The server chose that inopportune moment to come back to the table. "Can I get either of you anything else?"

"My grandson would like a big chocolate milkshake." Mildred clapped her hands enthusiastically.

Jason shook his head. "I don't want a chocolate milkshake." What was she up to now?

The server looked from Mildred to Jason with a confused look on his face. "So . . ."

"A chocolate milkshake." Mildred gave a firm nod, then smiled.

Arguing about this was pointless. The server looked at Jason, and he sighed, then gave a curt nod.

As the server walked away, Jason leaned forward. "Trying to run up the bill?"

She eyed him. "No. And if that's what you're worried about, you need to stop being so tight-fisted. I'm paying."

God, this lady liked to argue. "You're not paying." He was in a much better financial position than she was, so having her pay would be ridiculous.

"Yes, I am. I may not be swimming in tubs of gold coins like your grandfather, but I can afford burgers and fries for my grandson. I won almost six hundred on the slots this weekend. And I asked for the milkshake because you need to relax. Those were your favorite as a kid. You used to beg your daddy for them, and he'd split them with you."

Jason stared at her, trying to make sense of her. He hated his grandfather's voice in the back of his head at moments like these, spouting off wisdom about logic. She was driving him nuts, but she was flat-out honest, and that was appreciated. Strangely enough, he liked Mildred—much more than he'd expected to. She was a simple, eccentric woman but surprisingly funny.

"Is there a reason you want me to talk about my father?" Jason crossed his arms.

"Because you need to." Mildred wiped her mouth with her napkin delicately. "You're never going to be truly happy until you do, Jason. Look what happened to Kevin. It ate him alive. And even Jen couldn't fix that. She can't save you."

Jason winced at her words. At the parallel. "It wasn't Kevin's fault, though."

"He still blamed himself for it. It wasn't your fault either." Mildred coughed into her napkin. "And I can tell you still blame yourself."

Because she was wrong. It was my fault.

"I've talked to professional therapists." Jason held her gaze. "I've talked about it plenty." Not the complete truth, but she didn't need to know the details of his therapy sessions.

"Then you need your money back. You have a chip on your shoulder, and it's weighing you down so heavy you look like you're going to topple over."

Jason gave her a brittle laugh, shifting in his seat. "Mildred, this whole thing with the inheritance and Jen and Colby have nothing to do with my father's death. They're two separate issues."

She pulled out her purse and took out her wallet, counting out bills. "No, they're not."

"Yes, they really are." Now he was growing irritated. He felt it building in his chest. She was being stubborn and ridiculous.

Her bright blue gaze sliced through him. "You don't think that the whole reason you're so desperate to keep that company going, the main reason, in fact, is because deep down you know your daddy would be running things if he hadn't died?"

His throat went dry. His palms broke out in an aching sweat, and he rubbed them softly over his thighs under the table.

The waves broke over his head, and he was kicking, kicking, exhausted. Water filled his nose, and he felt himself pulled by the currents. Powerless to get out of them . . .

He sucked in a sharp breath. He squeezed his eyes shut for a moment, then looked back at that severing gaze. "People will lose their jobs if I don't save that company."

Mildred shrugged. "People lose their jobs every day, Jason. What you don't want is for the Cavanaugh name to lose its importance under your watch. Because you're the last man standing. And you don't think you deserve to be."

CHAPTER TWENTY-FOUR

"You're right. The view from the loft is better," Jason said, rolling over in the bed to look at Jen. She lay there, long hair over her shoulders, only half covered by a sheet, her body still flushed from sleepy sex. He loved watching her body's response to him. The way she looked in the morning. She was so naturally beautiful—one of the rare women who woke up looking like the same person he'd taken to bed. Not that she even used that much makeup.

"Remind me why I have to get up to go to church." She checked her phone.

He nuzzled her neck with a light kiss. "You don't. You can stay here with me, and I promise it'll be a lot more fun."

She laughed and swatted him. "You're practically wearing a red cape and horns." Sitting up, she brushed her hair from her face with her fingers. "You know, if you really wanted to impress my parents, you could go with me."

He interlaced his hand with hers. "I could, but then the church might burn down from that lightning strike when I go in. And then where would we be?"

Jen rolled her eyes. "I'm serious."

"Don't worry, I'll see them tonight. I think spending the entire afternoon yesterday moving boxes from your apartment with your dad and brothers *and* a family dinner tonight is probably all I should attempt at this point. Don't want to give them too much time to poke holes in our story."

"Or, God forbid, have them think you like me?"

"Well, I wouldn't want that." He grinned.

She climbed out of the bed. "I guess if I show up to church with you, they're going to know for sure that I spent the night here last night, anyway."

Grabbing his pants, Jason stood. "Or you could just tell them."

"Thanks, but no. Ever since your dumb brother, my whole family thinks I'm a screwup. My mom already gave me a talk about how it would be a good idea for us to 'get to know each other before we decide to be intimate,' and I really don't want to have another discussion with her like that again."

Considering the way Dan had acted, her church-going parents would probably despise him if they knew even a shadow of truth about their relationship. "At least they don't have the expectation that you're a virgin."

She gaped at him, her eyes widening. "Asshole."

He chuckled. "I'm serious. Lots of religious parents hold their kids to that standard." He came over to where she stood, still naked, and ran his hands over the smooth curves of her hips, cupping her ass. "And we both know you are anything but."

"So I'm just a slut, then?" She narrowed her gaze as though trying to decide if she was offended.

"No." He pulled her closer, kissing her jaw. "You're the perfect combination of innocent and dirty, exactly when you need to be. Which makes you unbelievably fucking hot." He swept her up into a kiss, and she gave a low, throaty moan before pulling away.

"If I don't hurry, I'm going to be late. And my parents like to sit in the front row with my brother Warren and his wife. I don't want to cross over everyone to get to Colby." She disentangled herself from his arms.

"The one time you worry about not being late." He gave her a teasing glance, lifting a brow.

"Oh, shut up." She laughed, grabbing her overnight bag and hurrying to the bathroom.

When she'd left, Jason made a coffee, grabbed his laptop, and returned to the loft bed. He opened the browser to the *Financial Times,* an old habit he'd developed in college.

He'd avoided the thought of another job while he was here in Brandywood, but it was something he'd have to think about soon. Ironically, as long as he'd been in the world of business, he'd never had to search for a job. He'd started going into the office with his father as a boy and later interned there in high school and college. As luck would have it, the CFO position opened a year after he'd graduated with his master's. Cavanaugh Metals was a family business. Of course, it was going to stay in the family.

Until it didn't.

With forty percent of the shares to the company tied up in an inheritance trust, who knew if there would be a company for Colby to benefit from in fifteen years?

The thought made his stomach clench with nausea. And there was little he could do to change things now. He was on the outside without those shares and fired. He'd watch Powell and Chad torch what his family had created—and it would die.

Just like everyone else did.

He rubbed his eyes, dropping back against the pillow, trying to get more comfortable. He could still smell the scent of

Jen's perfume against the sheets. Time was running out to settle the inheritance issue for Colby. And Ned was bound to find out the truth soon if he hadn't already. But if he told Jen about everything now and his idea to marry her and adopt Colby, would he lose her? He couldn't promise her the marriage of her dreams, but they seemed to be compatible. Sex was great, too. In a lot of ways, this was the best solution he could have come up with. It honored what his grandfather wanted to do with his will, in theory, while still allowing Jason the chance to save the company.

He wouldn't lie to her and let her make the mistake of thinking about this romantically. It was a business transaction. He'd never wanted to marry again, and he couldn't pretend the thought really appealed to him. Women changed when they were comfortably married—both in and out of the bedroom. But he cared about her and Colby, and she would want for nothing. If he could get Mildred to let him work something out with that hardware store, too, he'd give her the key to her dreams. She could stay in Brandywood, and he would . . . he'd find something somewhere. *It wouldn't matter. Jen didn't really need him.*

Cavanaugh Metals wouldn't lose its importance. He wouldn't be the Cavanaugh to let it fail. His father wouldn't have let it fail because his father never, ever gave up on the people he loved. Jason knew that all too well.

Swallowing a bitter sip of coffee, he turned his attention back to the computer and clicked through the headlines. Then he saw Bill Powell's photo. *"Bill Powell: Guiding Cavanaugh Metals Into the Future as its New President."*

Rage surged through him. *That son of a bitch.*

Closing the article, he slammed the laptop shut and sprang out of the bed. He was tempted to call the bastard and ream him out.

The phone rang in his hand. A number he didn't recognize popped into his call log, but from the area code, it seemed to be local to Brandywood. He answered.

"Jason." TJ's voice had none of its typical humor. "You busy?"

"Not at the moment." Jason sat on the edge of the bed, staring out the enormous window of the loft. Outside, the sky was a crystalline blue, the bare branches of the trees reaching into the cloudless view.

"I'm in jail. I need you to bail me out."

AS TJ WALKED out of the police station with Jason, he stuffed his hands into his pockets. "I'm going to kill you. I never gave you those cameras, thinking you'd turn around and *give them right back to Ned.* I'm facing felony charges, dude. Fel-o-ny."

The knot in Jason's stomach tightened. "I'm so sorry, man. I don't know what I was thinking."

TJ glared. "I know what you were thinking. You were thinking you could pull some macho, tough-guy move. Telling Ned we were onto him, I was fine with. Giving him the damn cameras, though?" He hooked his fingers into claws, shaking them in front of him as though he was strangling someone. "My fingerprints are all over those damned things!"

Jason cringed. He hadn't thought about that. "Doesn't water ruin prints?"

"Not necessarily. Especially if the objects don't stay in the water long. Vickers might be lying to scare me, but if he's telling the truth, I'm screwed."

"I'm going to pay for your legal fees." Jason unlocked his car as they approached it.

"Doesn't mean I won't go to jail. Stalking. Illegal surveillance. Threats. Not to mention the fact that I can't follow the dude anymore. I have a fucking restraining order." TJ opened the passenger door, plopped down into the seat, then slammed the door.

Normally, Jason would comment about someone slamming his car door, but TJ's anger was warranted. He got in the driver's side and sat, letting out a slow sigh. Ned had been quiet for too long. He should have known he was planning to strike a move.

"What now, then? What do we do about Ned?" Jason started the car. He felt a headache coming on, the muscles in the back of his neck and shoulders so taut that they felt as though they might stay permanently frozen like that. He tried to roll them out.

"I'm out." TJ shook his head in disbelief. "You can't seriously think I'm still going to keep helping you with this shitshow. It's over, Jason. I can't. I like you, you're a good client. Almost a friend, even. But you're in over your head with this one. My advice? Leave now. Before things get so fucked up, you'll never find a way to fix them. Space can be a good thing. You're too involved with that woman to think straight."

Jason didn't pull out of the parking spot. He rubbed his eyes. "What do you think Ned's endgame is? Just to get back at you? Me?"

TJ rubbed his hands together, then turned on the air vent so it hit him more directly. "Partially, yeah. But he's smarter than that. There are lines you cross in this industry only when necessary. And in this case, I've been in his way. My guess is that he wanted to get me out of the way."

Jason stiffened.

Jen.

He threw the car into reverse, feeling sick. TJ grabbed the handle above his seat. "Whoa, whoa, whoa! I'm not buckled."

Jason zipped out of his space, then put the car into gear. "Where's the first place you would go if you were Ned and no one was in the way?"

TJ's belt clicked into place. "I see your point."

Jason dialed Jen's phone number. It rang, but then went to voice mail after a few rings.

"Did she just decline your call?" TJ gave him a sidelong glance.

Maybe. Jason's heart hammered in his chest. If that sniveling snake got to Jen before he explained things, Ned could ruin everything.

His car zoomed through the streets of Brandywood. Luckily, Jen had texted him her parents' address the day before when he'd been helping her move—it was just one touch of a button to get his GPS to give him directions.

"Have I told you I get carsick?" TJ puffed his cheeks out as Jason took a hard turn.

They arrived within a few minutes, and Jason parked in the street in front of the old Victorian house. Jen's car was in the driveway, along with a few other cars, including Dan's police cruiser.

"Is one of those cars Ned's?" Jason tried to remember the car outside of Ned's cabin, but he couldn't.

TJ's lips set to a line, and he pointed—not at the driveway but across the street. The car was empty.

Jason dialed Jen's number again. The call immediately went to voice mail. Exchanging a look with TJ, Jason steadied his hands with a death grip on his steering wheel.

He didn't want to go in.

But he couldn't not go in, either. He opened the door.

"Can you leave the car running?" TJ called. "It's cold outside and I just spent the night in jail."

Jason tossed him the keys and started up the driveway.

Before he made it halfway up, the front door opened. Warren, a big, barrel-chested man—of similar stature and appearance to Dan, but bearded—stepped onto the porch. He stormed down the stairs and his petite, auburn-haired wife, Alice, appeared behind him. "Warren . . ." Alice said in a low warning tone.

"What the hell are you doing here?" Warren stormed up to Jason, and before Jason could get a word out, he threw a punch.

Jason ducked, springing back. Warren didn't stop, though. He looked like he should be a linebacker. And from the stance he took, he probably had been one. He leaned forward, then tackled Jason, flattening him onto the grass in front of the house.

The sky above Jason swam, his ears ringing from the blow to the back of his head. Something sharp—like a rock or a pinecone—dug into his back. Warren raised his fist to throw another punch, and a shadow crossed them. Dan was there, too, now. He caught his older brother's hand.

"You don't need this dick claiming you assaulted him, War." Dan held him back.

Jason blinked, his head feeling as though someone had taken an axe to it. The unyielding sun made his eyes water, and tears gathered on his lashes as he tried to see straight. "Get the fuck off me," he growled to Warren.

Warren heaved an angry breath but spit on Jason as he stood, shoulders heaving.

As Jason tried to sit, he caught Dan's gaze. He looked angry but troubled. He gave Jason a menacing look. "You fucking lied to me."

More people came out onto the porch of the Kleins' house

—Betty, Bob . . . and Ned. Ned gave Jason a satisfied smirk, then turned back and shook Bob's hand. "Don't forget, if you have any questions at all, please reach out to me."

Ned descended the steps in front of the porch, then sauntered down the front walkway in front of the Kleins' house. He practically glowed. Giving Jason a mock salute with two fingers, he crossed the street toward his car.

"Warren. Dan. Get inside the house," Bob said in a flat tone. "Now."

Jason gave Dan a pleading look. "I need to talk to Jen. I didn't lie to you."

"You're never talking to her again." Dan shook his head and pointed a thick finger at Jason. "I'm taking her to the precinct after this to get a restraining order. You stay away from her, you hear?" He grabbed Warren by the elbow and dragged him away.

Bob came to the top of the steps and stared at Jason as his sons passed him. Betty joined her husband for a moment, murmuring something, then went inside along with Warren's wife.

Jason stood, feeling unsteady. He turned toward Bob and walked a few feet forward. "Please let me talk to Jen."

Bob clasped his hands in front of him. He was like a bodyguard, except that he didn't remotely have the stature of his sons. He was much smaller. He took a few steps down. "Listen, Jason. Jen needs a little time to process things. It'd be best if you just went on home."

"To Chicago?" Jason lifted a brow.

"That'd be preferable." Bob shrugged. "I know you don't have any children, Jason. And it's hard to be a dad. Hard to see your little girl grow up and get hurt by a man who leaves her in the worst sort of position. But it's a little worse when that man's brother comes around and tries to pull a fast one over her."

"I swear to you that wasn't my intention. And I know how much you love your daughter—"

Bob gave him a stern look. "When my daughter came to tell me she was pregnant, I told her, 'Jen, that's my grandbaby, not bad news.' And that's the truth. I love that girl. And I love that baby. And I will not let anyone hurt them if I can intercede."

Jason drew a shaky breath. "I don't know what that man told you, sir, but he doesn't know the whole story. I want to take care of Jen. I want to marry her and adopt Colby—"

The door to the house opened.

Jen stood at the door, pale, eyes puffy as though she'd been crying. She wore an oversized sweater, and somehow, it made her look smaller, younger. The sound of her footsteps on the wooden slats of the porch caught Bob's attention, and he looked back at his daughter. "Jen, honey, I can handle this."

"No, Dad." Jen didn't look at Jason. "I want to—need to—talk to him."

Bob sucked air in through his teeth. Then he gave her a nod and went back up the stairs. "We'll be right inside if you need anything. And please"—Bob gave her a stern glance—"don't go anywhere with him."

"I won't." Jen wiped her eyes, then turned away from her father.

Jason crossed the yellowed grass on the lawn toward her. "Jen, babe, please listen to me—"

"Don't." Her voice was so quiet that he barely heard her. She turned a watery gaze toward him, not moving. "Don't call me that."

Jason clenched his teeth, a tightness closing in over his chest and heart, so fierce that it felt as though it would burst. "Jen . . . I . . . there's more to it than what that guy told you."

"All right." Jen crossed her arms. "Then answer a few questions for me."

Although she still had tears on her face, her words gave him the faintest notion of hope. "I'll answer anything you ask."

"Did you come down to Brandywood to make sure that no one would ever find out about Colby so you could inherit your grandfather's money instead of Colby?"

Wow. A trap right off the bat. Not a chance he could make this sound better than it was. He gave her a stiff nod, his neck aching from Warren's tackle. "Yes."

She choked back a sob. "And you had no intention of telling me that not only were you a *multi*-millionaire, but that Colby was your grandfather's heir?"

He came closer to her. Brutal honesty might be his best bet. "Not at first. I didn't think Colby deserved it. Or you." He saw the tears welling in her eyes once again. "But I knew nothing about you, Jen. I didn't know that Kevin loved you. Kevin liked to party hard and sleep around. The chance of you just being some chick he knocked up was pretty high."

She blinked tears away, her eyes narrowing. "And that's—that's what you thought I was when you met me? Just some 'chick' your brother knocked up?"

He put his hands in his pockets. "Yeah. I did. But it didn't take long for me to think differently." He cleared his throat, finding it hard to breathe. "Listen, Jen, I didn't know what happened to Kevin. With him dying of an overdose, I just assumed his life went on a downward spiral of drugs and God knows what else. But when I talked to Mildred last week, she told me the type of relationship Kevin had with you."

"Millie?" Jen looked at him in disbelief. "She knows about all this?"

He didn't want to throw his grandmother under the bus. "She knows some of it. Enough to tell me that Kevin left because he loved you so much he wanted to protect you and Colby from my grandfather. I don't know what he was thinking, but I can tell you that my grandfather was cruel and controlling. Even Kevin didn't want my grandfather finding out about you."

Jen absorbed this information with a dull expression. She pressed her dry lips together as though trying to form words.

Jason stepped even closer. "I know you don't need me in your life. But if Colby is named the heir to my grandfather's estate, control of the estate will go to a trustee—the CEO of Cavanaugh Metals, Chad Duncan—a man I deeply distrust. Most trusts work in a way that the minors don't inherit until after they reach adulthood anyway, but Chad's an asshole. The only thing Colby being the heir means is that Chad will control huge portions of his life and wealth—and yours, by extension, well into Colby's adulthood."

Squinting at him, Jen rubbed her collarbone, her fingers barely peeking out of the sleeves of her sweater. "So the money wouldn't help us at all now? Wouldn't make Colby's life better?"

"Not necessarily. It depends on the way my grandfather set it all up, but the trustee gets a lot of say in things. And I don't want that creep anywhere near you." Jason took a slow breath. "That's why I want to marry you, Jen. I want to adopt Colby. And I know it's a rush, but there's a ninety-day window for Colby to claim his inheritance, and it's almost closed. But if he's my son, we can take the whole thing to court. We can argue they should name me the trustee, which is what would happen if I had a legal son of my own. Then I can make life better for you both. Now."

"Just Colby and me?" Jen gave him a wary glance. "Or your life, too?"

His gut dropped. "It's not like that—"

"Isn't it, though? From where I'm standing, it sounds like you have a lot to lose—everything, in fact—if that's not what happens. The only way for you to get to your grandfather's money is what you just suggested." She covered her mouth, then lowered one hand to her stomach as though she might gag. "Is that why you've been sleeping with me? Because you wanted to make me think you cared about me so I would marry you?"

"No, Jen, no, I—" Jason dug both hands through his hair. Mildred's words about how he'd ruined things swirled in his brain. "No. I genuinely care about you. I can't get enough of you. I want you. Everything between us was completely real, I swear it." He drew closer and reached for her hand. "Even I couldn't fake a connection like you and I have. I promise—"

"Don't touch me."

Jason pulled his hand back.

She stepped back, her eyes wounded. "Please leave. Please."

"Jen, it doesn't have to be like this. What happened between us? It's been great. We get along well, and that's more than enough to build a life on."

"Are you kidding me right now? This isn't a movie, Jason. This whole thing more than proves we barely know each other. I am so sick of being taken for a ride, Jason. First Kevin, who proclaimed to love me and then bolted. And now you, asking me to marry you with even more to lose if I refuse you. No, I'm done. Just leave me alone. Get out!"

The last words tore from her throat with a savage torment that he closed his eyes, feeling her slip far out of his grasp.

When he looked back, she'd gone back into the house. Bob stood at the front window, his expression unreadable.

Jason's shoulders fell. He released the last suffocating sigh in his chest, then went back to the car.

CHAPTER TWENTY-FIVE

JEN STOOD in front of Colby at her parents' kitchen counter and wiped his tears away. "It's okay, bud. It's just a little scratch." She peeled the Band-Aid wrapper back and then placed it over his skinned knee. Bending down, she kissed his knee. "All better?"

He shook his head, tears still falling. "I tore my pants."

"Aw, buddy. It's okay. Pants tear sometimes. It's not a big deal." She pulled him off the counter and into a big bear hug. "It's better than getting caught in a . . . merry-go-round!" Then she twirled, spinning him until he giggled.

"Again!" he said with a wide smile on his face.

Jen steadied herself against the counter. "Mommy might fall over if she keeps spinning."

Her mother came in at that moment with Lindsay in tow. "Hey, look who I found outside."

"Miss Lindsay!" Colby squirmed from Jen's arms to get to Lindsay. "I missed you!"

Jen's heart squeezed to see Colby hugging Lindsay. He'd always loved her best friend, but after spending the fall in her class, he'd grown especially close to her. If only she could get Colby back in preschool.

Her mother stood in the doorway. "Hey, Colby, why don't you come with Mom-Mom back outside—get back on that tricycle?" She held out her hands for Colby, who nodded, and they went back outside.

Lindsay took her coat off and put it on the back of a chair at the kitchen table. She came over and gathered Jen in her arms for a fierce hug. "How are you?"

"Ugh . . ." Jen shook her head, determined not to cry. "You know the worst part about being a mom and going through a breakup?"

Lindsay bit her lip and shook her head.

"I can't just crawl under the covers and cry all day. I have to keep putting on a smile and try not to completely fall apart."

"But you guys were barely together." Lindsay squinted at her. "I mean, I'm not trying to downplay your feelings, but I'm just . . ."

Jen sniffled, then sank down into a kitchen chair. "I know. I'm an idiot. It was just so intense. Felt so real. Lindsay, he told me he wanted to marry me yesterday."

Lindsay sat across from her and took her hand. "Please, please tell me you were at least using protection with him?"

Grimacing, Jen covered her face with one hand.

"Jen!"

"I'm on the pill." Her voice came out more defensive than she intended. "It was the heat of the moment. It felt like a trusting thing to do."

"Right. A guy who tells you he likes to sleep around and have random hookups. Totally trustworthy."

Jen looked toward the kitchen door as though her mother might walk through, even though she knew she'd gone outside. "He said he always uses protection."

"Jen, I love you, but next time, just say no."

"I know, I'm so stupid. I just felt desirable." Jen slunk back in her seat. "I'm going to go to the doctor this week and get tested."

"Yeah, well, gonorrhea and chlamydia aren't desirable." Lindsay held out a hand. "Not saying you have that, but just please, please try to learn from this."

Her face turning warm, Jen said, "Lindsay, you're officially making me feel worse."

"Sorry, call it the teacher in me." Lindsay drew her hand down over the air in front of her face. "Turning that off and friend mode on. I'm honestly, so, so sorry. But I guess the good news is that you're rich?"

Jen combed her fingers through her hair. It felt greasy and tangled. She needed to go take a shower. "Yeah, I'm not rich. And neither is Colby. I don't want anything to do with the Cavanaughs or their money. I don't want it."

Lindsay's jaw dropped. "You better not tell me you're going to turn it down."

"I don't want his money." Jen shrugged and picked at the frayed edge of her shirt. "I spent all night last night thinking about it. And I don't want it."

"Are you crazy? That money could turn your life around."

"But I don't want it." The man who'd come the day before —Ned—hadn't given her a specific amount but said it was in the hundreds of millions. Along with the shares of a business and properties in Chicago. That amount of money sounded so absurd that she could barely process it.

Lindsay looked at her as though she'd completely lost it. "It's not like you can decline it."

"Actually, yes, I can."

"What? No, you can't."

"Yes, I can." Jen caught a flash of blue running across the

backyard. Colby was heading toward the swing set, her mother chasing after him. *Thank God for her parents.*

Lindsay followed her gaze. "What are you talking about?"

This part felt harder to explain, but it had occurred to her around three in the morning and the idea felt just as fuzzy in her brain as it had when she'd conceived it. "They told me they needed a paternity test to prove Colby was Kevin's son. And soon. Apparently, there was some stipulation that the heir had to come forward within ninety days and that window is nearly up. I'm just not gonna get one. Without proof of paternity, Colby doesn't inherit."

Lindsay squeezed her hand. "Please, Jen, please think about it. It's not your money anyway. It's Colby's money."

"No, it's not. It's Jason's." His name even felt bitter on her tongue.

"But it could solve so many of your problems." Lindsay held her hands out, motioning toward the kitchen. "Your parents are saints, but you said you wanted to give Colby a home. This money could change his life. Make you both a lot happier in the long run."

"Really?" Jen cleared her throat. She felt remarkably settled about this, despite everything else in her life feeling chaotic. "Look at Kevin. Look at Jason. Were they happy? I might not have a lot, but I have everything I need. I was blind and stupid; you're right. But what I was stupid about was thinking that somehow money would solve my problems. Make them easier? Yes. Solve them? No."

Lindsay lowered her chin, her gaze down toward the hardwood as she listened. Jen continued, "I don't want my son to grow up in a world where he thinks that the more money he has, the happier he can be. Where he doesn't understand that love and family are far more valuable. When I met Jason, he filled that giant void in his life with cheap sex and money.

Kevin tried to fill them with drugs. Colby has all he needs here in Brandywood."

Lindsay drew a sharp breath. "And if Colby gets to be an adult and finds he could have lived comfortably for the rest of his life and you took that chance away?"

"Then so be it. I'll cross that bridge when I get there." Jen stood and went to the fridge. She pulled out a can of seltzer and popped it open. "For right now, I have bigger things on my mind. I called Laura yesterday and quit my job at the cabins. And I think Bunny's upset at me for missing work today again."

Lindsay stared at her in shock. "What? Why? To avoid seeing Jason? You know he's leaving, right?"

Jen sighed. She'd been toying with the idea—wanting to avoid Jason was just the last bit of ammunition she needed. "The cabin job has become a lot less necessary with cell phones. And now that Laura and Mark live at the main house, they're what? Twenty seconds down the road? The main reason Laura kept that job going is that she thinks of me as family. And I realized recently that I can't keep bouncing Colby around all over the place. When every place is your child's 'second home'—it might be because he doesn't have a 'primary' one. So I'm going to give him one, even if it's right here. That's worth the six hundred bucks a week I make at the cabins. I can swallow my pride."

Lindsay came toward her. She hugged her again. "Jen, I feel so . . . I'm so, so sorry. Do you have any idea how much I admire you? You're like the hardest working person I know."

Giving a self-deprecating laugh that did nothing to ease the pressure on her chest, Jen sipped her seltzer. The fizz of the bubbles traveled down the length of her throat. "Linds, I'm a huge screwup, but thanks. I have thousands of dollars of rent and preschool back payments to figure out, not to mention credit card debt. And my only shot at paying off any of it—the baking competition—God, I'm so embarrassed about that. I have no choice but to withdraw."

"Which is why you should take that money." Lindsay spoke slowly, emphasizing her words. She released her and went back to the table for her purse. "Here. Tierney asked me to give you the invoice for the preschool." She dug through her purse and pulled out an envelope. "And I wasn't going to, but I want you to look at that number and then think about what it's going to take to pay it off. Don't throw away a chance at a life preserver when you're barely staying afloat."

Jen took the envelope and tore it open. She'd been avoiding all her bills for so long, that she didn't even know what she owed. Unfolding it, she blinked at the zeroes at the bottom of the invoice. She furrowed her brow and looked over the top of the paper at Lindsay. "Is this a joke?"

Lindsay sidled up to her and looked at the paper. Her eyes widened. "It says you have a zero balance. I don't understand."

"*You* don't understand?" What the hell did this mean?

"Your parents must have paid it off."

Jen shook her head slowly. "I never told them I was behind on the preschool payments."

"Who did you tell?"

Jen closed her eyes. *No.* Would he have done it? Every conversation she'd had with him felt so fraudulent. She gritted her teeth. "Jason." Then she ripped the invoice up into four long pieces.

"Honey, this is a good thing. So he paid off some of your debt. It's the tip of the iceberg with what he owes you." Lindsay gathered a piece of the invoice from the floor.

"No, it's not okay. I don't want to owe him anything. He had no right to invade my privacy and throw his money at me." Jen felt heat rising up her body. "But, Linds? Between him and Kevin, they completely and totally humiliated me. As much as

Kevin broke my heart, in some ways, Jason has hurt me more—he just came down here to screw with me and my life and—" She stomped her foot, crumpling the shreds of paper in her hands. She threw them across the room, where they bounced off the wall.

The thought of every encounter, every touch made her want to scream with fury.

Yet every hour that went by without hearing from him, she fought the urge to find some excuse to send him a message. Just to talk to him.

They hadn't even been in an actual relationship—had they?

Lindsay stared at her quietly, then said, "Jen, I think you really care about this guy. And he hurt you. But you're not making any sense. You say you don't want Colby's inheritance. You don't want the money he's given you. What is it you want?"

To find my soul mate. To find someone who respects me, loves me, and wants the very best for Colby.

She'd been foolish to think what she was missing was some fun in her life. Or even sex. And as good as that had been with Jason, what he'd provided was something much more meaningful—a soft place to land, someone to have an adult conversation with, friendship, even.

That day that he'd helped her with Colby at Bunny's, she'd let herself imagine what life with a proper partner and father figure for Colby would be like. Losing that, having to start that search all over again, made her feel like giving up altogether.

"Him." Jen gave a weak, defeated shrug, dropping her hands to her sides. Because for a moment, she had thought she'd found all those things in Jason. "I want him. The chemistry and fun we had together wasn't fake. At least, I don't think he could have faked that. All last night I kept tossing and turning in my sleep, wondering if anything he told me was true, but especially if he meant what he said about marrying me and adopting Colby. Because even if he just wanted me for money, I don't know . . . it still gets me him in the end, right?"

"No, not right. Colby deserves a dad, not a creepy uncle who married his mom so he could control his money. You deserve a man who *loves* you. Sure, sex with him might be good. For now. Until he decides he wants to go back to his life-style of brief affairs. How can you ever trust anything he says again?"

Jen wanted to agree—if only for the sake of having Lindsay not think she was foolish—but did she? She'd seen the hurt in his eyes, the desperation when he pleaded with her to listen to him.

Lindsay crossed her arms as though trying to figure out what she was thinking. "You know what? I take it back. He shouldn't have paid off that bill. Because I can see the way your brain is working. He probably did it so you'd think he's some great guy who cares about you. Don't let him use this to manipulate you. He's clearly good at it."

Jen narrowed her gaze at Lindsay, then whipped out her cell phone. She typed out a text to Jason before she could regret it.

Jen: *Did you pay off my bill?*

Three dots immediately appeared in a bubble. He was texting her back. That it made her heart lighten only helped to reinforce what she knew. She wanted to hear from him. Wanted to talk to him.

Jason: *Which one?*

Jen: *. . . which one??? Was there more than one?*

Jason: *Maybe.*

Her pulse pounded in her neck, and Lindsay drew closer, reading over her shoulder. Jen exchanged a look with Lindsay.

Then she clicked over to her bill pay system for her apartment complex. She logged in and then clicked on the balance.

Zero.

"What the hell?" Jen rubbed her temples hard with her palms. She had a headache crowning at the top of her head, radiating pain through her upper back.

"How did he even have access?" Lindsay stared, astonishment in her eyes.

"I don't . . . I don't know. I mean, I showed him my eviction papers. Maybe he took them? Though would that work? Or maybe he just went to the landlord?"

"I guess you could always ask."

The front door closed, and Lindsay glanced out the kitchen door. "Oh, hey, Mr. Bob."

Her father removed his jacket and shoes, then padded through the hallway in his socks. Mom had always required shoes be removed at the door, a habit that had driven Jen nuts until she'd had Colby. Now, with the amount of mud that came in with his shoes, she completely understood it. Her patient father had never once complained about the edict.

"Hi, girls." He smiled at Lindsay and grabbed his own can of seltzer from the fridge. "Good day?"

"Weird." Jen put her phone face down on the table. "Turns out Jason paid off some of my debts."

Her father's gray eyebrows drew in a puzzled frown. "Did he?" His voice didn't show what he thought about it. Her father had always been a quiet person, though cautious in making any sort of emotional response.

"But she wants to decline the inheritance. Refuse to get the paternity test for Colby." Lindsay's words were fast—as though she wanted to get them out before Jen could stop her.

"Lindsay!" Jen shot her a wide-eyed look. *How could she have betrayed her?*

Lindsay gave her a sheepish, apologetic look. "I know, and I'm sorry. I love you, though. And he's your father. He can give you much better advice than I can."

"I can't believe you right now." Jen crossed her arms.

The tab on the top of her father's soda can popped as he opened it. He gave Jen a thoughtful look. "Were you not planning on telling me?"

"No, it's not that—" She looked away from Lindsay, closing her eyes as her embarrassment crept up her back. "I just don't want you to hate Jason any more than you already do."

"I don't hate him, Jen. I don't particularly trust him with my daughter and grandson, but hate is a different story. I actually stopped by Millie Price's today to talk to her about him."

Of course he had. She glanced at the back window, wishing Colby would need her suddenly and that she could escape this conversation. "What did she say?"

"She told me a great deal. He's a complicated fellow, that's for sure." Her father lifted the can to his lips and took a sip. "It might be good for you to talk to her." Then he cleared his throat and gave a wary glance at the swing set outside. "Your mother probably wouldn't like me telling you, but she said that he told her last week that he was planning on telling you the truth about the whole inheritance issue. And that he wanted to do right by you and Colby."

"Then Millie knew about everything?" Her disappointment pierced her lungs, making it so hard to breathe that she grabbed the back of a chair to steady herself.

"Millie knew some things. Not everything." Her father set his seltzer down on the granite counter, then unbuttoned the top button of his collar. He glanced at Lindsay. "I know you're like a sister to Jen, Lindsay. But if you don't mind, I need a chance to talk to her for a minute. Thank you for bringing Jen's intentions up with me."

Lindsay bit her lip, her expression clear that she wasn't sure she had made the right choice. She mouthed, "I'm sorry," then grabbed her coat and went outside with Jen's mother and Colby.

Her father held a chair out. "Why don't you sit?"

Jen felt too agitated to sit, but she did anyway. Her knee bounced under her hand with nervous energy. "Dad, I'm sorry. It's not that I didn't want to tell you. I just"—she swallowed and looked down, her eyes filling with tears—"I know I messed up." She sniffled loudly. "I fell really hard and really fast for Jason, and I should have told you the truth about everything with him. Somehow, he made me feel less lonely, and I was just so embarrassed. Because I know it's hard to be proud of me—"

"Jen, I don't know where you got the idea that we're not proud of you." Bob reached across the table to the tissue box. He pulled a few out and handed them to her, then scooted his chair closer. "But if I've given you that impression, please forgive me. I'm in awe of you. You have blossomed into a wonderful mother and a very talented baker."

Jen let out a sputtery cry, then wiped her nose with the tissue. "But I keep messing up—"

"You are *human*. Don't you think you're being a little hard on yourself? If anything, Mom and I have failed you." He leaned over and took her hand. "You're kind. And compassionate. And stubborn as all hell—you won't ask for help when you need it—and we just sat back and assumed you were okay unless you said otherwise. I didn't know you were lonely."

His words made her cry harder. He came closer and wrapped his arms around her, tightly. She cried in his arms, feeling safety in her father that she hadn't really allowed herself to feel for so long. When she'd settled, she sat back, and he wiped her cheeks with a tissue. His own eyes were red-rimmed. "I'm so sorry, Dad."

He gave her a sad smile, then held her hands. "I want you to know a few things. The first is that you're welcome to stay here as long as you want. But you remember Price's Hardware store on Main? It's been available for rent for the last few years."

He dug into the pocket of his pants and pulled out a wrinkled envelope. "I talked to Millie today. She said you mentioned to Jason your interest in the property. She's having trouble renting or selling it because of the cost of the updates needed. But she's going to let you use it. Rent free. The contract is here, just to make things official, but there won't be a cost to you."

Jen stared at the envelope. *What?* "Why?"

"It's a good place. Prime location on Main. And it has a nice apartment on the top floor. The interior needs a lot of work, but I had Garrett Doyle meet me there. He's willing to do all the work it needs at a good price. To convert it to a bakery, that is. I know you'll need a business loan to get you started and pay for the updating, but I'd be willing to help by cosigning a business loan."

A bakery for her.

"Dad!" Jen pushed the chair back. "I can't accept this. You and Mom—you don't have the money to just give me such an enormous gift." And what if she failed? She was the screwup of the family. The one who was back at her parents' house with her hand out.

"I know it's a lot to consider. And if you're not comfortable with it, then we don't have to do it. And you know me, I'm not going to just jump into something like this without making sure we do our homework. We'll have to draw up a proper business plan, get your finances sorted, meet with a financial planner, my lawyer, and a loan officer at the bank. Think of a way to handle childcare for Colby. But those are all details we can figure out with hard work and diligence. And together, Jen."

Jen let herself imagine the possibilities for a moment. She'd been working for Bunny long enough to know that being a small-business owner wasn't easy, especially in the restaurant industry.

Yet she'd also daydreamed about it. What she would do with her own place. How she could balance being a bakery owner with being a single mom. Strangely, the obstacles her father mentioned didn't overwhelm her—they excited her. She cocked her head to the side. "But why are you doing this?"

He removed his glasses from his face and wiped them down with a tissue. "The truth is, Jen, I know you told Mom and me you want roots for Colby. And you will always, always have our home as an option. But I know how independent you are, too. I want you to be happy. And to give your son the home you want to give him. Sometimes you have to let other people carry you a bit. We do it because we love you."

Jen felt choked. Had she been so stubborn about accepting help? "I don't know what to say, Dad. And Bunny. Don't you think she'll be angry with me for setting up shop around the corner from her? I'd be competition."

Her father smiled lightly. "Well, think about it. And then talk to Bunny. She loves you a lot, Jen. And she's getting up there. She can't keep running that café forever." Then he drummed the table, the envelope flapping under his fingertips. "But I also want you to reconsider your position about the inheritance."

She'd known to expect this. "Dad. No. I'm not going to. I don't want Jason's money."

He gave her a wary glance. "Strictly speaking, it's not Jason's money."

"Cavanaugh—whatever. I don't want it."

Her father scratched his eyebrow. "I can't say I'm happy with Jason. And whatever his position now, he came down here with opportunistic, self-absorbed intentions. But I think you should know that I had a hunch about who Jason was when I met him."

What the hell was he talking about? She gawked at him.

He folded his hands in his lap. "Do you remember that time Kevin went hunting with us when you were dating?"

"Yeah, I remember." Kevin had looked so out of place with her father and brothers as they loaded into Warren's SUV. They all wore their hunting camos. Kevin had worn a red-and-black buffalo checkered shirt.

"On the trip, Kevin and I got to talking, and he let it slip that his last name was Cavanaugh. Just to me. He begged me not to tell anyone and said he came from a bad family situation, and I accepted that. Then after he left you pregnant, I didn't know if he would make the best sort of father anyhow, so I let it be."

Her father had known and had said nothing? Had he kept it from her mother? She tried to be attentive, keeping an expression devoid of her response.

"Anyhow, after Colby was born and you were so sick, and you ended up in such bad financial shape, I decided it was time for that boy to pay some child support. So I attempted to track him down. I tracked down Tom Cavanaugh, his grandfather, instead." Her father paused as though giving that information a chance to settle.

Jen gasped. The thought of her father doing all this behind her back was both endearing and hair-raising, which felt like a strange paradox. "That's when you met Jason's grandfather?" She could barely imagine her father doing all that. He was one of the least confrontational people she knew. "You knew about Kevin?"

"Yes. And he was floored to find out about you and Colby. He wanted to meet you. But as we talked, it became clear that Kevin left Chicago to get away from his grandfather. Tom was devastated. He blamed himself for Kevin's death and promised he'd make things right. Since it was clear that child support wasn't an option, I came home. Then I never heard from him again."

She shook her head, any anger that she would have felt choking in her throat. "Why didn't you tell me that my son's father was dead? That Kevin was never coming back?"

"I didn't know how to tell you. And you never wanted to talk about Kevin. I didn't want to open a wound when you seemed to have moved past it."

His explanation sounded reasonable, but at the same time, it wasn't. It spoke volumes that he'd felt the need to find Kevin's grandfather. Trying to think of what her reaction would have been was hard to imagine, given everything that had happened in the past few weeks.

Jen clenched her jaw, staring at the table. "You should have told me, Dad. That's a pretty big thing to have kept from me." Still, it was hard to stay too angry with him. Her father had always been protective of her—just like Warren and Dan. Sometimes to a fault. But he'd also always been supportive and loving. How could she complain when she'd basically won the lottery with the type of dad she'd been given? Look how he'd just stepped up for her, yet again.

"I'm sorry, sweetheart. You're right." Her father took her hand. "But the point is—I don't think it's a coincidence or luck that Tom put that information in his will. He knew Colby existed. Knew you could be found with ample digging—no matter how hard Kevin had tried to prevent that from happening. I think he meant for Colby to have it. It's not Jason's money, sweetheart. It's Colby's."

CHAPTER TWENTY-SIX

"You get your marching orders?" TJ stood at the door to his motel, wearing a floral Hawaiian shirt over a thermal. He'd paired it with sweatpants and flip-flops and looked ridiculous.

Jason peered past him into the motel room. Orange light illuminated the dated two-toned gold striped wallpaper. The bed was an unmade disaster, and open carry-out containers littered the floor and tables. "God, you're a slob. You gonna let me in?"

TJ rolled his eyes, then gestured Jason forward.

Jason shut the door behind him as he came in. "Turns out the owner of the cabins is related to Jen, so I was politely told my cabin rental couldn't be extended as I'd originally planned."

"Sorry to see you go, man." Gathering a few containers of food, TJ stuffed them on top of an overflowing trash can. "I thought you might actually pull out a win on this one." His sarcasm on the last part was dripping.

Jason cocked his head at TJ quizzically. "Why are you saying that like you're staying here?"

TJ flopped onto the hard loveseat in the room. "Because I

am. I've gotten to see a lot of this town while I've been here and, I don't know. There's just something about it. It's like a place where you feel like maybe if you stay long enough, you won't be alone. I'm sick of living out of crappy motels and eating like a pig. And I'm sure there are plenty of cheating spouses in the area who could use my services. I figure after you pay me—if I don't end up in jail from Ned's charges—I may try to take the domestic route."

Jason stared at him, blinking. TJ . . . liked it here? "Damn near a crime for you to use your talents on cheating spouses."

"All part of the job. And jobs like that sometimes lead to bigger ones, you know." TJ grinned widely. "I'm sending you your invoice via email later today. Make sure you're sitting down when you see it."

Jason smirked. As though he'd never seen a huge bill from TJ before. Or just in general. He nodded slowly. "Yeah, I will. I just wanted to thank you. For everything. You've been the closest I've had to a friend lately, which I know may sound ridiculous, but I want you to know I'm not going to leave you hanging with the legal issues."

TJ got up and walked over to him. Clapping him on the shoulder, he nodded, his eyes reflecting concern. "So that's it, then? What about that baking thing tonight? Isn't the last part of the competition tonight?"

"What am I supposed to do? Her brother said she was filing a restraining order against me."

TJ shrugged. "I don't know. Show up, make a grand gesture? *Say Anything* style. You know—boombox in hand, declare your love." His hands moved in wide motions to match his words.

"You're aware this is real life, right? That doesn't actually happen." After Jen had texted him to ask about the bills he'd paid the day before, he hadn't heard anything else. No thank you, which hadn't been why he'd done it. Not even outrage. Just . . . nothing.

Every notification from his phone since then had been torture.

"There's a reason those things have stood the test of time, my friend."

Jason gave him a cynical chuckle. "Yet one of the most famous lines to come from Hollywood is from *Casablanca* when the guy loses the girl and ends up with his weasel friend instead."

TJ dabbed his eyes in mockery as though he had tears. "Am I your Louie? I'm touched."

Jason couldn't help the genuine laugh this time. He sighed, then shook TJ's hand. "I'll see you around."

He left the motel and got back into his car. He had one more place to visit before he left. As he drove, the route took him right through Main Street. His heart felt as though someone had encased it in a sheath of ice. Unlike TJ, he couldn't think of coming back here. Every single corner of this town reminded him of Jen.

He pulled up in front of Mildred's house minutes later. Before he could get out, he saw her in the backyard of her house. On the top of a ladder, hand in the gutter.

His pulse quickened as he got out of the car. He came around, trying to make as much noise walking as he could. He didn't want her to get startled by him and fall off the ladder, after all.

"Look what the cat dragged in. I was wondering when you'd turn up around here. Don't tell me—you're leaving town?" Mildred looked down at him, then tossed a handful of leaves out of the gutter.

"Mildred, what the hell are you doing up there?" He waved at her to come down. "Can't you hire someone for that?"

"I quite like heights, thank you." Mildred grinned at him. "Only time I get to be taller than everyone else." But she began a slow descent.

Jason's palms hurt from watching her sway on the creaky old ladder. He held out a hand toward her as she drew closer. She took it, then climbed onto the leaf-covered grass. "Please promise me you won't do that crap anymore. I'll pay for someone to come and take care of this for you."

She frowned, then gritted her teeth. "Fine. If you insist. I don't know why you pretend to care."

"I do care." Jason squeezed her hand. "You're the only family I have, you know."

"You could have more family if you tried a bit. But as soon as you have a tiny setback, you flee."

Jason gaped at her. She'd told him so many times to leave Jen alone. What the hell was she playing at? "You told me to leave."

"And you're going to listen to a crazy old woman? Not to mention, I didn't know you loved the girl. You'd be a fool to leave now."

"Who says I love her?"

Mildred wiped her hands on her pants. "You're paying the rent on a firetrap on Main Street for her—which you begged me not to tell her father about. And you still haven't left yet. The Jason that showed up here a few weeks ago would have left for Chicago by now. You love that girl. Even if you won't admit it. You're just like your daddy, it turns out."

Loved her?

No, he was just filled with regret for what he'd done to her. Money was the only way he had to make things up to her. She wasn't making any sense.

"Well, I can't even see her right now. She's got a restraining order against me."

"Psh." Mildred blew a breath so hard out of her lips that her lips vibrated. "Her daddy told me differently. Says she refused to go get one. Then he called me back last night, tried to get me to call her and convince her she should take the money."

"What do you mean? The money is going to be Colby's. He's the legal heir."

"He's not the legal anything right now. She must establish paternity first. She's refusing that, too. Says she doesn't want your money." Mildred wagged a finger at him. "You want to convince her you're not in it for the money? Convince her to take it. No expectations on your part. Maybe then she'll believe you."

He almost smiled. The idea of Jen refusing hundreds of millions of dollars was just about the most "Jen" thing he could imagine. She'd wanted so badly to prove that she could make it on her own—and he'd let her down with that, too.

"Do you think she'd allow me to finish the baking competition with her? It doesn't even end for a couple of weeks, though, does it?" Jason raked his fingers through the hair at the nape of his neck.

"The final round is tonight—then Peter's announcing the winners during his 'Christmas Special.'" Mildred looked toward the heavens. "I swear if that man gets any more media recognition, I'm not even going to be able to tolerate him. He's been feuding with my friend Bunny for years. The two of them just need to schtup and get it over with."

He didn't want to think about those two elderly people schtuping. Cringing, he leaned over and pressed a kiss to her cheek. "Never change, Mildred."

Mildred whooped with laughter. "I tell it like it is, sonny. Now, you going to get your ass over to that baking competition? Jen deserves a shot at winning."

"She's not even going to go, I'm sure." Not to mention the idea of seeing Jen in public under the circumstances they'd left things was intimidating as all hell.

Mildred held out her hand. "Give me your phone. And open the dial pad. I don't know how to work those damn devices."

Jason frowned, then took out his phone. He unlocked it and handed it over.

Squinting at the screen, Mildred took a good minute to type in a phone number, then dialed it. She lifted it to her ear as it rang. After a moment, she said, "Bob? It's Millie. Millie Price. I'm calling from Jason's phone. Ha ha, got you there, didn't I? Anyway, can you get Jen over to that baking competition?"

She paused while Bob responded.

"Listen, Bob, I'm going to shoot you straight. I love Jen, and I love Colby. This dickwad grandson of mine . . . well, he's only been around a couple of weeks." Mildred gave Jason a laughing wink. "Jen doesn't deserve to be humiliated in front of the whole damn town by not showing up tonight. Everyone is going to assume something went south between them. And she deserves to win."

Another pause. Mildred nodded and then added, "We'll all be there. What can he possibly do? Also, he's going to do his best to convince her to take the money. Sound fair? Okay. Good boy. Now you get Jen there on time. Colby, too. Tell him Granny Millie is bringing him a big lollipop."

She hung up and handed the phone to Jason. "All settled. Bob's going to try to get her there. That's the best we can ask for, right?" She linked arms with him. "Now, seeing as you have two working arms and legs, and you want to help so badly, why don't you get up there and finish those gutters? I'll go make you some hot cocoa."

As Jason watched her shuffle back up toward the house without waiting for a response, he set his hand on the ladder. Her schemes were hard to keep up with. But for the first time in his life, he'd felt known. Understood. *Loved.* She'd seen so much without him having said a word. And he knew he'd miss that. He knew he'd miss her.

CHAPTER TWENTY-SEVEN

JEN CHECKED the time on her phone for the fifteenth time and slipped it back into her purse. "Don't you think you can drive any faster, Dan?"

Dan looked back at her and Colby in the back seat of his car. "You realize I'm a cop, right? I won't speed through Main to get you there faster when you're the one who took forever getting yourself ready."

She didn't know how she'd allowed her father to rope her into going back to the competition.

Okay, that was a lie.

A lie she kept telling herself and her family. *"I don't know how you talked me into this."*

Bullshit. She knew exactly how.

Because she was a glutton for punishment, and she wanted to see Jason. Not texting him, not talking to him was torture, and her family had sanctioned this. So she could do it and remain relatively guilt-free, right?

Go, compete, and give it her best shot. She was sure she had a chance to win that prize money. And then maybe she could seriously consider her father's offer for the bakery.

Plus, she'd have one last chance to see Jason.

Her nerves made her knees bounce, and she gripped Colby's hand tighter. She had taken longer. She'd spent more time on her hair and makeup than on any single date she'd gone on with Jason. Not that there had been many dates.

Ugh. Was it possible to fall in love so quickly?

Because this felt a lot like being in love, she had to admit.

It couldn't *all* be lust, could it?

They arrived at last, and Jen gave Colby a kiss in the parking lot, then hurried on ahead of him and Dan. Jason hated lateness; he'd told her that much. She didn't want to be late for this.

She hurried past the crowd at the front and then made her way toward the contestant holding area. Since only three couples were left, the area was far less crowded. The other two couples were already there. And so was Jason.

Her heart lurched, and she took a deep breath. She could play this cool if he could. After all, she'd need the money if she was going to get a head start on paying Jason back for the debts he'd paid off for her. No way she was going to accept a gift like that from him. But after she finished paying him back, she'd still have close to fifteen thousand dollars to put toward the bakery idea, if she did that.

My own bakery. The idea was surreal.

But it gave her a strange bubble of excitement she hadn't felt in a long time. A chance to prove she was more than just the bimbo from Bunny's. Just like this contest.

Jason lifted his cool blue gaze at her, and her legs felt as though they'd turned to liquid. Yup, total liquid. She stopped in her tracks, hesitating.

Maybe I can't do this after all.

They hadn't just been friends. Casual acquaintances.

They'd been lovers. And not like she'd originally suggested —they'd been lovers with no intention of slowing things down.

Her face must be going pale because her lips felt strangely cold and prickly.

Jason stood, gave her an amiable smile, and crossed the space toward her. "I'm only going to hug you so you don't fall over, okay? Plus, everyone thinks we're dating," he whispered. He gathered her in his arms.

Jen's arms felt limp, and she rested her cheek against his chest, relishing his familiar scent. She couldn't avoid the tears that stung her eyes and slipped her arms around his waist. "I've missed you," she finally responded.

"I've missed you, too." Jason didn't release her, and they stood in the middle of the store and the crowd, with the clock creeping toward the start time.

He seemed as unwilling to let go as she was.

Blinking back her tears, she finally pulled back and met his gaze. "Jason, I—"

"You don't have to say anything." He took her hand. "Everything that happened is my fault. I should have been honest with you about it all from the start, but I—"

"But that's the thing. I actually understand why you weren't. God, if my father was mega rich and left everything to a kid that was one of my brother's maybe random love children . . ." She drew a deep breath. "What you said made sense to me. You didn't know me."

One of the crew members from the magazine came by. "Contestants, if you could go over to your workstations, please."

She didn't want to be competing. She wanted to grab Jason's hand and leave and go somewhere else and talk to him until they figured this whole thing out. Now that she'd seen him, she had to face the truth—whatever it was—and work through this with him once and for all.

Instead, she avoided looking toward the audience and headed to the workstation with Jason. Even though they'd shown up to support her, she was certain her brothers would shoot daggers at Jason with their glares the whole time. Fortunately for her, even if someone in the town noticed, they wouldn't think anything of it. *And hopefully wouldn't put two and two together regarding the bruise on Jason's jaw.*

The show started without a hitch, and within minutes, she no longer had time to worry about any of the situations with Jason or her family. They had been asked to make a dessert that represented their relationship right now, but only had two hours to make it. Unlike cooking a meal, most of her best baking took hours.

Settling on a chocolate tart, topped with marshmallow whipped cream and strawberries, she started on a graham cracker tart crust immediately. Jason stood beside her, observing her quietly. "How is this going to represent our relationship?"

She gave him a side-eye and reached for the melted butter he'd brought back from the microwave. "You'll see."

"What are you going to serve it on, a broken plate?" His mouth twitched in a smile.

"No." She gave him a mock glare, trying to hide a smile. His ability to make her laugh wasn't funny under these circumstances, but it was one of the things she liked about him the most. *Sarcastic asshole.* Maybe that was her problem. The asshole part. She'd fallen for him despite that.

She dumped chocolate into a double boiler. "Take this over to the stove and put this on medium heat, between four and six on the dial. Then stir the chocolate until it melts. I have to make these tart shells." She found a heart-shaped mold that would work perfectly.

"Anyone ever told you you're bossy?" He lifted a brow at her.

She smirked. "Only in the kitchen."

He leaned closer to her and said in a voice only she could hear, "*Not* only in the kitchen." Then he turned toward the stove and started on the task she'd given him.

The feel of his breath near her ear made her shiver. She focused on her tart shells, feeling torn. She couldn't control the response of her body toward him. Not unless she willed herself to hate him.

But she didn't hate him.

She wasn't even sure she should punish him like this.

Maybe she was just stupid. Dan had given her a lecture, warning her to watch herself around Jason and be smart about him. But they didn't know him like she did either.

Wasn't that what every woman in a bad relationship said?

The next two hours seemed to fly, with Peter coming by for a few interviews once again and the crew focusing more on what she was making. Everything she did seemed like it had to be perfect, as a cameraman followed her hands, focusing tightly on the food she was making.

What if people watching this on television thought she looked like an amateur? Or, worse still, a hack?

Her brain felt fuzzy, weary, but Jason was there each step beside her, charming the camera, joking with Peter as though they were old friends, easing the pressure she felt mounting on her shoulders. He was careful to maintain a distance that probably didn't look awkward to others but felt like a chasm to her.

The timer ticked down toward the last minute, and Jen nodded toward Jason. "Fill that metal measuring cup with that spiced rum, will you?"

She'd pulled out the chocolate shell, shaped like a sphere, that she'd left in the blast chiller and set it on the ramekin she'd heated. The bottom of the sphere melted away and then she set the chocolate sphere over the plated chocolate tart covered with marshmallow whipped cream.

Just as she finished decorating with strawberries, the time was called and she stepped back.

Jason frowned at her. "I thought you said it was a chocolate tart," he muttered in a low voice as they carried it to the judges' table.

"It is."

"All I see is a chocolate globe. A beautiful one, but—" He stopped talking abruptly as they reached the judges.

Jen snuck a glance at the desserts the other couples had made. One of them had made a sugar cookie house, complete with little cutout sugar cookie people. *Why hadn't she thought of something like that?* It was cute and fit the Christmas season perfectly. Maybe it was because she hadn't really felt in the Christmas spirit lately.

The other couple had made what appeared to be bread pudding with ice cream, which while it looked delicious, also looked homemade and messy. She bit her lip. She wasn't in any position to be snarky, really. The judges might not appreciate the showy surprise she had for them.

One by one, they explained their desserts, and the judges tried them—and once again, Jen and Jason were last.

When it was their turn, they stepped in front of them. The judges stared at them with blank expressions, but it was hard for Jen to look at their faces. Even Peter, whom she'd known all her life. She'd gone on vacation with the Yardleys, for goodness' sake. Lindsay had been her best friend since kindergarten.

Jen cleared her throat. "I—we made a chocolate tart with marshmallow whipped cream, because . . . even though our time together has been limited, every time we're together, time is what we want s'more of."

The audience chuckled. The cheesy line had sounded just as bad in her head, but whatever. *Go with it.* She should have told Jason to say it—he would have done a better job.

"But all I see is a chocolate ball," Peter countered.

Jen nodded, then smiled. *Please let this work.* "It's because there's s'more to it. A visual depiction and surprise." She pulled a lighter out of her apron, then lit the rum on fire. It lit into a brilliant blue. Tilting the flaming rum over the chocolate ball, she covered the outside of the chocolate with the fiery liquid. The chocolate sphere melted around the tart and coated the whole thing with chocolate.

The audience gasped, then burst into applause.

"Wow," Jason murmured beside her. She met his gaze, and he winked at her. "Well done."

Peter gave her a pleased look. "So can we say this is burning just as brightly as your love?"

More like our relationship is up in flames. Jen's voice caught in her throat.

Jason gave a smooth grin and grasped her hand. "Something like that."

Jen barely heard the judges' comments about the dessert. She couldn't stop thinking about Jason standing there, hand in hand with her, putting on a show. He'd come through on this whole thing for her sake?

Maybe because he felt guilty, maybe because he hoped she'd be satisfied with $25,000 instead of his inheritance.

Peter told the audience that the winners would be decided and announced on his Christmas special a few days after Christmas, and then it was over.

As the audience rose from their seats, Jason released her hand. "Listen, I know we didn't have the chance to talk much, but do you mind sticking around and talking for a few minutes? I hear you're considering not taking Colby's inheritance."

She sighed. And they were right back to this. "I'm not."

"You should, Jen." He gave her a hard look. "It's what's best for both of you."

Jen stared at the shiny, lacquered wooden floor of the Depot. She turned her head to answer Jason, but before she could, Lindsay and Travis were around her, hugging her. Considering how awkward they were with each other, she couldn't help but give them her full attention. "That was brilliant," Lindsay said.

"My grandmother wants to know why you haven't been making those at the shop," Travis said with a laugh, then pointed back at the audience, where Bunny was talking to Millie.

Jen shifted. "Because I need to save some things for my own place someday." She grimaced. "Speaking of which, do you think you could spare some time to meet with your grandmother with me? I have something to tell you both, and I'd rather do it in person."

Travis eyed her. "If I think it is what you're implying, that wasn't even slightly subtle." He winked. "I'll text you."

As they let her go, Jen turned to find Jason once again. But he was gone from her side.

She frowned and looked around the Depot. Where was he?

The crowd was still too thick for her to see over, so she went back onto the stage area to see if she could see him. *Please don't let him have left without talking to her.*

That was silly. He'd asked her to talk to him.

Then she saw him. He was standing just outside one of the front windows, talking to a tall woman with dark brown hair. She was slender, with striking features, and Jen didn't recognize her.

Removing her apron, she pushed through the crowded store and went out onto the sidewalk. "Hey," she said, coming up toward Jason.

Jason stiffened, and a worried expression crossed his face.

The woman turned toward Jen. Her eyes narrowed. "Oh, just who I was hoping to talk to. The woman who's been fucking my husband." She arched a perfectly shaped brow and held out her hand. "Didn't Jason tell you? Amanda Cavanaugh, nice to meet you."

CHAPTER TWENTY-EIGHT

JASON RESISTED the urge to strangle Amanda and stepped between the two women. "Ex-wife."

The look on Jen's face made the panic rising in his torso feel completely justified. She looked from Amanda to Jason, a mixture of confusion and anger on her face. She didn't accept Amanda's proffered hand and stepped back. "What's going on?"

Jason's words were venomous. "You don't know what the hell you're talking about."

Amanda shrugged and dropped her hand to her side. "Fine, but Ned Vickers has plenty of footage of you two together to prove otherwise." She rolled her eyes. "I'm his soon-to-be ex-wife. We're on the verge of divorce but still technically married. But Jason is the father of my soon-to-be-born child. Is that better?"

Jason gave her the iciest glare he could muster. "Don't even start with that." He held out a hand to Jen. "She's lying. Listen, I can prove this one. I don't know what the hell she's doing here, but we're getting divorced. We signed a prenuptial, and it's uncontested so it's just a matter of weeks, really."

Jen placed her fingertips to her temples as though her head hurt from the information. "And you didn't think to tell me this?"

Amanda just set her hands on her hips, arms akimbo. She tilted her head to the side, watching them with interest. The people leaving the Depot stared at them and Jason spotted a skulking Dan Klein by the door. He didn't look happy that Jen was outside with him.

This couldn't be happening all at once. *Not today, Satan.* His gaze narrowed at Amanda once again. "I need to talk to Jen. Alone. We can talk after." He pointed at Yardley's. "Meet me at that bar in a half hour."

Amanda sighed. "Don't you think I should be here for—"

"In a half hour or not at all, Amanda." He wasn't in the mood to negotiate with her.

She pressed her lips together. Without responding, she stalked away, the heels of her boots smacking against the sidewalk. She'd toyed with modeling in her early twenties, an attribute Jason had considered a turn-on when they'd started dating. Her power strolling was less appealing these days. His fury at her bringing up that paternity issue had him ready to burst.

One glance at Jen, though, told him he had a lot more to be worried about.

She hadn't come out with a coat on, and her glance back at the Depot made it clear that she was considering fleeing back to its safety.

"Jen—wait. Let me explain."

She didn't look at him, raking her fingers through the knots in her messy bun. A passerby squeezed her forearm, giving her congratulations and a wide smile.

Jason stepped closer to her. "Can we talk somewhere more private?"

She gave him an odd look, then shook her head. "I don't think so."

"Look, I didn't tell you I was still married to Amanda because I don't really love to talk about her. And we're almost divorced. It was a brief marriage that meant little to me. The dumbest decision I've ever made. And a few months ago, I hired a private investigator to track her odd behavior and discovered that she's been cheating on me with my best friend from college since before we were married. She's with him now, and he's the CEO of my grandfather's company."

"Great job, you two!" Another woman shook both their hands. Jason and Jen pasted polite smiles on their faces, then watched her go.

Jen still said nothing, so Jason continued. "Anyway, because we hadn't officially separated when my grandfather died, she was present when they went over the will with me. She knows about the inheritance stipulations. And now I'm pretty sure she's trying to make up a pregnancy to take me to court for the whole thing."

Jen blinked up at him, looking confused. "So she's not actually pregnant?"

"No, well . . ." Jason cleared his throat. "I think she's pregnant. I'm just saying I'm not the father."

"And you know this for sure?" Jen gave him a sharp glance.

"Pretty positive."

Jen stared at her own reflection in the Depot's window. "You know, Jason, I'm not saying I don't believe you. It's just that we've only known each other for what? A couple of weeks? And every few days, I find out something new. Some big surprise that has the potential to devastate me." She swallowed hard, then met his eyes. "I can't keep doing this to myself."

"Jen—"

"No, I'm serious. It's not fair to me. And it's not fair to Colby. I need to be a functioning person, you know? I don't get to just stay in my pj's and cry all day eating ice cream. Not to mention, I must think of him first. Who would be good to have in his life." Jen straightened, but the hurt in her eyes brimmed with her tears. "And you're just not that person."

"Jen, please. I know I lied about so many things. And if I could do it all again—"

"You would do the exact same thing!" Jen's words broke out in a cry that was clearly louder than she intended. She scanned the vicinity with an embarrassed flush on her cheeks. "Think about how many times you had the opportunity to tell me the truth. And you just couldn't bring yourself to it, could you, Jason? You took the easy route because you're a liar. Because you never cared about me in the first place."

"That's not true." He tried to think of a way to prove his point, but how could he? Mildred had been convinced he loved her because of the damn hardware store, but if he told her about the bakery plan, she might refuse it.

"It is. Thank you for paying off my debts. If we won tonight, then I'll pay you back as soon as I get the winnings. Otherwise, it might be a while. And thank you for showing up tonight. But it's really over. I can't trust you or your intentions." She struggled for a steady breath. "And I don't think I ever will."

He reached out to her, but she slipped out of his grasp. Then she turned and hurried back into the Depot, wiping her cheeks of tears as she went.

AMANDA WAITED for Jason in a booth in the back of Yardley's. He regretted having told her to come and wait for him immediately. The restaurant was crowded, and from the way people looked in his direction as he walked through the place, they knew who he was.

Which made sitting down at a table with his ex-wife particularly uncomfortable. Not that other people knew who Amanda was. But they didn't really seem to care either. Jen was clearly a beloved member of the community. He was an outsider.

He always would be an outsider.

Amanda had already ordered a drink—a Coke—which wasn't like her at all. She sipped it, then lifted her eyes to him. "This is about the only thing I can stomach lately. Coke and soda crackers."

Right. Because of the pregnancy. He gave her a sharp look. "Are you really pregnant?"

"Yes." She paled some, which wasn't the easiest thing considering how pale she already was. "But you knew that. I didn't exactly try to hide the fact from your PI when he was snooping around my personal business."

"It's not mine." Jason crossed his arms and leaned back in the seat. "And Jen's son is first in line to inherit, so you may as well drop the sham. That baby is never going to even have a chance. And frankly, I don't want to embarrass you in court."

A server interrupted their conversation, and Jason ordered a beer. He watched Amanda sip her Coke again, her gaze downcast. She'd always exuded confidence. But she seemed strangely muted. Even the fact that she'd come to Yardley's without protesting was a change of pace. When the server had left, she played with the edge of her paper coaster. "It's your baby, Jason. We already did a paternity test. It's not Chad's. In fact"—she didn't meet his eyes—"he dumped me for cheating on him with you."

He suppressed an ironic laugh. *Cheating on Chad with him?* The absurdity of the phrase made him raise his brows. "So you—who never wanted to be a mother, ever—just so happened to conceive that last time we were together when it conveniently aligned with a viable opportunity at a substantial inheritance? What are you playing at? I'm not an idiot, you know."

"I've never thought you were an idiot. But nothing about this is convenient for me, Jason." Her face looked a bit pinched, as though she was on the verge of tears, something he wasn't sure he'd ever witnessed. Or had he? Who knew? "But believe it or not, I want this baby. I had stopped taking birth control because Chad and I were talking about getting pregnant, but I didn't think it would happen so quickly or with you. I should have told you, and it was wrong of me not to. And I'm sorry. I don't know—it's probably the hormones or something—but when I found out I was pregnant, I was really, really excited."

"If it's not about the inheritance, why'd you do a paternity test?"

The edge of her coaster was fraying badly. "Because I told Chad that I had slept with you when I found out. That it might not be his. And he asked for a test. He said if it was his, he'd consider staying together, but no way in hell was he raising *your* child."

Even though she'd told him a few times now that the baby was his, something in her words now hit him differently. Made him almost throw up.

His pulse quickened, his throat going dry. He needed that server to come back with that beer—now.

He was going to be a father?

The breath he drew was shaky. "How do I know you didn't sleep with someone else?"

"I didn't. But if it makes you feel better, you can do a paternity test, too. There were only ever two options. It's not Chad's, so that leaves you." Amanda shifted in her seat. "Think about it. What possible reason would I have to lie about this? We didn't exactly end things on good terms. Co-parenting with you is just about the worst twist of karma I've ever heard of. And you've said it yourself—it's not about the money. Maybe, just maybe, you can admit that leaves the obvious fact that I'm telling you the truth."

He set his hands down on the edge of the table, pushing his weight into them. The server returned with his drink, which he stared at, watching the amber bubbles rising up the side of the glass. He was going to have a kid.

With Amanda.

"Holy shit," he breathed out, but his head felt light. Too light. Was he getting oxygen? His throat felt choked, his collar too tight.

Amanda gave him a wary look. "You okay?"

"I'm processing."

She nodded, then returned to destroying her coaster.

He chugged his beer. He might need a few of these with this news.

A father?

He couldn't visualize that. A kid Colby's age—okay. They could walk and talk and watch cartoons. But diapers and midnight feedings? Wait—would he even be around for that? They were on the verge of their divorce being finalized. "What does this mean? Are you trying to get back together?"

This time, Amanda laughed. She shook her head. "No. Maybe you are an idiot." She cleared her throat. "No, I think we were together long enough to realize we don't work. I don't believe any child we bring into this world would benefit from a life being spent in our sham marriage."

"It wasn't like that—" Their shouted words during their breakup, the night he'd moved out of their house, came back.

"You should have told me you wanted out."

"How can you talk to someone who's never there, even when you manage to see them? You checked out of this marriage long before I did. I'm not even sure you were ever in it. You're incapable of actual feeling, Jason! Grow up, already. Your life has been the exact opposite of hard."

"You knew who I was when you married me, Amanda. You just didn't care because I still came with a good stock portfolio and an address in Lincoln Park. Nothing changed."

"How do you just not get it? I changed! I realized I wanted something more. Someone who actually gave a damn about me."

And he hadn't had a response for her because he hadn't given a damn.

The truth was what he'd felt when Amanda left was annoyance and anger. Not sadness. Not hurt.

Not loss.

The exact opposite of what you're feeling right now with losing Jen.

Amanda sighed, twirling her straw. "I should have told you about Chad before you found out the way you did. I hated myself for a lot of that, you know, especially since you were always a lot nicer to me than he was, and I don't know. I guess in the end, it's better that I didn't get pregnant with his kid."

"Chad's an asshole," Jason agreed. It had taken him a long time to see it, but he'd never look back at their years of friendship the same way.

"You were an asshole to me, too, at the end." Amanda shrugged. "But I probably deserved it. We were making each other miserable. And that's a good sign that we shouldn't ever be together again." She sucked her cheeks in. "Besides which, you apparently have moved on."

Her claims about Ned having footage brought back his anger with her. "Why in the hell would you have Ned take footage of me with Jen?"

She blinked a few times, her long lashes lifting as she looked at him. "Because I had him do it in general. I was angry after you hired that PI to follow me and Chad. And I wanted revenge. I wanted to contest the divorce. So I had Ned gather evidence, and wow, there was a long string of women for a couple of months, Jason. I'm not going to lie. That astonished me.

Until you got here. And then it all stopped."

"Then if you know I care about that woman, why would you introduce yourself that way?" Jason's voice was strained.

"I don't know. I was jealous. She's pretty. And obviously talented. I watched the show last week, and the way you looked at her? I don't know if you even looked at me that way on our wedding day."

That she'd been jealous was odd. But it gave her a vulnerable side he didn't normally associate with her. "And you never looked at me the way you looked at Chad. You definitely never considered having a kid with me."

She grimaced. "Touché."

Fighting with her no longer held any note of satisfaction, strangely. For the first time in a long time, Amanda somehow seemed more . . . human. Maybe it was the fact that she was pregnant. Or maybe that they were having a conversation that felt civil.

How long had it been since they sat and talked like this?

Had they ever?

He took another swallow of beer. "And what are you planning on doing with that evidence you gathered?"

"I don't know." She met his gaze, her blue eyes thoughtful. "I think it sort of depends on how you choose to proceed with the baby. I'm not exactly a fan of dragging my child's father's name through the mud in court. But if you have no intention of stepping up . . ."

He should have expected her to have some sort of endgame. Amanda was as risk-averse as he was. It was part of the reason they'd gotten married. They were safe options for each other. Her decision to have an affair had only been proof of how much she'd loved Chad.

Jason was silent for a few moments. The restaurant was noisy, which he was grateful for. The likelihood of them being overheard was too high otherwise. "If it's actually my child, then I want to be involved." The relief on her face was palpable. "I'm not going to ignore I have a baby, Amanda. I don't know exactly what that means for you or the baby, but I'll be there to support you in whichever way I can."

She breathed out, then reached across the table, offering her hand. He reached for it and grasped it for a moment, not caring who saw. Even if their marriage had gone up in flames, they didn't have to continue the cycle. Her eyes were shiny, and she squeezed his fingers, then released them. "I guess we can figure out the details later. Especially now that you've made a new life here in Maryland. I want you to have enough time with him." She bit her lip. "By the way, it's a boy. I tested for gender. I didn't want to wait to plan things."

He was going to have a son.

He closed his eyes, breathing out.

Then a scene came to him, an imagining from his brain, of Jen and Kevin sitting here a few years earlier. Or maybe somewhere else in this town. When his brother had found out he was going to be a father.

He didn't know how the conversation had gone. Had it scared Jen to tell Kevin? Had it excited her? *Had he been excited?*

Whatever the circumstance, the news must have tormented Kevin as much as it moved him. Kevin's reaction hadn't been the right one, but Jason couldn't entirely fault his brother. And if Jen had been as instrumental to his sobriety as Mildred had suggested, losing her must have been more than Kevin could bear.

The problem was that it had left Jen vulnerable and abandoned.

And she'd fought back, shown a resilience that was so . . .

His jaw clenched.

. . .*it's what you love about her.*

Jen and Colby deserved that money. Every cent. He was ready to let it all go now, no matter what it meant for him.

His chest tightened.

He didn't want to leave Brandywood. Didn't want to imagine a future where Jen and Colby were here—without him. And with Amanda having his baby, it's not as though he could ever imagine leaving Chicago permanently again.

But he'd tried so hard to figure out a way to make any of this right, and he'd failed.

No amount of money he could spend, no grand gesture could undo the harm he'd caused, the trust he'd broken. He could never repair that. Never convince Jen he loved her.

He had no choice but to leave.

He would never be worthy of Jen and Colby. Because his grandfather was right: he'd never been worth the second chance at life he'd been given. He didn't deserve Cavanaugh Metals, and he sure as hell didn't deserve Jen and Colby Klein.

All that was left was for him to stop fighting the inevitable and walk away from it all.

He looked at Amanda, and the breath he expelled felt like hope leaving his body. "Actually, I think it's time for me to go back to Chicago."

CHAPTER TWENTY-NINE

JEN SAT in a booth at Bunny's, watching Colby as he downed a sugar sprinkle cookie. His ability to get crumbs everywhere never ceased to amaze her. Half the time, she was convinced he got more of the cookie on the floor and table than in his mouth. She returned her gaze to Travis, who sat across from her waiting for his grandmother to finish with a client behind the counter.

Travis gave her a quick wink. "It's going to be okay, you know that." She'd already told him about the bakery her father had proposed—he'd texted her impatiently asking to know.

"I know, but I've worked here since I was sixteen. I feel like your grandmother is almost my grandmother at this point."

More than that, she thought of all the work she'd poured into things the last week. The meetings with her dad at the bank and to see his lawyer. Staying up late into the night reading everything she could get her hands on and building a business plan. She'd also met Garrett Doyle at the hardware store to gain a proper estimate on the cost to fix the place—that number still made her break out in a cold sweat.

Her plan might still be in its infancy, but she'd worked harder on it than she'd worked on anything for a while. And a part of her didn't want to let that go now. Jen stretched her arms out on the table in front of her, then folded them across each other while she set her head down. "What if Bunny hates me for this?"

"She won't hate you." Travis chuckled sardonically. "You know her. She's going to have your back."

"Really? When I'm thinking of setting up a shop a few doors down?" That was the part of this that worried her the most. That Bunny would never want to speak to her again. After all, whatever had sparked her feud with Peter Yardley had lasted for decades now. And they'd spent most of that time always trying to outdo each other. "What if I'm the new Peter to her?"

Travis lowered his voice, leaning closer. "Peter's become his own thing. I think even my grandma must claim defeat on that one. He has his own show on that network that does all the celebrity food shows. A classic American show. How can my grandma compete with that? He's moved his whole Christmas special to the lighted flotilla at the lake, so it can coincide with the festival and fireworks, and he's going to make the announcement then."

She gave him a curious look. "Who told you all that about the flotilla?"

A sheepish expression crossed his face. "Lindsay."

Her draw dropped. "Have you two been talking again?"

He rubbed the back of his neck. "Maybe. I don't know. It's so complicated with her. But we did text after that baking competition last week. But see? You're the glue that brings the Yardleys and the Wagners together. The one thing we can agree on."

Bunny started toward their table, still holding the cloth

they used to wipe down the espresso machine. She shook her head when she saw she still carried it and set it in front of her. "I swear I've put more than one of those in my purse before." She sat beside her grandson.

Jen smiled. "I think I've done something similar." She gave Bunny an apologetic look. "Though it probably doesn't help that you've been having to pick up so many hours that I couldn't work for you."

"That's what happens when you use that preschool that Yardley girl recommended." Bunny folded the cleaning cloth into a neat square. "But that's beside the point. With Christmas only a few days away, things are just busy, you know how it is. I would be here anyway. Now, what did you want to talk about?"

Jen didn't want to think of Christmas being a few days away. Her life had taken such a strange turn in the past few weeks that Christmas didn't feel quite real right now. She'd been able to buy Colby some presents and had wrapped them, thanks to Jason paying off her bills, but her spirits didn't match. That was also thanks to Jason.

She put the thoughts of him aside, and her gaze darted briefly to Travis. He gave her an encouraging look. Thank goodness she'd asked him to be here. She glanced at Colby, who was still chewing the cookie. "Well, Bunny . . . you know I've always appreciated everything you've taught me and how I give you credit for everything I've learned."

Bunny gave her a puzzled look. "Are you quitting?"

She felt the need to ground herself in something safe. For as many conversations that she'd had with Bunny, telling her this made the possibility of it real. If she moved forward now, she was on the hook.

She put her hand on Colby's back. "Millie Price has agreed to rent me the old hardware store on Main. And my father has offered to help me get a loan to fix it up and create my own bakery."

Bunny was silent. She blinked, her face thoughtful as she seemed to weigh her response. Tilting her head, she asked, "When are you opening?"

Jen cleared her throat and her fingers curled around Colby's thin shoulders. "I'm not sure. I wanted to talk to you before I made a final decision. There's no way I could move forward if you were angry with me. I'm making a business plan right now. But, hopefully, if all goes well, sometime next summer."

Bunny squinted, then she exchanged a look with Travis. "Did you know this?"

Travis nodded.

Bunny smacked his forearm lightly. "And you didn't tell your own grandmother?" She shook her head as though disappointed. She looked back at Jen. "All right. Well. Tell me when you start taking orders." She slid out of her booth as though she was going back to work.

"Wait—what does that mean?" Jen scrambled out of her booth. "Are you mad at me?"

Bunny scanned her face, and then a slow smile spread on her features. "Silly me." She pulled Jen into her arms for a strong hug. "I tell you, the Christmas season has my brain upside down. Mad at you? Are you nuts?" Then she laughed. "Well, considering I've been in this business for so long, you are a little nuts to want to do it, too. But that's not the point. The point is it will be a relief to outsource all our baking to someone I trust. Then maybe I can finally start cutting back on hours here."

Outsource her baking? "You're going to sell my products here?" Jen blinked, trying to wrap her head around what Bunny was saying.

"Of course. And don't worry, I'll still give you credit." She dipped her chin and pointed out the window. "You should get Lindsay to help you talk to Peter. He'd probably be interested in throwing some of your products on his dessert menu, too. And in the Depot."

She winked, then caressed Jen's cheek gently. "I'm proud of you, kiddo. Never taught anyone with as much talent as you. You go get them." Then she turned and shuffled back toward the counter.

Jen watched her go, her lips parted, mouth hanging half-open. "Told you you'd be fine," Travis said behind her.

She turned and gave him a warm smile. "Thanks for being here anyway." She reached for Colby. "Hey, bud, want to go for a walk? I have something I want you to see."

Colby abandoned his crumbs, jumping onto the seat of the bench excitedly. "Is it a toy?"

She grabbed a napkin and wiped off his face, then she quickly cleared up the table as best she could. Travis shooed her away, though. "No. It's better than a toy." Putting him down, she took his hand. She waved goodbye to Travis, then hurried outside with Colby. Despite the frosty December air, a potent force propelled her forward, and she broke into a jog up the sidewalk. Colby laughed, trying to keep up with her.

They stopped in front of the hardware store. Digging into her purse, she found her keys and then looked for the key her father had given her. She slipped the key into the lock, picking at the peeling navy blue paint on the door frame. "What is it?" Colby asked.

"Just look." She pushed the door open. "This used to be your great-grandfather's store. A long, long time ago."

Colby looked wary, hanging back by the door. "Like yesterday?"

Jen chuckled. "No, a little longer than that." She squeezed his hand reassuringly.

The inside of the hardware store was cold and dark. Uninviting. Plastic lined some walls, and the smell of dust was strong.

This place was going to take a ton of work.

"Does he still live here?" Colby asked, looking a little worried.

"Hey, where's my favorite nephew?" Dan's voice came from behind them, startling Jen. She gave a slight jump, then turned, releasing a relieved breath.

"Uncle Danny!" Whatever fear Colby had felt moments before seemed to vanish as he whirled around and leaped into Dan's arms with childish excitement.

Jen gave him a taut smile, tucking a strand of hair behind her ear. "I doubt Warren would be glad to hear you have favorites. What are you doing here?"

"All my nieces and nephews are my favorite when I'm with them." Dan winked at her. "I was just down the street. Saw you two stop here." He shook his head at the decrepit interior. "I've had to chase some squatters out of here before. You probably shouldn't go in there alone." He set Colby down.

"I just wanted to show Colby the place. Did Dad tell you about his proposal for me?"

Dan shifted, rubbing his clean-shaven jaw. "He did. Can't wait to see what you do with the place." He tilted his head, a troubled look on his face. "Feel like walking to the playground? There's something I wanted to mention to you."

Jen nodded and locked up, pushing away the disappointment she felt at not showing Colby the space. But Dan was probably right. It might be better to wait to show him the building when it was less scary. But she'd felt so enthusiastic after her conversation with Bunny, and losing that feeling was heartbreaking.

The playground wasn't too far away. When one of the oldest buildings in town had burned to the ground a few years earlier, the lot it had been on had been converted into a community space. With a playground for kids and gardens with plenty of seating, it was especially popular in summer. As they drew closer, Colby broke out in a run toward it.

Jen watched him climb up a ladder. "What's up?" she asked Dan, not taking her eyes off Colby.

Dan grimaced. "You're going to be mad at me. But you're my sister, and I've messed up a lot with you. And I want us to trust each other like we used to."

She crossed her arms and raised both brows. "Uh . . . what is it?"

"I looked Jason Cavanaugh up before you came to me that day at the precinct asking me if I could investigate him. And I didn't tell you I'd already found out he was Kevin's brother. I had already paid him a visit and asked him not to tell you about his connection to Kevin."

"Wait, what?" Jen stiffened. She remembered Dan's reassurances when she'd gone to the police station. That he couldn't use his position to look into people like that. *That was a lie, too?*

Dan gave her a squinty-eyed look. "He said he was leaving. That he was in town to see Millie Price. And I didn't want to bring up Kevin because, well, you know. You were doing a lot better with that whole thing, and I figured you're old enough to make your own decisions."

"Mommy, watch!" Colby cried, clamoring at the top of a twisting green slide.

Jen didn't bother to look at Dan, going closer to Colby as he slid down it. "Wow, bud. That's a tall slide." She helped him off and he ran around to the ladder to go back up. She felt Dan come up behind her. A heavy feeling weighed down her chest.

Jason's face flashed in her mind. She couldn't allow herself to think of him. To think of the time they'd spent together. Jason's wife—with all her beauty and glamour—haunted her dreams. The lies from his lips mocked every memory that snaked its way into her brain. Her mistake had been to think she knew him when really, she didn't. Just like she'd never really known Kevin. So many things she didn't know. "So you told Jason not to tell me anything? Or threatened him?"

Dan turned her to face him, then set two brotherly hands on her shoulders. He ducked his chin, frowning. "A bit of both. But I'm starting to realize you don't need protection. Not really. And my interference probably made a confusing situation even worse. Jason told me he was going to tell you everything. And I told him not to. I didn't know about the inheritance stuff, of course. No way to know about that. So I still feel like he wasn't honest about what he was doing here in town."

"And you didn't tell me about this sooner?" Jen pulled herself free from his grasp as irritation bubbled inside her. "Dan, if I had known who Jason was from the start, things could have been really different." Honestly, she didn't want to think about how things would be now. She wasn't over Jason— not by a smidge—and it was too easy and unrealistic to think about what might have happened if he'd told her the truth when they'd met. She could never really know that.

After catching Colby at the bottom of the slide, she set him down on the ground. He ran over to a climbing pole with a grin.

"I thought I was doing the right thing. I shouldn't have looked him up, really. I knew how mad it might make you. But then once I knew the truth, I felt stuck." Dan motioned toward Colby. "I love you guys. You know I'd never let anyone hurt you, but I think it's time for me to hang up my hat as the enforcer of that. So I wanted to tell you the truth. Start with a clean slate."

Jen crossed her arms, grinding her teeth. "It was an awful thing to do, Dan." She checked the playground to make sure they were relatively alone. Only another mom appeared to be in the vicinity, but she was busy swinging her kid on the swing set. "And I'm having a hard time believing you're being sincere about not interfering in my business. But I'm also really, really sick of being mad right now. It's Christmas, and I don't want to be fighting with my big brother. So if I let you off the hook this time, swear to me this will be the last time."

Dan's broad shoulders fell as he released a sigh. "I promise, Jen. You know, Warren and I really took the news of you being our baby sister seriously. Probably because we were so excited to be part of a normal family. And you're the one who brought us all together in a way. But you're not a baby anymore. You're not even the girl you were when you got pregnant."

He gave Colby a fond smile as he ran by to the other side of the playground set. "You're really admirable, Jen. Hell, I think it's pretty safe to say you're a lot more mature and smarter than I am. Look how much trouble I've caused you." He reached out and squeezed her shoulder once more. "So I swear it. You don't need me trying to look after you. You're doing just fine on your own. And I'm not the only one who thinks so. Mom and Dad wouldn't be offering to help you with that bakery if they didn't believe in you just as much as I do."

Jen's eyes misted unexpectedly at his words. "I don't know about that."

"I'm serious. How many other people do you know who could juggle two jobs, do an amazing job raising a baby all on your own, and be a hot-shot baking contestant on a television show while charming the pants off a billionaire?"

"Multimillionaire." Jen winced.

Dan winked. "After five figures, you're talking about zeroes most people have and will never see in their bank accounts. It's all relative." He slung his arm around her shoulder, drawing her in for a bear hug. "You're doing great, Jen. We're all proud of you. You just have to believe it for yourself." Dan kissed her temple and then released her. "I should get back to work. I have a whole town to look out for instead of you."

As Dan walked away, Jen felt a surprising tug of loneliness in his absence. Almost how she pictured one of those scenes from the movies where the parents helped their college student pack up the car and waved goodbye while they left. Dan had been towering over her all of her life—and not just because of his tall stature. Despite their age gap, he was the big brother who took the time to play with her. Who watched over her when she got home from school.

His uniformed figure retreated down the sidewalk, and she fought the urge to call him back. Maybe she needed him more than she thought, after all. Hadn't she just shown she wasn't the best judge of character . . . *again?*

And here I am, considering trying to run my own business. I keep letting minor obstacles steal my security.

"Mommy, look!" Colby was groping for the monkey bars and Jen's heart dipped with worry. She crossed the space to his side in a flash and then helped him across. As he reached the last bar, he let go and slid into her waiting arms.

"I did it!" His babyish voice was filled with excitement, his innocent joy melting her heart. He didn't care whether she'd helped him or that he'd basically taken a trust fall in the end, which still had her palms feeling slick. He was still proud of his attempt.

Maybe that's how things are supposed to be with the people you can count on.

Colby's arms were tight around her neck as she set him on

the ground. She kissed his forehead and decided right there. "You know that building I was showing you when Uncle Dan showed up?"

"Yeah?"

"That's going to be Mommy's new bakery." She swiped a cookie crumb from his collar that she'd missed. "I still have to fix it up. But I'm going to have someone make it pretty and paint it. What color do you think it should be?"

Colby grinned. "Yellow!"

"That sounds good to me." She searched his eyes, knowing he couldn't possibly understand entirely what she meant. She didn't know if she would succeed, but she knew she wasn't alone, even if she'd never met another man again.

Or if she'd ever have another baby.

She didn't know if this bakery would work or how to manage childcare while running a business.

But all she could do was wrap her arms tight around the little boy who had been the best decision she'd made. And just keep moving forward.

CHAPTER THIRTY

CHRISTMAS EVE HAD NEVER BEEN Jason's favorite day of the year, but today it was particularly miserable. Pouring himself a glass of scotch, Jason studied the amber liquid, the musky, rich scent filling his nostrils. He sipped, his eyes roving the view from his high-rise.

The familiar buildings of Chicago blinked with the electric pulse of the city. When he'd first come back to Chicago from college, some of his friends had called him crazy—telling him he should try another city. New York, they said. Finance capital of the world.

But Chicago was home. Chicago, where he'd gone to baseball games with his father and Kevin as a kid. Where they'd gone boating on Lake Michigan every summer.

He squeezed his eyes shut, sipping his drink. It burned his throat.

Since he'd been home, he hadn't shaved once. Hadn't gone for a single run. Hadn't flipped on the television. He'd gotten a note slipped under his door that his mail was piling up in the mailbox. But he still hadn't gone to check it.

Nothing about this place felt like home.

Each time he closed his eyes, he was haunted by thoughts of the betrayal on Jen's face. Or worse still, thoughts of the good moments. The times she'd melted into his kisses. He missed her, and Colby, too. One night he'd visited Jen at the guest lodge, and Colby had woken up with night terrors, like Kevin.

Colby was undeniably Kevin's son, and not just because of night terrors and his looks. His obsession with trains, his quirky sense of humor. Even his laughter reminded him of Kevin.

He missed Kevin, too.

He'd considered finding a date for the evening, just so he wouldn't be the pathetic loser alone.

But maybe he deserved it. Deserved to be alone. He'd killed them all, hadn't he?

At Kevin's funeral, his grandfather had given him that sharp look like he was thinking it, too. Mom's broken heart. Kevin's depression. His father's accident.

All his goddamned fault.

He turned. He'd barely even moved in here. A decorator had arranged for some furniture, but most of his things were still in storage. He didn't even have a single photo of a family member here.

The picture he treasured the most—one of him, Kevin, and his parents—was still in his office at Cavanaugh Metals. The last picture they'd taken together.

He wanted it back.

If he couldn't have family, couldn't have anyone with him on damned Christmas of all nights, he was going to have his picture. The Powells may have taken everything else he had—but they couldn't take that.

He set his drink down, then grabbed his keys. He headed out of the apartment without bothering to grab a coat. He punched the button beside the elevator, nodding a hello to a neighbor in the hallway. Not that he knew it was a neighbor. He didn't know any of his neighbors.

What was it that TJ had said about Brandywood? It was a place where you wouldn't be alone? Something fruity like that. But that didn't make it wrong, either.

The drive to the corporate office for Cavanaugh Metals wasn't far—it was part of why he'd chosen his apartment when he separated from Amanda. Just a couple of train stops on the L. With it being Christmas, he pulled up in front, the street parking more open than ever.

Hopefully, they wouldn't have disconnected his badge. Then again, he didn't have to try it. The doorman saw him approach and opened it. "Mr. Jason! Haven't seen you around for a few weeks."

"I had some out-of-town business." He nodded toward the elevators. "Any chance you can swipe me up to the office? I just came for some papers, and I think I left my badge at home."

The doorman grinned. "Working even on Christmas, eh? Sure, no problem."

Although he'd spent most of his childhood coming through these doors, Jason's heart pounded as the doorman let him inside the office. Jason slipped toward his office. When he arrived, he noticed the door nameplate had been changed again. *Chad Duncan, CEO.*

Damn jackass.

Jason's key worked on the door, regardless. If they'd disconnected his badge, they probably wouldn't have thought they needed to change the lock.

Chad had made himself at home. Jason's things appeared to be shoved into a few paper boxes by the closet. He paused in front of the giant desk, tempted to piss in the chair. No matter how terrible his grandfather had been at times, Chad didn't deserve to be in his chair.

Jason's eyes fell on the quarterly report on the desk and he lifted it. He hadn't seen it come through the mail yet, but then again, he'd been gone and hadn't checked the mail.

Flipping it open, he stared at the numbers.

Then he frowned.

What the hell was this?

There was no way in hell they were posting profits like that. He'd run these numbers right before the last meeting with Chad and Bill Powell. These weren't even close.

Taking the report, he moved over to where they had apparently stashed his things. He lifted the lid and checked—the picture with his family was on top. He lifted both boxes, then edged his way out of the office.

Instead of going back to the main door, he headed for an intern's desk. The interns were the only ones who had computers he might successfully use to log in to the internal database. He knew the password they were issued—and the software for accounting was loaded onto their computers, even if they didn't have the passwords to get on.

Jason set his boxes down on the floor, then booted the computer. He logged on without a problem, then went into the applications. Opening the accounting software, a pop-up displayed instantly, asking for the username and password.

Would his old one work?

He tried it. An error message displayed. He tried once again, in case he had mistyped.

Still an error message.

Leaning back in his seat, he narrowed his gaze at the screen. Only a few people had credentials. Bill. Chad. Jason's assistant. The IT guy.

His grandfather.

His grandfather . . . had had the credentials.

What if they hadn't removed his information from the system yet?

Jason still remembered helping his grandfather set everything up. And his password. Typing in his grandfather's username and password, he hit enter.

And he was in.

Jason fist-pumped, then grinned. He clicked through into the panel he was looking for, checking the numbers.

Something was seriously off.

Time seemed to fly as Jason continued his search, printing and taking screenshots as he went. He doubted he'd have another chance to get into the system like this. The simple fact that he'd come on Christmas Eve when no one was here was a future circumstance that was rarely duplicated.

And who knew how long it would take the IT guy to see that his dead grandfather had logged on to the system when he returned after Christmas?

When he finished, Jason emailed himself the screenshots. He logged off and gathered a stack of papers from the printer. Then he grabbed his boxes and slipped back out.

AMANDA OPENED the door to her house, then did a double take at Jason as though shocked to see him. She crossed her arms. "Did you get lost?"

"Hilarious," Jason snapped, breezing past her. Being back in their house had a strange vibe to it. They'd bought this place together. But Amanda had liked it so much she hadn't wanted to leave. He stopped just past her in the foyer, then turned to face her. "I'm going to give you one chance to tell me the truth, and if you don't, I swear I will never trust a single thing you say again."

Amanda stared at him in confusion. "What the hell are you talking about?"

"That Chad's been fudging the numbers. He's inflating profits by overestimating the value of the product being sold to Duncan Motors but then selling the goods to Duncan at a discount. I'm sure it's to show a more optimistic forecast for the shareholders and keep the stocks from dropping. Now look at me and tell me the truth—did you know?"

The shock on her face looked genuine. "What? He wouldn't be that stupid, would he?"

Jason stared at her.

"How do you know?" she gasped.

Would she lie? She had every reason to. This could sink Powell Enterprises and Cavanaugh Metals. And Chad could face jail time, possibly even her father.

But she was the mother of his child now. Whatever he did with this information would affect not only Amanda but his son, too. It complicated things in a way that made him uncomfortable and unsure of how to proceed. He had no problem seeing Chad in jail. He had a major problem with his son's mother facing that situation.

The ethics of it all made him sick. How far would he be willing to go to protect Amanda if she was involved?

How far would he be willing to go to protect his son?

The only way to find out would be to offer Amanda a smidgeon of trust.

Jason handed her the quarterly report he'd found on Chad's desk, open to one page he'd circled. Amanda scanned it. She stared at it. When her hand lifted to her mouth, there was a quickness to it. "Hang on. I have to go throw up. I get really sick this time of day."

She dropped the report and rushed off to the powder room, gagging. She didn't close the door, and Jason stepped to the side, trying to give her privacy. Had they still been together, he would have gone after her, but a strange awkwardness settled over him. Navigating how to be around the mother of his child would probably present many more moments like this.

When she came back out, she looked shaky and pale. She dabbed a tissue to her lips and waved him over to the sitting room. Slipping her long legs to the side, she sank into a chair there. "I didn't know about the numbers, Jason. I can understand if you don't want to believe me, but it's the truth."

Could it be? He trusted her less than anyone else. And she had a lot to lose here. Jason followed her and sat beside her. The last time he'd been in this room, they'd been yelling so loudly at each other he'd worried the neighbors would hear. "I don't know exactly what our plans are, but we have to be honest—"

"I'm being honest." A weary look crossed her face. "I didn't even see the report yet."

If he believed her, and that still felt like a big *if*, it would be a major relief. Either way, she was going to have to lawyer up and expect other people to assume she was lying because of her relationship with Chad. Fortunately, her job was with Powell Enterprises and not so much with Cavanaugh Metals. Her excuses just might hold.

"What about your father?" Jason lifted the report. "There's no way he hasn't seen this and doesn't know."

"Agreed." Amanda shifted in her seat. "At least, that would be my assumption. You realize this will ruin him?"

"I know. And as much as I don't like your dad, I also wouldn't wish that on your family." *Not when they're going to be tied to me forever.*

Jason rubbed his eyes. He didn't want to deal with this, especially not on Christmas Eve. Most of the people he would even contact wouldn't be around right now. Then he gave her an odd look. The Powells always held a big Christmas Eve party. "You're not with your family tonight?"

She sighed. "Not feeling that great, to be honest. Besides which, my parents aren't thrilled that I've decided to have a baby right now. They say it's embarrassing to the family. I mean, I'll still show up at their place tomorrow morning. But I didn't want to schmooze with all their friends tonight."

"When my daughter came to tell me she was pregnant, I told her, 'Jen, that's my grandbaby, not bad news.'"

Her words were strikingly different from what Bob Klein had said about his response to Jen's pregnancy. Maybe it was why Amanda had sought him out. He'd never really seen her behave so vulnerable before. Without Chad or her parents, she probably needed the support.

His brow furrowed. Speaking of Bob Klein—he might be a good person to ask about what he'd discovered regarding Chad.

"I can't really keep this information to myself, Amanda. If your father knows about it—it'll mean serious consequences for him. This is accounting fraud. It's what took Enron down."

Amanda released a slow breath, then sighed. "I understand. But be careful, Jas. My father doesn't really hesitate to take revenge. And right now, he's got enough about you to torch your name. Starting with the fact that your mother's name wasn't Sutter."

Because of Ned Vickers. To be honest, he didn't really care what Bill Powell said about him. And if his mother's real identity was found out, so be it. Mom wouldn't suffer the consequences, and he doubted anyone could do anything to Mildred. *But Jen . . .* He turned toward her. "Did Ned give you everything he gathered from Brandywood?"

Amanda hesitated. Then she smoothed her hand over her abdomen. "No." She cleared her throat. "He still has most of it." She appeared divided in her loyalties between Jason and her father. It was a surprise, actually. Amanda had always put her family first. They both had.

She'd told him she changed. That she wanted love and a family. It didn't pardon her for having an affair with Chad, but it gave it context.

Context, he was learning, was everything.

Jason focused on the bare spot on the wall above the fireplace, where their wedding picture had once hung. She hadn't put something new there yet. Or if she had—maybe she'd taken it down when she broke up with Chad. "Did you really mean what you said about wanting to keep our relationship friendly? For the sake of our child?"

She sighed and nodded. "I mean it, Jason. You may not have been the one I picked to have a child with, but I'm not stupid enough to think that means you won't care about your son. Who knows? Maybe you'll even extend some of that family mercy to your son's mother."

He took her hand and squeezed it, for the first time feeling a twinge of guilt about the way he'd dressed her down whenever he'd spoken to her since the separation. They might never be friends, but they could be friendly, couldn't they? And if he was being a fool for trusting her, so be it. He'd spent enough of his life putting himself first. "I think I can manage that. But I'm begging you, I need to talk to Ned Vickers. And if you can, I need your help."

CHAPTER THIRTY-ONE

When he'd left Brandywood almost two weeks earlier, Jason hadn't ever expected to be driving back here so soon—especially not on Christmas. Yet here he was, turning off the highway exit onto the road that led to the small town.

He'd never gone back home the previous night. After he'd left Amanda's, he'd gone to his grandfather's house. Spent some time in the attic, poking around his mother's old things. Then he'd packed up his car with a few dust-covered crates he'd trekked down from the attic and driven through the night to get here. He'd stopped at a couple of rest stops to get some sleep when he felt too tired to continue, but he was mostly fueled on caffeine and adrenaline.

The streets and houses that had once seemed so foreign to him came into view. If he turned in about a mile, he'd only be a few turns away from the Kleins' house. At this time of morning, he imagined Jen opening Christmas presents with Colby.

As much as he wanted to text her, he wasn't here for that. And he wasn't going to disrupt her life.

But he was determined not to spend Christmas Day completely alone without family, either.

Within minutes, he'd pulled up in front of Mildred's dilapidated house. The split-level home wasn't ugly—just old and devoid of upkeep. Maybe he'd stretch his visit next time to address some issues. He didn't know a damned thing about home improvement, but Mildred didn't seem to like the suggestion that he'd hire people to help. He'd learned a long time ago that anything he wanted to learn to do, he could learn from watching videos online or reading—even if he didn't do it perfectly.

He popped the trunk and swung around to the back of his car. Grabbing the crates, he lifted them. The canvas sheet that covered them flapped in the cold breeze.

He made his way to the front of the house and rang the bell.

No one answered.

He rang it again and . . . still nothing. At last, he tried the doorknob. It opened. *Didn't Mildred lock the door?*

"Hello?" Jason's deep voice echoed against the large face of the wall over the steps that led to the lower level. He slipped inside, using his foot to edge the door closed. What if something had happened to her? She wasn't young, by any means, and she lived alone.

Setting the crates down by the top of the steps, he looked around. Not a single Christmas decoration.

"Mildred?" he called out.

At last, he heard a soft voice call, "Back here."

He moved down the hallway. At the end, on the right, a closed door led to the small master bedroom. Jason opened it. Mildred was sitting on the edge of her bed, zipping up a long blue robe. She gave him a surprised look. "What are you doing here?"

His relief at seeing her was greater than he'd expected. "Were you still asleep?"

She rubbed the sleep out of the inside corners of her eyes. "Yes, sir." Clearing her throat, she stood. "I wasn't expecting company."

Jason crossed his arms and leaned against the door frame. "I wasn't sure I'd find you here. Thought you might be at church or someone else's place for the holiday."

"Went to church last night." Mildred slipped her feet into slippers. "And I had a few invitations but . . . let's just say Christmas isn't my favorite holiday anymore. You ruined my plans to stay in bed all day." Despite her words, a pleased look shone in her eyes.

Jason's mouth turned up in a smile. He took a few steps into the room, then sat on the edge of the bed. "I aim to ruin things for you. There I was, sitting in my apartment like Ebenezer Scrooge, all alone and miserable, and I thought—now who can I share this misery with?"

She ducked her chin at him. "You came to the right place."

Even though they'd never had the type of relationship that included hugging, he gave in to the urge to slip his arms around her frail shoulders and pulled her in for a hug. "Merry Christmas, Gran."

She returned his hug. "I like the sound of that."

"Oh, the presents don't end there." Jason stood and held out his hand for her. "I have something else for you. Something I remembered last night while I was on my journey with ghosts of Christmases past."

"If you stretch the metaphor too far, it loses its impact." Mildred grinned at him. "But what do I know? I'm just a back-country old coot. Did I ever tell you I taught high school English for forty-six years?"

He blinked at her, clasping her hand. "No, you didn't. But I have a feeling we have a lot of catching up to do." He led her out of the bedroom, feeling more certain than before that he'd made the right decision to come down here.

Imagine if he hadn't? Mildred would have spent the whole day in bed, alone and lonely.

He guided her past the crates, then onto the worn paisley-patterned sofa in her living room. "One sec."

Jason left her there, then went back for the crates. Setting them down beside her, he knelt in front of them. He was practically at eye level with her this way. He pulled the canvas back. "I went to my grandfather's attic for these last night—I had a faint memory of my grandfather storing them there after Mom died."

The crates were filled with art canvases, neatly fitted inside.

Mildred eyed the canvases suspiciously. "What are these?"

Jason pulled one out, running his thumbs over the text of the dried oils. The smell of them brought him back to another era. Entering his mother's dark rooms, her silhouette against a window.

The sharp sting of turpentine, the paints smudged on her hands.

"After Dad died, Mom took to painting a lot. I never really knew what these were, but look." He pushed a stack of ten canvases into her hands.

Mildred's grip was shaky. She motioned toward the coffee table with her nose. "Hand me my reading glasses, will you?"

Jason fetched them for her and she unfolded them. Putting them on, she stared at the painting on top. *Main Street, Brandywood.*

Mildred put it beside her, then gazed at the next one. The backyard of Mildred's house—at least as it had probably looked thirty years earlier. In total silence, Mildred sorted through the ones he'd handed her. One by one, images of the world Martha had left behind came into view.

Mildred had been right—his mother was a talented artist. And her renditions of these places had been crafted with care and diligence. These were not places that appeared dark or unloved.

Jason took Mildred's hands. "It occurs to me you've spent the last fifteen years thinking that your daughter hated the world she left behind." The wrinkled fingers curled against his. "I don't think that's true, though. She was depressed, and her mental health suffered, but I think she thought about you a lot. Missed you. So she kept coming back home—in these paintings." Jason motioned toward the crates. "Mi—Gran. They're all of Brandywood. Every single one."

Mildred still didn't respond, but her eyes looked watery.

Had it been a mistake to do this? Jason felt the knot of worry tugging at his gut. "I don't know if I ever really apologized for turning you away when you came to her funeral, but I'm sorry. You deserved to be there. Deserved to say goodbye. And I didn't realize just how true that was until recently. I'm sorry I was such an ass for so long."

Mildred chuckled. "I suppose you get that on all sides, no? Maybe even from me." She reached out and touched his jaw gently. "But don't tell me you came all this way just to make an old woman cry on Christmas?"

He shook his head and gave her a smile. "I came to be with my family on Christmas." Then he moved the paintings and sat beside her again. "And maybe stay for a little while after that."

She slipped her arm into his and leaned against his bicep. "What about Cavanaugh Metals?"

"Chances are Cavanaugh Metals won't exist within a few weeks." Jason didn't want to think of the conversation he still needed to have with Bob Klein. But if anyone could figure out his next steps, a consultant for the FBI financial crimes department could.

Mildred gave him a wary look. "So if Colby is inheriting and the business goes under—won't you be in the poorhouse before long?"

Jason threw back his head and laughed. "Maybe so. You have a room I can rent? By now, I'm pretty sure I'm persona non grata around here."

Mildred puffed up her chest and sat straighter. "Do I have a room? You could have stayed with me for free this whole time if you had just asked, you know."

"After you shot at me? I think I'd have been sleeping with one eye open." Jason exchanged a laughing glance with her. He put his arm around her shoulders. "By the way, you're going to be a great-grandma. Again."

Mildred whooped with laughter. "Jason?"

He gave her a sheepish glance. "Yes?"

"You need to learn how to keep it in your pants, sonny."

JASON PACED through Mildred's living room. When he'd sent a text message to Bob Klein on Christmas Eve asking to speak to him, he hadn't expected Bob to respond on Christmas. Now he was on his way over here.

Did he think Jason was trying to intrude on the holiday? Cause a scene?

Probably.

Mildred was in the kitchen, making a last-minute Christmas dinner for the two of them. She'd sent Jason to the grocery store with a list, and he'd even found the small ham she'd asked for. Finding an open store meant going a few towns over to the nearest big-chain grocery store open on Christmas, though. Everything in Brandywood was closed.

The soft thud of a car door closing made Jason lift his chin. *That was fast.* Bob strolled up the front walk, wearing a Christmas sweater. Jason smirked. That didn't surprise him in the least. He went down the steps and opened the door as Bob approached.

Bob greeted him with a curt nod. "Merry Christmas." He held out his hand to shake Jason's.

Jason returned the handshake, inviting him in. "I appreciate you coming over. I honestly didn't expect you to respond so quickly. This could have waited another day."

"Eh. I'm in Betty's way, and the kids all went to some of their family's houses for lunch." Bob went up the stairs with a familiarity that made it clear he'd spent time at Mildred's house before. She was like family to them, after all. He popped his head into the kitchen at the top of the stairs. "Merry Christmas, Millie. Smells good in here. Sure we can't tempt you to come by for dinner?"

Mildred came over toward the doorway, wooden spoon in hand. "Not a chance." She gave Bob a kiss on the cheek. "Can't you see I got myself a handsome beau for the evening?" Her exaggerated wink toward Jason beamed with pride.

Bob chuckled, then followed Jason to the living room. He sat in an armchair across from the sofa. "Can I get you something to drink?" Jason offered.

Bob scrunched his nose. "No. Thank you, though." He clasped his hands together, then leaned forward. "What can I do for you? I must admit, it surprised me to hear you were back in town." His wary glance made it clear he was worried about Jen.

"I came to see my grandmother for Christmas." Checking back over his shoulder toward the kitchen, he lowered his voice a bit. "And, before I say anything else, I just want you to know that I have no intention of bothering Jen while I'm here. As it so happens, what I was hoping to speak to you about is something else entirely."

Jason pulled out a file folder where he'd placed the quarterly report, as well as screenshots he'd taken from the software. "I went into Cavanaugh Metals last night and I stumbled across a problem. Well . . . take a look." He handed the folder to Bob.

Bob slipped a pair of glasses out from the top pocket of his shirt under his sweater. Without a word, he scanned the documents. Jason cleared his throat. "The printouts"—he left his seat and squatted beside Bob—"those are directly from the accounting software we use. There's a system in place that logs each user any time a change is made."

Bob flipped through the papers silently. At last, he took a sharp breath in through his nose and closed the file. "You realize I can't be silent about this sort of thing."

Jason nodded. "That's why I came to you. I figured you might give me guidance as to what the next steps are."

"Someone is going to jail." Bob set the file on his lap. "I can contact my boss about it later tonight if you'd like. And more than likely, once this sort of thing comes out, shareholders will sell en masse." He looked directly at Jason. "Don't think about dumping anything beforehand, by the way. You don't need that sort of trouble."

"I know." Jason had already thought of that.

Bob lifted the file. "Mind if I take this with me? So I can go over it in more detail?"

"I made multiple copies." Some of the tension in Jason's shoulders dissipated. The matter was out of his hands now. "And what do you think the chances are of having to declare bankruptcy?"

"They're high." Bob's lips pressed to a tight line. "But

chances are more will come out about how long this has been going on. I know your grandfather had relinquished control of the company a while ago, but things like this rarely happen overnight."

Jason frowned. "Are you saying my grandfather knew about it?"

Bob shook his head. "I doubt it. His sense of morality might not align with my own, but I don't think he was a criminal." He cleared his throat. "Speaking of which, I should probably tell you something I told Jen. About how I met your grandfather."

He set the file on the small end table beside the armchair and began telling Jason of his trip to Chicago to find Kevin years before. Jason sat back on the sofa, listening without interruption. His grandfather had known about Colby?

Why hadn't his grandfather just said something? Or made it more clear in his will what he wanted if he knew the truth?

Then again, he and his grandfather had only sparred more and more as time went on. Would Jason have tried to put a stop to the inheritance question if he'd known about his grandfather's idea beforehand?

His grandfather would have thought so.

When at last Bob finished, he said, "I don't know what your true intentions with Jen are, but I will say that I've seen the light in her eyes dim since this whole thing with you. This has taken a toll on her in a way that's been hard for Betty and me to see. We didn't know how much she was struggling—and I don't mean financially—but in feeling alone." Bob cleared his throat. "Betty is sensitive to it because she was left in a similar position years ago. When I met her, she had two small boys and didn't think she'd ever marry again."

No wonder Dan and Warren looked nothing like him. They were his stepsons.

"I love Dan and Warren as though they were my own kids,

you know." Bob held Jason's gaze. "And someone loving Jen is important to us. Of course, it is. But she's not a one-person package. Whoever loves her needs to love Colby just as much, you understand? Not put Jen in a place where she feels like she can't trust."

He'd liked Jen's father before this, and the parallels made the hair on his arms rise. "I understand." Not that Jen would ever want to speak to him again. He glanced away from the intensity of Bob's gaze. "I didn't know much about any of this when I first came to Brandywood. And I was angry with my grandfather's decision. Angry with Kevin for what he'd done. But now, with Jen, I truly believe she and Colby deserve everything my grandfather left Colby. And I may have started out unsure what to make of her, but she spun my world upside down. I love your daughter. And if leaving her alone is the best for her, then that's what I'll do."

Bob searched his face, then nodded a few times. He stood, holding the file. "I'll be in touch about this."

Bob called out another warm wish for Mildred, then left. Jason closed the door behind him.

Time to move forward.

CHAPTER THIRTY-TWO

"Why haven't you gotten yourself ready to go to the flotilla?" Lindsay asked, sitting beside Jen in her parents' living room. The room appeared as though a tornado of toys had whirled through it—despite Jen's efforts to clean it up the past few days.

Jen glanced over at the light snowfall, still coming down. "You don't think they'll cancel?" The snow was supposed to be ending sometime soon, but the flotilla was scheduled to launch just past sundown when the boats in the lake could all light up with the Christmas lights their owners had used to decorate them. In the past day, the television producer had called Jen about ten times.

The producer hadn't been happy to hear that Jason wouldn't be there with Jen. The weather must be making her miserable. She'd promised to send word if there was a cancellation by noon and hadn't. The weather had worsened since then, though.

"Not a chance you can get out of it that easily." Lindsay scooted closer to the fire. "You would have heard by now if they were, but my dad said they were setting up propane heaters and making a few more firepits. My bet is that the food trucks will run out of hot chocolate and cider."

Colby came racing by then, one of Warren's kids following quickly behind. The two boys weaved their way through the messy living room, then started upstairs, yelling as they went. "Boys are so loud." Jen shook her head with a grimace.

"Girls are just as loud, believe me." Lindsay smirked. "Especially when they get to screaming. Then it's just a bunch of shrill shrieks that make you feel like you've lost part of your hearing."

Jen considered Lindsay's perspective, then scrunched her face up. "Fair point." She shifted under the throw blanket, stretching her legs. She didn't want to go anywhere, but she'd entered that damn baking competition, and if she'd won, it would change everything for her. But the idea of being there without Jason made her sad and nervous all at once. Especially because she didn't know what to say when they asked why he wasn't there. It was one thing to tell the producer that they'd split up. Quite another to tell the entire world. "Do you think I'll be disqualified because Jason isn't there?"

"I'm not sure. I mean, you did the contest as a couple. Tonight is just about seeing if you won, right?"

Except they hadn't really been a couple. Though it had almost felt like it at one point. She groaned. Lindsay was right. She should probably start getting ready. The boat launch was at five. It was already two, and the producer wanted her there at three thirty.

The doorbell rang, and Jen got up for it. A man, close to her own height, with a trim beard and longish brown hair, stood there and turned toward her with a wide smile. "Hi, I'm TJ." He held a box in his hands.

Jen frowned at him. "Can I help you?" He didn't look like a deliveryman. His clothes were . . . *unique*. Bright orange pants were matched with a teal blue plaid top poking out from under his coat. Instead of snow boots, he appeared to be wearing camo galoshes. Snow accumulated on his hat.

He held the box out toward her. "This is for you. Merry Christmas."

Jen took the box and then closed the door as he scooted away, leaving tracks in the snow on the front walk.

He stopped at the end of the walk, then turned back, cupping his hands around his mouth as though to speak.

Jen opened the door. "What is it?"

"He's in town." TJ shrugged, then stuffed his gloved hands into his pockets. "Just thought you might want to know." He gave a quick wave, then turned away.

Who?

Staring at TJ's fading form, she closed the door again, the snowy weather a stark contrast to the warmth of the living room.

She returned to her seat by the fireplace. The box wasn't a delivery package, or at least didn't appear to be. It wasn't taped shut, but the four flaps of the lid had been folded shut.

Lindsay gave her an odd look. "What is it?"

Jen scanned the outside of the box for some clues. Not even one mark on the cardboard. "I have no idea." She moved to open it.

Lindsay's hand shot out. "What if it's like a trick package? It could be poison or a bomb or something."

Shooting her a laughing gaze, Jen shook her head. "You watch way too much true crime TV."

"There's no such thing," Lindsay defended.

Jen opened the package under her protest. Several manila envelopes and a few thumb drives were inside. And on the top, a single sheet of paper, folded in two.

She opened the paper, her eyes skipping to the name at the bottom.

Jason.

Her heart gave a painful thump. She swallowed, turning away from Lindsay. Jason's handwriting was printed neatly with thick, bold, and masculine handwriting.

DEAR JEN,

There will never be a way for me to make up to you for what I did by not being honest about everything from the start. This is the truth:

I love you. I know it's crazy to think that you can fall in love with someone after a few weeks, and if you had asked me when we met if I thought it was possible, I would have laughed. But then I met you and you changed my whole world.

And I love Colby. He and Mildred are literally the only family I have left. When I look at him, I think of the Kevin I knew as a kid —and how much my brother missed with the decisions he made.

I can't give back to you what we lost with my dishonesty. I'm not asking for another chance because I know I don't deserve one. Turns out, I'm going to be a father, and that's made me realize, more than ever, that my actions don't exist in a vacuum. I earned the consequences here.

My ex mentioned to you she had footage of our time together. I didn't want you to ever worry about that coming to light, so I asked her to please allow me to purchase it from the PI her family hired. To make peace and move toward a better future as divorced co-parents, she's agreed. He's signed an agreement and turned everything over to me. This is all of it. There are no other copies. That's all in the envelope that's marked with a one.

And this may be stupid, but I included everything else he

had on me in the second envelope. All my secrets are there, everything I'm most ashamed of. Not that I really want you to see all my bad decisions. But you wanted to know who I am. So it's there, in your hands, if you ever wanted to know more about the man you spent two weeks with.

Those weeks were the best two weeks of my life. I don't know if this is all stupid, or if this will atone at all, but I'm sorry, Jen. I wish I could take it all back, but then I'd also have missed that time with you. And I will never regret the moments I spent with you and Colby.

If you ever need anything and feel like you can call on me, I'll be here.

Jason

AT SOME POINT IN READING, Jen had covered her mouth, her eyes misting at his words.

She handed the letter mutely to Lindsay, then pulled the first manila envelope out, holding it gingerly.

She didn't want to know what was in here. Didn't want to look.

At either envelope.

Before Lindsay could even finish reading the letter, Jen had pulled back the grate to the fire. She tossed both envelopes and the thumb drives into the fire.

Lindsay lifted her gaze sharply. "Are you sure you want to do that?"

Jen nodded. Both envelopes sat on top of the logs, smoke curling under them. Then a bright burst of flame caught them, filling the fireplace with a yellow glow. The flames licked higher, the envelopes consumed by fire and smoke.

Lindsay folded the letter and handed it to Jen. She stood

beside her, watching the envelopes burn. "You're a better person than I am. I would have been too curious not to look."

Jen shook her head. "I don't want to know." She looked down at Jason's letter, her heart feeling painful.

"Do you think he really loves you?" Lindsay whispered.

Jen wiped a tear from her cheek. She sucked her lips in, between her teeth, until they hurt. *Does he?*

Who knew? She shook the thought away, then looked back at Lindsay with a sniffle. "I'm getting ready to go to the boat. You want to come with us? It might be a good idea for us all to go in my dad's truck."

"Sounds good." Lindsay scanned her face with a worried expression.

Jen folded the letter again, then put it in the back pocket of her jeans. "I'm going to hop in the shower and do my hair and makeup. You know, for my ten seconds of fame. Can you keep an eye on Colby if he needs anything?"

She hurried up the stairs, leaving Lindsay in the living room. She headed straight to the bathroom and locked the door. Turning on the shower, she closed the lid to the toilet, then sat on it.

She stared at her hands.

Jason claimed to love her.

God, what she would have given to hear those words from him if things hadn't gone the way they had. The thought of him still made her want to scream and cry and stomp her feet and talk to him all at the same time.

Because the truth was, it wasn't hard for her to believe someone could fall in love quickly. A part of her loved him. There was no use denying that.

. . . maybe not just a part.

She was less angry now, though her hurt hadn't diminished.

But she loved him. Even though he was selfish and had lied

to her, she'd seen a side of him that told her there was so much more to him than that. Something had hurt him—maybe his ex-wife, but probably something before that, given that Kevin had struggled, too—wounded Jason so deeply that he guarded himself. Some of his behavior was an act.

Thanks to Kevin, she also knew that she couldn't heal that pain herself. Whatever had caused Jason to feel like he was "no good," he was going to have to make his peace with.

Yet love sometimes helped you want to be the best version of yourself, doesn't it?

. . . but he was going to be a father.

Jen's heart gave a little tug and she closed her eyes, feeling guilty as hell and awful.

He'd be bound to his ex-wife forever. And Chicago. What would that mean for him? Would he stay in Chicago permanently? The thought of never seeing him again made her ill, despite everything. She didn't want him to be anyone else's.

But how selfish and terrible was she for even thinking that?

She wanted someone who would fully and totally embrace being a dad to Colby, the way her father had stepped up for Warren and Dan. But Jason's son deserved to have his father's full attention, too.

The fact that she didn't want to share him told her she wasn't done with him. She didn't want him to move on without her.

She didn't want to move on without him.

He'd tried to be honest with her now, even if it was too little too late. Or maybe too much, too late. She didn't need to know all his secrets, after all. She'd be mortified if he ever found out all her secrets.

And TJ said Jason is in town.

Before she could overthink it, she whipped her cell phone

out. Steam fogged the bathroom, and she wiped the screen, unlocking it. She dialed Jason's phone number.

The call went straight to voice mail. As his pre-recorded voice came onto the line, she closed her eyes, tempted to hang up.

The line beeped. "Jason, it's Jen. I got the package you sent and . . ." She hesitated. "I want you to know I burned the whole thing. I appreciate you trying to be honest, and I appreciate you getting rid of anything that might embarrass me in the future. I'm not sure I needed all the stuff about you—and I didn't look at it."

She kicked off her slippers, sweating in the foggy, damp bathroom.

"If you—" She rose, the steam billowing so thick she could hardly breathe. "If you really meant it, I'm going to be on a boat tonight at the lake for the announcement of the baking competition. It'd be nice if you could be there with me. Call is at three thirty, and the launch is at five. Please come."

THE FESTIVAL AREA for the townspeople watching the flotilla from the shores of the lake was thronged with people, despite the snowy weather and it being an hour and a half before the launch. Jen's hand tightened around Colby's as she followed her parents, who carried sports chairs over their shoulders. Lindsay had a stack of blankets under her arm. "Do you think Colby will be warm enough?" Jen asked her mom.

Her mother gave her a smile. "I think he won't even notice it's cold outside between the hot chocolate, the firepits, the lighted boats, and the fireworks."

Her parents found the firepit where Warren and Alice and Dan had set up their chairs and held space for them. Peter had arranged for two big screens to be positioned near the front, where the crowd could watch his Christmas special and see the announcement of the baking competition.

Jen cringed. She hadn't given too much thought to being on screen during the competition—hiding behind a workstation and her apron had made it easier to forget. Plus, Jason had been there with her.

She scanned the nearby crowd, looking for him. She hadn't gotten a phone call or text back from him. It felt as though more than Brandywood had come out for this, and she wouldn't be surprised if they had attracted people from the tristate. The line of cars to get into the lake area had been ridiculous. Thank God Lindsay had encouraged her to leave early. She never would have made it.

No sign of Jason.

Her heart felt heavy. She shouldn't have asked him to be there. Taking that chance just gave him one more opportunity to disappoint her.

Not too far from them, Bunny and Millie were gathered near a group of their church friends. Millie was in the middle of animated conversation. Wouldn't Jason have come with her?

Jen took a breath. Maybe she knew if Jason was coming.

She left Colby playing with his cousins in the snow and crossed the space toward Millie. Millie broke into a wide smile when she saw Jen, then left her friend. "Jen, sweetheart!" She gave her a tight hug. "We all have bets on you, you know. That sugar cookie house was a good one, but you were brilliant."

Right. She was here to see about the baking competition.

Funny how that seemed so unimportant.

"Millie, I hear Jason's in town."

Millie nodded, wrinkling her nose. "Sure is. He came to surprise me on Christmas. I've been busy fattening him up."

Was he staying with Millie, then? She couldn't imagine Jason there. "Do you know if he's coming tonight?"

Millie's pleasant expression sobered. Then she gripped Jen's forearm tightly. "Here, sweetheart? No, Jason won't come near here tonight. Not a chance."

"Oh, I just thought . . ." Jen stared at the plain gold wedding band Millie still wore on her ring finger. "I asked him to."

Millie stroked her cheek. "Did Jason ever tell you about the accident?"

Accident?

"His daddy drowned in a lake."

CHAPTER THIRTY-THREE

Twenty years earlier

THE TASTE *of barbecue chips clung to Jason's lips as he sat on the pier, feet swinging off the side.*

The waters of Lake Michigan stretched in front of him, glistening in the sun. They'd been up since four o'clock, when Jason and Kevin had snuck into their parents' bedroom. "This is the best time to go fishing." They'd wheedled and whined—until their dad had promised them that if they didn't wake up their mother, he'd take them.

But they hadn't caught anything.

Four hours of sitting there and nothing. At least the July temperatures hadn't made it so bad. And their dad had let them stop at McDonald's for breakfast.

Dad wound the fishing line up, tying it off as Kevin climbed the rails of the pier. "Jason, I'm going to go pack up the car with this stuff here." He pointed at some of the gear and chairs they'd brought. "Keep an eye on your brother until I get back, and then you boys can help me carry the rest."

Dad was barely out of view when Kevin hopped up on the top of the rails. "Watch my balance," Kevin said, grinning with two big front teeth that didn't match the rest of his mouth.

"Get down. Dad doesn't like you climbing up there." Jason stood, frowning down at the churning waters below.

"You're a sissy." Kevin laughed, then stuck his arms out wide. "I won't fall. You're just afraid to do it."

"I'm not afraid." Jason puffed out indignantly.

"Fine, then you just can't do it." Kevin continued his balance beam act, walking the length of the rail until he reached the corner.

Jason rolled his eyes, then climbed up onto the rails. He put one foot securely on the top plank, then the other and stood straight. "I've been climbing since before you were born."

Kevin lifted his leg. "Okay, then let's see who can stand here longest on one foot."

Before Jason could respond, Kevin wobbled. He tried to put his leg down but missed, his foot catching the air behind him.

Jason watched in horror as Kevin's face froze in shock. Then he plunged off the side of the pier, legs and arms flailing, into the deep waters below.

The yell that ripped from Jason's throat sounded as though it had come from somewhere else. Had Kevin yelled, too? Jason took one step forward, his palms sweating, hands aching. He jumped off the rails, then squatted, looking for Kevin's head to come up. Circles rippled in the water where Kevin had dropped.

Jason didn't see him. "Kevin!"

He looked back toward the parking lot. It was too far away for his father to have seen. And the other people on the pier were several feet away. When Kevin still didn't turn up, Jason jumped, feet first.

The fall was faster than he expected. He plunged into the cold water, bubbles around his eyes and nose and face, the water dark. His arms immediately went into action, clawing toward the surface until he broke free and gulped a deep breath.

Where was Kevin? "Kevin!" He called his name repeatedly. Where had he gone? Swimming out farther, he looked back toward the pier. Then he saw him. Kevin was climbing out onto the rocks near the base of the pier. He waved toward Jason.

The relief that filled Jason made his arms and legs shake. Kevin was safe. He wasn't dead.

Jason started the swim back when something brushed his leg. He shivered, then went the long way around the pier instead of the dark water under it. The more he swam, though, the more he didn't feel as though he was going anywhere. The water seemed to tug him along, pulling him in the direction it wanted rather than where he wanted to go.

Jason pushed harder. Panic slid up his body, his arms and legs exhausted from the struggle. He couldn't get out.

A wave crashed over his head, and his head went under.

The waves broke over his head, and he was kicking, kicking, exhausted. Water filled his nose, and he felt himself being pulled by the currents. Powerless to get out of them.

As exhaustion increased, so did his fear. Water filled his nose, choking him, stinging his throat.

Then powerful arms locked around him.

Dad's voice was in his ear. "Hang on tight, Jason. I'll carry you."

Dad swam, but they kept getting pulled out, farther and farther. Still, Jason clung to his neck, his body shaking, his muscles relaxing in the strength of his father. He was no longer alone.

Another wave nearly ripped them apart. "Dad!"

The water felt choppier, the current faster. "We're going to do this together, okay?" Dad said, breathing hard. They couldn't tread water, couldn't stay still. The more they lost themselves to the current, the farther it pulled them out.

Jason sucked in a breath as his father pulled him away from his neck, taking his hand instead. "Swim that way!" His father pointed. "Hard as you can now, Jason. I'm right beside you. You just keep going without stopping. I'll be right here the whole time. Next to you."

Jason gritted his teeth, water in his mouth, stinging his nose. He coughed, then sucked down a deep breath. They swam forward. Occasionally, Dad grabbed the back of his shirt, pulling him forward. Then Dad gave one last big shove, and Jason felt the grip of the current loosen around his legs and torso.

He flung his body forward, weeping and sputtering, kicking and breathing until his hands hit the rocks.

A small crowd had gathered and a man pulled him out, hooking his arms under Jason's armpits. Jason turned, scanning the water for his dad.

"Dad!" He lunged toward the water, but several sets of hands held him back.

"Let me go. I have to get my dad!" He searched the churning water. "Let me go, let me go! Dad's still there. He was right next to me. Right beside me."

But he was alone.

JASON RAKED his fingers through his hair, then pounded the steering wheel with the fleshy part of his palm. He was late. He couldn't remember the last time he'd been late anywhere, and the feeling was suffocating.

And this might be the most important thing he'd ever tried to be there for.

Damn cell phone reception at Mildred's house meant he hadn't gotten Jen's voice mail message until he'd taken a break from work and gone into town in search of a sandwich since he'd skipped lunch. By then, it was already past four thirty, and he'd turned the car and driven straight here.

Jason resisted the urge to stop staring at the clock on his dash, his eyes flicking back to the parking lot. There wasn't a single spot available. And the half mile up to the parking lot was equally crowded, lined with parked cars on each side.

The boats—he shuddered—were going to leave without him.

He saw a sign for the boat launch and drove toward it. Maybe if he left his car near there, he could just worry about the fine later.

He drove straight to the launch, pulling his car to the side. A group of people near the launch gave him strange looks. He jumped out of the car, leaving his phone and keys inside it. He'd tried calling Jen about twenty times. Now that he was here, he realized why. No service.

Some things in Brandywood he wasn't going to get used to, that was for sure.

He ran onto the launch. "Has Peter Yardley's boat gone?" he asked a passerby, who stared at him as though he was a maniac.

Maybe he was a maniac.

He didn't have a coat, for starters. He'd left it in Chicago. And the only clothes he had were old things that Mildred had dug up from her attic that had belonged to her husband, his grandfather, John. His grandfather had been close enough in size and stature that Jason hadn't rushed out to buy clothes.

"All the boats are gone," the man answered, then pointed out to the water to the right. "But they're not far."

Jason took off running alongside the water's edge. What

was he hoping to do exactly? Wave them down? Have them turn around and come back for him?

The colored twinkle lights from the boat blurred in his vision. The cold air filled his lungs, and he dodged people by the water's edge, not paying attention to the stir he was causing.

He had to get out on that boat.

If Jen was out there, he wanted to be with her.

The thought was singular in his mind, pulsing with an urgent beat as he ran out of shoreline to run along. He stopped, watching the boat gliding into the water.

The gentle lapping of the lake brought terror to his heart.

She was out there, slipping farther away.

Peeling his shoes and socks off, his heart continued pounding in his chest.

He hesitated, his bare feet aching in the icy mixture of snow and mud by the water.

He couldn't let her down again. Couldn't let her think he'd failed one more time.

Jen can't save you. Mildred's voice rang through his mind. *You're the last man standing. And you don't think you deserve to be.*

What did he deserve? He'd spent so long thinking he deserved nothing, deserved to be dead instead of his father—the words that his grandfather had put in his head that awful summer day at Dad's funeral.

But his dad had died for him. He'd given up everything so that Jason could be here right now.

And what had he done with that gift?

He'd spent the last twenty years letting himself become hard, selfish, and focused on making himself feel happy, even at the expense of others. He'd been bitter, angry that he hadn't saved Kevin. Angry that his son-of-a-bitch grandfather would take Cavanaugh Metals from him because he blamed Jason for

Dad's death. Angry that Mom hadn't had the strength to be there for them.

Angry at being alone.

But he wasn't the last man standing. There was Colby. And his future child. Cavanaugh Metals had failed anyway, outside of his control. His grandfather had done that—not him.

He was done squandering his father's gift. Even if it took the rest of his life, Jason was going to spend it like he was worthy of the sacrifice Dad had made. Mildred had taught him he could be someone different than he'd believed. That all wasn't lost with the people who deserved his love.

And maybe if he could be worthy of Jen, be the man she deserved, he could start toward a different future—one he longed for more than anything he'd ever known.

He ran out into the water to audible gasps behind him. People had been watching him, and now if they'd wondered if he had lost it, he'd just confirmed it.

I probably have lost it. I'm just not going to lose her if I can help it.

The water was so cold, he clenched his jaw. His entire body broke into a single sheet of gooseflesh. The pins and needles on his skin felt like knives poking in from all sides.

He was about to dive under when he felt arms wrap around his waist.

"Jason, stop!"

He swung around. Jen was in the water, holding him back. He trembled, then pulled her up and out. He wrapped her legs around him and buried his face in her shoulder. Cheers of applause broke out on the shore. The tears in his eyes were from an equal mixture of freezing pain from the icy waters and his relief at seeing her. His teeth chattered as he asked, "What are you doing here?"

"I didn't get on the boat." She wrapped her arms around his

neck tightly. "Not once Millie told me about why you hate water. I'd never have asked if I had known. I think I love you, Jason Cavanaugh. I would never do that to you."

Jason pulled his face back, scanning her eyes.

He could barely think with the cold.

She said she loves you.

He dropped a kiss on her mouth. As she kissed him back, Jason's legs started to go numb, his body shaking in response to the cold. She laughed, then pulled away. "Should we go to the shore?"

He nodded, and the ice that had been strangling his heart for so many years melted away at last. "I'll carry you."

CHAPTER THIRTY-FOUR

THE SECOND JEN's feet hit dry land, the surrounding crowd broke out in more raucous applause, the people of Brandywood hooting and hollering. Dan approached with blankets for them, and Jen looked away from Jason's shoulder toward the bank of the lake. One member of the camera crew was still on shore, his camera trained on them. Her eyes flitted to the big screens. She and Jason were in focus on them.

They'd captured that on camera?

She glanced at the microphone still strapped to her sweater. It was live!

Oh my God. When she had talked to Peter and explained why she wouldn't get on the boat at the last minute, she'd never expected this. She hadn't even known if Jason would show up. Then she'd seen him wading into that lake . . . she gave him a sidelong glance. What type of crazy person jumped into a mountain lake at the end of December?

She shook with cold, her jeans freezing her. Thank goodness she'd followed Jason's lead and taken her shoes off.

Dan wrapped the blankets around them both, and the view

from Peter's boat split the screen. Peter's face came into view. "Well, folks!" Peter said a big grin on his face. His voice boomed from the speakers set up near the screens. "I don't think I could have made this more exciting if I tried. Nothing like a little trouble in paradise to bring that drama, huh, folks? As for the winners of the Brandywood Baking Competition sponsored by *This Charmed Life* and Happy Home Channel, I think these two lovebirds have already won, don't you agree? But sadly, Miss Jen Klein came to me earlier this afternoon and requested to withdraw from the competition."

A collective murmur of shock and disapproval broke out from the crowd. Someone near them booed loudly, and a quick glance revealed Millie Price standing with her group of girlfriends, hands cupped around her mouth. Jen's face warmed.

The camera panned over their stunned expressions for a few more seconds, then cut back to Peter's show on the boat. "Why did you withdraw?" Jason asked in a low tone, his teeth chattering.

"One of us had to be on the boat to win," Jen explained, still aware her voice was being picked up by the mic. "When I couldn't get in touch with you to tell you not to worry about coming out here, I realized I'd rather risk the prize money than ever make you think I'd ask something like that of you."

The screen showed Peter beaming at the camera. "And that's among the many reasons Jen Klein deserves to win this show—because let's be honest, folks, she carried that team with baking."

The crowd laughed.

Peter lifted his hands to ask for silence and then said, "So I've decided to reject her forfeit. And I have it on good authority that if you want any of the delicious treats she made for the show, you'll have to go no farther than Main Street in

Brandywood because she's opening her own bakery next year! Jen, when do you start taking orders?"

Jen stared at the screen, blinking with shock.

She'd won.

$25,000.

. . . and . . . what?

"We'll keep you up to date, Peter," Jason said smoothly, answering the question for her.

"Ladies and gentlemen, the winners of the baking competition . . . Jen and Jason!" Peter's voice rang out.

Jen covered her mouth. As the crowd cheered and music played, Jen turned to Jason, who shivered beside her, his arms still tight around her waist. "I won?" Her voice shook. "Oh my God, I'm freezing. I can't feel my legs."

Jason kissed her once again, and the cheers grew louder.

This all felt so surreal. Like someone else's life.

But she'd earned the prize, hadn't she?

And Peter had just told everyone about her bakery.

Jen pulled away from Jason, setting her cheek on his chest, her excitement making her want to jump, but the cold she felt made her knees wobble. Despite the cold, Jason held her steadily.

Jason was *here*. He'd come down here anyway and jumped like a crazy man into that lake, even though he was afraid of water.

That spoke volumes. As the show on Peter's boat continued, the camera guy came over and put his camera down. "Here, I can take the mic off you now." He looked sheepish. "I'll have to put it back on you later when we interview you. Just meet us back here at seven."

He reached into the blanket, then lifted the back of her sweater and pulled the battery pack off, then unclipped the cord. He gave them a nod, then left them there.

Jason pulled her closer. "Thank God I didn't say anything about what I'm going to do to you as soon as I get you alone," he teased. "Though it might be a while. My balls have retreated into my stomach."

She laughed, her face warming, and checked to make sure Dan had stepped far enough away that he couldn't hear. "If you don't mind driving me back home real fast, we can go get out of these wet clothes and then come back."

They stooped to put their shoes on. Leaving Jason with the blanket, she went over to Dan. "I think we're going to go back to the house and change."

Dan shook his head. "You're both nuts, you realize that?"

"You're not going to kill him, right?" Jen gave him a laughing look, despite her worry. Dan and Warren had a way of holding on to grudges that sometimes got the worst of them.

Dan lifted his gaze over Jen toward Jason. He raised his chin. "No. We had a friendly talk once. I made it clear the way you deserve to be treated."

Jason came up behind her. "And I completely agree with you. But if I don't get into some new pants, there's a good chance you'll have to take me to the hospital for hypothermia instead."

"We'll get that city boy trained up real good soon." Dan winked at her, hesitating as he started to turn away. He smiled. "Congrats on the win, little sis. We all knew you had it in you. I'm gonna go help Mom and Dad with Colby. Make sure they don't let him have too much sugar."

Releasing Jason, Jen took a few steps toward her brother and hugged him. "Love you, big brother. You really are the best uncle in the world. And Colby's lucky to have you."

Dan squeezed her wordlessly and ducked his chin. He didn't have to say anything for her to know how much the words meant to him.

As she went back to Jason, he lifted a brow. "What about me? I get no best uncle credit?"

Jen scrunched her nose. "You know, when you put it that way, it makes it sort of weird." Then she laughed, interlacing her fingers with his. "Should we go?"

"The faster, the better."

They hurried through the crowd, and Jen's legs ached from the cold. Moving helped, but she could only imagine how uncomfortable Jason must be. As they approached the boat launch, they saw a few men hanging around Jason's car. She gave him a wide-eyed look. "Did you leave your car on the launch?"

"We already called the tow truck," one man said, standing in front of the driver's side door.

"Man, you people are tow-happy in this town," Jason muttered.

"How do you think we fund all the parades?" Jen quipped and then gave the man a pleading look. "Please. I know he wasn't supposed to park here, but can you let it slide for now?"

"Yeah, yeah," the man said, shaking his head. Then he sighed. "I guess. But this isn't a parking spot, you hear? How are the boats supposed to get out of the water if someone just leaves their car sitting here?"

Jason thanked them, and they hurried into his car. Jen loosened her snow boots as she sat, legs still out, then removed them. "There's mud caked on the bottoms of my shoes," she said, holding them up as she put her feet into the car and closed the door.

Leaning over, Jason took the shoes from her and set them on the floor in the back of the car. "It doesn't matter. If I'm moving to Brandywood, I don't know how practical this car will be. I almost skidded off the road ten times while racing over here."

Moving to Brandywood?

She gaped at him, her jaw dropping. "What do you mean moving?"

"Uh, long story. But it's what I was dealing with when I got your phone call."

"I have time to hear the story now." She crossed her arms. "And is that why you were late?"

He backed the car away from the launch, then began the slow trek through the snowy parking lot. "I didn't get your message until like four thirty. It's been a really long day of phone calls. I found out over Christmas that some illegal activity's been going on in my family's company, and I spent a good portion of the day talking to the FBI and the board of Cavanaugh Metals. The CEO has been fired, and they hired me as a liaison as we file for bankruptcy."

"Wait, what?" Jen's eyes widened. He'd never talked about this part of his life with her. "I'm not sure I'm following."

Jason glanced over at her, the dimple in his cheek showing as the corner of his lips turned up in a smile. "I'll try to see if I can summarize, but it's all a shit show." He cleared his throat, his eyes returning to the road. "A few years ago, my grandfather sold over half the company to a larger company called Powell Enterprises. Against my advice. My grandfather retired as CEO, and a man named Bill Powell became president of the company and then hired another man, Chad Duncan, heir to Duncan Motors, as CEO."

"You don't have to go that much in detail." She got the feeling Jason wasn't the best at putting things in simple terms.

Jason drew a sharp breath and then said quickly, "Okay so, Powell and Duncan arranged with Duncan to sell steel to Duncan Motors for a lower value than it was worth. But Cavanaugh Metal's profit statements didn't reflect that. They fudged the numbers so it looked as though Duncan paid the appropriate price to inflate revenues and not alarm shareholders. A year ago, there was also a lawsuit that factors into the why of it all, but that's probably more detail than necessary."

Jen studied his profile. "Are you okay, though? What does it mean for you? You should talk to my dad. He might help you." Given the seriousness of his words, he seemed calm.

"I'll be fine. Cavanaugh Metals won't. At least, it's not likely they'll survive. But I have some thoughts on that. And I did, actually. That was part of the reason I came back to Brandywood."

He'd talked to her father? "How long have you been back in town?" The weeks without him had felt unusually long. So much had happened since then.

"Just a few days. Since Christmas. I'm probably going back to Chicago again soon, but I plan on selling my place and buying something over here. In fact, there are a whole lot of buildings around here, especially on the outskirts of town, that look like they could use an investor. Who knows. I might even salvage some portion of Cavanaugh Metals and make a smaller, leaner workforce down here. And if not, I think I'm ready to move on from that business. With Peter Yardley bringing this town to national attention, I might be right on time to get in here before everyone else does."

She didn't doubt he'd be successful wherever he went. He was smart and charming when he wanted to be.

But that he wanted to come here made her heart melt. "Just to be clear. You're planning to buy here because of me, too, right? For Colby and me? Not just for the wonderful investment opportunities?"

He looked across at her and she saw love in his eyes. "Yes, Jen. The time away from you both was the worst kind of torture. I love you. I love you both. You and Colby *are* my home."

Relief. That's what I feel beyond anything else right now.

Still, one last thing worried her. "What about your ex-wife and the baby?" She didn't want to admit that it was hard to think about that, but it was. Her heart gave a sad dip. "I love you, Jason. But I could never ask you to be away from your baby."

"Turns out, I'm not the only one who found something to like in Brandywood." Jason sighed. "When Amanda came here a few weeks ago, she really fell in love with the town. And her family was already giving her hell about having a baby on her own. Her father is Bill Powell."

Jen arched a brow. "The shady guy involved in your grandfather's company?"

"The one and the same. And with the news breaking about his involvement with the Cavanaugh Metals scandal, it's been a media circus for Amanda's family. Amanda doesn't want the stress of it all to affect her pregnancy, so she's decided to move to the area to ride out the storm. She's planning on coming down to hunt for a place after Christmas. So at least for the time being, she and the baby will be close by."

His ex-wife was moving here, too?

Jen couldn't picture that. Or how that would work. "And you all are—"

"Completely and totally done. We signed the divorce paperwork while I was back in town. The whole thing should have been a lot faster, but she got a bit carried away with the inheritance question and sending a PI after me."

Celebrating his divorce seemed strange, but she couldn't help the relief his words brought her. "You swear it?"

Jason chuckled. "I swear. And I'm going to do my best to never lie to you about anything again if it helps. By omission or not. In fact, you'll be so sick of hearing the truth from me you're going to probably wish I would lie to you. Fortunately, you're a superb cook so you never have to hear me tell you how much I don't like something you made."

"Um, you can fib to spare my feelings about food. You're also welcome to use the phrase 'you're absolutely beautiful' to any question I have about my appearance in any circumstance. Like when I was pregnant with Colby, I had serious cankles—"

"But you *are* absolutely beautiful in every circumstance." As they exited the lake area, Jason pulled over to the side of the road. He shifted into neutral and pulled up the parking brake. "Don't mind me. I'm going to take off my pants."

She laughed as he wiggled out of his soaked corduroys. Then it didn't seem like a half-bad idea, and she joined him, taking off her own pants. "When they pull us over for fleeing from a tow truck, they can drag us pants-less into jail." Her thighs were ice cold, her skin feeling unnatural. She reached over and playfully flicked his bare thigh. "If you hurry, I can guarantee a steamy shower will be waiting for us."

Jason unlatched her seat belt, then pulled her onto his lap so that she was straddling him. His eyes settled on her lips, then he dipped his mouth to hers. *God, she'd missed this.* The taste of him, the way their mouths fitted together so perfectly, how quickly he made her melt into a puddle that just wanted more of him. He groaned, then pushed her back. "You know, I'm fully committed to continuing our visits of all the best side-of-the-road locations for hot car sex. But first, I want to make sure I'm not dreaming and heard you say you love me back in that lake. Because it was freezing. And I'm not sure my brain didn't stop working."

His words made her own desire for him lurch, and her heart ache for him. Whatever tough exterior he'd shown, asking her to tell him she loved him showed a vulnerable side. He craved to hear it just as much as she'd needed it. Her lips curved over his, delicately, intimately, so featherlight tingles rushed up her arms. "I love you, Jason Cavanaugh. I love you . . ." She kissed his forehead. "I love you . . ." She kissed both of his closed eyelids. "And I don't know that I can stop loving you."

His warm breath mixed with hers as they kissed again. "Dammit, woman, I'm serious about not being able to restrain myself." His eyes glinted as he shifted his hips so she was pressed against his hardened length. "Although it feels like you want me, too."

She smiled, her lips brushing his jaw and neck. "Did you ever stop to think that the fact that my underwear is wet might be because your boxers were just in a lake, and I'm sitting against you?"

He gave her a mischievous grin, then pushed himself past the fabric of her underwear and between her legs. As he slid against her wetness and inside her, she let out an electrified moan, sinking her mouth onto his collarbone. "You want to stick with that story?"

She shook her head, kissing his jaw. Lifting her face, she met his eyes and shook her head slowly. "Welcome home."

EPILOGUE

Jen covered Jason's eyes. "Keep them closed. I'm serious." She positioned him near the door of the bakery.

She'd closed it for the day, even though it was so close to Christmas. Baked goods could wait. This couldn't.

While she'd stuffed the bakery with balloons, Amanda had done her the favor of watching Colby. After the birth of Blake, Amanda had been a lot like a deer in headlights, unsure of how to do anything. Jen wasn't sure Amanda had ever even been around children before. Unlike Jen, who'd spent most of her teenage years babysitting, Amanda had never even changed a diaper.

But like so many things the past year, Amanda had surprised Jen. She'd adjusted to life in Brandywood beautifully and been humble enough to ask for help, and not just from Jen. Mom had helped Amanda a lot, too. Her parents blended families in a way that made Jen proud and had treated Blake's birth like the birth of a grandson. After all, he was Jen's stepson now.

Amanda and Blake would even be at the surprise party

tonight. She'd gone from here to Bunny's, where Jen's parents and family were setting up.

But Bunny's could wait. This moment with Colby was something Jen had been dreaming about since she'd set eyes on her baby boy. She pushed Jason into the bakery, then flipped on the main light.

Jen winked at Colby, who stood on the counter of the bakery, and released Jason's eyes. "Surprise!"

Jason did a double take. His eyes flitted from the white and blue balloons to the streamers, to Colby, who held up the sign Jen had given him proudly, a big smile on his face.

I Love You, DADDY!

Jason took an almost involuntary step forward, his jaw dropping open, and looked back at Jen. His eyes looked red-rimmed. "Does this mean . . .?"

Jen's hand came up to her throat, her own eyes filling with tears. She nodded. "The paperwork all went through. He's Colby Cavanaugh now."

Jason leaned over and pressed a swoon-worthy kiss to her lips before releasing her and flying over to Colby. He swung him up into his arms. Jen couldn't hold the tears back, and she ran toward them, catching them in a hug.

After a year of Jason having to do battle in the courts, first with the Cavanaugh Metals trial and bankruptcy, then with Colby's inheritance issue, where they'd managed to get Jason named as the trustee, then the sale of his grandfather's mansion—this was the first time all year that news from the courts wasn't something that had taken a battle.

Not that the entire year had been tough. With Jason and her father's help, Jen had secured a loan and spent all spring getting the bakery ready. And thanks to Peter Yardley's endorsement, her website had crashed from orders the day it went live.

Then on a warm summer's day shortly after the bakery had opened, Jason had proposed to her at Redding's Bluff. They'd married in October, and TJ had been Jason's best man, which was fitting because he'd become his best friend, too.

"Two kids in one year," Jen teased Jason as he set Colby down. Colby played with the balloons like Jen had promised he could do as soon as Jason came in.

"What can I say? Domestic life suits me." Jason reached for her hand, interlacing his fingers with hers. "I'm married to the hottest baker in town and proud owner of two rug rats. All I need now is a dog and a white picket fence."

"We have both of those." They'd just moved into their new house, just a stone's throw from Millie Price. She even helped Colby get to preschool a couple of times a week, though Jason had been forced to tell his grandmother that her flipping off other parents in the parking lot had put them on the receiving end of a stern email. Thankfully, she'd reined it in after that.

"Then I don't need anything at all. Turns out I have it all." Jason kissed the back of her hand.

Jen wiped her cheeks and slipped her arm around Jason's waist. "The fun's not over yet. I wanted this moment to be just for us, but everyone else is waiting for us over at Bunny's. Including Amanda and Blake."

Jason pulled her in close and kissed her again. He lowered his lips to her ear. "Sure we don't have time to sneak away for a few minutes first? I hear there are some excellent spots around Brandywood for a quickie." He pinched her ass.

Jen swatted him away, although he'd already turned her knees to Jell-O. "Oh, we'll definitely have our own celebration tonight."

She let out a contented sigh, kicking away a balloon that Colby punted toward them.

Almost four and a half years earlier, she'd walked the

streets of Brandywood, wondering how Kevin's leaving would ever be anything other than a black hole in her heart. Sometimes she still wondered how things would have turned out if Kevin had stayed.

She'd never have believed his leaving would end up like this—with Jason in her life, her future bright. Kevin may not have intended to, but he'd saved both Jason and her in the end.

The door to the bakery swung open, bells clamoring, and they looked up in surprise as Millie rushed in. She wore a wide grin, a camera that looked ancient in her hands. "I know you wanted a few moments alone, but I'm an old lady who needs a picture."

Jason rolled his eyes, his smile making it clear that her antics didn't bother or faze him in the slightest anymore. "All right, Gran."

"Right over there." Millie directed toward one long wall filled with local artwork. Framed neatly in the center of it all were the pictures Jason's mother had painted. She'd brought them framed like that to Jen while the drywall was going up, and it had inspired the idea to put local artwork up for sale.

They posed for a picture. "Say banana hammock," Millie chirped cheerfully.

"Gran!" Jason and Jen said nearly in unison as she snapped the picture.

"See you at the party." She left with a smug grin.

"Sometimes I can't believe I'm related to her," Jason said, shaking his head.

"I think she does it to see you squirm. And you know you secretly love it." Jen squeezed Jason's hand. "Ready?"

Jason lifted Colby onto his shoulders, then drew her close. "With you?" He winked playfully. "I'm ready for anything. By the way, I hear *A Christmas Carol* is this weekend. We should take Colby."

She leaned against his arm, her heart lightening at the memory from last year's play. "It's a date."

NEWSLETTER AND NEXT BOOK

Want to keep up with me and hear what's going on in my world? Join my newsletter on my website! I have freebies and giveaways, exclusive content and, of course, you get to hear all about upcoming book news, my life, and my small army of children.

I hope you enjoyed Jason and Jen's story. Thank you so much for reading; my readers really are what make this possible and I am so grateful for you! If you enjoyed this book, I'd love it if you took the time to leave a rating or review at your favorite book retailer. It truly goes a long way.

And if you'd like to stick around and see more of the world of Brandywood, you can! Dan's story continues in Once We Met, available April 11, 2023, available now for preorder!

ACKNOWLEDGMENTS

While my love for Jen and Jason and Millie (especially) practically caused this book to write itself, it wouldn't be here without the hard work of an incredible amount of people.

They include:

Marion Archer, my fantastic editor who has not only been wonderful to work with but an amazing mentor. Thanks so much for your keen eye and brilliant suggestions. You polish these pages to an absolute shine and I'm so grateful for you.

I also could not have done this without the top-notch editing talents of: Julie Simms, Amanda Coleman, and Julie Deaton. Thank you for your wonderful edits and feedback and always being consummate professionals.

My beta readers, ARC and Street teams: you all rock. Thanks for loving these story world as much as I do.

Lisa Boyle who has been my cheerleader with this whole project, thank you for your feedback and support.

Patrick Knowles, for yet another cover design that made me cry tears of joy. Thanks for always putting together exactly what I envisioned without me even knowing it.

And to my wonderful family, for being patient with me when I'm working on these books, for cheering me on, and for loving me. You really are my dream come true, so thank you for helping make these other dreams a reality. I love you Patrick, Cora, Andrew, Evie, Victoria, and Graham.

ALSO BY ANNABELLE MCCORMACK

The Windswept WWI Saga:

A Zephyr Rising: A Windswept Prequel Novella

Windswept: The Windswept Saga Book 1

Sands of Sirocco: The Windswept Saga Book 2

The Brandywood Contemporary Romance Series:

All This Time

I'll Carry You

Once We Met (Available February 14, 2023: Preorder Now)

To find out the latest about my new releases, please sign up for my newsletter! I love hearing from readers and have some great offers lined up for my subscribers.

ABOUT THE AUTHOR

Annabelle McCormack spins you tales of epic historical adventure, heartfelt romance, and complex family dynamics with strong female protagonists to make things interesting. She is a graduate of the Johns Hopkins University's M.A. in Writing Program. She lives in Maryland with her over-worked husband, where she is a professional comedienne and short-order cook for her (yes, I know how it happens) five children.

Visit her at www.annabellemccormack.com or http://instagram.com/annabellemccormack to follow her daily adventures.

CPSIA information can be obtained
at www.ICGtesting.com
Printed in the USA
LVHW091922050123
736467LV00003B/348

9 798986 529431